D1046532

THE DIVINE ECONOMY OF SALVATION

THE

DIVINE

ECONOMY

OF

SALVATION

Priscila Uppal

ALGONQUIN BOOKS OF CHAPEL HILL   2002

Published by
ALGONQUIN BOOKS OF CHAPEL HILL
Post Office Box 2225
Chapel Hill, North Carolina 27515-2225

a division of
WORKMAN PUBLISHING
708 Broadway
New York, New York 10003

Printed in the United States of America.
First published in Canada by Doubleday Canada,
    a division of Random House of Canada Limited.

Lines from P. K. Page's "Autumn" are from *Hologram*, Brick Books, 1994.
Lines from Paul-Marie Lapointe's "Poem for Winter" are from *The Poetry of French Canada in Translation* (John Glassco, ed.), Oxford University Press, 1970.

This is a work of fiction. While, as in all fiction, the literary perceptions and insights are based on experience, all names, characters, places, and incidents are either products of the author's imagination or are used fictitiously. No reference to any real person is intended or should be inferred.

Library of Congress Cataloging-in-Publication Data
Uppal, Priscila.
    The divine economy of salvation / Priscila Uppal.
        p. cm.
    ISBN 1-56512-365-4
    1. Nuns—Fiction.   2. Violence in adolescence—Fiction.   3. High
school students—Fiction.   4. Female friendship—Fiction.
    5. Initiation rites—Fiction.   6. Boarding schools—Fiction.
    7. Teenage girls—Fiction.   8. Guilt—Fiction.   I. Title.
PR9199.3.U59 D58 2002
813'.54—dc21   2002018467

10 9 8 7 6 5 4 3 2 1
First Edition

for my mother
  wherever she may be

&

for Christopher
  without doubt

For thee, who, mindful of th' unhonour'd dead,
Dost in these lines their artless tale relate;
If chance, by lonely contemplation led,
Some kindred spirit shall inquire thy fate,—

—THOMAS GRAY,
"Elegy Written in a Country Churchyard"

~ Autumn ~

Wearing a smile or frown
God's face is always there.
It is up to you
if you take your wintry restlessness into the town.

—P. K. PAGE, "Autumn"

My name was Angela H. then. You may remember me. We went to school together at St. X. School for Girls. I had long brown hair, cut at the waist in a single straight swipe, and I used to wear a tiny silver chain with a faux-gold locket in the shape of a heart, a picture of my mother inside. We knew each other. We all did. By name or by deed. Or at least I thought so at the time. I've had plenty of time here, plenty of time to think about the past and what we did know, or thought we knew, about what we, what I, have done. The air is thick as the stone walls with memories, with ghosts of us. I do not think it sacrilegious to speak so about ghosts. Jesus Christ is a ghost, the Holy Spirit is a ghost, the Bible tells us. I imagine God too, omnipresent and without form, is a ghost haunting my night. A wind in this darkness. I have food and water, a bed and paper. This is all I need.

You may remember a few of the girls began a group, The Sisterhood, and we snuck out of our dormitory rooms to meet. You and I, we were invited to join. We met in the dark of the hallway, our movements anxious, almost animal, feeling our way to Room 313, Rachel's room, the girl with the shoulder-length blonde curls and light-green eyes, the one we wanted so to impress, the one we believed was the strongest. I can still smell the sweet perspiration, girls' clean preadolescent sweat. It is different from the sweat here, a grown woman's sweat we try to hide by doing the wash early in the morning after pacing in our rooms, restless, alone. The hard sweat of layers of clothing, the heavy habits if we choose to wear them, the blankets we pile on top of our bodies to keep us covered at night. Or the cold, blank sweat of the nightmares many of us have. Before I moved in here, I never would have thought so many nightmares should fill a place of God. Prince of Peace. But I guess we did know. We lived one of our own at St. X. School for Girls. Our sheets were washed then too. The stains of sin, Sister Marguerite would have said, her large chest pounding like a needle on a sewing machine. No one ever found out what happened in Room 313. That's the part that disturbs me most in the middle of the night in this tiny basement room, a single window the height and width of one of the bricks at ground level. I watch feet go by, have come to identify the different boarders and visitors by the kinds of shoes or boots they wear. By the noises they make treading on the grounds. How our footsteps changed. No one confessed, you know. The crosses that hung over blackboards and bulletin boards in the classrooms and the adjoining church were oblivious to our crime, and the nuns only punished us for the ordinary sins of daily living, the banal trespasses of girlhood. No one confessed, until now. If you choose to remain hidden, I will not expose you. But I must confess. It's time. Don't turn away. We held hands once in the dark. You may remember me.

SISTER BERNADETTE CAME BY to see me this morning with a package. I nodded when she entered, from where I was kneeling on the white square-tiled floor, reciting my morning prayers in white cotton pyjamas, the late autumn air crisp after having left the window open a crack in the night. She smiled, laid the brown wrapped box in the middle of my already-made bed, and shut the door gently, her sneakers echoing softly down the empty basement hall. I had known she was coming because of those shoes; the left one squeaks on the tiled floor. The package held little interest for me, as I assumed it was from my sister, my real sister, Christine, who married a lawyer and has two sons. I washed my hair and ate my breakfast without opening it, compelled to get out, to see the changing leaves of the maple trees on the front lawn. Their thin, flat bodies, forced to fall for the coming winter, have always attracted me. After it has rained, if you hold a leaf tightly, sometimes the colours run onto your hands.

Before returning to my room I went upstairs to the second floor of the convent to help Sister Irene with her pills. She has been in and out of the hospital, back and forth, the last three years. There was discussion about giving her a room on the first floor, so that stairs wouldn't be a problem when she needed to go back again, but she's settled in her room now and the next trip, we know, will be her last. The doctors can do no more, and they insist she'd probably rather die here, though she has few friends among the other Sisters, the ones left. So many she had known when she first entered this convent, back in the years of World War II, have already died, passed on to where they believe themselves to go. With the onset of her sickness, Sister Irene turned rude and ill-mannered, rushing into rooms without knocking, yelling at a Sister for the tiniest inconvenience she might have caused, muttering under her breath every time she saw a Sister leave the main entrance, implying they were involved in something sinful. In the early stages, most refused to walk by her room, avoided her in the dining hall when she still took her meals there, pretended to have other engagements when she'd try to talk to them in the recreation room. With her time drawing nearer to an end, however, some Sisters have taken it upon themselves to light candles in her name, recite a specific prayer in her favour before bed, or drop off a treat, a bag of butterscotch candies perhaps, which she likes to suck. A few requested Father B. say a weekly Mass for her health. Still, most avoid her room, refusing to pass directly under the archway between her death and our lives.

I too have little affection for Sister Irene, though I am compelled to witness the change in her. Since the stroke, she has lost feeling in her legs and in the left side of her face. Her single bed with its twenty-year-old box spring and mattress is her sole domain. I hold her bendable drinking straw to the good side of her mouth when I feed her a liquid meal, her dark lips large and soft from inactivity. They used to be so thin, tight, well-sealed, those lips. Now she tells me things. Or she tries to, mumbling incoherently, her tongue unskilled and numb against her teeth as she struggles to form simple syllables. She grips my arm at the wrist as if she would snap it like a twig in her frustration, but she lacks the strength, tries to attract my attention with her brown eyes, while the wrinkles on her face deepen like etchings in stone. She tells me addresses and telephone numbers, listing them off without including names, and I've given up prodding her to remember whom they belong to. She doesn't seem to care anyway. She just enjoys reciting the numbers themselves over and over as if they are well-loved people. It is almost comforting, except the strong spice-like smell of her keeps me at a distance on the stool beside her, her body leaking, forcing itself to the outside. The pills calm her, put her to sleep, her hair thin against her pillow, olive scalp tough as hide. I've touched her scalp as she's slept, pushed my hands against its surface petting her, an attempt to unleash what has become trapped over time. Once, she bolted up, holding her hands in front of her, confused, as if she couldn't understand who these hands, the skin over the knuckles white and bumpy like curds of milk, belonged to. "Death is backwards!" she cried. "Backwards!" It's the only thing she's said to me in the last month resembling a sentence. And I've wanted to ask her what she meant, but it seems as she sleeps, her head pressed against the cloth of her pillow, that she will be taking her secrets with her.

Only in the afternoon, after leaving Sister Irene to her drug-induced peace, did I notice that the address of the convent on the package was typed, and no return address announced itself. I could not decide at first whether to open the package, although besides the unfamiliarity of the typing, there was no reason for my hesitation. We frequently receive packages from elementary schools, the social services department, or from thoughtful parishioners in thanks for our work or time. A particular man or woman may simply have believed I'd helped them personally, beyond my call of duty, and made out a gift to me. I'd just donate the contents to the convent, inform Mother Superior. She might even praise me, I figured.

Yet deep down I knew. I knew it was no gift I was about to receive. My hands trembling, I was sure my face had lost its colour, though there is no mirror hanging in my room to check such things. I could feel blood leave my cheeks, pump quicker to the heart. I tried to reason I'd exhausted myself with Sister Irene and needed a good nap. Cold, I wrapped the grey wool afghan from my bed around my shoulders. A tiny ceramic hand-painted statue of Mary, a gift from my mother when I received First Communion, which I sometimes hold in the palm of my hand when I think of her, seemed to forsake me from her central place on my dresser. *Do you know who has come for you?* I heard the season's wind ask, beating against my low window, a yellow leaf's face flattened against the glass. I did.

The box was wrapped first in plain brown packing paper, the kind you can buy in rolls at the post office for a couple of dollars. The stamps were Canadian, standard red maple leaves, totalling $7.35, the postmark illegible. When I shook the package, an object grudgingly slid from side to side, the weight comparable to a medium-sized pot. I tore at the paper with my blunt, bitten finger-nails, the bits of packaging on the bed like pieces of bark scraped off a tree. The actual box was made of white cardboard, void of logos, but the type found in department stores, easy to put together, flimsy, the edges folded into wings and taped shut. I checked the door. It doesn't have a lock, but I made sure it was firmly closed. When it is left ajar, my entire enclosure can be seen if someone happens to walk by, the room being only nine by seven feet. Not that many people come by here. To see others I usually need to seek them out by going upstairs. I am the only one living down in the basement. The room was assigned to me when I entered the convent because renovations were being done to the second and third floors due to weather damage. All the Sisters were grouped together on the first floor until construction was finished, bunking like girls, two or four to a room after years of sleeping in their own quarters. The bunks were all filled up. Besides a bathroom, furnace room, and storage area, there is only one room in the basement suitable for living. I took it. When the other rooms became available, I clung to the excuse that I was accus-tomed to my space and didn't need to move. Mother Superior didn't mind. Better to use the space than leave it vacant. And I honestly felt comfortable in the small room, encased and protected. A single bed, an oak dresser like the kind my father crafted for my mother when I was a child that I found at an antique store, a single folding chair, photographs, a few other mementos, and a large leather tote bag for my sister Christine's letters are all I own. My room doesn't even have a closet. Now I wished there were more places to hide.

The tissue paper inside the package was white and had a faint perfume smell. The strangely familiar scent forced me to take my hands off the box. Lilies. I had accompanied Mother Superior once to the mall to visit the wig lady, a woman who helped the older Sisters, the ones who had lost their hair from too-tight wimples, brush out their wigs. The wig lady wore a similar scent that day, and I ran out of the store without explanation. How could I tell them that the smell made me see blood, blood spilling over the glass counters like fountain water, blood on my hands, my habit, my shoes, on the holiday decorations, blinking in the lights, the store windows, the exits? Blood on the wigs, on the faces of the manne-quins, on their Styrofoam lips, and on Mother Superior's scalp, down her round cheeks as the hairnet was fitted. No, I couldn't tell them of the sights occasioned by a woman's perfume. Though it is my belief, if the dead come back to earth, they travel by smell. Lilies.

It was at that moment I knew for sure. I swallowed hard, in an effort not to choke. The box open, the only thing left to do was to look. The room took on a yellowish hue, like that of old photo-graphs. I tried to blink it away and rubbed my eyes vigorously, thinking I might be allergic to the scent. An unacknowledged ache forced its pressure against my stomach. For the first time in years, I longed for a companion, someone who would comfort me for no reason except that I asked. For the first time in years, I longed for God to announce Himself, to speak in a language I could under-stand. As if in a dream, compelled to continue, I unfolded the white tissue. The silver candle holder lay at the bottom of the box like a slender body frozen in the snow.

A KNOCK AT THE door startles me. I cough, clearing my throat, and throw the tissue paper back over the silver candle holder. I'm not sure how long I've been sitting here in a daze, staring at the offensive object, when Sister Bernadette arrives.

"Come in," I invite.

Sister Bernadette's white forehead peeks through the doorway. My attention distracted, I had missed the squeak of her left shoe.

"Come in," I say again.

Sister Bernadette is the youngest nun at the convent and loves to chatter. The two usually don't go together, as the young tend to keep their secrets well-hidden, revealed only to their confessor, one of the resident priests at R. Catholic Church. However, few young women have been admitted here in recent years, so the tide might have shifted in this respect without my knowledge. Regardless, Sister Bernadette is of another ilk. Those who take vows out of optimism, instead of shame. A social brand of nun, who want to save the whales and protect the ecosystem. She is always passing around flyers and petitions, reciting a litany of statistics and studies. Her belief in fact is apparently unshakeable. She keeps meticulous records and files detailing her various projects and photocopies them at the church for Mother Superior's office. Sister Bernadette has been rallying Mother Superior and Father B. to allocate some of the parish's money to ethical mutual funds, citing examples of Sisters in the United States who hold shares in large companies solely so they can disrupt the annual shareholders' meetings and control the morality of businesses. I wonder how Sister Bernadette will possibly survive in this world. Who has protected her for so long? Most of us can't save even one person, let alone an entire species. She smiles often, though, her braces removed before she came to live here, her teeth perfectly aligned, and her brown eyes are quite pleasing, large and round like amber. Within a week of Sister Bernadette's entrance into the convent, she took over the mail delivery from Sister Maria, whose knees are stricken with arthritis. There is no need for anyone to deliver the mail, but Sister Bernadette claimed it was "such a lovely way to say hello to everyone in the morning." Mother Superior is amused by her, I gather, though Mother Superior herself is rarely visible in the mornings. She is efficient and incredibly organized. Perhaps because of this, she is rarely social with anyone when it doesn't directly serve a greater purpose. It is rumoured she composes long religious sermons on the deterioration of the laws of the Church, on contemporary evils such as genetic engineering and plastic surgery, and that she packs them up and sends them to her brother in England who looks after her finances. Sister Maria says Mother Superior receives mail from academic religious journals under an androgynous pseudonym, but Sister Maria doesn't read very well, English being her third language. The truth of Sister Maria's claim is difficult to prove. Sister Maria also thinks Mother Superior wishes she had been born a man.

Sister Bernadette, twenty-four years old, tiny-hipped and small-breasted, her face scrubbed clean and makeup free, lowers her head in a mock gesture of guilt.

"With such a large package to deliver this morning, I forgot to give you this little letter," she says, her left arm extended towards me on the bed.

The candle holder occupying my private thoughts, weighing

heavily upon me, I try not to tremble as I take the letter from her hands. If there is any outward change in my behaviour or appearance, Sister Bernadette doesn't seem to notice. Relieved, I let out a sigh, louder than I mean to, when I see the writing on the envelope. Christine always prints on her envelopes or packages, usually in bright pens or markers: purple, green, yellow, as if the sender were a child. She says she wants to brighten up the convent a little, add some colour. This particular letter is addressed in mustard yellow, and Sister Bernadette recognizes the distinct presentation too.

"From your sister, Christine, right?"

I nod cheerfully for Sister Bernadette's benefit. My sister's letters and visits rarely make me happy. We see differently. Even discussions about the weather leave us on opposite sides of a fence. The first time she came to visit me here, she walked into my room and gasped. "Couldn't you ask for a nicer room, one with a little more light? What will you do in the winter? Did they give you this room because you're new? Is there really nothing left? How about this floor, it's going to be impossible in the cold. You'll get sick. You'll never get any fresh air from that window," she ranted.

"Who sent you the package?" Sister Bernadette asks as she rocks toe to heel, the white sneakers peeking from underneath her habit. Months earlier, I had made a mental note to ask her if she wanted me to take hers to Sister Humilita for hemming; Sister Humilita mends the habits and orders new ones when she decides they need replacing. Sister Bernadette's are all an inch too long, but I forgot to mention it, and I almost wish she'd trip to detract attention from my package. She waits for me to show it to her.

Do you know who has come for you?

"An old ... an old friend."

"A gift?" she asks with excitement.

There is no use hiding objects. The Sisters find out sooner or later if there are any new items in your room, even if your room is in the basement. Purchases are noted, gifts from friends and family brought out for others to see, especially during the holidays. They are considered tokens of love and goodwill. Blessings that should be acknowledged. Books are frequently shared, as well as any item deemed to have communal benefits, like bread makers or coffee percolators, sewing machines, board games or decks of cards, large packages of baked goods or canned preserves. When Sister Katherine's brother sent her an electric typewriter, she immediately offered it up for the church's use. This is proper procedure. Only thoughts can be concealed, and I've hidden my share. Enough for two, enough for this innocent Sister Bernadette. I remove the box from the bed, the weight resting on my forearms, and she approaches me eagerly.

"It's a little heavy," I tell her. "You'll have to lift the tissue paper."

Her fingers move delicately, as if she realizes the solemnity of the gift. If initially I wanted to hide the candle holder, now, equally desperately, I want someone to touch it, leave fingerprints on it. Prove the object is made of matter. That it won't disappear or crumble when taken out into the light.

She takes it out of the box, relieving my burden, cradling the silver in her arms like a baby, her eyebrows arched in appreciation. A strong rain pounds against the windowpane. The afternoon has grown dark under the threat of a storm. Normally there should be snow this time of year, but rain and autumn have won out. My window leaks and the drops come down, some caught by a coffee mug kept for that purpose on the inner ledge. I shiver, anticipating another cool night.

"It's beau-ti-ful," Sister Bernadette hums.

That it is. I often thought so back then, before everything else began. I had coveted that very silver candle holder or one exactly like it twenty-five years ago. It spoke of another world, with its crafted austere elegance, sitting attentively on Rachel M.'s bookshelf. It was a gift from her father, purchased on a downtown street in Rio de Janeiro, where he'd vacationed. He had brought her back silver necklaces and chocolates, thin cotton dresses and wooden-faced black dolls with haunting orange circles around their eyes, but she asked for the candle holder. Made of real silver and quite valuable, her father told her to be careful with it. The features are the same as I remember: a square base with four squat legs, its body vertically converging to the mouth where a candlestick would be inserted. There is a wick melted onto the silver. At the four bottom corners are black burned etchings, intriguing but foreign, strokes in a language I don't know how to read: a loop swallowing itself, a type of cross with two horizontal arms, a star with a jagged edge, and an oval like the outline of an eyeball. When polished, the candle holder's shell reflects like a mirror. In the dark, lit by a single wax candle, it dominates the room, the light contained but threatening to break. The days at St. X. School for Girls were like that shell. The nights were like that light.

I could lie and tell you I've never thought of those days until the arrival of the silver candle holder, but I won't. I've thought of my time at St. X. School for Girls every single day, and if a day does pass and it occurs to me that I haven't thought about it, then for the next couple of days I'll be haunted by little else. The gift is no surprise, but a sign I have been waiting for these twenty years in this small convent in Ottawa. At least I can bless the fact that it has finally come.

WE MOVED TO OTTAWA because my mother was ill. The long straight hair my sister Christine and I inherited had thinned upon her scalp to strands of black thread. Her eyes, circled with dry patches and puffy as blisters, were most of the time wan and dazed. She applied lotion to the skin on her face three or four times a day, and she wore rose-tinted glasses to shield her hazel eyes from the sun, the only thing the doctors had ordered that seemed to help. My father loaded us into a rented van, and my mother slumped in the front seat like one of our hastily packed bags. She slept most of the way, her weak groans drowned out by the classical radio station she had requested for the trip. "Ave Maria," sung by young boys with high girlish voices, propelled us forward through the farmland and small towns with family-run grocery stores and cheap gas stations where we would all get out, except Mother, to stretch our legs and take another look at the map. Three hundred miles of driving that took all afternoon, the exhaust from the van filtering into our noses, my mother coughing, her head and mouth against the glass, my father's foot at intervals solid, then teetering on the pedal, changing our speed.

Christine was excited by the possibility of city life, pointing at the signs announcing the number of miles left, pronouncing the names of the towns we didn't drive through, rocking in the seat beside me, ritualistically eating a single potato chip from her bag each time we reached a new town name. I wanted to be back in my bed, the one my father had made from the trees on our property shortly after I was born. Eventually, my feet fell a couple of inches over the edge of the red oak frame, but I refused to let him build me a new one. I had crawled underneath and etched my initials into the wood. I felt the bed and I were a part of each other, even if I'd outgrown it. We left it for sale like all his other handiwork: rocking chairs and shelves made of oak and pine, birch dressers and maple chests, cabinets and sewing tables. My haven of privacy, where I would lie under the covers reading or daydreaming about when I would be married and have a house of my own, was abandoned like our home. I made a fuss to my father about it, wringing my hands and crying, holding onto the bedposts as if they were part of the family and couldn't possibly be left behind.

"We'll get a new one, Angela."

"No! I want this one!" I had cried.

Generally a gentle man, my father shocked me, clamping my shoulders in his large arms and pulling me up, my feet dangling above the floor. I was afraid he was going to hit me. My eyes shut, his cracked voice blurted in my ears: "I can make a new one! Don't you understand? I can make you a new one! I can't make you a mother! Do you hear me?"

He dropped me and left the room, slamming my bedroom

door, a few hangers on the doorknob falling to the ground, tinkling. I pushed against the headboard, beating the wood with my fists. The bed, like our home, like our farm property, was going to remain without us. We would go on without the things we had come to rely on, and I knew instinctively that once we left, nothing would be the same. What I didn't know then was that I would never sleep again in a bed that was solely my own.

When we entered the city limits, the highway twisting down into a concrete valley with high-rises and numerous bright street-lights, Christine, ten years of age, four years younger than me, let out a childish squeal, slapping her now empty bag of potato chips across her knees.

"Stop it, Chrissy," Father silenced her.

Mother, startled, woke up. She shifted her weight on her seat and I could feel it against my knees, the top of her head peeking out of the headrest.

"Joe, I can't see. I can't see," she panicked, her hands fumbling over the glove compartment in front of her and onto the windshield.

"It's dark, Anna," my father told her, veering the vehicle to the curb and stopping, covering my mother's shaking hands with his own, eyes searching hers for recognition. "It's night. Only night. See, I'll turn on the light."

He flicked on the small reading light located on the roof of the van and waited as my mother, the instant tears which had come with her fear drying upon her cheeks, put on her rose-coloured glasses and waited for the shadows to adjust.

"Oh, Joe, your eyes," she exclaimed. "Your eyes!" And then she slumped back down in her seat, breathing heavily.

My father took longer to recover, unfolding the map again, tracing the route we had taken with a pencil, periodically staring blankly out the windows at the new signs. Cars were passing us, their headlights on, anticipating arrivals, and I wondered how many drivers or passengers knew where they were headed on this night or if there were others like us, finding bearings in a new place.

"Daddy, do you know where this new house is?" I asked, while Christine busily pointed to a row of pine trees along the roadside.

"Look at them, they're all so small!" she cried. The ones on our old property were three times the size and could only be decorated outside at Christmas, being far too large to fit in our living room.

"Of course I do," Father assured me. "Can you girls just relax and let me alone 'til we get there? Please," he added, feeling my mother's forehead beside him for temperature. "Your mother needs her sleep."

"She's always sleeping," Christine muttered, pressing her hand against the window, outlining the dusty print it made with her fingers.

"Shut up," I told her.

"You're no better, always moping around. Can't anyone have some fun?" She leaned forward, jutting her head into the front of the van. "Can't we have some fun, Daddy?"

My father reached back with his right hand and ruffled the bangs of her hair. He was probably at the end of his tether, but he adjusted the rear-view mirror to offer us both a sympathetic smile and then started the engine again. "Soon, Sweetheart. Let Daddy drive now."

Christine leaned back into her seat and, astonishingly, was asleep within minutes. I always envied her ability to meld into her surroundings, no matter how foreign or strange. Her ability to adapt. My eyes remained open the whole trip, keeping watch over Mother's breath, Father's erratic driving, the scenery passing us, as if I might be able to find my way back if needed. Reflected in the window, my face was as grave as the dark pines we were passing. I did not like this city, this new house, before we ever arrived. The air, thick like gas, and the smell of burning pulp from the paper mills in the town we had driven through just a half-hour earlier had left me nauseated. The city's being rose up like an animal out of a hole. *How does it breathe*, I wondered, *under all this dirt?* Then it started to rain.

Ashbrook Crescent, a street with grey concrete curves that wound around the houses as if protecting the lights in living rooms with drawn curtains, possessed humble homes with one-door garages and short, stubby driveways, almost all split-level bungalows made of red or grey brick, townhouses, split into two. The autumn foliage was the only hint of nature's stubborn intrusion. The windows were untrimmed, the backyards hidden by fences, the front entrances ornamented modestly with dried cornhusks or wooden plaques. Three streets earlier a park with a miniature baseball diamond and a neglected plastic playground had stood vacant, with crossing signs that read "Watch Out for Children," though none were playing there, and I didn't see any on the streets as we drove.

Not a single person was outside when we arrived. Our new street, though worn with age, had the appearance of being temporarily erected, a place to recuperate between moves, not a place to move to.

When our new home came into view, with the fresh rain slipping down the windows, I saw it first like that, as though through a veil of tears. From that moment on, I think my own eyes took on the vision of that glass, with single-second moments of clarity, but mostly a view lacking in focus, causing me to venture with caution. We had a corner lot near the end of the winding road. Obviously the bungalow had been abandoned quickly: cardboard boxes on the curb, many of the window shutters open, a single porch light at the entrance hanging in vigil, the scuff marks on the red bricks exposed. The street numbers painted in gold, however, were apparently new, and glittered against the peeled skins of the plaster and stone. The number 40, the exact age of my mother, hung oddly unattached, removable like the plastic ones we had pressed into her birthday cake two months earlier. Christine had blown out the candles for her.

After my father and I got out of the car, shielding the rain from our heads with our hands, we helped lift my mother out of the front seat. She had lost weight over the last year, had become brittle in her bones, and the slightest bump or nudge left bruises on her skin. Three days before we finished packing, she'd stumbled on a stair and hit the banister. A purple bruise, the shape of a plum, was still visible on her arm. Christine, who had woken up when we stopped, jumped along the driveway, her feet splashing in and out of puddles, her coat, flattened from the long trip, flying open and rising in the wind. She was eager to open the locked front door, and pulled at the handle.

"Stop her, Joseph, she might get sick," my mother feebly managed as my father covered her with his jacket, his white shirt plastered from the rain, curly brown chest hairs tight against the thin fabric. He moved like a man delivering a fragile package, with short steps, her body held up in his arms. My father too had transformed over the last year, his hair a shade darker from store-bought dye, his face pinched, his torso firm. His body was so taut it appeared to be conserving space. At the top step, he pointed to the mailbox, where Christine found the key in an envelope soaked with rain.

I was in charge of bringing in the sleeping bags. Our first night at 40 Ashbrook Crescent would be spent in the living room, the small brick fireplace burning damp wood and crinkled newspaper, the thermostats defrosting after having been shut down for a couple of days. The floor was orange-brown, carpeted, and dusty. Mother spent most of the night coughing, keeping us half-awake. The previous owners had left various things in the home: a plastic table in the kitchen, mismatched bowls and cutlery, a broom in the linen closet, an end table, a painting of a sailboat left crookedly attached to a nail in the living room, a pail under the kitchen sink, and a couch with a large stain and an offensive odour that Father had to drag outside to the curb with the rest of the garbage before we could sleep. I noticed nervously as we unrolled the sleeping bags that there were only two bedrooms and one bathroom off the hallway adjacent to the living room and kitchen doors. There weren't enough rooms for us to live as we had before; I didn't want to share a bedroom with Christine. My sister slept curled up in a ball, my father's face close to hers, my mother's angled towards the hallway. I resigned myself to the corner, near a single window slapped with rain, asking myself dumbly what this place would offer me, counting the half-dying embers of the fire.

It was two days later that I was told about St. X. School for Girls. My mother had since been put up in the larger of the two bedrooms on a fold-out cot made comfortable by unmatched sheets and blankets, her dry face peeking out amidst the colours, her short hair flattened to her scalp with bobby pins. Her usual pitcher of water sat on the carpeted floor. We had made sure to keep it handy in the van for when we arrived. I knelt beside her while my father, who had made the arrangements, spoke to Christine in the kitchen. I had already grown weary that no attempt had been made to set up the other bedroom, and no one had mentioned who was to sleep there. Father had filled it with unopened boxes while the three of us continued to sleep in our bags in the living room.

"You will have your own room there," my mother told me calmly. "And your father's new work will be taking up too much time, and you know I can't get around like before."

Her breath was laboured, wheezing in and out like an old fan, her lips chapped, matching the white creases on her forehead and cheeks. She sweated continually, the mildest movement, however delicate, acting against the desire of her body to keep still. "At least it isn't her mind," I overheard Father say to a nurse at the clinic we had visited in the nearest city to our old home. The nurse nodded back, squeezing his arm comfortingly, and exited the room to escort an older man with a cane in for tests. My mother was too young for such a place, I thought, the room filled with grey hair and wrinkled faces, signs in large print. Yet, relegated to her cot, she did seem old in her body, and I wasn't sure she wouldn't have preferred to trade a little of her mind for a piece of her younger body back. She was slowly being erased. I feared if I left her, she would simply disappear.

"I could help out here, Mommy, please." I held her hand in mine, tracing her knuckles, the fine bones delicate as the beads in her rosary she kept beside her pillow, a plain silver chain with tiny white beads, the silent companion of her hours, a Confirmation gift from the nuns she had lived with in Ireland when she was a girl. The Sisters of Mercy. They had taken her in as a toddler after her parents were killed in an automobile accident. The grandparents had disowned her mother for marrying a Northerner. However, she had been baptized and the nuns welcomed the young girl. "They were strict women," my mother told me. "But they did good work. They saved me from a destitute life. They gave me a sound education and moral values. I owe them more than I can ever repay."

"No, God will watch over me, Angela. You must have faith in Him. You must get an education. The school is very good, well worth the money—"

"It's too expensive," I begged. "Daddy hasn't sold all the woodwork yet. I heard him—"

"That's not your concern," she replied sternly, taking a deep breath, the air struggling into her lungs as she removed her hand from mine and motioned to the window. I rose and opened it. A gust of wind shoved itself against my neck.

"You be a good girl for your mother. I'm too tired to argue with you," she added, as if she were the one defeated in our argument. "It isn't far and we'll see you on weekends when your father is home. It'll be like the school I went to when I was a young girl. It will be an important time in your life, Angela. Trust me."

I gave up and stopped listening to their reasons for sending us to private Catholic boarding schools. I stared through the window at the flowerpots filled with the week's rain, a hummingbird ornament dipping its wings in and out of the water in monotonous thirst. Christine would be enrolled at an elementary school closer to the house, and I would be enrolled in one downtown for junior girls. We had never been to separate schools before, and I heard Christine slam the back door, my father running after her, trying to calm her down. After a time, my mother took off her rose-coloured glasses, rubbed at her reddened eyes, and slept, her breath so barely noticeable she could have been mistaken for dead. My face turned to our new backyard, to that nailed-down hummingbird, I almost wished she were, and I could go back to our old home, my old bed, back to the life we had been living. But then I realized if my mother were dead, I'd never be beside her again, and my shame at the thought of her unburdening us of this place made me bite back tears. I tucked her blankets underneath her chin and went to ask Father when Christine and I would be leaving and what we would need to bring with us. Luckily, we had not unpacked.

The following evening we joined together for a parting dinner, a scarce affair since we had made only a quick trip to the grocery store, but we ate a cooked ham and corn and savoured small, bell-shaped dark baking chocolates, my mother's favourite treat, for dessert. Christine and I sat with Mother by the fireplace and listened to the radio after packing up a few of our clothes and bathroom supplies. Father would drive Christine in the morning and, to save time, I'd be taking the bus downtown, the route map passed into my hands, underlined in blue ink, about an hour's trip with stops from Ashbrook Crescent. I was to ask the bus driver to announce my stop and enter the grey stone building, part convent and part school, and ask for the Mother Superior. "She's the head nun, the one in charge," my mother instructed me. "They have a lot on their minds, organizing everything, so don't be upset if she doesn't spend much time with you. You'll meet the girls your own age soon enough." As the night crept up on us, the autumn air filled with the scent of pine, my mother asked us to pray, her head bent, her rose-coloured glasses reflecting the flames.

"Let us thank God for all His blessings. Watch over these children, and bring them into Your grace. Amen." When she lifted her head, she was smiling with a vividness unseen in the past few months, her eyes turned towards Christine and me with hope. I was about to return her humble amen with one of mine until I noticed the shadow of my father in the doorway, large and fumbling, backing away from us to grapple with our luggage in the semi-darkness. He bowed his head in a gesture that I can now, after years of observation, recognize as despair.

When I left my sleeping bag that night to get a glass of water from the bathroom, I heard his voice through the white walls.

"You're not going to die on me," he said.

I was shocked by his words. I realized my mother was ill, but death had never crossed my mind as a real possibility, only a childish fantasy. The sounds of crying seeped through the wall, but it was my mother who was crying, whimpering like an injured animal, and not my father.

"What am I being punished for?" she asked him. "What did I do?"

These were the only words of doubt I had ever heard from her; she was to me a pillar of faith, reading the Bible, reciting her rosary, and humbly thankful for every morning when she woke. She had given me a faux-gold locket with her picture inside, a photograph taken just after she was married, her face strong and clear of lines, her eyes confidently turned to the camera. I am in her belly at this time, although the picture doesn't show it, and her face, even in a black-and-white photograph, seems to glow with a secret serenity. There is freshness to both her appearance and the angle of the shot, as if she had been caught off guard enjoying herself in the summer season. I couldn't believe the woman on the other side of the wall was the same person who had played with me outside—running through the fields with her skirt in her hands, stepping through mud—cooked elaborate dinners, and kept house. My ear against the wall, I briefly sensed movement underneath the plaster. The new house seemed to sigh, letting go of us all. I took my glass of water back to the living room and wrapped myself tightly in my sleeping bag. I remembered how we had discovered a nest of robins in our maple tree back home and gone to visit them each day, offering seeds, monitoring their growth. Christine once even brought out an umbrella to cover them in the rain. Then one weekend, the mother disappeared. Father told us our attentions might have disrupted the natural order of things. The tiny scared bodies, lifting their blind eyes up to an absent beak, huddled together for warmth. Brothers and sisters fought, pecking each other and drawing blood to get near the one most equipped to survive. The weakest, not able to make his way to the warmth and food, died, and we buried him beside the tree under the soil. The following morning, a hole was left in its place, another animal probably having dug it up for food. I decided that at St. X. School for Girls, I would need to find a new family to survive the season, curl up next to the one who seemed the strongest.

My strategy would prove more necessary than I knew. Though my parents hadn't exactly lied to us, I was unaware at the time that Father's new work did not involve any employer. Renting the bungalow on Ashbrook Crescent was an act of hope on their part. He would admit her to the hospital the day after we left and spend all his time and energy trying to get her well. Christine and I were to be kept away until the money ran out.

THIS MORNING, FATHER B. speaks to us Sisters about a young pregnant Korean girl shut out of her house by her parents. He found her weeping against the confessionals at the end of Mass last night, holding her stomach. She did not have a coat, a loose blue cardigan was draped around her waist, and her jeans were worn and tattered. There are services that could take care of her, but she refuses their help, and Father B., not afraid for her as much as for the baby's health, asks that she stay with us while plans are settled for her future.

We have come to R. Catholic Church to discuss the upcoming rummage sale. I am in charge of organizing rummage sales, and on the day of the sale I work specifically at the clothing booth: marking the clothing, printing a fair price on tiny white stickers, and jotting in a little notebook what has sold and what is left over. I specialize in things, not in people, so I'm anxious about having a new ward to take care of at the convent. So are some of the other Sisters. Sister Maria, in particular, complains that the girl ought to find a halfway house or women's shelter. Sister Ursula, our resident doctor, counters with the virtues of a challenge, reasoning that God might be putting her in our path for a specific purpose and we ought to rise to the occasion. The discussion grows fairly heated at points, but Father B. manages to convince the majority. I was supposed to speak today, and feel both cheated and relieved. Although I realize the rummage sale is not the greatest of accomplishments, it is mine, and I want to make sure it runs as smoothly as possible. At the same time, however, I am nervous speaking in public, even to a group of Sisters that I converse with each day at the convent. When I know every eye is watching me, I can't help but feel exposed.

As Father B. talks about the girl, I review the accounts I've kept of what there will be for sale. Collecting items months ahead of time, I am astounded at what gets thrown away—or "donated," as we are supposed to say—but it is rare that someone donates something they actually want to keep. Only children do that, offering up an old favourite toy or a pair of well-worn shoes, a proud parent standing behind, beaming at the proof that their strong moral values have transferred to their children. But really their children have demonstrated an act of giving beyond their own. Adults lose that generosity somewhere along the way, determined to keep anything they deem useful for themselves. Instead, they offer boxes filled with scratched pots and pans, broken blenders and vacuums, outdated fondue sets and radios, old trinkets with cracks in the clay or paint. Even what might at first appear to be overtly generous, in terms of value—silks and cashmere, angora sweaters that have never been worn, underwear still in its packaging, blouses and shorts with the price tags from the store still on them—are usually gifts that didn't fit or impulse buys that have stayed in the closet for so many years that they can't be given as gifts to friends or family. There are also boxes and boxes of books, though most parishioners donate mysteries and Harlequin romances, not really appropriate, I think, their gory or sleazy covers out of place in a church basement. But when I mentioned my reservations to Father B., he made it clear that he doesn't mind. "They probably never even read them," he said, although the sad condition of the spines tells otherwise. Besides, they only sell for a quarter or a dime, and they take up a lot of space. The bake sale is the most popular, especially for the women who don't have time to make Rice Krispie squares or chocolate cake for their children, who are too busy running around building up careers and working out at the gym to keep their husbands happy. We make the largest profits on the food—the items of the least material value, requiring only time.

After Father B.'s announcement about our new charge, Sister Bernadette passes around an animal-testing petition to be mailed to a pharmaceutical company, and the rummage-sale meeting is reset for the following morning, after ten o'clock Mass. Apparently the girl in question (fifteen years old, I find out later, although without breasts and as skinny as a rake, she looks closer to twelve or thirteen) is waiting outside the church in the coffee shop. A few of us sometimes stop by there for lattes and cappuccinos. A couple of Sisters object to the smoke, and a strict few feel it might reflect badly on the Church to see Sisters engaged in leisure activity, but more of us think it's harmless and enjoyable, and the caffeine keeps us moving. We have no espresso machine at the convent. The girl has told Father B.

her name is Kim, but he's unsure whether or not she is telling the truth. "The father of the child is dead, she claims. This, of course, is probably untrue as well," he continues, "and I doubt very much that she is Catholic, but probably picked our parish to be away from her own community." He seems proud of his insights, stroking his collar pensively, his eyes scanning our attentive faces for reassurance. But he also seems tired. I often wonder if he gets any sleep.

Father B. performs Mass almost every single day, conducts meetings, and makes himself available to the community for private consultations and guidance. He hardly ever recycles his sermons, and delivers Mass in Italian once a week on Saturday afternoons. Older women in the audience sometimes approach him afterwards to correct his grammar, but they are pleased he tries to communicate with them in their native language, since many don't have an adequate grasp of English. He is always helping out with the functions our parish sponsors, and his hair has grown the whiter for it. When I first came here, he was the second priest, but after ten years he took over for Father K., who, old and exhausted by the pressures of his vocation, finally retired to another city. Father B. had thick black hair then, and many of the Sisters commented on his fine and rugged appearance. Now it has thinned somewhat, and his visage has taken on a contradictory state of hopeful dejection. He tries so hard to keep in touch with all walks of life and age groups. He's even started to conduct informal meetings with his altar boys after Mass to find out about their schools and what they think of current events. When the boys are ignorant of a news report or can't name the political leaders in the area, Father B. can't comprehend it. He wonders how they spend their time and whether they understand what the Church is meant to accomplish. I think his determination to take on Kim is partly due to his failure to connect with those boys. At least she needs help and has asked for it. "A group of caring women can do a lot for her health, for her soul," he says.

The day is warmer than when I received my package. Although attired in my winter coat, I could be comfortable in a lighter jacket. Winter has stalled this year. I had mentioned the lateness of the season to a woman who sells newspapers to aid the homeless on the street corner outside. "Winter comes when it comes," she replied. "I've been in this country long enough to know that." She has an Eastern European face, with stark features and a thick neck, a sunburn in November, red scraped skin across her nose and cheeks. Her hands are covered by black knitted mittens, the kind children wear, without fingers. When money is inserted into her palm, it disappears down her jacket right into her pocket. She may be sure of the weather, yet it seems understandable to me that I could be fooled by the clouds and the temperature and the weathermen on television. Nothing in my life is in order, so why should nature be any different? But I don't want to be fooled by the person who sent me that gift, the person who must be looking for me. After Sister Bernadette finally left my room that afternoon, I handled the candle holder for the next two hours, trying to determine whether it was a copy or the original. The exercise proved futile. I know little about the authenticity of objects or how to weigh real silver or judge when the candle holder was engraved, where it was made. Everything on the surface indicates it is the original, but this is little comfort. In fact it is worse. I thought it had been buried. I thought no one was going to dig this up again. My instinct is twofold: to run or to hide. To run would mean an investigation, probably involving the police, as the Sisters would worry about my absence and fill out a Missing Person Report. They've done it before. Eight years ago, Sister Olivia went "over the wall," as we say. She was found in Edmonton, working in a restaurant as a cook. She simply told the police she'd had enough of working for free. However, for me, if my crime becomes known, running would be seen as akin to guilt. And to be found guilty in front of the world is a decidedly different judgement than the private guilt I've carried for years. To hide is the best solution to me at the moment. To hide as I have been hiding among these women for years. To do the work I have been doing for our community. Go about my ordinary routines while keeping my eyes open for another sign of who might be tracking me down. I have certain suspects, but I can't quite resign myself to the notion that they would want to expose me and thereby expose themselves. The people I suspect were also involved. They'd be implicated. Who wants to drag all this back into the light? Years have passed in silence. The dead shall remain dead no matter what we might do.

Although I do enjoy a latte now and then, I had no plans to retire to the coffee shop after the meeting. However, curious and weakened by my own worries, I feel the distraction might be good for me. On noticing our entrance, the pregnant girl tries to regain her composure. Her small face is scoured and red from the napkins used as Kleenex; her tiny hips support a small bulge the size of a cantaloupe. We decide to send only Sister Bernadette over first, as a group of six of us congregate at a table with our drinks. Most of us are in our habits for Mass, and we think the uniform might intimidate her if she feels shame over her delicate condition. Sister Bernadette, although also sporting a habit, has a better chance of welcoming her because of her youth. Kim does respond to her, accepting a decaffeinated coffee and letting her sit in the seat across from her. Gradually, one or two of us follow suit. Her face is oily, and she smells as if she's slept in her clothes the night before. We tell her she can take a shower and eat and watch television in the recreation room if she likes. She must have stayed in Father B.'s rectory, I conjecture, and a night in a church after getting kicked out of one's home could not have been a good night of sleep. We tell her about the orchard in the front of our convent and how it still has flowers in bloom at this late date, and about Father B.'s kind words in her favour, that he thinks she is a good young woman and that we will all get along well together in the interim of finding her a place to live. She nods, gratefully, but is clearly overwhelmed and flustered by the information. She barely speaks back, only to ask if she can come with us right away or if she has to wait for Father B. to finish his parish duties and escort her later in the day. Her eyes reveal despair and suffering, her body an acute ache. She did not come to us to build strength, but to lose the little she has left. I think about the silver candle holder sitting on my dresser, waiting for me, its single burnt wick like a singed eye.

ST. X. SCHOOL FOR GIRLS looked like a jail. In fact, the public
school for boys down the street had been a military establishment; an
old mess hall was their cafeteria and the detainment building one of
their classroom structures, a relic from the War of 1812. There was
even a spent and preserved cannon in front of the school, in which
many of the boys would hide their drugs and packages of cigarettes.
Our buildings were less obtrusive, but historic as well. The convent
for the nuns and teachers had been a hospital during the nineteenth
century, an institution completely run by women. Our residence had
housed sick children. It was believed that many of those children's
bodies, orphaned or unclaimed, had been incinerated in the boiler
room or buried under the floors. Any unaccountable noises in the
night, cries heard through the walls or knocking sounds, were attrib-
uted to the ghosts of these children. It was further believed that if
you crossed yourself and asked forgiveness, the children would then
be able to sleep peacefully for the night.

The building housing the classrooms and dormitory was
erected in the early 1920s for a convent school. A courtyard on the

south corner, which contained a miniature garden of lilies and daffodils, tufts of sunburnt grass amidst the green, and a few wooden benches built by altar boys, was as bare as the willow trees as I approached that autumn morning. Those trees were said to have been planted by women in order to appease the children they heard screaming down below. Rachel told me once the tree roots were red, made of blood, and if the trees were ever cut down, the children would rise up from their graves to replace them. The walls were grey stone, imposing and sterile, and there was a brass plaque over the front entrance with the school's name in plain block letters. The few windows on the main building were its only gesture of friendliness to the outside world. A black iron fence, five feet high, enclosed the entire plot of land, there to protect the young women in the night. But when I entered, and the black iron gate whined shut, I feared I would never be let out.

Mother Superior was waiting for me as my mother had promised. She resembled the war monuments I had passed on the bus, heavy and solid, her facial features square and thick. Her nose in particular, protruding at a right angle, could have been cut out of stone, and her breasts moved up and down with her breath like large steps.

"Welcome," she began, and motioned to a cardboard box filled with clothes.

"Find two uniforms that fit. No more. That's all we can offer you at this time. You'll need to start wearing them right away." She spoke all her sentences as if she were listing rules, jutting out her chin in tandem with the first syllable of each line, stressing it by stretching out the vowel sound.

The uniform consisted of a navy blue cardigan with a crest bearing the motto of the school, "Our Eyes to Heaven," stitched in fine gold-coloured thread, a plain white blouse with buttons up to the neck, and a grey wool skirt to be worn at calf length.

"Socks must be white or blue. You may not wear nylons."

I didn't own any nylons, and all the socks I'd packed were white. My mother had guessed the nuns would require white socks, and I felt somewhat comforted by the fact she had been right. I sorted through the box, checking tags for sizes and claiming the clothes without measuring them against my frame to determine whether they would actually fit. I didn't want to appear finicky in front of Mother Superior or to take up too much of her time. She seemed in a hurry to get me out of her office.

"Sister Marguerite will give you pencils and notebooks and the textbooks for your classes. She teaches you in the mornings. Sister Aline teaches you in the afternoons and runs the choir. I teach you History. This is the way with your grade. Sister Marguerite will answer your questions, if you have any."

She smiled then, and it didn't suit her face, her lips abnormally wide, though she had a regal handsomeness about her. With my two uniforms, hand-me-downs, draped over my arm, I awkwardly grabbed my luggage and was directed to wait in front of Sister Marguerite's classroom until she had finished teaching the hour. There was no window on the classroom door, and I stood against the wall. When the bell rang for lunch, Sister Marguerite welcomed me and immediately led me to my room in the dormitory section of the building. The uniforms on my arm informed the passing girls that I was staying. Their eyes glanced over me as if I were only slightly noticeable, possibly irritating, like a leak in the roof.

I passed my introductory week in an anxious state. Never having slept away from my family before, I found the nights terrible, alone in my room, unsure of whether or not to speak to girls in the communal washroom area for our floor or ask directions when I had trouble finding my way around to classes, the cafeteria, and the library. I began having nightmares, waking up in my foreign surroundings, sweating in my new sheets, afraid the wetness might mean that I'd peed myself. I dreamt of my mother. She appeared in the room beside me, tended by a child, a little girl in a nurse's outfit, a stethoscope hanging like a necklace, the monitoring device a locket against her chest. I tried to tell the girl that it was I who should be there, administering medicine and water to my mother, but she just ignored me. My mother told me angrily to leave; I was not wanted here. Two large orderlies shoved me out, warning me that I'd be taken to the police if I continued to bother her. I'd wake upset that my mother had not phoned to check up on me. I had tried to phone in the evenings to ask about coming home for the weekend, but no one had answered. I cried into the sheets until it was time to prepare for class.

Although the classes were not as difficult as I had first imagined they would be, they too filled me with dread. It took time to discover the correct decorum and protocol. I learned that putting one's hand up to answer a question did not necessarily mean the teacher would ask you for a response. The nuns liked to pick on those students whose hands weren't up, and even when they called on you, and you stood to answer, you would not be allowed to sit down if your answer was wrong. You were required to stay standing, in front of all the girls, until someone else provided the correct answer to save you from further embarrassment. The lunch bell rang every hour since the classrooms had no clocks, deemed to be distractions. This did not indicate that classes were over, but that one hour was up. The nuns could extend class if they felt like it, and on my first day, Sister Aline did so because she said the class had spent time being introduced to me and summarizing material that should have been mastered by now. I hated being singled out; the other girls were tired of studying and wanted to go back to their rooms. I became the cause of their frustration.

At the end of my torturous week, my father telephoned to inform me that as the new man at his company he would have to work on the weekend. I was told I wouldn't be able to come home for a while, and certainly not that weekend. I tried to hide my disappointment from him, to act like the grown-up girl my parents expected me to be, but I had been looking forward to seeing them both and couldn't conceal the anger in my voice. Without seeing Mother for myself, I could only wonder if her eyes were less sore or if she was able to take walks on her own again. Father told me she was fine and could even read a little bit when the afternoon light came in through the window of her bedroom. He told me to be a good girl and use the time to make friends. Surely there would be other girls staying on the entire week. Other parents must work out of town or on the weekends. I wasn't listening. I was remembering the card games we used to play as a family on Friday nights, drinking hot chocolate with whipped cream even in the summer. It was a tradition that went back as far as I could recall. Mother's illness hadn't changed that; she'd get Christine to help her decide how to play out her hand, or we'd play a three-person game instead of one that required partners. Every once in a while I would drink too much and go to bed with a bellyache, suffering through it so that I wouldn't be scolded for complaining for what was my own fault. Father didn't mention what he and Mother would do now without us. He also didn't ask how I liked the new school or how the nights had been without my family. I wanted to tell him I was miserable and this was all their fault. I wanted to tell him I was meant to be at home, that God had made it clear to me that I should be at home. Anything to get out of here. But he didn't ask.

When Friday classes finished, I returned to my floor in the dormitory. Bella, a girl who wore her hair in braided pigtails, roomed beside me. She was difficult not to notice, although she wasn't physically striking in any way, merely pleasant. She had black hair and a smooth, milky whiteness to her skin, a few tiny beauty marks at the corners of her eyes. But if she was not the most popular with the girls, she was clearly the favourite of the nuns in the school. Bella had the right answers. Bella was attentive and responsive to instruction. When they inspected our hands to make sure we had washed, Bella had no dirt under her fingernails. When Sister Aline handed out music sheets for choir practice, Bella was delegated all the solos, though I had yet to hear her sing. It was obvious she liked it here, and the nuns liked her for it. She was polite to the girls too, in a reserved adult manner. Passing others in the hall or the washroom she would say hello and carry on her way without fuss.

With her mother waiting downstairs for her in the lobby, Bella asked me how I liked my first week at St. X. School for Girls.

"It's all right," I replied, noticing that she had packed a book for an assignment handed out that day and not due for a couple of weeks.

"You staying?"

I shrugged. "My father works on the weekends."

Bella flung her bag over her shoulder, catching her hair. She groaned and lifted the strap to release the braid.

"I've heard it can be fun here on the weekends. Mr. M. comes down and takes some of the girls to the movies and stuff."

I didn't yet know whose father Mr. M. was, or if he was someone's father at all. But it was an indication to me that there might be some advantage to staying at the school and I was interested, although Bella was eager to greet her mother.

"Yeah?" She was friendlier to me than some of the other girls, so I wondered why I didn't feel the urge to befriend her. Perhaps I felt we weren't the same kind of girl. I had no idea whether to define Bella as a potential friend or an enemy.

By informing Bella I was staying because my father worked on weekends, I'd hoped to demonstrate my superiority, my parents' belief that I was capable of being on my own. Instead, Bella saw through me and offered some comfort.

"I'm sure the girls will find something to do together," Bella replied, and walked off to meet her mother, leaving me at the door of my empty room without any idea of what I was going to do next.

I watched the other girls packing up their tote bags and small suitcases or simply carrying a few books outside with them to their parents' cars. They broke out of the gate like horses, sprinting to be on the outside after being kept in. They would have the pleasure of sleeping in their own beds and eating at their dinner tables instead of in the cafeteria. Perhaps they would choose what they wanted to eat instead of being served whatever the staff made. I imagined they had the luxury of two sets of friends, those at school and those in their neighbourhoods, and the knowledge that they were missed at home, for it didn't cost parents any extra to keep their kids at the school for weekends. Tuition, plus room and board was a blanket price. It cost more money for parents to take their children home, for the travel, the outings they might have, and for the extra food. The girls were aware of this. When their parents came to pick them up, they knew they were wanted.

"I SPENT MY WHOLE allowance already," said Rachel. "But we could go window-shop until tomorrow. My dad's gonna take us to see a movie."

"I don't know," Caroline, the tall girl with a French-Canadian accent, wavered, swinging her dark ponytail from side to side around her shoulders while she dried her hands. "Maybe we should just stay in. It's no fun if we can't even get Cokes and sit by the fountain. They'll ask us to leave."

"We could have our meeting tonight then," said Francine, a girl with almost orange hair and with freckles on her cheeks, nose, and forearms.

I ascertained that the two girls who were with Rachel relied on Rachel's money, or at least couldn't keep up with her escapades without it, as neither offered to pay her own way. These two girls leaned against the wall of the washroom as Rachel put on a layer of pink lipstick, smacking her lips in the mirror, betraying annoyance. I knew who they were because I'd jotted down their names in class. Rachel commanded attention, an incredibly pretty girl with curly blonde hair cut at her shoulders and light-green eyes. The other girls in the class deferred to her when she spoke, and no one snickered when she stood to answer a question and got it wrong. Even the nuns were a bit less strict. On my second day of class, Sister Marguerite did not ask her to write the answer to a geography question she had missed three times on the blackboard, because Rachel claimed she hadn't understood the question properly. The classroom went silent. No one except Rachel would have dared turn the blame around on one of the nuns.

Rachel, Caroline, and Francine had a club. I'd heard about their club while they were talking about it in class: The Sisterhood. Their classmates were envious, even a little scared of them, I gathered as I watched from my desk or cafeteria seat, eavesdropping for information about who hung out together, who was well-liked and who was shunned. As Sister Marguerite wrote with chalk, her black back merging with the blackboard, I copied her handwriting in my notebook but kept my attention on the girls.

I saw Rachel the day after my arrival. I came in through our classroom door and stood near the radiator, waiting to see which seat was free. She strolled in, her bookbag held underneath her arm, her blonde hair catching the autumn light coming in through a small window at the far end. Her green eyes flickered. She waved to Caroline, whose dark hair was tied back into a neat braid, hanging down to her tailbone. Caroline's cheekbones were high and pronounced, her skin abnormally pale. She had harder facial features than most of the girls her age, strong lines and a rectangular jaw, dark bushy eyebrows. She resembled a horse and, compared to her,

Rachel was reminiscent of a wild bird. Rachel sat beside her and sifted through the contents of her bookbag, removing her cardigan and shaking it out like a feather pillow. I could tell she was the kind of girl who cared little for things that didn't affect her directly, and the glint in her eye alluded to a continual search for amusement. Caroline appeared more serious and was the tallest girl in the room, almost six feet. She held herself without slouching, which made her height doubly pronounced. The seats around them were quickly taken up, and I was left to sit at the other end of the classroom, Sister Marguerite directing me to an empty desk with a small crack in its wooden seat. The desks were lined up so that two sets, on opposite sides of the classroom, faced each other, while the desks in the centre faced forward to the blackboard. The white tiled floor was slippery, recently washed, and dirt from our shoes instantly clung to it. The radiator gurgled on behind us and Sister Marguerite lectured loudly, tapping her pointer against the desks at the front for emphasis. Initially I was disappointed to be far from Rachel, but when the lecture began I realized I would be able to view her every movement, admire Rachel from afar.

It was Francine's association with Rachel and Caroline that I could not quite comprehend immediately. She was a mousy girl compared to them, a little more like me in that respect. Her reddish-blonde hair had unruly ends that curled in opposite directions, and the freckles on her face were unsymmetrical and blotchy. She squirmed in her skin whenever she moved, and she spoke demurely when forced to. Only later would I discover that Francine and Rachel had gone to elementary school together and their parents had lived on the same street before Francine's father got a job that required him to travel, his wife accompanying him on the business trips. Out of the four of us, Francine was the one who wasn't always forced to stay over for the weekend. She chose to and her parents didn't complain, were perhaps thrilled that their unspectacular daughter had friendships, and didn't want to interfere. Rachel genuinely liked Francine, and protected her as she would later protect me, but you could sense if they hadn't shared a past and had met for the first time at St. X. School for Girls, they wouldn't have been friends. It was from Francine's mouth that I heard about The Sisterhood. After a grammar lesson on active verbs and a short quiz on the Confederation of Canada from which I was compassionately exempt (it being my second day), we were excused for lunch. The bell clanged loudly in my ears, the noise escalating instantaneously as shoes shuffled and voices called to each other, desk chairs screeched across the tiled floors, and doors opened and closed down the hallway. Francine rushed by me, knocking my arm as I swivelled out of my seat, while I worried about who I might sit with at lunch or if I'd be alone. She quietly apologized and continued scrambling to the other side of the room, where Rachel and Caroline were gathering their pencils and books.

I waited outside the class like a shadow without an object as girls from other grades breezed by me. I caught the girls discussing their club as they exited.

"We'll have The Sisterhood meeting on Saturday," Rachel said.

"After the movie?" Francine asked, eager to keep pace with Rachel and Caroline, who walked side by side down the right side of the hallway as girls walking the other way came by on the left. I shoved my loose-leaf papers into my binder without ordering them and followed behind. The hallway was narrow. A new row of orange lockers had recently been installed, and their shiny rectangular boxes jutted out, forcing girls to brush arms and offering a stark contrast to the dullness of the white tiled floors. The cramped hallway worked to my advantage, because there was no room for someone to steal my place in the line.

"Should we invite Yvonne?" piped Caroline, her long braid swinging along her waist.

"Nah," said Rachel. "We don't need her any more."

Francine laughed uncomfortably. I judged at the time that she had not been part of their group long enough to make any decisions or offer her own opinions. But that was just the way Francine was, content to follow. I learned quickly that most girls were cruel unless you could force them to respect you. They didn't want to suspect you needed them. They needed to feel like they needed you. And I didn't have anything to offer. As they turned the corner, Francine shuffled alongside Caroline. If the girl named Yvonne wasn't invited, it was apparent Francine could not invite her herself. I wondered what she had done to displease them, but my locker was not near theirs, and I lost sight of them and could no longer hear their conversation. At lunch in the cafeteria, after standing in line for my food and scanning the area as I stood with my plastic tray in hand, content not to get bumped and spill my juice or mashed potatoes on my new uniform, I ended up sitting beside two girls in a grade lower than mine. They asked me questions about where I was from and how long I'd be staying, what I liked to do, if I'd seen this movie or that one. They seemed like nice girls, polite and friendly, offering me advice on which meals to avoid (they were right about the mashed potatoes, dry and crunchy) and how to know whether Mother Superior was having a good day or a bad day (depending on whether she used the long pointed stick when she taught); but I guess I'd already decided which camp I wanted to be part of, and watched as Rachel, Caroline, and Francine ate quickly and left the dining hall to go outside, Rachel's blonde locks leading the way.

"They won't ask us to leave," Rachel said, untangling her hair with a round brush and handing a dark-blue scarf to Francine, who proceeded to tie it around her neck.

I sat listening in the toilet stall, peeking through the crack between the door and the hinge, dreading the thought of another night by myself, reading and catching up on class material the nuns had produced for me in piles. They claimed I was behind in school because I hadn't received a proper education in the country. I felt like a dog they needed to house-train. I wasn't sure if the girls knew I was in the stall, finished but holding my breath, hoping to come up with a way to interrupt them, step out without making myself unwelcome.

"What's your sister up to?" The question was directed to Caroline.

"She's got a date tonight. She left me a note in the wall. A tall Frenchman who works at a club."

Rachel sighed. "Oh, well. I guess she'll have a good time."

I could see Caroline applying powder to her face in the mirror. "She tells me French guys are for the birds. But she does make exceptions. She'll get free drinks and stuff."

"Can we get in?" asked Rachel, nudging Francine, who looked a bit afraid at the possibility of older men and alcoholic drinks.

"Not tonight. I already asked. There's a lot of cops around the Market lately. Some fights. She's going to do LSD."

"What's LSD?" asked Francine.

"A drug that makes you see colours and stuff," Caroline replied proudly. "She says you feel like you are in another world. A pretty place where you feel good." She bent over the sink, examining her face close up, and frowned. "I wish I was as pretty as Aimée. Maman calls her dangerously pretty."

"Maybe the boys from G. will be in the Market. We could check," Francine piped up.

Rachel rapped her fingers on the sink in agitation. "You're right, Caroline. It's no fun to go without any money."

I flushed and quickly opened the door. The girls looked me over the way you might a scab on your elbow. Francine chuckled and Rachel held her lipstick tube in front of her like a potential weapon. Caroline continued to powder her face and splash some water on her eyebrows, brushing the hair with her fingertips into an even line. She was like a stick figure, a straight back and long legs, her hair equally straight along her backside.

My father had slipped twenty-five dollars into my jacket pocket, which he told me only to use in an emergency, when I left to get on the bus for the school. I hid the money underneath my mattress. The guilt I knew I would feel spending it, weighed against my loneliness, seemed justified. I took a breath, wishing the girls would miraculously change their expressions of annoyance. Their strength in numbers drew me towards them. Their makeup bags filled with cosmetics also fascinated me. I had only used makeup on special occasions. My mother would apply a little blush to my cheeks and a clear lip gloss across my lips. I wasn't allowed to wear it outside.

"I have some money," I said, still dressed in my uniform and feeling a little childish compared to their framed eyes and shiny lips. "If you want ... I don't know what there is around here.... I'm new ... and ... anyway." I tried to appear casual, but my hands were shaking. My fingers linked around the back of my skirt, and I checked to make sure my zipper was closed.

Rachel and Caroline turned towards each other like twin marionettes and shrugged in unison. Francine pushed her heel against the wall, waiting for them to decide. At this point I had no idea whether we were even allowed outside the walls of the school or whether the girls had to sneak out. Getting into trouble so soon would not bode well for my time here, I surmised, but I also didn't want to appear to be afraid of following them. For all I could judge, they might be applying makeup to pass the time and would then wash their faces and go to bed fantasizing about LSD, colourful places, and boys who bought you drinks in bars.

"Yeah, OK," Rachel said. "We could show you around." She smiled then, and I was struck by the softness of her face, the way her smile caused her green eyes to beckon warmth. Some of my nervousness left me. *They're just girls,* I thought, *like me. They want to go out and look at dresses and pick out makeup and bracelets. They want to talk about boys. They are nothing to be afraid of.* Still, my hands continued to shake as I returned Rachel's smile. Heat ran through my body in a rush. I may even have blushed.

"Great," I said, a little too eagerly. "I'll change then and come back here?"

Rachel and Caroline didn't respond, but Francine nodded enthusiastically. Rachel was already conjuring up a map of where we would go. "We've got three hours before we have to be back," she said, and the girls tallied up on their fingers places we might visit. I was trying to think of whether I had any clothes that might impress them—a bright scarf or an interesting necklace—but I knew I didn't. The dresses I had brought with me were mostly ones my mother had sewn, and they went down to my ankles. She was afraid I would outgrow them too quickly and made all my dresses long so they could last me a couple of years. This was before her fingers had begun to burn. She stopped sewing after that, and a few of the dresses weren't even hemmed; I couldn't wear them without tripping. The dresses that didn't fall to my ankles and were bought at stores had frills on the hems and bows in front and were meant for church. I hadn't packed everything, I thought bitterly to myself, because I thought I'd be going home to pick up more things. I'd have to cut up one of the longer dresses some night, one that would leave a straight clean edge, I decided, taking note of how these girls rolled up the material on the waists of their skirts to bring the hems above their knees. I owned a single tube of lipstick my mother had let me keep, ground down to a stub and dried up. I could barely get any colour from it to transfer onto my fingers. It wouldn't do. But I couldn't do everything in one night, and I accepted that I'd just have to catch up to them later. There were other things besides "proper" schooling that I had missed out on in the country. Back home there were rumours of what certain girls did, ones who were already wearing makeup and short skirts and running around at night near the strip of restaurants and bars in the nearby town that fancied itself a city. Those girls were condemned. Here, it was clear, the opposite held true. I was upset that I'd never had the experiences these girls obviously had; they'd aged ahead of me. On the morning I'd left my parents, before taking the bus and entering the school unchaperoned, my mother had commented: "You are such a young lady now. A real young lady." Maybe this was part of what she knew I would come to learn. Why hadn't she prepared me? How would I be able to handle it all at once?

"I didn't know you were a Leftover," Caroline said just as I was about to go to my room and rummage through the clothes I'd only recently unpacked. She held out her makeup brush to me and I applied a little powder to my cheeks, which made me look pale because her complexion was naturally lighter than mine.

"A Leftover?" I replied, handing back the brush, worried they might be making fun of me.

"Someone who stays on the weekends. Your parents don't come for you?"

"Oh? No," I said, feeling worse that they knew I had been abandoned. "My mother doesn't leave the house."

I don't know why I didn't mention my father instead of my mother as I had to Bella. I certainly didn't want to have to explain that my mother was ill and none of the doctors had been able to help her and my father had to work harder to afford life in the city. I didn't want to get into it with them. I was ashamed. But no one asked me for an explanation. I wondered why each of them, especially Rachel, was here.

"Mine doesn't leave the house either," said Rachel to the mirror without turning around, pressing her index finger against her eyelashes to curl them.

But her father did. She said he was going to take the girls to a movie the following day. Bella's mention of a Mr. M. came to mind, and I concluded it must be Rachel's father who liked to treat the girls who stayed on the weekends. I wanted him to take me too, so I knew I'd have to make Rachel think I was worthy of their company. If I couldn't do this with clothes and makeup, I'd do it another way. I was determined to be one of them. To latch on to their group. Leftover or not. It hadn't yet occurred to me to think of them as Leftovers too. They had each other. All I had was a dormitory room with concrete walls and a carpet that curled at the corners, worn out and ill-installed. The room was furnished (as the pamphlet for the school had promised), and I had a bed and a single mattress (lumpy in parts, which I was slowly adjusting to by curling up on my right side when I slept), a black-painted table made out of cork and used as a desk, a bedside lamp, and a dresser with two drawers. My closet was half the size of the other girls' because my room was in a corner and the angle had cut off space during the dormitory's construction. There was enough room for a few hangers, and I had stashed the rest of my things on the floor in three shoeboxes left by the last occupant. A large maple tree whose leaves slashed against the glass whenever the wind blew blocked my view from the window. Oddly, although the room had been scrubbed clean with disinfectants and vacuumed before I moved in, it still smelled of dust. There was nothing I desired more than to avoid being confined to my cramped quarters for another evening, staring at that bulky tree.

"I'll go get the money," I said and sprinted down the hallway, nearly tripping over my own feet.

The market's stores were lit up in the dying light of the day as we strolled by. Rachel and Caroline linked arms in front, and Francine and I exchanged awkward smiles and giggles following behind. We had our jackets on, but the air was humid enough for us to leave the zippers and buttons undone, or at least the other girls were more interested in showing off their shirts and accessories than in fending off cold. The Market comprised a square area enclosed by four roads in the downtown core. Cars moved slowly to accommodate the people who didn't wait for "Walk" signs or streetlights to cross over, crowds who were strolling around and browsing merchandise in the windows or in booths erected outside, their owners bundled up and sipping coffee, children and adults with snacks in their hands: a glass of lemonade, a caramel apple, a chocolate bar, or a fried pastry. The Market was buzzing, and we swarmed around the clusters of fresh foods and handmade jewellery, tourist shops full of postcards and T-shirts, the cafés and restaurants lining the square, the electric lights with their hum calling us in. I was mesmerized. A night out in the city, and I was without an adult and with a group of girls I desperately wanted to call my friends. My need was as immense as the city itself, with its hand-to-hand exchanges of money and goods and services. My father had said that the city of Ottawa was built in a valley. It had become the capital of Canada because it was a centre geographically. *Anything that gets inside, stays inside,* he said. *The cold, the heat. The city contains it.* The city grew in front of me, in the dark-blue twilight, opening its hungry mouth.

Rachel and Caroline tried on silver jewellery in front of an old woman who sat stiffly behind the table, counting out change in her pockets, a baggy beige coat puffed out around her. She kept one eye on the change in her hand and her other eye on them. Francine and I rifled through a rack of colourful cotton dresses from India, monitored by a dark-skinned man who wore a white turban on his head and smelled of strong spice. There were so many things to attract my eye that I couldn't concentrate, unlike Francine, who picked out an orange and purple dress with embroidered stitches resembling fruit along the hem and edges of the sleeves. She paraded in front of the mirror nailed to the makeshift wall of the booth with the dress held in her arms, dancing with the cloth as if it were an invisible woman. Rachel and Caroline laughed, discarding their jewellery to circle around her mockingly. "I'm an Indian princess," they chanted. "Look at me!" The dark-skinned man rose from his seat, agitated at first, but relaxed when he saw their jabs weren't directed at him.

I had my money in my pocket. Twenty-five dollars. I didn't know how to spend it, if I should offer it up all at once, or if they would ask me for it when they wanted to purchase something. Everything in the Market was for sale, and everything pleased me with its novelty and up-to-date style: the synthetic fabrics and cheap designer copies, the pungent food fare encapsulating all. I had been to the city nearest our old town and realized that markets in all cities were probably alike, but to me this was the grandest and most exotic market I had ever seen. It was Rachel's market, and she and her friends were showing it to me. The girls were content just to look for a while, retracing steps from previous weeks, accustomed to the regular merchandise and searching out newer, just-in necklaces or shirts. We walked around the square, past flower stands of irises and pink roses, carnations and sunflowers, and vegetable stands with baskets of squash and corn, large pumpkins lining the sidewalk waiting for holiday tarts and pies and salted seeds.

Rachel suggested we visit an Italian café on the corner where they had desserts and coffee, and which was one of the few establishments besides the restaurants that would admit underage girls in the evening. The circular glass case in the window turned electrically and was filled with treats, the slices carefully removed by the young woman behind the counter, who seemed less interested in the chocolate and caramel cheesecakes and the bowl of whipped cream into which she dipped her spoon to top off the slices than in two young men who flirted with her each time she strode by, which was often.

As soon as I saw the double-chocolate cheesecake with carved chocolate flowers on top, I knew I had to have it. Rachel had one too, I remember. I felt as if we had shared a secret when we both pointed to the same cake and smiled with anticipation at the same time. Again, I was struck by her beauty: the way her cheekbones lifted when she smiled and how the skin around her eyes stretched into half moons. She had the brightest blonde hair I'd ever seen, like gold thread, without a hint of white or brown. When she looked directly at me, I could feel myself go slightly numb.

The young woman served us our cakes and milkshakes and we dove in, hardly speaking for a few moments as we enjoyed our dessert. The music from a couple of the clubs had started, taunting us a little, but for the moment we were happy where we were. I was beginning to relax in their company, not to feel so guarded, when Caroline asked about my mother and father again.

"So what do they do?"

"My father's a carpenter," I said, placing the cloth napkin over my lips so as not to talk with my mouth full and wide open. "My mother doesn't work."

I hoped my answer pleased them. I had no idea what their parents did for a living, and I still didn't want them to know about my mother's illness.

"My mom works on the weekends. She's also taking a class to learn English. She can get by around here. Ottawa's full of French people anyway, but she wants a promotion," Caroline said. "It doesn't matter that she knows English. Because of the rules she has to have a certificate."

I was relieved that they might not all be as well off as I'd first thought. I knew the school was expensive, but it was evidently not out of reach for parents who really wanted their children to go there, if they made sacrifices. Like my own parents had supposedly done.

"Maman says she doesn't want me to turn out like my sister. That's why I'm getting a solid Catholic education." Caroline tightened her lips and pointed her finger at me in imitation of her mother as she furrowed her brow. The girls laughed so I joined them.

"Aimée's not so bad," Francine blurted between mouthfuls. "I mean, from what you've told us."

"No, but Maman thinks she is. Says it's why she's all over the boys. That she's never going to get anywhere wasting her time working in a store and going to the clubs at night. Maman's old-fashioned."

"You should hear my mother," Francine said, putting her fork down and speaking quickly as if afraid she wouldn't get another chance. "My mother wants me to become a nun. She said that would be her greatest achievement, if I became a nun like her Aunt Madeline!"

Rachel folded her napkin around her head like a wimple. Caroline followed suit. As I didn't want to offend Rachel and Caroline by assuming I could participate in their teasing, I simply chuckled. Francine took it well.

"Who wants to be like them? Sister Marguerite's freaky and Sister Aline's a bore! I don't even want to know what Mother Superior does in that office of hers all day."

"You'll see," added Caroline to me. "Those nuns are nuts! All they do is think about God and keeping their fingernails clean. Maman says they should tell us about their lives and we'd be fascinated, but I tell her they don't do anything, so what do they have to tell except spelling lessons and choir sheets?" Caroline placed her makeshift wimple back down on the table.

"Well, my mom's probably never thought about it," Rachel said and then went silent, as if she didn't like where the conversation was headed. She didn't pout, but she used her fork to poke through the layers in her cake without eating her icing. I hadn't yet learned what Mr. M. did for a living or what kind of relationship Rachel had with her mother. I couldn't imagine her having any troubles, though. Her mother wasn't going blind and losing all her energy like mine was, of that I was sure. And her father probably didn't have conversations with his wife about what God might be punishing her for. Rachel seemed to have everything she wanted. I got up to use the washroom.

By the time I returned, they were speaking about a girl named Adrienne. I sat down and Rachel eyed me up and down. I checked to see if I had any crumbs on my shirt, but there weren't any. She snickered.

"Adrienne was a good friend of ours," she said. "You have her room."

"Oh," I replied, wondering if they resented me taking her place, filling her room with new things except for the shoeboxes. "Where did she go?"

"Her mother won the lottery, took her out of school that very week. School just started."

Caroline thumped her hand on the table, shaking the sugar dispenser. "Maman's played ever since I can remember, and Adrienne's mother wins the first time she plays. Can you beat that?"

"Sister Aline says it's not Christian to gamble," mumbled Francine as she sipped on her straw, her front teeth holding it in place.

"Who cares?" Rachel snapped back. "My father says that since they won so much money, they should have donated some to the school like he does. But they went to live in France instead. Bought a vineyard or something ridiculous."

"I'd go live somewhere else if I had all that money," Caroline said wistfully, her elbows on the table. She'd finished her cake and her drink. "Wouldn't you?"

"I don't know," I answered honestly. "I've never thought about it."

"Nobody likes to be broke," she continued.

"No, I guess not," I replied.

The cakes were expensive when buying for four and with a milkshake each, but I didn't care. We were out on the town and I felt grown-up sitting at the table being served without being chaperoned. We were eating in a place that had tablecloths and candles and where I would receive the bill from the waitress. The double-chocolate cheesecake melted in my mouth deliciously. I can still taste its sweetness if I concentrate hard enough.

LATER THE SAME EVENING I found my opening. Although the girls were treating me well, I was painfully aware it was due largely to the fact that I was treating them all. Since it was the emergency money my father had given me, and because I'd never received an allowance and didn't know how long it would be before my father or mother would give me any more, I knew I couldn't count on money to keep me in their company. For the night, however, I enjoyed being able to provide for our short-term happiness. We went from the café to the Hudson's Bay Company, the largest store in the city, located near the Market where the canal passed. Boats lined the sides of the canal, some with their lights on, others dark, attached by ropes and buoys to the concrete shore. With winter approaching, their residents would soon need to vacate their temporary homes. I wondered where those people went and where the boats were taken when the canal froze over. I bought the girls Cokes and plastic bags filled with candy to take home. I also bought them each a fashion magazine from the newsstand near the store exit. This way we could all trade after reading them and enviously admiring the glamorous women on the covers and in the layouts, their bodies thin and attractive to men, not much unlike our own except that they were comfortable in them. The male clerk gave us a wink and we amused ourselves by speculating on what his girlfriend might be like, whether she resembled any of the women in the magazines we had just purchased.

By the time we browsed the clothing, I hadn't much left in my pocket, and we resigned ourselves to window-shopping. We touched the alluring fabrics on mannequins and tried on some of the complimentary perfume at a stand. I picked a lily scent, knowing it was my mother's favourite flower, spraying the liquid on my wrists and under my ears as I had watched her do before her skin became so sensitive she no longer could. Rachel managed to get us samples from a clerk she knew because her father bought perfume for her mother there. "She doesn't leave her room in the morning without it," said Rachel, flinching at the sight of the bottle, one of the most expensive brands, kept in a glass case with a key. The clerk gave us each a small tube of skin lotion and explained how to brush it in an upward motion on our cheeks to avoid lines and wrinkles. "They come sooner than you think," she said. We practised in the mirror, taking her directions as seriously as if she were explaining procedures to follow during a medical emergency or a fire. I circled the cream around my eyes, aging myself in the process, imagining what I would look like when I started to get wrinkles like my mother. Whether I might end up with skin as sensitive as hers.

I was thinking about using the last of my money to buy Rachel the cheap perfume in a cute yellow glass sitting on the counter until we saw the red satin bra. Rachel was the first to notice it. She had rushed ahead to the women's underwear section and was pointing at the skinny mannequin with the large breasts who was wearing it when we caught up to her. We were pinched with envy at how elegant and beyond us it was.

The bra was bright red and the cups only covered half the plastic breasts, the cloth stopping just above the nipple line. There were two layers, one of satin and one of lace, both the exact same shade of fire hydrant red. Rachel stood behind the mannequin cupping its breasts with her hands.

"Could you imagine wearing that to a club?" she cooed, fingering the material.

Caroline, Francine, and I were speechless. It seems a bit ridiculous now, the fuss we made over a bra in the department store. Even if it was red. We were wearing bras; my mother had bought me two, although mine were white and completely cotton, and because of my late development the cups were flat as doilies. The other girls, from what I could gather through their white blouses in the washroom in the morning and the changing rooms for gym class, were sporting bras of similar practicality. But the red bra attracted us with more than just its exotic fabric and flashy colour. You would need to be a woman to wear a bra like that; you would need to wear it for a man. When a middle-aged saleslady with feathered hair walked by, eyeing us suspiciously, Rachel took her hands off the mannequin and smiled.

"It's so pretty," she said to her.

"It is, isn't it?" the saleslady replied, pushing her glasses up the bridge of her nose and herself examining the cloth between her fingers. "It's new."

She left us, her hand lingering on Rachel's shoulder as she turned to adjust a display on the other side of the racks. She had decided we were harmless.

Rachel grabbed the price tag.

"Twenty-five dollars," she read, the exact amount I had started the evening with. There were duplicates of the bra on the table beside the mannequin, and she sorted through them. "I don't think they have my size," Rachel said.

"They probably don't make them that small," Caroline replied.

"Who asked you?"

"It should be here for a while if it's new," Francine offered.

Rachel let go of the price tag and pouted. The saleslady glanced at her sympathetically and then went back to work. Rachel fumbled through the bras on the table with a fierceness that made us all silent. Then she pushed Caroline aside as she went to the other racks. But she flipped the underwear on the hangers with disinterest. She even checked her watch. Our good time was threatened by the simple knowledge that we were not old enough and didn't have enough money to wear a red satin bra.

"My dad will never buy me one of those," she said to me, walking back over to the table with the red bras. "Look." She grabbed one with cups that were barely curved. "I know this would fit me." She held it up against her chest, pressing the cups against her shirt and prancing in front of the display mirror. Then she handed it over to Caroline, who stroked it a little, folded it, and returned it to the table. Rachel made her way to the exit, buttoning up her jacket.

"Well, are you coming? We don't have any more money, so we might as well go back."

Caroline exchanged an annoyed expression with Francine. Then she whispered to me, "She can't stand not having something she wants. Her father spoils her rotten." But they followed her command nonetheless, edging towards her.

"I'll meet you in front," I said. "I've got to use the washroom." I followed the sign that directed me left of the women's underwear section.

When we returned to the school, the large iron gates closing behind us as we held our magazines and candy, I was bursting with pride. Although Rachel was disappointed by not getting what she wanted, Caroline and Francine had warmed up to me, and they thanked me for the stuff I'd bought them before they settled in their rooms for bed. Sister Marguerite was monitoring the dormitory building, but she was barely alert. She perused a newspaper and didn't speak to us as we passed. The girls shut their doors and turned off the lights, but they had flashlights hidden in their beds so they could read after hours, and I was sure Caroline and Francine would do just that, flipping through their new magazines, shoving toffees and mints into their mouths until their teeth hurt.

I waited a few minutes, getting up my nerve, then left my room still wearing my jacket. Rachel's door was closed, so I knocked as silently as possible. She opened the door.

"What do you want?" she said, already changed into a pink cotton nightgown, her body blocking my view of her room. Her bed was

all I could make out, with a matching pastel pink afghan on top, waiting for her to slip inside. She placed one of her hands on her hip and
sighed, as if we had returned hours ago and I had interrupted her sleep.

"I have something for you," I replied.

I'd never stolen anything before. I couldn't believe how easy it
had been, how natural when I set my mind to it, when there was a
reason for doing so. When I left for the washroom, I zipped open the
large right-hand pocket on my jacket. The thought crossed my mind
that with Rachel's foul mood the girls might leave without me, but
I decided to risk that too. The timing was perfect. As I exited the
washroom, the saleslady had her glasses off and was intent on cleaning them, wetting her fingers across her lips and rubbing them over
the lenses. She didn't see me as I snatched the bra from the table and
shoved it into my pocket. The bra had a wire, but Rachel's size was
small enough that it fit snugly, without a bulge poking out to give me
away. I kept a Kleenex hidden in my palm, which I planned to use to
wipe my nose in case the saleslady became alarmed by the movement
of my hands digging into my pocket. But she didn't register me at all.

When I met the girls outside the store near the canal, waiting for
the bus back to St. X. School for Girls, Caroline eyed me strangely.

"Your face is all red," she said.

Rachel scowled but led us home. It would be all right, I told
myself. I began to relax. I had something Rachel wanted.

"It's yours," I said now. "I ... stole it."

I extracted the bra from my jacket and handed it gently to her,
as if it might tear. She received my offering, darting her eyes up at
me and then back down at the bra with amazement.

"I never would have thought that you ..."

She didn't finish. She pulled me inside her room, which I could see now was larger than mine, but cleaner than I thought it would be. She had movie posters on the wall. Aside from a few trinkets on her dresser, her school books piled on a wooden desk, the silver candle holder displayed on one of the bookshelves, most of her personal items were in her drawers and in her closet. Her plastic bag with the candy and magazine were already out of sight.

She lifted her pink nightgown, tossing it on the afghan on the bed. Even though I knew she was pleased, I shook with nervousness. Her body was bare except for her full-brief white underwear. She fastened the red bra to her chest and faced me. It was out of place with her ordinary cotton underwear, and it was still a size too large, but she was beaming, adjusting the straps and twisting her hips from side to side. To me, she looked like a young movie star from one of her posters, her white skin striking against the bold red.

The plan worked. Rachel slapped my back and tried to hold back giggles so as not to attract attention to her room. I told her how beautiful she looked. She told me the bra was the best gift she'd ever received. I had to resist the urge to touch the satin fabric while she was wearing it, the lace against her budding breasts. Rachel was thankful, but she knew there now existed a debt on her side. My gesture was genuine, yet nothing comes without a price.

THERE IS NOTHING LIKE a pregnancy to get a bunch of child-less women stirring. The Sisters try to entice Kim to eat fresh berries and other fruit bought at the local market or the organic food store a few blocks farther away. They ply her with cartons of two-percent, homogenized, and lactose-free milk, and different kinds of rye, honey-grain, and cinnamon breads. "Have just a bite," Sister Josie says, holding up a Granny Smith apple, bright green and round. "Please, for the baby's sake." And Sister Sarah, directly behind her, nods her approval like a mother. They are going about this business all wrong. Kim flinches at the word "baby," is keeping thin, I believe, on purpose. The skinnier she stays, the less likely to accept the inevitable. At lunch, as we sit in the cafeteria, she rests her head on her folded arms, her eyes red with sleeplessness, the olive skin around her cheeks pinched and uneven in tone. Besides, I think, when has an apple ever brought a woman any good? It's not going to save her.

She fingers the slices of tangerine on her plate, rearranging them into indistinct patterns, and replaces the green apple in the fruit bowl set in front of her on the table. She smiles politely at the Sisters, her teeth unusually white, like a newly painted wall, but it is clear she cannot bear the attention. She seeks to melt into the surroundings: her chair, the long cafeteria tables, the windowsills where there is a view of a corner of the orchard and the street outside. Times have changed. Two women walk side by side holding hands when I look over. A young man with piercings in his nose and eyebrows stops to point at the rhododendrons in a planter near the entrance to our convent. I wonder if he knows what he's pointing at. The building is frequently mistaken for a school, a hotel, or an old-age home, depending on who happens to be visible from the windows or sitting outside the entrance, depending on what they're wearing. Possibly because of our penchant for black, the most frequent assumption is that it's a funeral home, though I remember once a woman stopping to ask me if our convent was the battered-women's shelter rumoured to be going up in the area. "No," I replied. "We've been here forever." "Funny, I never noticed what this place was," she said and kept on her way. We have a sign on the entrance doors like those on office buildings, but we have no sign on our gates. You must enter to know where you are. Returning home from an errand or from church, I've often thought that our convent could be mistaken for a mental-health group home where patients reintegrate slowly into society. Mr. Q., who is Father B. and Mother Superior's favourite social worker, took us on a field trip to one located in the west end of the city, and it seems similarly set up. There is a fence there too, dormitory rooms and a cafeteria, as well as a recreation room and a garden outside for the patients. We had tea there, and apart from a few of the patients' odd demeanours, and the time required to instruct them on how to perform the most ordinary tasks (how to use a bus transfer or how to clean up the coffee machine after use), the home was a somewhat familiar place. They live closely together too, grow accustomed to the particular habits of their peers. The only major difference was the men. We rarely house visiting male relatives, only when there is really nowhere else to board them. Otherwise, it's women only.

Kim scrunches herself into as tiny a space as she can manage, her elbows tight against her rib cage as she eats, her posture hunchbacked. Talking about her past is out of the question. There is little about her any of us have been able to discover in these couple of weeks. She's a smart young lady, the way she hoards her memories. She converses with us, but she skilfully avoids the Sisters' questions.

"Where is your family?" I overheard Sister Claire ask her, suspiciously taking a trip to the other side of our dining hall, pretending to admire the orchard through the window behind Kim, after commenting, as many of us have, on the lateness of the snow.

Kim simply took up her fork and replied, "Not sure. What about yours?" Most Sisters, eager to speak about themselves to someone new, answer her and forget about their initial question. Sister Claire went on about her grandfather's piano business and how her mother was a schoolteacher, her father a dentist. About ten years ago he successfully urged one of his colleagues to furnish her with braces for free. Sister Claire had been a comical sight with her metallic smile and her dark habit, but her teeth were perfectly straight afterwards, unlike mine, with their small gaps. When a few of us accused her of vanity, she claimed she needed braces for medical purposes, but I've seen her smiling into the mirror in the cafeteria washroom at her new set of teeth. Kim feigns interest in the Sisters' histories, asks a follow-up question to keep them talking. Background noise for her silence here. Within a short time, she has it down to a routine. Many of the Sisters will tell her about how they entered the convent and the reaction their parents had when they did. Sister Katherine's brothers disowned her immediately, as did her mother. "The gates in convents," she explained to Kim, "were originally set up not to keep us in, but to keep others out. I heard of one woman back in my country who had broken ribs because her father had tried to drag her out against her will before she took her vows." "You'd think they'd be happy that they wouldn't have to worry about you," Kim had responded, genuinely intrigued. "Worry? They were worried we wouldn't be under the control of men. Allowed to just be ourselves under God. A lot of women here were made to feel ashamed for their calling. Not wanting to get pregnant was seen as unnatural. You were supposed to have babies. You weren't supposed to give up your father's name until you found another father's name to claim you," she said. "Under the sanctions of marriage, of course." "Of course," Kim replied and got up to get some juice.

Kim has also managed to keep Mr. Q. at bay. Generally, Mr. Q. is quick as an eagle, swooping down to collect the unfortunate in his claws. "That man," Father B. says, "is a miracle worker." He finds shelter for the battered, food for the homeless, and Christian counselling for the mentally ill or distraught. He signs them up for programs: Get Well Get Work, Fear of Failure Group, Alcoholics Anonymous, Incest Survivors. He comes regularly to church, sits attentively in the first-row pew, has tea with the parishioners after Mass, and homes in upon his subjects. Of course, he doesn't attend on weekends, doesn't seem to mind losing that demographic. But he tells us that those in need of help tend to arrive when you least expect them, during the days, not at peak hours of worship. They are self-conscious of their problems and don't like to be watched, he claims. Sunday Mass is for those who have their act together. He reminds me of a medical doctor, the way he tries to diagnose a soul in trouble, ascertain the problem within an hour or two, then sign them up for tests. He has his own office, in a room in the back of the church for confidentiality. Father B. gave it to him three years ago. He has a phone in there and a picture of his wife and two kids smiling in front of their two-storey home. He thinks the photograph sets a good example. I think he's rubbing it in their faces. Kim has threatened to run away if she is sent to see him, says she distrusts men, and Father B. bends to her will, but he tells her she will soon have to think of the future. Mr. Q. advised Father B. that Kim would begin to open up if her self-confidence was raised, that he should assign her some light responsibilities to make her feel useful and integral to the community. Father B. immediately gave her work. She is going to help with the rummage sale, the proceeds from which will pay for the turkey dinners we send to the Catholic food bank at Christmas. She will be paired up with me, though really I've been rather unsociable since the arrival of my package. I've been spending my nights with a notebook and a copy of the telephone book, trying to remember the full names of the girls I went to school with. It must be one of them trying to expose me. Someone else must have witnessed what happened that night in Room 313. Someone who must have been scared all these years to confront us, but has finally found the strength or else can't handle the stress of keeping secrets any longer. The telephone book has offered few clues. People move so often these days. And those who were girls then are now women in their early forties with maiden names changed to married names and plane tickets and careers that might have uprooted them from here. I wonder how it is that I was located, without a last name. Two weeks of nightly searching under any lead I could think of has turned up nothing solid, nothing I'd want to act upon by phoning or staking out an address. Plus I've found it exceedingly difficult to remember family names, since in my profession we use them so rarely.

Father B. asked me after Mass if I've been having any sort of trouble, but I managed to brush him off. "I haven't been feeling well," I said. "Might be a cold. I'm not as young as I used to be." He chuckled but said if I required his assistance, I knew where to find him. Father B. probably thinks supervising Kim will do me good too, so I hoped to divert his curiosity by adding, "I am concerned about her." He accepted my explanation, and I was momentarily thankful. But I'm not looking forward to working with this pregnant girl, her belly holding us both down like a stone caught in our throats. I pray to myself, *Kim, do not let your own weakness join with mine. Seek out the strong, or we will both drown.* I have my own burdens that have nothing to do with her predicament, and they are plenty for one person.

As I eat a bland egg-salad sandwich, I watch her, Sister Claire usurped by Sister Sarah, whose hands are curled, thumbs touching the middle fingers on either side, painfully attempting to convert Kim to her new yoga regimen. She tried with me too a few months ago. I found it unbearable to listen to my own heartbeat for that long. *Da-dum. Da-dum, Da-dum. Da-dum.* Like hard footsteps coming closer and closer. I'd started to panic, dropped out with the excuse of an acute headache.

Kim indulges her, sucks on an orange peel, biting the skin as if it were her own.

I HAD INGRATIATED MYSELF to Rachel, which meant that I had ingratiated myself to The Sisterhood. After only a couple of weeks we established a routine that was fairly regular. We had our meetings on Wednesday nights and on whichever weekend night Mr. M. did not take us out. These meetings consisted of opening Rachel's window to smoke cigarettes, writing fake notes, and making sketches of the girls in the class and of the nuns, then tearing them into little pieces to dispose of in the garbage at the end of the night. We applied make-up and did each other's hair, we read fashion magazines and stole pornographic magazines, which we hid underneath our mattresses. We read the articles on kissing and new trends in music and movies. We played games that seemed risqué, daring each other to take off our clothes or make a crank call from the phone in the lobby next to Mother Superior's office. We told each other the swear words we overheard the boys who passed by the school using. Then we told each other the names of the boys we fantasized about dating. We tried to hypnotize each other and conduct séances, and we made messes out of ourselves eating junk food and drinking cans of pop into the night. When asked, we acted like we were doing worse things than we were, implying various horrible sins the likes of which we couldn't speak aloud. We dropped The Sisterhood into as many conversations as we could. The other girls were nicer to me now, even tried to get on my good side by asking if I needed help with any of the school assignments. The girl Yvonne, whom I had replaced, didn't betray us. She seemed to think she might be invited again.

With various holidays about to begin, the choir sheets were put to use. I understood immediately why Bella had been given all the solos. None of the girls teased Bella about her talent. I'm not sure if that was because she was so good or if they were afraid of the nuns, who were enormously proud to have such a gem to show off to the parents. We all enjoyed her singing; it was impossible not to. When she sang, it was nearly impossible to think. She had the ability to clear one's thoughts with her voice, which filled the church, and she could hold a single note for what seemed like an eternity. When we passed each other in the hallways of the school or the dormitory, I was amazed that such an ordinary creature could move others so effortlessly, with nothing but her voice. Bella and Rachel were complete opposites, but I suspected Bella possessed a power even Rachel didn't. I just couldn't put my finger on it. There was a calmness to her face when she sang, not unlike the look of serenity she had in the classroom busy at her work. I'd never seen that look on someone of my own age before, only on my mother when she spoke of God.

On Mondays, Tuesdays, and Wednesdays, we had choir practice in the afternoons and calisthenics in the mornings. On Thursdays and Fridays the activities were reversed. It was said that

Mother Superior liked to send the girls home a little tired, to prove they had studied hard during the week, that the nuns had earned their keep. There were many tests, and lots of little reports we had to write on a weekly basis for school, but the tests Rachel set up for us girls were more rigorous and anticipated and held much more anxiety for me than a future report card to my parents. As I relied more and more on The Sisterhood, pleasing my parents mattered less and less. I wanted to please Rachel. We all had to come up with new ways of amusing ourselves, ways to go further in our advancement as young women. One night we kissed our arms until we produced bruises, wearing our sleeves proudly rolled up the next day in class; on another night we each came to the meeting with a boy's real telephone number; on a third we had come prepared to strip down to the nude, but we didn't entirely, cracking up in our underwear before uncovering our pubic hair. One night, I remember, Rachel found a condom and we unrolled it together, sticky on our hands, and filled it with water in the washroom. My idea of what a penis would actually look like was warped by this experiment; I thought it was round with a tip on the end like a breast. We acted like we knew everything.

Caroline, at sixteen, was the oldest among us. She had been kept back a grade when she first moved to an English school. Francine was the second oldest, fifteen, and had the most developed body of the four, her breasts larger than her hips, her armpits and legs requiring shaving twice a week instead of every other week like the rest of us. Rachel, like me, was fourteen, but I was younger than Rachel by three months. Regardless, Rachel acted as if she were the oldest; she claimed to have lost her virginity the year before, and this left the three of us in awe. When we filled the condom with water, Rachel said she hadn't used one that first time because the boy was too excited and dirtied it by dropping it on the ground. Then she burst the condom on the floor and we howled back to her room, unsure whether she was joking or not. I was the least womanly in our group; I hadn't yet gotten my period. I was beginning to fear I never would. The girls and I tried everything we could think of to speed things along: a hot bath, doing a headstand after a shower and then getting up quickly, wearing a tighter bra and pants in the hopes I'd produce the proper cramps, drinking three cups of tea a day. Nothing worked, and I began to fear that despite my biology I might end up being no different from a boy.

By Thanksgiving weekend, a few weeks after my arrival at the school, I still hadn't returned to my family. When I phoned home, my mother said that Christine had visited earlier in the week but my father was being paid overtime for working on the holiday and the extra money was needed. I was about to point out that all this money wouldn't be necessary if they hadn't sent both their daughters away, but decided against it. I hated upsetting my mother in her condition, though I did feel she deserved to feel bad for leaving me alone on a holiday. My loyalty had shifted over the weeks, The Sisterhood becoming a new family to me, yet it hadn't disappeared. The holiday triggered an immense longing to be with my real family again. I tried to hide my disappointment. "Your father's taking good care of me," she reassured me. There was a great deal of static and background noise, and my mother coughed several times during the conversation. "It's the television," she said, and quickly got off the phone.

Caroline and Francine went home for the holiday, but Rachel stayed behind. Her father came to join us for a special meal with the nuns. I'd met Rachel's father when he took us to the movies the day after I stole the red bra for his daughter. Since then he'd taken us to the Market for milkshakes and on other short excursions. I was one of a group of six or seven girls on those occasions, so he offered me little individual attention beyond asking my name and whether I liked the school or wanted any popcorn. He paid for us all, and I was flabbergasted by the amount of money he seemed to have on him at all times. I also noticed that he never asked the price of anything before purchasing it. When we strolled down to the cafeteria together for the holiday dinner, Rachel and I were practically the only girls left, except for twin sisters in the youngest grade whose mother was in the hospital delivering another child.

"What a beautiful way to celebrate Thanksgiving," Sister Aline said warmly as we ate our turkey dinners. The nuns themselves had prepared the meal, the cafeteria staff off for the holiday.

"Yes," said the twins in unison. But they didn't seem happy or thankful. Neither was I.

"Angela," commented Mr. M., "You don't seem to be enjoying this delicious cranberry sauce." He was dressed for the bank, where he worked as the manager: a three-piece suit with a tie and a silver lapel pin with a miniature carnation tucked inside. His auburn hair was parted to the right and a bit greasy. He smelled strongly of cologne.

"It's good," I replied, scooping another spoonful to prove I believed what I'd said. Rachel was having no trouble eating; she acted like it was any other day.

"Are your parents on a trip, Angela?" Mr. M. asked absently.

Rachel poked her father's arm. "Is Mother on a trip?" she said wryly.

"Rachel," scolded Mr. M. "I'm asking Angela a question." Rachel returned to cutting her turkey meat into thin slices, her head bent.

The question caught me off guard. Regardless of the presence of Rachel and Mr. M. on this day, I felt so alone in the cafeteria filled with nuns and without my parents, I barely managed to contain my tears. I'd never spent a holiday away from them. We always ate together at the table, my mother saying grace, and afterwards we would watch television together, play a game, or go for a walk. Thanksgiving was my mother's favourite holiday. "The Sisters of Mercy taught me the value of every thing in God's world. Every living thing is worth giving thanks over," she would say. I wanted to be thankful for everything she loved, but I wasn't. I was resentful.

I turned to Mr. M., hoping he might save me from my loneliness if he knew the truth. "My mother's very sick, Mr. M., and my father works a lot."

Rachel stopped cutting to scrutinize me, to figure out if I was putting her father on. I hadn't told her or anyone about my mother yet. I broke open a dinner roll and laid a thick mound of butter upon it with my knife. Mother Superior asked me to hand over the butter dish when I was done, a request I obeyed automatically, passing it across Sister Aline and another nun at the table whose name I didn't know. They waited until Mother Superior had finished garnishing her meal before adding seasoning to theirs.

"Say a prayer for them then. I'm sure you'll see them soon." Mr. M. dumped more of the sweet cranberry sauce onto my plate. "It'll do you good."

My sadness must have been palpable, because Rachel accepted what I'd said about my mother. "Father," she said, spooning another helping of the dry mashed potatoes, "why don't we take care of Angela until her parents are able to come for her? She's been here every weekend, you know."

I whipped my head in Mr. M.'s direction. I was shocked by Rachel's suggestion, but also deeply touched. "You can be sisters," Mr. M. said, smiling broadly in the direction of the nuns at our table, who seemed neither pleased nor displeased but returned his smile with polite nods.

"Sisters," said Rachel again.

"Sisters," I echoed, sounding the word on my tongue. Rachel and I were choosing to be sisters. The word meant something more to me now. The Sisterhood was a club name; ours was a pact. If I could have no mother, then I'd have a sister. As we ate, I didn't know which I longed for more. I felt love for Rachel then, genuine love. I felt blessed.

Sister Yolande, the religion and geography teacher of the grade lower than ours, who was a little hard of hearing, turned around from her table, wondering who it was that might be calling her.

PARISHIONERS ARRIVE EARLY FOR morning Mass, determined to have first choice of the rummage-sale items. The Sisters working at the event run like chickens, pecking here and there through the boxes, putting together the final touches. They pour the complimentary tea and coffee, find extra chairs for some of the booths, retag the items whose labels have disappeared in the shuffle. The parishioners bring in the cold, shivering, as the weather has grown aloof, the sun hiding behind the clouds, a chill wind blowing. Snow has finally fallen, flecks of white on the hibernating ground. Father B. has to go out on the ladder to rehang one side of the white banner, which has gone askew in the night. It reads "Rummage Sale" and is hung over the regular banner, which declares "Returning Catholics Welcome." The Sunday school children made the banner as an exercise for the church. They filled in the letters with dark-blue paint, and most of them miraculously stayed within the red outlines, the youngest students sent to paint on sheets hung up in the basement classroom and not meant for public display.

Regardless of our regular banner's mandate, the rummage sale draws our most loyal worshippers as well as people from the neighbourhood who've never attended Mass, who aren't returning Catholics or Catholics at all. You can tell the latter by the way they avoid Father B. as he weaves around the tables chatting about other upcoming spiritual events sponsored by the church—a marital seminar or father-son outing. The outsiders chat with the Sisters about the items for sale, asking whether a colour suits their complexion, if we've read the book, or how many pieces are missing from the dinner set. The regular worshippers do the same, but are more cunning about it because they know they will run into us again in the following weeks. They check underneath linings, examine shirts for stains or missing buttons, read the backs of the novels and cookbooks feigning disinterest, tell the Sisters they will buy a damaged item at the asking price in order to help charity. The doors on rummage-sale day are open to everyone. We don't care where the money comes from as long as we can put it to good use.

Kim insists on letting me sit on the stool, although her back has been bothering her. She went to see Sister Ursula about it and is supposed to be doing exercises in the morning to help alleviate the pain. She showed me her pamphlet with crude stick drawings of pregnant women kneeling and stretching on the floor and against the wall. The instructions are highlighted in yellow ink. Sister Sarah even acquired a blue mat for Kim to do her exercises upon. Kim drinks the decaffeinated coffee that Sister Josie has made especially for her, ignoring the cup of ginseng tea that Sister Celeste brought and which Kim sniffed with a forced smile.

"She thinks I'll drink it 'cause I'm Korean," she says, pushing it to the side of our table. "It smells like dirty socks."

I am getting used to Kim. She has slowly seeped into my routine. Father B. knew this would happen. It is difficult when living and working with someone not to form attachments of some kind. I'm prone to hiding out, and being responsible for Kim has forced me to leave my room, go through the motions of a day. I find myself walking past Kim's room on the second floor when I have no other business to do there, sitting near her at meals, or waiting in the orchard for her to come out, hoping she'll keep me company as I watch the people going by. I'm worried about her and her baby and what will become of them. I know she has spoken to Father B. about the possibility of adoption. Sister Maria let that get around. Apparently Kim dropped the subject when Father B. told her she should speak to Mr. Q. if that was her decision. Abortion, of course, has never been discussed. The Sisters know there are ways to make it appear like an accident, and this is part of the reason we never leave Kim alone for too long—and part of the reason no one questions me about seeking out Kim's company over theirs. Alone at night, in the privacy of her room, however, Kim could probably do much damage. There's no telling what her dreams reveal, trapped with that baby in her belly. There's no telling if she feels the least responsible to this life, something inside her she's not seen, doesn't know. She won't be able to avoid Mr. Q. and his programs forever, but she does her best, and I admire her resolve. She is determined to do things her way.

I even brought her with me when I went to the library, under the premise that books would help her use her time in a valuable manner, but really so that I could use the computers there. I asked the staff if they could help me locate addresses on the Internet, thinking it might be more fruitful than the telephone book. But the World Wide Web proved equally unproductive. There were too many entries for each name, and I had no way of knowing whether I'd identified the right person without actually sending an e-mail message. To do that, the librarian explained, I would need to open an account. It would have my name on it. I didn't like that idea. I looked around and saw countless young people glued to their terminals, pressing keys and changing screens without anxiety or bewilderment. I realized then that the people I'm looking for might be as unfamiliar with the Internet as I am. I had brought Kim with me but I couldn't ask her for help. How could I explain my predicament? That I am filled with dread because I am sure someone is looking for me to accuse me of a crime. I almost wished she were my partner in this search, so I could share my burden with her, but she is only my alibi, and an unwitting one at that. It's becoming clear that I am a bad detective, whereas the person wishing to contact me has done so without leaving a trace. No other anonymous messages have been received since; no other clues. At the library, Kim ended up in the horror novel section but had the good sense not to ask me to take out any of those books on my card. If you want those, I told her, there will be plenty at the rummage sale. Before we left, she haphazardly selected a pile of recent best-selling novels and a book about the emotional life of animals. The cover had a picture of an elephant holding white bones in its trunk. I shook my head at her taste but checked them out anyway.

One hand flat on the table to support her weight, Kim bends to rearrange a bunch of sweaters at the front of our rummage table.

"You want to put the colours on top," she tells me as I check the price tags. "To attract the eye."

I let her have her fun. She is enjoying herself for once this morning, the feel of the fabrics in her hands, occasionally picking up a shirt or dress and pressing it over her body to see if it will fit her. The church basement has been transformed into a thrift shop, void of the solemnity it generally emits even when the Sunday school children meet here. The effect is good for Kim's health. I don't know much about pregnant women, but I do think a baby is better off if the mother is healthy and relaxed, so I am glad. She doesn't yet know I have put away a box for her. I've already sifted through the clothes to find things in her size. Father B. gave me his blessing when he caught me assembling the hand-me-down wardrobe. He thinks we women have a duty in such things.

The basement is packed a half-hour before morning Mass is due to begin, and Father B. reminds some of his regulars of the time, rolling up his sleeve to reveal his watch, then heads upstairs to robe and prepare the altar boys, to bless the wafers for Communion. We working Sisters are allowed to stay below. Yesterday, as we collected the boxes, I told Father B. the rummage sale was as popular as ever, informing him that many people had stopped by to inquire about the hours and what items would be up for sale. A young woman with her "partner," she said reservedly, elusive about her marital status, mentioned they were in need of furniture. A regular had a christening to attend and wanted to know if there were any baby items for sale. There were people looking for dishes, antique furniture, and jewellery. Many women asked about the bake sale.

"Yes," replied Father B. "It seems to be, but I went down to see one of ours at the hospital, recovering from a liver transplant, and I drove by the United Church at the corner of the General Hospital, and they had posted on their billboard: Sunday Worship and Bar-B-Q. All welcome." He stroked his collar absently, as if it were fur. "It's something to think about."

"A barbecue?" I said. "Isn't that a bit crass? I mean, the rummage sale at least goes to charity. The items are recycled by the community. Who would be converted by a hot dog?"

"I know, I know," he said, a bit distraught. "But times have changed. Does it matter really what we do, as long as they come?" He picked up one of the shirts I had just placed on the table, a white T-shirt with a pink heart on it and the single word "Hole" written across the chest. A rock band, Kim had informed me when I laid it out. "One day they get a shirt, the next something else they need. It's only our duty to provide it. Jesus did it with fish and loaves. We need to be practical. That seems to be the mandate." Then he headed over to speak with Sister Greta, her stack of Harlequins in a neat row at the front of her table.

Kim asked me, somewhat hesitantly, after overhearing us talk, why I had become a nun. I brushed off the question, not wanting to divulge the truth, just telling her it was difficult to explain and that I didn't regret my decision, if that's what she was wondering.

"That's three dollars. A real deal," Kim argues beside me to a woman turning over a yellow silk blouse, the loud spiral design indicating its age. But the seventies are in style again, Kim told me as she went through a garbage bag full of vintage pieces. An elderly widower sent the bag. His wife died almost five years ago, but he hadn't been able to send them before now, couldn't bear to remove her things. There are many like him, who finally give in around this time, Christmas season approaching. I didn't bother to tell Kim the vestments were a dead woman's. She still doesn't eat much and keeps to herself about her past, her dark hair like a shroud over her thoughts. But she has been perking up over the last week, knowing the sale would bring a bit of the outside world to her. Why tell her we're in the business of selling the leftovers of the dead? Such knowledge might destroy the little pleasure she has managed to cultivate for herself.

The buyer in question, a regular, met Kim last week at Mass. She is surprised to see her behind the table, unaware that we have taken her in as our own. She holds the blouse across her arm to determine the sleeve length, but her eyes are focussed on Kim's stomach. If only Kim weren't so skinny, her pregnancy wouldn't be easy to detect, as she is not that far along. The woman snickers and openly reveals her disgust by sending me a stern look of disapproval.

I ignore her, pretend I'm looking for change for the five-dollar bill Kim has been handed for the purchase. Kim notices, though, and asks to switch places; she can hide her stomach underneath the table if she sits. She takes her Styrofoam cup to her lips and sniffles. I get up and count out the change.

"Mass is starting any second now," I say.

"Oh, yes," the buyer replies, slipping her coins into her purse. "I'm on my way up." She is wearing a green blazer and holding a white wicker purse. Her gait is that of a patron.

"You think you are," I mutter to myself, amazed at the anger she has wrought in me over the girl. I have the scandalous desire to ask the woman to open her bag so I can check whether she's been stealing.

Kim is finished with her coffee and places the empty cup by her feet. Her head is bent now, and I feel like comforting her, knowing at the same time that she must expect the treatment she receives. We can't protect her from everyone. Child or not, she has her sin marked on her skin and will pay for it, regardless of the more liberal attitude the Church and society have adopted in the past decades.

Even though Mass has begun, the basement is still full of people. Money changes hands. Goods and services are provided. Many shoppers are hoarding items underneath the tables until they can return for them.

"You know the story about Jesus in the temple?" Kim asks me.

"I'm a nun, you know," I reply, handing her the ten we just received for a winter jacket, somewhat taken aback that Kim has knowledge of the Bible after all.

"Don't you think it's a little strange?" she asks, jutting her chin towards a group of women at the ceramics table who are fighting over a lamp as politely as possible, each insisting they know someone who is Catholic and perfect for it and doesn't have much money.

"Father B. no longer reads that passage at Mass," I whisper to her, afraid I might be betraying one of our secrets. "Because people leave less in the collection plate."

Kim eyes me warily, trying to determine whether I'm serious or not, which I am. I then point to the cardboard box underneath the table that I've saved for her. It is unmarked, but I know it is the right one because I placed it there myself. I even hid it in the broom closet for a week so she wouldn't see the surprise coming. The box has a picture of a television on it.

"The things in there are for you," I tell her. "I thought you could use some new clothes while you're here."

She smiles weakly, close-lipped, but I can tell from her fidgeting hands that she's eager to open the box. I've made sure there are enough dresses that are loose around the middle, elastic-waistband skirts and pants that she can wear throughout her pregnancy, but perhaps afterwards as well. Kim being so slight, they were difficult to find. Most of what seemed the right size were children's clothes. I had to gauge how childish some of the frills on the dresses appeared and take a closer look at the magazines lying around the convent to become current with what's in style. Strangely enough, a lot of the women's styles portrayed in the magazines were closer to a child's wardrobe than an adult's. Models in baby doll dresses sucking on lollipops or wearing cut-off shorts and halter tops with butterflies and unicorns on them. Barrettes with bobbles glued to the spines and sprinkled with glitter, short skirts with polka dots, and nylons in offbeat colours, including gold and bright pink. Although I find the trend somewhat unnerving, my research enabled me to salvage more of the children's clothes than I had first imagined. What Father B. doesn't know is that I also went to the department store and bought a few more things for Kim out of my own pocket—a dress, a sweater, and a pair of baggy pants as well as socks and underwear—tearing off the price tags and throwing them in the outside garbage bins near the window to my room. Kim cannot have this child in rags. This is not the age of perfect births in mangers. I figure sometimes what we need, we must seek out ourselves.

"Go on," I tell her. "Take a break. Try them on. If they don't fit, we can put them on the table. But keep the ones that are a little large, because you'll need them in the next few months."

Inwardly I wince. I shouldn't have mentioned the child even if the child is on my mind. Kim drags out the box now as if hauling a stone across a bridge. There is always a catch, she must be thinking. These are for the baby, not for me. I have made the gift a practical matter like the other Sisters who tell her to take her vitamins, stretch out her legs, drink milk; I've taken the joy out of it. She opens the cardboard box and sorts through it with her hands.

"Remember when you asked me why I became a nun?" I say as she unfolds the dress I bought for her at the department store, long and purple with spaghetti straps crisscrossed at the back. "I think it was for the clothes."

She smiles then and takes her new dress to the washroom to try it on. I watch over the table, pleased that, at least for a moment, we are able to find the humour in it all.

BELLA IS SINGING, HER thin body like a candle in the darkness of the church, her braids like curls of melted wax. Her arms are raised up to the heavens, and a bright white light shines down from the rafters. There are other singers, hazy outlines swaying in the background, their voices muffled. Bella is clear, her voice piercing the air like a swift bird flying through an open window in winter. She sings with confidence, as if the church were empty, her own heart fixed on a spot beyond this time.

Lamb of God, You take away the sins of the World
Have Mercy on us

The song is a round, but all the voices are Bella's. She is her own chorus, the notes sombre and haunting, the pubescent girl growing older as each new voice enters the chant. I am alone in the confessional, gazing at her through the screen that should house the priest. "The Lord be praised," I whisper, but there is no man there to receive me, only Bella's lungs filling with air and exhaling her song.

Lamb of God, You take away the sins of the World
Have Mercy on us

As she nears the end of the hymn, her many voices slowing, steadily softer in tone, the white ghosts behind her lower themselves onto their knees. Bella screams, her hands against her stomach. Blood appears and she looks down at them with her dark eyes as if her fingers have sinned against her, their tips like foreign objects in her sight, bloody wet flowers sprouting from the nails, pricking her flesh. I try to open the door to the confessional to help, but it is locked. I can hear the trampling of footsteps towards the doors. "Why are you leaving her there?" I yell, pounding the weight of my body against the wood, the small compartment filling with smoke, the screen sizzling. "She's burning! She's burning!"

I wake to the deep rumble of thunder breaking in the winter sky outside. Wet snow against my window in the darkness like tiny hands. I am parched, my throat sore and scratchy, the air in the room dry. A flash of lightning, and the silver candle holder on the dresser is momentarily illuminated as if standing in judgement. I put on my housecoat, turn my back on my accuser, and decide to fetch a glass of water from upstairs.

The hallway on the first floor, unlike mine of grey stone, is plaster. There is a washroom in the basement, a single toilet and basin, but no shower. I walk between the white painted walls, lined with wooden engravings of palms and crosses, and pause by Sister Josie's door. Sister Josie and Sister Sarah, both in their fifties, comprise a convent of two. They are virtually inseparable: take their meals together and say their prayers in unison. It is fairly common knowledge that in the night one might make her way into the room of the other, stay until morning. Mother Superior has never mentioned anything to me directly, but every once in a while, if Father B. has been by, the women make an effort not to sit together at Mass or gaze at each other over bent heads in prayer. I have come by their rooms often in the night, pressed my ear quietly against their doors, my heart pounding, in order to hear them. Though I have never heard a single noise except snoring, I imagine what they might be doing, Sister Josie's uncovered head perhaps caressed by Sister Sarah's smooth round hands. Sarah's modest bosom upon Sister Josie's swollen one, their bodies exploring, attaching to the other like roots. I have never heard two women making love. I have never heard a man and a woman making love, for that matter. Except once, with Rachel, when I was invited to come and watch.

Rachel picked me and Caroline, who had just sneaked us cigarettes because the delivery boy liked her, to watch her have sex with Patrick. Francine wasn't allowed to come because Rachel thought she wouldn't be able to keep it a secret. But I knew Francine was the most likely to stay silent in such a situation, so I thought her exclusion had to do with Rachel impressing us. Francine was so devoted to Rachel that she never needed any more reasons to be in awe of her. So was I, but Rachel might not have known the extent of my loyalty.

Patrick went to the boys' school nearby and was in the grade ahead of ours. He was lanky and tall but had learned to swagger when he walked, which made him seem tougher, a bit dangerous. He parted his hair in the middle and blow-dried the sides so that they flared out, and he smirked often, his continual banter contagious.

His hair was brown with a hint of blond on the sides, and he told us he shaved twice a day. Rachel met Patrick in the washroom one night at the movie theatre. He had left his seat and gone to hide in the bathroom stall nearest the door. Apparently oblivious, Rachel sat herself down in the next stall and lifted her skirt. When she went to reach for toilet paper, his pink lips inched underneath the barrier. Noticing his hand supporting his weight, she crushed it with her boot. He screamed, and startled by the voice of a boy, she pulled up her stockings and whipped open the door. He stopped her by holding her arms back in a twist, begging her not to tell on him. "Then act like a man, not like a boy," Rachel told him, a line straight out of the spy movie we were watching, spoken by a red-headed dancer in an expensive bar. "If you want to see something up close, then we'll talk." Surprised, he let her go and she ran back to her seat beside us. "He smelled like the aftershave in the department store," she said and giggled. "I would have let him have me right there, but I didn't want to look like a tramp." At least that's how Rachel told it, looking behind her every few seconds to see if he was watching—her face, even in the darkness, flushed.

Like me, Caroline admitted she'd never had sex, though she had let the delivery boy feel her breasts underneath her shirt when she wanted an extra pair of nylons for free. I spent extra time that morning in the shower, examining my young body, circling around my bulkless burgundy nipples and bony waist and allowing my fingers to mysteriously and intentionally waft through the new coarse patch of hair between my thighs, the dark brown fur like some small tame animal I had discovered, the opening underneath a cave. With the palm of my hand foamed with fresh soap bubbles, I forced one finger inside myself, ashamed by the wetness, amazed by the warmth. The flesh wrapped around the tip protectively and I quickly took it out, afraid someone could see me through the thin plastic curtain. I couldn't imagine anything larger going inside there, was convinced there wouldn't be room for it to roam. Unlike Caroline, I had never let a boy touch me at all, though I imagined one doing so as we watched, thrilled at the movies, when hands touched or lips pressed against cheeks and closed mouths, when women in low-cut dresses showed off their cleavage or undressed behind curtains. But I was little prepared for what sex would look like in front of me.

Along the east side of the school, where the building met the street and where we could sit and chat while people walked to the store or stood for the bus, were a couple of loose bricks that girls used as mailboxes. Rachel's was easy to find, marked with a splash of tar at the bottom of the corner, a thin slit visible when you bent down. She left her messages for Patrick there, written on plain white paper, rolled up like cigarettes. Because of her father and his open chequebook, she had made friends with all the staff, tipping them for special services, an extra dessert or a women's magazine, and for their silence whenever she might break one of the many relatively inconsequential rules we lived by. The laundry girl, Esperanza, a Spanish teenager only slightly older than we were, was an easy ally. Rachel had given her little favours—trinkets and junk earrings— over the course of the last year and planned to call all of them in now. She needed Esperanza to get Patrick in and out of the building. She needed a schoolgirl uniform in a tall size.

On the night of Rachel's scheduled performance, Patrick was to walk behind the grocery store located a block away to the east and pick up the plastic bag that would be waiting for him by the garbage bin in the parking lot. Then he was to hide in the trimmed bushes and put on the grey wool skirt, white blouse, and navy blue cardigan with the St. X. School for Girls crest on it. Esperanza would wait for him by the back door of the residence. Rachel was careful to pick a night when the nuns would be gathering for a meeting in the common room at the other side of the building.

"Are you sure Patrick's gonna put on girl clothes just to come over here?" I'd asked Rachel.

"You've obviously never done it," she taunted. "Boys will do anything you ask them to just to get it."

I was startled by her sureness, thinking back to my morning shower, baffled by what could possibly compel boys to do anything you asked them to just to feel a little warmth and wetness.

"Isn't he afraid, though, that you won't let him in and he'll just be left in a girl's uniform? That he'll get caught?"

"Oh, probably," laughed Rachel. She shrugged. "I thought of doing that, too, but I like Patrick."

"Really?"

Her face turned instantly serious; her eyebrows dropped. "Don't you?"

"I don't know. I guess … I don't really know him."

Rachel's green eyes perked up. "Maybe he has a friend for you."

Secretly I was both thrilled and anxious at the thought, but tried not to show it. The time was drawing close for the event, and

I sensed that after tonight I would never be the same again. It was as if I were entering womanhood, but without the right equipment or the proper knowledge. I envied Rachel's brassy confidence, her overt desire. I knew I looked awkward and childlike beside her, stuck with my ignorance of boys. Even the thought of letting a boy see me naked was enough to send me into strange nervous spasms.

"Let's wait until you manage this first," I said, staring at the curled ends of her hair, as if my gaze alone could protect them.

Esperanza received a carton of cigarettes, three chocolate bars, and a small red beaded necklace from Rachel. She put them in her laundry basket, underneath some white blouses to be cleaned, and left Rachel with her prize. Rachel had the lights off and the window open, a brand-new white candle in her silver candle holder shining like a solitary star in her room. Caroline and I were in Rachel's closet, the door slightly ajar, waiting for them to begin. Patrick stood looking ridiculous, the white blouse wrinkled and rolled up over his elbows, two sweat patches underneath his armpits. His breath was laboured and quick, and if he hadn't been smiling as he scanned the contents of Rachel's room with his eyes, I would have suspected he was crying. Rachel helped remove the skirt Esperanza had found for him. Patrick had wrapped his leather belt around it, and the grey wool fell to the floor as her hands, shaking I noticed, undid the buckle. He pushed his bangs off his face with his hands, revealing gold freckles on his nose in the soft yellow light.

"It's cold," he said.

"I gotta keep the window open for the smell," whispered Rachel, indicating the candle.

He nodded, and Rachel patted the baby blue afghan on her bed for him to sit down. He was now dressed in white undershorts and the blouse, crossing his legs over where we could spot a bulge.

Patrick pulled the edge of the afghan over his lap and knees. Head bent, his hands fiddled with the wool, moving his fingers through the holes in the design as if he were going to rip it, the fine brown curly hairs on his calves peeking out.

"Should I take off my shoes?" he asked.

"Sure," said Rachel, leaning backwards on the bed, her back against the wall. Her blonde hair had been pinned up by Caroline into a French twist, which Rachel slowly unwound, placing the bobby pins on her dresser beside a photograph of her father. The photograph was taken outside their home, and her father's face was worn by the sun but happy, with a large grin for the person holding the camera, his hand waving. I almost called out to Rachel to get rid of the photograph; it seemed sacrilegious to have her father watch, his bright blue eyes intent and sparkling, Rachel's old tree swing empty behind him. Over the next silent minute, as Patrick kept playing with the blanket, his eyes stuck on his sneakers beside his feet on the carpet, Rachel's confidence seemed to drain away. All of a sudden, the rouge she had smudged on her cheeks made her look like she was playing house, her own uniform skirt hiked just above her knees and a silk orange scarf wrapped around her neck. She batted her eyelashes to the air, Patrick still not turning towards her. She started to cough, covering her mouth with her hands. Caroline nudged me in the ribs, her eyes restraining laughter, and she stuffed one of Rachel's shirts into her mouth, biting on the cloth to keep from being heard. In the cramped space, which smelled of laundry detergent and mould, I hid behind Rachel's thick winter coat, regretting that we had come, hoping Rachel would call the whole thing off, that we could go back downstairs and find Esperanza and get Patrick out of here. I was starting to shiver from the winter wind blowing straight into the closet from the window. I was afraid of catching a chill.

"Aren't you going to kiss me?" Rachel finally asked coyly, yet obviously agitated.

Patrick shrugged, his skinny shoulders angling towards Rachel regardless. Rachel closed her eyes and slid her legs over the edge of the bed. Patrick bent over her, his hands covering her shoulders, and placed his lips on hers.

Caroline whispered, "He looks like a girl."

He did; with the white uniform blouse on and his short puffy hair hiding his features from us, the two figures on the bed could both have been schoolgirls as they touched each other lightly over their clothes. But a minute later, when Rachel started giggling and helping Patrick off with his shirt, his sex was noticeable, the bulge in his shorts shoved up against Rachel's midsection.

"You know what you're doing, don't you?" asked Rachel, her head emerging into our view again from underneath his chest.

"Course," Patrick mumbled. He looked stunned, his eyes avoiding Rachel's, his bangs long on his forehead.

"You gotta pull out before."

"Yeah. I know. I know."

Patrick pushed Rachel's skirt up above her waist and pulled down her cotton underwear. We had helped her dress earlier, and it was the bra we had counted on him admiring. She didn't want to wear the red bra I had stolen for her because she thought he might think she was easy and had done it with tons of boys; it was too flashy. Instead she wore a delicate white cotton bra with lace around the edges, the most elaborate bra her father had purchased for her, but Patrick didn't bother taking off her blouse. His undershorts were already discarded on the floor, and Rachel shifted positions to lay back with her head against her pillow, as if she were alone and too awake to sleep, her face to the ceiling, her eyes wide and anticipatory.

Caroline breathed against my neck and it tickled, but I didn't dare move. I could feel her moving, trying to get a better view over my shoulders, pushing some of the hangers to my other side, shifting her weight onto one foot and then the other.

"He's not gonna pull out in time," she whispered.

"What do you mean?" I asked.

"The boy's gotta pull out or else ... *bébé*!"

Rachel moaned and bit her lower lip, her teeth like clothespins. Patrick was bobbing up and down on the bed, his face strained, not even watching Rachel, his bony knees pinching her sides together. He was moaning too, a lower grunting sound interspersed between loud breaths. I couldn't imagine he would be able to leave that place, warm and wet, before he released himself. Though I didn't know what that involved, I understood Caroline's warning that Rachel could have a baby on her hands if he didn't. Rachel had spoken to me about it, saying that buying rubbers was too risky and boys didn't like wearing them anyway. It was like a game, she told me; you could get pregnant or you couldn't. God just chose.

"He's too loud," I said to Caroline, turning for the first time to see her. She had her fingers covering the opening of her mouth.

"Shhhh," she replied, her left hand snuggled around my waist so she could lean in. "I want to hear."

Patrick placed his left hand squarely on Rachel's right breast as he started to bob faster, his breath whistling in and out through his nose. Rachel still had her teeth clipping her lip, but her face had relaxed a little, the baby fat on her cheeks loose. For a brief time I wished it were me underneath Patrick, with Rachel and Caroline admiring me from the closet, my breast being rubbed with his hand. But as the wind entered bitterly, and Patrick kissed her clumsily, smearing part of Rachel's pink lipstick against her cheek, sucking the skin on her neck in his mouth, I wouldn't have traded places with her for anything. Patrick hit her absently with his hand as he tried to regain his position, and Rachel caught his hair in her hands and pulled. He continued to bob, straining against Rachel's body. They were messy and inelegant: pressing, slamming, sweating, heaving. I could clearly make out a mole on Patrick's back and some large pimples on the flesh between his buttocks and his thighs, and the marks on his skin, the unevenness of it, bothered me. The smell bothered me too—their smell, of fresh cold sweat, and the scent of the musty clothes in the closet, and Caroline's close salty breath near my neck, her left hand tugging at my waistband in her fixation.

"He won't pull out in time," she said again, directly into my ear, her voice high-pitched and pained.

She was right. He gave out one last grunt, louder than all the rest, his upper body arched, with his head almost hitting the far wall, and collapsed on top of Rachel. In those last seconds, with her blonde hair fanned out against her pillow, all of Rachel's facial features drooped downward, and her shoulders and head doubled over. I wanted to push Patrick off her, make him leap out the window where the wind was disturbing her curtains. I grasped my locket in a tight fist. Rachel's expression frightened me. Her face wore the same anguish my mother's did when she'd say her eyes were burning and ask for pills.

And then the candle blew out.

Patrick had fallen asleep, or so we thought, by the time Rachel got up to relight the candle. I could hear her fumbling to find her matches on the dresser. When the room was once again filled with light and shadow, Rachel tiptoed to her closet in pinched steps, her hands pressed against her belly, her skirt crumpled and her blouse transparent in patches. Her hair was tousled, the usually curled blonde hairs frizzy and tight. She had pink lipstick in a line down her chin like dried juice. Caroline and I had waited patiently in the darkness, holding hands, our palms damp, her face burrowed in the nape of my neck, mumbling the opening lines of the Our Father.

"He's asleep," Rachel whispered. "But will probably wake up any second. Esperanza will be coming soon. You need to leave."

I glanced at the clock on Rachel's dresser. Caroline and I had been in Room 313 for half an hour; Patrick and Rachel's act had lasted less than five minutes.

Caroline pushed her way out of the closet in front of me, scratching the skin around her neck where her sweater stopped. Patrick's legs were bare, spread out in almost the same position as when Rachel had been underneath him, only his eyes were now closed, his breath even, his body inert. Though he never acknowledged us, I think he knew we were there and was waiting for us to leave. I don't think he would have fallen asleep so easily in a strange building and a girl's room, knowing he could get caught by one of the nuns at any moment. Plus, I could've sworn I saw him wink in our direction, but he may merely have been adjusting the angle of his neck, placing his hair between the wind and his reddish skin. I felt like a scared animal sheltered in Rachel's clothes, unwilling to move out of the warmth towards the open palm in front of me.

Relenting, I took her hand, cool with perspiration and stronger than my own, and came out of the darkness. Rachel's breath was hurried.

"Did you see ... see his thing?" she asked, her eyes wide, glistening in the candlelight.

"No. I don't think so."

"Too dark?"

I nodded.

"Oh well," she sighed. "Maybe next time."

Then she whispered in Caroline's direction, "Funny little thing, it throbs. Beats like a heart and then just bursts." Rachel made an exploding motion with her hands. "My legs are wet," she added uncomfortably.

Caroline giggled and grabbed my arm as I tried to make out Rachel's legs. I couldn't see where the wetness was, but suspected it had escaped from her insides when his thing exploded.

"Let's get out of here," Caroline said quietly, and Rachel opened the door to her room, her body barring the view to her bed.

I took Rachel's hand one last time, stroking it gently as I did my mother's when she was in pain. *I want to take this away from you,* I thought, without knowing why. Rachel didn't seem upset, and neither did Caroline, but I felt as if she had just suffered a wound, a wound that would open up in the coming months instead of clotting, a wound without the possibility of healing. Meanwhile, Rachel radiated a new power, even in her awkward steps, her tentative movements. She seemed to be floating.

The stringent scent of the hallway carpet and walls assaulted me as we moved towards our rooms. As each room number greeted us, I thought about the secrets trapped within their walls, wondered what had occurred in each of those rooms before we entered them or while we slept. Were the other girls engaged in similar acts or worse ones? Did we have nightmares because of them, their whispers and smells permeating the air, wafting forcefully into our dreams?

"She'll probably feel sore tomorrow," Caroline whispered conspiratorially as we reached the door to her room. "That's what Aimée told me happens your first time."

I assumed Caroline had been misinformed. Rachel had done this before, though not in front of us. Did it hurt more if people knew and saw what you did? Was there a first time for that? "First time? What do you mean 'first time'?" I asked.

"The first time you do it," Caroline said, turning her back to me to twist the door handle.

"But Rachel told me she did it before." I was raising my voice, and Caroline fumbled with the handle, jiggling it in annoyance.

"Shhh. You want to get us caught?"

"But she told me—"

"She told me that too, but a couple of days ago she admitted she hadn't. She thought I was lying that I had never done it. She thought I'd done it with the delivery boy. But I asked my sister what it's like so I told her. Aimée says the boy has to pull out."

As Caroline went into her room, tears welled in my eyes. "Good night, *petit chou*," she said warmly, closing the door, leaving me alone and disoriented. And yet I did not wish to be with anyone, least of all Rachel or Caroline. Even if my mother had invited me to return home at that very moment, I'm not sure I would have. Everyone seemed to possess knowledge I didn't. When would I no longer be in the dark? I climbed into my bed, the perfect size for one, and slipped on my warmest, thickest nightgown. The cloth around my body like a bandage. I tried my best to sleep, unsure whether Rachel had offered me a gift or a burden.

WHEN I WOKE UP in the morning, I saw the blood. The first thing I thought to do was phone home, but there was no answer. If Sister Aline hadn't been sitting nearby, I would have slammed down the receiver. I knew what it was, my stomach bloated and cramping. The other girls frequently rattled on about their periods to each other in the washroom, but it was my first one, and I wanted my mother to come and help me. She had bought me a belt and the proper bulky paper pads, which I had packed, and yet, like an infant, I wanted her to strap them on, make me smell sweet like talcum powder, hold my stomach as I slept, like I held her hand sometimes when she was in pain. Why was it when I was in pain there was no one to help me?

Dismayed by the endless ringing at the other end of the line, I sought refuge in the washroom, stripping off my nightgown and showering. The hot water stung my skin, and I scrubbed my thighs rigorously as if cleaning a stained carpet. Luckily it was Saturday and I didn't need to go to class, only to choir practice in the morning. It was meant to keep us Leftovers busy and out of trouble, even though we could in fact accomplish very little without Bella. We practised notes and breathing techniques; songs just didn't carry when Bella wasn't present to guide us. The last thing I wanted to do was sing, but I didn't want to draw attention to myself by missing practice, so I waited for Esperanza to enter the washroom on her morning rounds. I hid myself in the shower stall, listening to a couple of girls come and go, water running, teeth brushing, and morning chatter. I heard Rachel say her father would take a few of us to the movies tonight; a new picture was showing at the theatre in the Market. A fresh white towel wrapped under my armpits, I watched the lingering drops of water spiral into the drain, my feet growing colder on the wet, beige-tinted tiles, and thought about my blood mingling with the dirt and sewage of the city streets like a dirty secret, travelling back to the canal.

Finally I heard the rustle of the hamper and the depositing of the washroom garbage into a bag. Through the curtain, I saw Esperanza in her grey uniform, starched stiff as living-room curtains. She bent over the sink, and her long skinny arms like cleaning brushes grazed over the floor, picking up stray towels and facecloths.

"Esperanza," I called from behind the curtain.

She looked up, her face in the mirror, her eyebrows arched in confusion, trying to decipher the direction of the noise. She had not noticed anyone was in the washroom; she inspected the vent.

"Esperanza, please," I said again, and she ventured over to the shower stall, abandoning her baskets and her grey cart with the tiny wheels on the bottom that she dragged up and down stairs and along hallways. Her body was older than she was, her hands wrinkled from astringents and cleaners, the skin on her fingers calloused. A couple of the girls called her witch behind her back, for the way she rubbed her hands together with lotion as if casting a spell; some also teased her by anglicizing her name to Esther, which made her scowl. She approached, not with friendly concern, but not with disapproval either. The pockets of her eyes were deep, and I imagined she saw right through me.

"What do you want? I don't have extra shampoo to give you."

I held out my nightgown to her, displaying the bloody stain, a deep reddish-brown splatter like rust. "Do you think this will come out?" I asked, close to crying, as if I had wet my bed in the night and were showing her my sheets.

"Sure. What do you want to give me for it?" she responded instantly.

I hadn't thought of that, but I knew Esperanza didn't do any favours for free. Still, I half expected, with an entire school of young girls, that my request would be a fairly common one, not one that required immense secrecy, although due to my innocence in these matters, I wasn't sure. Again I wished for my mother, who should have been beside me, who could have helped me wash the stains herself. The idea that I'd never experienced a period before might not have crossed Esperanza's mind. It was probably the shame emanating from my washed body that made me suspect.

"Rachel's father is taking us to the movies tonight. Do you want to come?"

Esperanza leaned back against the stall door, her light-brown skin dull in the brightness of the bathroom, twisting my nightgown in her hands. She had never accompanied us to the movies before, but I knew she wanted to go, had seen her regard Rachel's father longingly as he left with a bunch of girls down the street, his stride fatherly and grand.

"All right," she said, and placed the nightgown underneath some white towels in her basket, hiding the stain. She was shaking her head, waiting for me to get dressed maybe, to leave her alone and go to choir practice like the others. I was going to be late. As she opened the door to leave, her cart squeaking on the wet floor she had just sprayed with cleaner, she threw back her head and laughed.

"Your friend Rachel's very strange," she said. "Paying me off to bring a boy up for you. For you!" Her head bobbed faster up and down in laughter as Patrick's body had against Rachel.

Rachel's father accompanied the girls to dinner in the cafeteria that evening, promised us ice cream after the movie, and advised we skip dessert. He sat with the nuns instead of with us, discussing plans for the Christmas pageant with them. There was no lineup to speak of on the weekends, so we quickly received our plates of food and headed to a distant table. The women who worked in the cafeteria were immigrants, newly arrived in Canada, and many were Chinese. They spoke little English and no French, and we simply pointed to the potatoes and beans, ham or fish that we wanted on our plates.

"My father says they were traitors in the war," Rachel said.

"I think those were the Japanese," Francine muttered between mouthfuls. "And not the ones in Canada."

"No matter," Rachel claimed. "They are all going to hell anyway. They're not Christian, you know. None of them are going to get into heaven. My father says so, no matter how many dishes they make for us. Besides, they get paid for it, it's no act of charity."

Considering what Rachel said about her father's dislike for the Chinese, I was surprised at the kind and polite manner in which he dealt with them. He even joked in their company, playfully poking an elbow into a rib, slipping a few quarters to them over the countertop. From the bank, he would bring Rachel a whole roll of quarters, wrapped in brown bank paper, at the beginning of each week, which she would unroll carefully, hiding the coins in her drawers, in socks and shirts, in envelopes. It was from these rolls that she could afford to buy cheap jewellery or makeup from Woolworth's, or get us cigarettes and candy from the delivery boy. Every time she took out a quarter, she wove it in and out of her fingers like a magician, a trick she had learned from her father. In his heavy pockets, you could see the bulge of other rolls, dimes and nickels, that he kept close to treat us at candy machines or to dispense as little prizes when we pleased him. Rachel walked beside her father as if he were God, her eyes orbiting him, and the rest of the girls privileged enough to be on her list of friends followed suit. And he looked the way I imagined God would, towering over even Mother Superior, whose face relaxed as much as it was able to in his presence. He had made large donations over the years. The school couldn't have continued without him. When in his presence, one felt honoured to be received.

Rachel knew the power her father possessed. His frame was robust, large around the chest, and he sometimes wore his dress shirts open a button, where crisp brown hairs protruded like dried grass from the collar. The hair on his head, parted perfectly to the right, was a slightly darker auburn than that of his beard and moustache. He wore large navy blue blazers with silver buttons and solid-coloured silk ties and he smelled of money. When he would sit beside me, his thick musk cologne filled my nostrils, reminding me of my father before my mother got sick and he stopped wearing anything that might aggravate her lungs or sting her eyes. Rachel's father called me Angel when I pleased him, in a lingering Irish accent that made his sentences seem like short songs. He loved movies and enjoyed taking the girls on weekends to see them. Sometimes we would see the same movie two or three times if we liked it. Mr. M. didn't care what kind of movie it was, as long as we wanted to go with him. He easily forgot which movies we had seen, but he could remember in exquisite detail what we had worn. The best days, like that day, we would be giddy with excitement to see the new film advertised in the paper, for the nuns rarely let us watch the single television in the recreation room. We expected spies and intrigue, death and murder, sex and love—the bright colours of the adult world we hoped to be entering.

When Mr. M. arrived, Mother Superior and the nuns swarmed around him, displaying the new banners for the church or the classroom textbooks they had purchased with his last donations. He nodded vigorously as if he adored each new item, exclaiming in brassy tones, "You ladies are really outdoing yourselves this time." Sister Marguerite, so pale she was practically transparent, would turn a deep red and fumble with the object she was holding. He also supplied the nuns with blankets, the crocheted afghans Rachel's mother made—between one and three in a week. The nuns loved them; each had their own, and they would keep extras for the girls and guests, donating the older ones when they became worn to the Salvation Army. Once Mr. M. had even offered to take all the nuns to the movies and out for ice cream, but they refused. He brought back a small tub of vanilla. "They can't get offended by the colour white," he joked, and Mother Superior accepted it kindly. I imagined the delicious pleasure the nuns must have had dipping their spoons into the soft cream and savouring the sugary taste that night, their habits stripped off and their hair running along their shoulders, tucked into warm beds with their reading lights turned on or gathered together in Mother Superior's quarters the way The Sisterhood gathered in Rachel's room.

I was late to meet the girls after dinner, trying to get myself accustomed to the sanitary belt, practising the quickest and cleanest manner to get it on and off.

"You're usually the first one out, Angela. Angel?" Mr. M. called. "What's keeping you? Choosing the right shoes?"

He always treated the girls like budding women, tormenting us with jests that we had secret boys in our lives whom we were dressing to impress, that this was the reason we went to the movies.

"Not to be with an old man like me," he would say, "that's for sure." But Rachel was the only one who had actually spoken to a boy on any of our outings with her father, and I was sure he knew nothing about it. When Mr. M. was around, we gave him our undivided attention.

The door handle turned, and then Mr. M. in his heavy fall coat stood obstructing the doorway in front of me. I blushed and dropped the pads I had been about to throw in my closet, spilling them onto the carpet. Mr. M. fell to his knees and started to pick them up for me as I fumbled with the cardboard package. Horrified, I slapped his hand.

"Don't—" I squealed and started to cry, shoving the pads haphazardly into the flimsy box and stowing them under the bed. The room trapped me, and Mr. M. approached without hesitation, his smile wide, his teeth as white as the pads, his gums the colour of my blood.

"No need to cry," he spoke softly. "No need to cry, little Angel." And he stroked my hair, while I, frozen, let him, his pungent cologne wrapping around me. I felt a tingle where the blood was, an ache, like the way I felt when we looked at pictures of men in magazines with their shirts off, but stronger. I wanted to push myself away from him, protect that feeling for pictures and not for real male bodies, but I couldn't. "It's a natural thing, you know. You don't think I do, but I do know about these things. I'm a married man. I've known girls in my day."

His words swarmed me and I wanted to swat at them like flies, but the stroking soothed me.

"I want my mother," I said, and buried my head in his chest, his warm skin close enough that if I quivered I'd be kissing him, his hair in my mouth. I was utterly flustered to have Rachel's father discover I was having my period, and afraid at what I was allowing myself to feel for him in the process, but I parted my lips slightly and tasted salt. I'm sure I felt him tremble.

Rachel found us in this way, me tight in her father's arms, and she kicked her shoe against the door, annoyed we were keeping her from leaving for our outing. Ashamed, I burrowed deeper into Mr. M.'s chest to avoid her gaze. I didn't know what she would think of me seeking comfort in her father's arms, whether she would tease me or force me to stay away from him. I envied Rachel for her father, who always wanted to be close to her.

"Dad," she said forcefully. "Let's go."

Mr. M. rose to attention. His entire body stiffened, abandoning with it the illusion of continuous movement that he normally possessed. Rachel traipsed back down the hallway and Esperanza, wearing her new red beaded necklace, followed. Mr. M. wiped his hands across his pants, mumbling under his breath words I couldn't quite make out, except for the end of a sentence: "she doesn't know."

"She doesn't know," he said then in a louder voice, "what it's like to be lonely." He patted my shoulder and placed a couple of quarters into my palm, whispering, "You get yourself something to make you happy."

We joined the other girls, a group of about eight Leftovers. Rachel was a Leftover too, technically, but no one treated her that way. She seemed, of anyone, the most loved daughter. I tried to take my mind off the new pain I was feeling in my abdomen, my mind off the blood, off what it might lead to, off of Rachel's newly broken body. Esperanza had thought it was I who was changed and I was secretly pleased by the mistake. But she was wrong. And I wondered whether Mr. M., who had known girls in his day, sensed the change in Rachel, if that's why he rose to attention when she spoke. Because she was now a woman, and I was still only a girl.

When Rachel introduced an anxious Esperanza to Mr. M., he welcomed her in as large a voice as he could muster within the school walls, "Well then, since you are new, you must sit beside me in the theatre." The sparkle from his gold cufflinks transferred directly to the irises in Esperanza's eyes.

THE POLICE COME BY early in the morning to take Kim to the station. She had been forewarned a couple of days before, but still appears shocked as two officers pull up, their car's siren turned off, in the back lot of the convent. She wears fresh clothes, washed by Sister Josie and donated by Sister Bernadette, who is close to her in size, and her hair is brushed back into a short and stubby ponytail. She appears much younger than fifteen, despite her swelling middle. One would almost think she were afraid of her first day at school, the way she clings to my hand as we walk towards the lobby, her hands nervous, her voice high-pitched and slightly pained, trailing half a step behind.

"I'm going to come back, right?" she asks me, her eyes, generally oval, round with fear.

"Like I said, as long as you don't have a record and no one's filed a Missing Person Report, you'll be back before you know it." I try to make my voice sound cheerful. I am, however, exhausted, deprived of sleep by nightmares about the past and the quest to discover who wants me to remember it. At evening Mass I almost grabbed a woman from behind, her voice reminding me of Caroline. But she stopped to chat with another woman and I saw that she was far too old. She had a wider nose and higher-set eyebrows as well. Notwithstanding the mistake, the hint of familiarity around me has been consistent and palpable; I can taste it, the way you can taste the seasons changing in the air. A hair colour, or a scent, an inflection in a voice, a mannerism in the hands or in a person's stride—anything and everything is feeding my imagination to couple the present with the past. The woman behind the counter at the grocery, the woman who bent her head and opened the confessional at church, a woman's feet outside my window: all hammer the same question, *Who has come for you?* We have a lot of Spanish families who attend church, and I could have sworn there was a young woman whose hands were exactly like Esperanza's. I forgot to do the math. Esperanza would not be nineteen with calloused fingers any longer. She'd be a woman only slightly older than me, with kids and a husband most likely. But I eyed the Spanish families suspiciously. If Esperanza did send the candle holder, she'd have done it like this. Let me wait in silence, torturing myself. She'd have enough bitterness welled up in her, I'm sure, to strike out at the most inopportune moment. I'd nearly forgotten about her. But she knew everything that transpired at St. X. School for Girls. She knew what was in our hampers, what was in our garbage. I used to wonder how she kept so many secrets to herself. Then again, I had something on her too. I suppose it is all important now, if there's a debt to be paid. In order to carry or uncover a secret, one must first determine its worth.

"I don't have a record," Kim states defensively.

I trust her on that account. She's a good kid. A little too trusting maybe to some boy who told her she was beautiful and he'd love her forever, or a little too curious or stupid to take the proper precautions she could have obtained at a medical clinic, from a drugstore pharmacy counter, or from the metal dispensers in public washrooms. She isn't rude or disrespectful, and blushes when anyone asks her a personal question. It's as if it's never occurred to her that the day might come when she would need to explain her situation. As if she herself has no idea, has been struck unwittingly with a bulging middle, a Virgin Mary without an angel to explain the grand purpose of her pregnancy.

"So," I repeat, releasing my hand from hers as we approach an officer, a man in a bomber jacket and beige slacks leaning against the wall beside the convent door, the other officer in the front seat of the car. "Unless someone's looking for you, they're going to bring you back here."

I've salvaged a jacket from our Lost and Found to keep her warm, as it has started snowing and the winds have picked up force over the last two days. She arrived here with nothing, this girl, like an orphan dropped off on our doorstep. *An orphan going to give birth to an orphan*, I think. *The blind leading the blind.* The rummage sale over for another season, I am now required to go through the items in the Lost and Found. My method involves dating the items. A one-year time limit, because there are those who only come to church on the festive occasions of Christmas or Easter. The usual things are left over: black umbrellas, odd mittens and gloves on church pews or buried underneath snowbanks that become visible in the spring, scarves and skull caps, bus passes now expired, small pieces of jewellery such as earrings or bracelets thought to have been lost somewhere else, a binder or datebook, the events since transpired. Purses, of course, are always retrieved, and with complete relief and thanks. As are jackets in the spring or autumn, which tend to be left behind because the weather has warmed for the day. These things are expensive to replace. Yet people do return for things I wouldn't think twice about. Once a woman took a cab to the church to retrieve a lip balm, asking me to keep it aside with her name on it in case I wasn't here when she arrived. A man lost a button from his coat and came every week to search for it, because each button had been stitched on by his late wife. An older woman who could barely manage to walk down the hallway to the Lost and Found booth was nearly in tears one Sunday because she had lost her bus transfer. I've learned you just can't tell what people will want back. I am no closer now than I was when I started this duty fifteen years ago to discovering what people value most. Whenever I remove things from the box, I'm worried someone, some day, will come back and accuse me of depriving them of their ownership rights. Even though the jacket I gave Kim has been ownerless for only about a month, I rationalize that if anyone had needed it, they would already have come back to get it. If anyone asks now, I'll say it was never here.

I lead Kim through the cold air, which tastes of the brutal winter to come, over to the cruiser with its motor running. I try to keep my face hidden, wearing my wimple purposefully, keeping my chin down. But the men, as usual, seem to have their attention on the young girl, on Kim. I am just the deliverer.

"No one's looking for me," Kim says, settling into the back of the cruiser, behind the screen. For a second, it seems almost possible that she is in one of the church confessionals and not in a police car. I'd never thought of it before, but it occurs to me now that both are used for similar purposes. I hope the policemen will be good to her, not ask too many questions, not force her to speak directly about her past.

I shut the passenger door and walk back to the convent entrance. The falling snow melts into my collar. If no one's looking for you, Kim, I think, you're luckier than you know.

ESPERANZA'S ROOM WAS LOCATED on the ground floor of the dormitory beside the furnace room. She said she liked it, bragged her room was the warmest of all, although we knew that wasn't the case. Her room was even smaller than ours were, barely housing her bed and the end table she used as a dresser. She had no closet; her clothes were hung on the inside doorknob and her uniforms in the staff room, where she was allocated a locker. Her underwear and socks and other personal items were kept in a nylon suitcase that was never closed, because she required these things on a daily basis. Once, Rachel told me, Esperanza had asked for a room in the dormitory with the older girls, but the nuns had refused, told her she needed to keep her distance. No matter. Esperanza still managed to keep abreast of what happened in the school. And not from eavesdropping or by any special power the girls sometimes accused her of possessing, a dark mysterious ability bred in generations of women in her Spanish family. No, she learned a great deal from access to our rooms and the washrooms; she learned the rest from Rachel.

Rachel met Esperanza immediately. Mr. M. had arrived with

Rachel in tow the day she'd been admitted to the school, three years before I was enrolled there. Esperanza had just completed the minimum amount of required education before accepting the job, and Rachel needed an ally. Esperanza knew Rachel's father was rich and held sway with the nuns. It was a simple exchange on both parts. Rachel had always been a curious girl, and Esperanza's age and experience appealed to her. Esperanza made sure Rachel was happy. She waited on her especially, bringing her treats and ensuring she was well looked after by the nuns when her father wasn't around. She handled any of her requests through the delivery boy, and as to any indiscretions occurring in Rachel's room, any breaking of the school and boarding rules, Esperanza kept quiet. In exchange, Rachel gave her gifts and money, and ensured her job by speaking well of her to the nuns on occasion. Although Rachel did not encourage Esperanza to have any contact with her father when he came to take the girls out for cake or to the movies, Esperanza still benefited from Mr. M.'s generosity.

The day I caught Esperanza and Mr. M. together, we were suiting up for a skating expedition on the canal. The ice froze early that year, and city officials opened the canal to the public a month ahead of schedule. Many of the local merchants who set up booths on the ice were pleased. The canal remained frozen for four full months before spring arrived to melt it. A big band played on the night of its opening. We could hear the music from our dormitory rooms, leaning out our windows, breathing into our hands for warmth, trombones and saxophones belting into the night sky. We gathered for a Sisterhood meeting the Friday before, and instead of our usual games we decided to dance in Rachel's room, pretending we were with the skaters on the canal. Caroline claimed her sister was dancing there for real as we listened. Earlier that day we had witnessed a troupe of women with picket signs marching down the street to the Parliament Buildings. They wanted the crowd heading to the opening of the canal to join their protest. A women's group, fighting for equal pay for equal work. They marched in front of our school, chanting to us girls as we watched them through the iron gates. The women, dressed warmly, held aloft cardboard signs that read "Women Are People Too" and "Feminists Unite" and "Working to Live and Living to Work." A skinny woman who stepped out of line for a moment to scan us girls pushed her sign against the iron gate: "I Am NOT a Baby Factory." The overlooking nuns did not return the chants or acknowledge the picketers, but they didn't actively disapprove of them either. The nuns worked for a living; they had no children themselves. They let us watch without reproach.

Rachel got fired up by the excitement and the anomaly of the experience, throwing her own arms into the air when the nuns' backs were turned to demonstrate her support for the women on their way up the hill.

"That's what I'm going to be," she said. "A feminist."

"Aimée says 'feminist' is just another word for an ugly woman," Caroline jeered, pointing to a couple of unattractive picketers in snow pants and one in denim overalls whose hair was completely tied back, revealing pimples on her face. "See?"

"You're being stupid," said Francine, who didn't seem to want to join the women, but didn't want Rachel to be proven wrong. "There's plenty of pretty women who are feminists."

"What does your sister know?" Rachel asked Caroline. "You know, I've only ever seen her come visit you once. When does she tell you all these things?"

Caroline frowned. "Aimée and I are very close! She knows more than you do! She knows all about this stuff!" Her usually white face turned completely red, and she bounced a bit on her toes, bending her calf as if threatening to kick Rachel if she was further provoked.

"Aimée has to say that. She works in a bar. She makes less than Esperanza, I'll bet." Rachel then turned, dismissing Caroline, who was fuming, trying to rally me to her side by pulling on my jacket. I'd never seen Caroline angry with Rachel before.

"It's not how much money you make," she said, her jaw shaking. "It's not."

"Tell that to them," Rachel replied, indicating the last of the protesters hoisting their signs in the cold.

Caroline said she was going back inside to get a drink of water. But she was definitely upset. By the time our Sisterhood meeting convened, she had calmed down, and Rachel handed out pink candy hearts from Woolworth's as if nothing had happened. Rachel always won. There was no way to break her confidence in what she believed. At that stage in our lives there was nothing contradictory in needing boys to find you attractive, desiring foremost a husband and children, and thinking of yourself as a feminist. Rachel wanted the world at her feet. And she generally got it that way. Caroline was content to inform Rachel that her sister was skating on the canal while we were cooped up inside the school, and Rachel had to admit she would like to trade places with Aimée for the night at least.

The next day Mr. M. came to take us to the canal with him.

"We'll skate the entire afternoon," he said. "So make sure you have a good lunch. You'll need your energy." He patted his pockets to indicate his usual rolls of coins. "And if you're all good, I think there might be some surprises in your future."

Rachel and I ran down to the cafeteria, but we could barely eat, the excitement affecting our appetites. Although Rachel went every opening weekend to skate on the canal, and her father had bought her white skates with tight laces and small picks in the front like the ones figure skaters wore, she acted as if she had never been.

"I'm going to get a huge hot chocolate with tons of whipped cream," she blurted. "And a Beaver Tail. A cinnamon one with lemon. Mmmmm."

I could almost taste it myself as Rachel described the French-Canadian pastry sold from makeshift wood cabins on the sides of the canal, along with steaming beverages that warmed up numbing limbs, and hot dogs and hamburgers grilled right there on the ice. At first I worried I wouldn't be able to go because I had no skates of my own, but Mr. M. assured me there were rentals available and we would find a pair in my size.

"You can rent skates for the day?" I had guessed skates weren't the kind of thing people would reuse or lend out to others. They seemed to me items of luxury, not of necessity, so I had nearly accepted an afternoon of sliding along the ice in my winter boots while Rachel spun gracefully in circles or skated backwards out of my reach.

"Sure, you can rent just about anything you need," Mr. M. said, nudging my shoulder. Rachel poked him back. She never mentioned the day she found me in her father's arms, so I didn't mention it either. Mr. M. treated me with the same kindness as before, but I wondered if he thought of me buried in his chest, my tears hot against his skin, like I did. If one day he would tell me how much it meant to him to protect me.

"Do you think there'll be music?" I asked Rachel.

"No bands today. I asked already. But they play music over loudspeakers in some sections of the canal. Last year there were races."

As my excitement grew, I was reminded of my mother stuck at home on her cot with her jug of water and rosary beads. I wanted to bring her along to experience the twinkling lights strung along the railings and the restaurants where people unlaced their skates and walked up stairs for dinner or a nightcap at a table with a view of the canal below. My mother would have appreciated the tall pine trees, trimmed with ornaments, tinsel, and glittering Christmas lights, and the red velvet bows tied around the necks of the street lamps. She would have loved to see the families skating, parents teaching the younger ones how to balance on the ice, the falls that would inevitably occur, the laughter at running smack into a snowbank along the edge of the canal; the large Parliament Buildings, their tops green as the trees, standing watch over all, the clock the tallest point in the city. Before my mother was confined to the house, advised by her doctor not to venture outside unless absolutely necessary and then only after wrapping every inch of her body in numerous layers of clothing and covering up her mouth with a scarf, her eyes with rose-coloured glasses, Christine and I had watched her dance in a restaurant on her wedding anniversary. My mother made a little fuss about leaving us girls alone at the table, but my father convinced her we could handle being quiet and eating the complimentary slices of bread and butter. They held each other close. Mother's arms around Father's waist, her cheek against his, and they rarely strayed from that position or from a box-sized four-tile area at the side of the floor. And yet they were quite appealing to the other patrons, who turned away from their dinners to watch; it was obvious my parents were still taken with each other, found joy in holding hands and looking into each other's eyes. My father brought her back to the table a bit exhausted but in good spirits, and he made a toast to the grace of being joined with her for life. How she would have loved a celebration on the canal.

As we girls gathered together after lunch, zipping up snow pants, pulling on thick sweaters over long-sleeved shirts and mittens with tiny packets tucked inside (supposed to react to body heat and keep our fingers warm), and stringing long knit scarves around our necks, Mr. M. was nowhere to be found. The Sisterhood convened in Rachel's room. Francine was having trouble with the zipper on her jacket. Rachel, frustrated, tugged at it and eventually ripped the zipper pull right off. As Francine struggled to contain her dismay, Rachel offered to lend her one of her own autumn jackets, suggesting she wear another sweater underneath. Esperanza could fix the zipper later, she told her. Because I was already dressed and ready to go, Rachel sent me down with Francine's jacket to Esperanza's room. I was to meet up with them in the school lobby shortly afterwards.

Esperanza and I had rarely spoken, and not since she had taken my stained nightgown to be cleaned. Whenever our paths crossed, she gave me the impression she found my existence amusing, her lip curling up into a half-smirk. If she spoke to Rachel, and I happened to be there, she treated me as if I were a plant or a picture frame, part of the banal decor of the hallways, not worth a second glance. Rachel said Esperanza took time to get used to and not to worry about it. I thought Esperanza was just biding her time before circulating rumours about what had gone on in Room 313 the night before I asked for her help in the washroom. She wouldn't do anything to harm Rachel or her reputation, but I figured she couldn't care less about me. My parents hadn't bothered to show up since my arrival, and I had no clout with the nuns. I didn't want to approach Esperanza or risk bothering her. But I also didn't want to explain my predicament to Rachel. She would tease me if she knew what Esperanza thought happened that night. She might even tell Patrick.

Esperanza's door was closed, and none of us had doors that locked. I didn't knock. I turned the door handle expecting to find her room empty. Instead I found Mr. M. sitting on the edge of her bed, his shoes placed apart on the floor, his back slightly arched and his eyes closed. Esperanza knelt in front of him. His belt buckle was unfastened and the zipper on his suit pants was open. I watched, frozen, from the crack in the open door. Esperanza's black hair, let loose of its net, shielded her face and hung over Mr. M.'s knees. He bent to kiss her scalp where the hair parted in the middle, his hands on her uniform, rubbing her breasts together. She moaned, breathing heavily. He coughed in her hair, grabbing her ears and pulling her face towards his lap. She brushed some strands away from her mouth and moaned again. Her eyes closed. If she had been alone, I would have thought she was singing. Or praying.

Mr. M. was sweating and his forehead and cheeks were flushed. He was catching his breath as if he had run a long distance and had now collapsed, needing water. Esperanza's hands, wrinkled by the soap and water she was constantly dipping them into, were firmly clasped around his knees. This was different from what Rachel and Patrick had done. Esperanza didn't seem self-conscious or in pain. Mr. M. hadn't removed a stitch of clothing from Esperanza, her white apron with a blue and yellow stain on it sweeping the floor, but I could tell what was going on between them was as intimate as if they were both naked. She was kissing his lap and he was kissing her hair. Mr. M. and Esperanza moved together as if part of the same body. They had no need of candles, blankets, or witnesses. Heat welled up inside me. I was an intruder. And like an intruder, I wanted to do them some harm, but I knew I would end up on the other side of the door.

I backed away and closed the door, hooking the brown rabbit fur collar on Francine's jacket to the outside doorknob, and stumbled to the lobby. Rachel and Caroline and a couple of other Leftovers were waiting. When her father visited, Rachel was nice to girls she normally wouldn't give the time of day to. He liked to treat as many girls as possible. When Rachel insisted only her close friends be invited, sometimes he would relent, but other times he would resist. "How would you feel, sweetheart, if you were left out?" he'd say.

Francine was changing her clothes because the new jacket didn't match her snow pants. Rachel had told her no one who mattered would see her anyway, but Francine ignored her.

"She thinks romance will bloom between her and some guy in charge of the skate rentals," Rachel said, crooking her hands underneath her chin in coy imitation and fluttering her eyelashes.

"Does she?" I asked, fiddling with my scarf.

Rachel was sharing a tin of shortbread cookies with the girls around her; when she offered me the tin, I didn't take any. She broke hers into smaller sections and ate them one by one. "I'm just joking. What's wrong with you?"

"I got my period," I blurted.

"Really?" Rachel whispered. I hadn't told her why her father had been comforting me that day. I just told her I'd not been feeling well. I'm not sure why I didn't tell her, as I should have been relieved to prove I was now like the other girls, but I wasn't. I was too embarrassed to explain that Rachel's father knew before anyone else, before my own mother. I didn't feel proud of the blood.

"Yep. I got it this morning. I'm worried people will know."

Rachel motioned for me to turn around. I spun in a slow circle as she inspected the snow pants I was wearing, navy blue with white stripes, which Rachel teased must have been bought at the same store the nuns shopped at, because they resembled our uniforms.

"Can't tell a thing," she said.

"Good."

"So you're no longer a little girl," she proclaimed, grabbing my arm and smiling broadly. "Have a cookie."

I took one.

"What about Francine's jacket?"

"Esperanza wasn't there, so I left the jacket," I said, trying to appear casual. I thought talking about my period might have made her forget where I'd been.

"It's ugly anyway," Rachel said, picking crumbs from her palm, then licking it with her tongue.

"Yeah," I replied, taking another from the tin. "Ugly as Esperanza."

Rachel laughed, smacking my mittened hand, and my cookie fell to the floor. I crunched it with my boot and Rachel swept the crumbs under one of the chairs in the lobby by using her boot as a broom. Finally Francine arrived. She had managed to find a brown sweater that matched her jacket, if not her snow pants. The top of the sweater curled out over the end of the zipper. Rachel stood, rubbing the soles of her boots on the floor, and spoke to some of the other girls. I stood aloof; I could not get Esperanza and Mr. M. out of my head. When their breath rose in front of me, I couldn't bear to watch any longer for the release they seemed to be searching for. They appeared to want to become each other, to get outside of themselves. With Rachel and Patrick it had been only Patrick who had needed release, but here there were two. What went on inside a woman, I had no idea. I imagined it was the thought of being loved, protected and cared for, but Esperanza did not love Mr. M.; she didn't know him. Nor could I accept that Mr. M. might love Esperanza. I remembered over and over his lips near my hair, me up against his chest, him telling me Rachel didn't understand loneliness. The scent. Musk on my cheek. I couldn't tell Rachel what I had seen. And if the nuns found out, Mr. M. and Esperanza would be punished, I was sure. Rachel might even have to leave the school, notwithstanding the large donations Mr. M. made. I wished for numbness, instead of the confused stirring within me that wouldn't let go. I wrapped my scarf around my neck. It was tighter than it needed to be.

"Now we just need to wait for Daddy," Rachel said cheerfully.

RUMOURS SPREAD EASILY IN a house of women. No underground system is necessary. Doubting Thomas, a man, needed proof of Jesus' Resurrection. At the foot of the cross, and at Christ's well-guarded tomb, it was the women who believed he had not died, that he would not abandon them. They told each other so. Men, like Peter, looked out for themselves, forsook their Saviour to save their own skins. And Jesus appeared first to Mary Magdalene, a woman, knowing she would tell, not able to keep the news to herself. Her faith unshakeable, she ran around the village to inform the men of the truth. They didn't believe her. Men need proof beyond the shadow of a doubt. Women talk to make things unseen heard. It has been this way for centuries.

Here the women believe in rumour, give it the respect it deserves. I hear that Sister Sarah and Sister Josie have one recurring argument: Sister Sarah enjoys attending the weddings held at the church, and Sister Josie enjoys attending the funerals. Sister Josie says it's her duty to mourn the dead, and Sister Sarah responds by saying it's her duty to bless the living. They both like to bring flowers. I hear Sister Ursula did her medical residency with a man she fell in love with and who rejected her. She spent three years in his service, tunnelling into his heart, until he shocked her by marrying a patient she herself had tended. I hear Father B. spends much time with a young prostitute who comes to evening Mass on Tuesdays before she goes out to work. It is believed this young girl is his niece and the rest of his family has no idea of her whereabouts—another runaway on the city streets. Are these things real? Are they the facts? I suppose it all depends on whose story makes sense to you. Sister Josie and Sister Sarah can be caught sitting in their respective pews for weddings and funerals, but do they fight about it? Sister Ursula avoids speaking about her residency, only says she left because she couldn't stand their rules. Father B. has provided clothing, food, and medication for the prostitute who shields her face with her hair and calls him Uncle when she greets him. Who knows whether she has chosen the name for him because he is kind or because he is related by blood? Does it matter?

I'm sure I could find out more about Kim if I probed deeper, if I asked the right people. If, perhaps, I followed up with the police who kept her for the day. But talking to the Sisters, I collect rumour. I collect mystery. Sister Katherine says Kim's parents were originally contacted and demanded that Kim not return to their home in her condition. They insisted they no longer had a daughter. Sister Maria says it is good Kim is not younger than she is, because we would be forced to hand her over to Children's Aid, and the foster parents who take on teenagers do it for the free money and labour, not out of love or charity. Sister Humilita suspects Kim's father may have been the one to bring Kim into such a state, which is why he threw her out. Mother Superior believes the unborn child's father has come searching for Kim, because there was a twenty-year-old Korean man hanging around the back of the church last Sunday, dousing himself periodically with the holy water. But why Mother Superior should believe the father is Korean doesn't matter. Something has happened. Is noticed. Is told. The rumours encircle Kim without her knowledge. She is the newest reason for faith. And I find myself mesmerized by Kim's skinny body and the way life grows despite its confined surroundings. I try to envision how large the child is, if it has fingers yet or knees. How it breathes underwater. A rumour. *The Lord works in mysterious ways.* She bears our mystery.

Esperanza was a mystery at St. X. School for Girls. We knew little about her thoughts or feelings; she kept her opinions to herself and rarely revealed anything about her past. But Rachel loved spreading rumours. We knew Sister Gabrielle, the nun who acted as school secretary, kept a flask of gin in the top drawer of her desk. We knew Mother Superior's family tree traced her ancestry back to royalty during the age of Mary, Queen of Scots. We knew Patricia took medication to stop her from falling down and having fits, and Olivia, a girl in the grade below us, wet her bed weekly and was told to light a candle each time and pray for the Virgin Mary to keep her sheets clean. Esperanza cleaned her sheets, but it was the girl who slept in the room beside hers who confessed the secret. Not Esperanza. Esperanza knew the value of silence. Despite all the rumours circulating about the torrid affairs and sinful practices of Esperanza (that she met the gardener in the shed on Fridays, or that she put arsenic on the toilet seats hoping it would seep through our delicate skin and give her one less body to fuss over, or that she and Mother Superior were mortal enemies because of an incident that involved the iron gate surrounding the school, a bar of soap, and a letter, the contents of which we could never uncover), Esperanza's real life was hidden from us. Never once had a rumour involving Mr. M. passed through the lips of the girls. I wasn't going to start one. There was no mystery in that. There was only truth. And I would be implicated; I had watched and done nothing. I didn't want to be responsible for the truth.

So I kept the secret sealed, only opening it in the privacy of my room to fantasize about when I'd find myself in front of a man, kneeling between his legs, kisses against my hair, my ears, my neck. The scene I'd witnessed both attracted and repelled me. Esperanza in control, and Mr. M. at her mercy. His pants open, his belt like a limp snake. I was angry at Mr. M., not for his deceit, but for his choosing Esperanza. Waiting for her. For her to bring him salvation. The nights I spent holding on to my secret were long and lonely.

WE ARE TRAPPED BETWEEN our responsibility to the past and the demands of the present. This is a summary of Mother Superior's argument on this afternoon as we are gathered in the cafeteria, our conference room for the day. The fishy smell of the cod we've had for lunch lingers over our long tables, designed like picnic tables but made of fibreglass instead of wood. The bustle and chatter of lunch-time after our morning prayers brings a certain excitement for us. Although prayers are usually recited quickly (Sisters pray faster than anyone else), as the words of the prayers are not as important as the meditation that prayers provide, today we executed them even more quickly than usual. Father B. and Father G., the younger priest who has taken on some of Father B.'s duties and tries to provide a bridge for the younger parishioners, encouraging them not to think of church as an antiquated place run by the old-fashioned or the harsh and bitter, are also here, seated near where Mother Superior, flushed with the power of her own oratory, clings to a series of notepads and presses the Pause button on the videocassette machine whenever she wants to make a point without the distraction of moving images.

She has been collecting data in order to help us recover from our present financial circumstances, although she veils the economic concerns under the gauze of the moral ills of contemporary society. There are empty beds in the convent. Beds that haven't been replaced by Sisters dead or gone "over the wall" for decades. The video we are watching, which has been kindly copied by another group of Sisters from the United States who are currently implementing the new procedures, demonstrates, as Mother Superior puts it, the transfer of the spoken Word to the Image. Transubstantiation, she might have said, but that would provoke too much argument, and might be considered blasphemous. But she comes close to it when she speaks of our need to embrace the Image as a new holy vehicle, destined for our use as much as for regular society's. As it is, a number of Sisters look very nervous as Mother Superior runs through her statistics and graphs, as this new mode of conversion reaches our eyes and ears through the wonders of modern technology. A few turn, periodically, to Father B. and Father G. to gauge their reaction. Sister Josie sits beside Father B., taking notes for him because he left his reading glasses back at the church. Father G., however, doesn't seem perplexed in the least; he's enjoying himself, smiling and eating one of the sugar cookies left out for snacking during the meeting as if watching an engrossing movie and not a video entitled *How to Advertise the Catholic Life*. For Father B., his forehead glistening with sweat, the signals on the screen are clearly pressures on his side.

"The Sisters of the Order of K., the Sisters of U., and the Sisters of the L. Valley in the United States have made an enormous impact by working together with the full support of their clergy on this advertising campaign. We do not want to be left behind."

Mother Superior, in full-habit regalia, is set for war. There is a moral impetuousness about her stance. She defies the crowd to refute her. I've rarely seen her back so straight, as if she's placed a ruler against her spine underneath her clothes. Her movements are quick and sure, practised, and orderly. She takes out her pen, flicks the cap off with her teeth, holds her notebooks up in the air for authority. The lines on her face are hawklike, her wimple a hood. There is a hint of the sinister in the aggressive mode of her attack, but her tone is not condescending. She preaches, and I think of what Sister Maria said about all those packages she receives from academic journals, under androgynous pseudonyms, and the rumour rings true as I watch her. Mother Superior was made to be in front of a crowd, talking as she does. The convent chose her wisely as the leader, and the majority of Sisters listen to her respectfully at our own inclusive meetings. But the company of men is different; whenever men are invited within our walls, it is usually the men who speak. And today a woman stands preaching about the future of Catholicism.

Mother Superior pauses the machine to examine in detail one of the billboards used during the campaigns. Within the frame are fluffy snow-white clouds in a clear blue sky and a large pink hairless arm protruding downward, extending a large, perfectly unblemished hand. This is, as Mother Superior explains, a recognizable image of the hand of God coming down from the heavens. He holds in His palm a black cellular phone with the green signal light flashing. The caption in bold black letters across the bottom reads, "Is there a call you should be answering?" Underneath the caption is a toll-free telephone number and another caption stating, "Brought to you by your Sisters of the Roman Catholic Church."

We are encouraged to take notes, so I flip open a prayer book on my lap and write in the margins, "Advertising is the way of the Future," quoting Mother Superior herself. I underline the word Future. Beside my marginalia is a section from the book of Ecclesiastes. *There is no remembrance of former things; neither shall there be any remembrance of things that are to come with those that shall come after!* The word Advertising is right beside the citation: Ecclesiastes 1:11. As I lift my pen, Father G. points to the television screen and is about to speak, but perhaps sensing that Mother Superior is on a roll, he humbly lifts his hand to be acknowledged like a student.

"Do you believe the Sisters could send us some of the actual advertisements if we requested them?"

"Oh, yes. Certainly. I can get on that right away, Father." She turns to Father B. and nods to indicate that she will provide him with copies as well, but he stares blankly at the screen and at his own notebook, which has been divided by a black line into two columns: Pros and Cons. Up to now, I notice, sneaking a glance over Sister Sarah's shoulders, he's written nothing on either side, only a doodle resembling a sun with spikes around the globe. Sister Josie has copied down two or three pages of notes for him already. Mother Superior, indicating her earnestness, pauses to write on a yellow Post-It note Father G.'s request.

"Good. Good."

She presses the Forward button. The next billboard features a young woman, her hair tied back in a straight ponytail across her neck, held by a white barrette. Her hair is blonde and shiny, as in the advertisements for shampoo and conditioner that we see in magazines and on the samples that Sister Katherine obtained at the mall. "They were just giving them away. For free!" she said each time she dispensed one of the little packets. "I asked for a box for us Sisters. You should have seen their faces. I told them we use tons of shampoo to keep our hair healthy." The girl in the picture is beautiful, approximately twenty years of age, probably the same age I was when I entered here, although I wasn't half as good-looking. "Airbrushed," I hear Sister Sarah whisper to Sister Maria beside her, and I wonder if it's sacrilegious to use the technique on a religious ad, whether it's dishonest. Scattered across the picture's background are flowers and animals, a red rose and a white rose crossed over one another, a dolphin and a sheep—the former leaping out of the water, the latter jumping over a fence. Written in a vibrant green on top of this collage is: "Are you living the Good Life?"

"The ads are particularly directed at the youth, the future of the Church. As you can see, these ads comprise aspects of their own culture in order for them to be able to imagine themselves as a part of ours. As the statistics demonstrate ... "

Mother Superior turns to smile fondly upon Sister Bernadette. She is the representative demographic. Who cares about recruiting old spinsters and bitter women when you can entice socially conscious bright young teenagers into believing they can change the world, that living inside these walls is living the Good Life? They are do-gooders, and as such, like Sister Bernadette, they make things happen. The only other young woman who's shown any interest in our convent in the last year is Kim, and she's desperate with nowhere else to go. This state of affairs makes me think that the responsibilities to the past ought to be discarded for the demands of the present. The thought that I might be part of this past both frightens and thrills me. In the year that Sister Bernadette has been here, after two years as an acolyte before taking her sacred vows, she has outsolicited the other Sisters—except Mother Superior herself, who has thirty-five years of established contacts—in fundraising drives. Sister Bernadette sold the most tickets to our raffle, collected the most donations for the homeless shelter being built in the south end of town, and managed to start up a fund for Catholics who are ill and request alternative medical treatments. She knows the right angles to pull; heartstrings that open purse strings. I take notes. Mother Superior is right; she is the future.

ONE OF MY LETTERS has been returned. Sister Bernadette slipped it under my door this morning, because I did not wish to get up. I'm feeling under the weather, I said. With the stamped and addressed return envelope now back in front of me, I cannot believe it. I had visited the City Archives to filter through the papers from St. X. School for Girls that ended up there after the school went bankrupt. There had been talk before the school filed for bankruptcy about allowing boys into the school, as a way to increase enrolment and revenue. But it was decided that the income generated wouldn't outweigh the income lost from those parents who desired a same-sex education for their girls. The school was sold to the Catholic school board of the city two years after I left it. The nuns were relocated, the rent being too high to remain there, and new teachers were hired through the school board system. Although the more sensitive material in the files of the school is with the diocese, public archival material, such as school yearbooks, was given to the city. I made do with what was available there.

Organized by year, the yearbooks were in boxes marked with faded labels. The crest we used to wear on our uniforms was copied on each cover, but the rest of the cover was bland—nothing but a white, blue, or black background and the years it covered. Black-and-white photos of girls from age eleven to sixteen, nuns, and teachers filled the more recent editions. The older yearbooks were more like pamphlets, with a few pages listing various events and transcribed snippets from church services, a Psalm or a quotation from a poet, plus a group photo of the graduating class all dressed in their uniforms, which didn't change much over the years except that the skirts became slightly shorter. After World War II, instead of a single group photograph there were separate shots of each student and beside each, a name. Checking the yearbooks against some of the school enrolment records, I was able to link names with addresses.

I told the gentleman who helped me track down the boxes from the archives basement that I was searching out the alumnae of the old school for a reunion. Since the school is now defunct, I said we needed the records in order to make the event happen, and that we planned on holding it at our convent. I told him I realized many of the addresses would be old ones, but it was sometimes surprising the number of people who don't abandon a place once they've put down roots. Perhaps parents, if alive, would forward current information. The post office might be able to track others down. I wore my habit to gain credibility, and it seemed to work. The gentleman, who had a handlebar moustache, quite rare for these times, responded to me with quick attention and an endearing manner. He brought me a cup of coffee and told me not to tell anyone, because they didn't like food or drink in the archives, then he stopped on his own coffee break to see if I'd made any progress. I wondered if he was Catholic, since my habit hadn't unnerved him at all. He seemed lonely; there was only one other person on the floor, a city official checking on some blueprints in another room. Although it's been a while since a stranger flirted with me, I think he might have been as he brushed against my arm, turning the pages of my own year's yearbook with me.

My picture wasn't in it, because the photographs had been taken the first week of classes. I did, however, find Rachel and Francine and Caroline, as well as other classmates whose names and faces had almost vanished from my memory. It is amazing how you can simply forget another human being if she hasn't affected your life in any significant way. Yet I was also surprised by the accuracy of my memory; like first love, I had not forgotten a detail of Rachel's face. Her green eyes held my attention even in the black-and-white photograph in the book, taunting me to take things further.

I longed for her, for the girl she was, my only comfort being the proof she and I had lived for a time together. At the outset, I noted down each name and address because the gentleman was looking over my shoulder and I was unwilling to blow my cover for being there. I continued because it occurred to me that even if I had forgotten someone, they might not have forgotten me. How could I tell what knowledge someone else possessed? How could I tell whether someone in a photograph had witnessed a key part of the events on that winter night in Room 313? So I took down all the addresses. The gentleman said he hoped I'd return if I needed anything else. I admired his moustache once again, dark brown with straggling red and white hairs, before I signed out, thankfully giving my first name only, as Sisters do, and left.

I typed the letter in Sister Irene's room while she nodded off in her regular drug-induced sleep, snoring with huge gasps. I used to panic when she'd fall asleep, her chest rising and falling with an energetic frequency she can no longer display while awake, and call for Sister Ursula. Then I'd stay an extra hour, checking her pulse, putting my finger against her nose to see if I could readjust her breathing, laying my head against her chest to make sure the heartbeat sounded healthy. Now I know this is just what her body does and it is easy to ignore. On the day I typed my letter, Sister Irene received a double dose of her sleeping pills.

I mailed the form letter to each person on my list and included a self-addressed stamped return envelope. The letter stated we were searching for donations for our Catholic Convent-sponsored charities. It described some of the causes we have supported over the years, including the diabetes foundation, cancer research, drug and addiction counselling, homeless shelters, and our local humane society. Also enclosed was a donation card with a list of possible amounts under the headings Gold, Silver, and Bronze sponsorship, plus a blank amount for a lower donation under the title Friendship Sponsor. My name typed and signed was at the bottom of both the letter and card as the Head of the Donation Committee for the convent. Even though there is free use of the photocopier at the church, donated by one of our parishioners to help with the costs of making a newsletter and posters for upcoming events, I decided not to take my chances there. I used the photocopier at a corner store run by an elderly Polish couple and their adolescent grandchildren. How I would explain what I was doing to Mother Superior or Father B., I didn't know. I figured if someone was searching for me, this was the only way to offer myself up to them in surrender; they'd know I'd received the silver candle holder and was asking for my accuser to present herself. I also secretly hoped listing the good works that I'd been involved in might work in my favour for mercy. But I didn't expect to receive any real donations. Perhaps I've grown too cynical. I didn't expect anyone to care about our convent. I wasn't thinking ahead.

With my first returned envelope in front of me, it is difficult not to let my mind race with fear as I get up the nerve to slice it open, even though I know the chances are slim that the addresses have proven to be the correct ones. The donation card is filled out at the Silver level. A cheque is included and a note: *My address has changed. I just happened to be visiting my mother for the weekend. Your causes are very worthwhile and I applaud the church for sponsoring them. I work with deaf children myself. I ask you kindly for a receipt for tax purposes. Send it to the address indicated on the cheque. Best Wishes, Francine L.*

She didn't recognize my name, but I can cross her off my list. I recognize hers.

THE VIRGIN MARY WAS a silent role. I got the part. Sister Aline was pleased I wouldn't be singing a single note through the entire Christmas pageant, I'm sure. Honestly, so was I. My voice was nothing less than a disgrace. After endlessly tormenting me by striking the organ keys and then asking me to mimic the sound emitted, Sister Aline soon advised me to hum bars instead of singing them, and eventually to simply mouth the words. The thought of humiliating myself in front of the nuns and students' parents, or opening myself up to endless taunting and teasing from the girls themselves as I croaked lines of music wearing makeshift wings or a wise man's robe was enough to make me sigh with relief as Sister Aline announced I would be playing the Virgin Mary and I realized I wouldn't have to sing at all. What I didn't think about in that instant was how I would be tormented in another fashion until the play was over. Now I was The Virgin of the school. Named and fitted for the costume. A blue and white frock made out of felt and a tablecloth. The girls laughed as Sister Aline squealed that the powder-blue robe and white veil were a perfect fit from last year's pageant. I cringed under the mark of The Virgin, although her role in the Bible had intrigued me; Mary was a teenager herself, ostracized by her own family and community. Who could believe her strange story? The news of her pregnancy both a blessing and a curse. Who was the man who had come for her in the middle of the night and left her pregnant? An angel? How could she stand the ridicule of those who were sure she had tricked her dense husband and made him the fool of the town? And now I was named after her, and the nickname stuck until the winter term, until the catastrophe. I couldn't shake it off as easily as the light snow falling to blanket the outside world.

Bella was Gabriel, the part with the most singing. She would be present in nearly every scene, joining the choir in their hymns of praise and providing the solos when Gabriel flies in through Mary's window to tell her the sacred news and when Jesus Christ is born. She practised a version of "O Holy Night" that gave the girls chills and brought tears to Sister Aline's eyes. Even Mother Superior, at the back of the church, stood mesmerized upon hearing Bella's voice. She said she needed to speak to Sister Aline in private and to continue on with our practice, but she had really come to check on the pageant's progress, making sure that her paying parents and patrons would be thoroughly pleased with the education their daughters and the daughters of the community were receiving. When Bella sang, we were directed to watch, to appreciate her carriage as well as her voice, how she projected by bringing the air in through her nose and out through her mouth. Sister Aline used her as one might use a textbook in class, to demonstrate how the songs ought to be sung, how

we might strive to be like her. It was the same way my father sometimes spoke of my mother to Christine and me. "Look at the way she
accepts all life with grace," he said once as she bent over in our
garden to admire a nest of ants. "Look at her face, children. It is the
face of someone absolutely blessed by life." Bella's face radiated when
she sang; she accepted her gift with the same humility with which my
mother accepted my father's compliments. "Grace can be learned,"
my mother said. "You're not born with it." But it was difficult to see
how Bella might have learned so much more quickly than the rest of
us; we were sure her singing voice had been given to her, and sure
that there was nothing we could do about it either.

We knew the pageant was important. The school wasn't as
popular as it had been in the past. Most girls went to public school
and to the co-ed separate schools. A private school, taught mostly
by nuns in a convent, was a dying breed, and we sensed this, even if
we were not acutely aware of it. Rachel said if it weren't for her
father, the school would have closed long ago. But that was a lie, or
at least an exaggeration. His money wasn't enough to cover the
expenses. The school was in massive debt, although the nuns tried
not to show it. Mother Superior acted as if the school would be
under her jurisdiction for another fifty years, rallying us with the
claim that one day we would be proud to send our own children
there. But Sister Marguerite slipped one day as she supervised recess.
She took a long, forlorn look at the entrance of the school building
and said, "I'll regret the day the gates close for good." It was only a
matter of time.

"If there are angels," Sister Aline stated proudly at the bottom of the altar steps while Bella let out a final high note until the organ went silent, "she is certainly one of them here on earth."

Mother Superior applauded. The rest of us were aware that we were merely earth dwellers, Bella's celestial graces out of common reach. Bella didn't need us to convince her she was worthy or special. Her mother and father picked her up every Friday, her father speaking briefly to the nuns, who always commented on Bella's studious nature, excellent grades, and singing talent. Her mother, who spoke almost no English, had Bella translate to her in Portuguese. In pride, her mother would flatten her hands against Bella's cheeks, then place a kiss inside her palm and bestow it upon Bella as they left the school. At the end of practice, Bella's mother came to collect her. They crossed themselves at the holy water as they left. That was the moment I knew I hated her. Bella was Gabriel delivering a great message. All I could do, as a mortal, was step out of her way.

On the day of the pageant, what we called "Opening Night" although there would only be one performance, Sister Aline rallied us around her like an athletic coach—the girls in costume, jittery about performing in front of their parents and friends—to recite the Our Father prayer. Rachel tugged on my blue tunic. When I turned around to greet her, the other girls' chins bent to their chests, Rachel, her eyes sparkling with mischief above her silly fake beard and moustache, opened her wise-man robe and flashed me. She was wearing the red bra I had stolen from the department store, her breasts cupped in its delicate lace and satin. I felt myself blush, and she had to shoot me a stern look to stop me from gawking at her newly re-covered bosom and return to the prayer. Virgin, she mouthed, shoving out her chest as if it weren't hidden in a formless yellow and navy blue blanket turned cloak for the night. We're too old for this, I thought. Dressing up in costumes and makeup, pretending to be religious characters riding into cities on donkeys to pay our taxes, the wise men with breasts bunching up their robes. Still, I couldn't believe Rachel's nerve in flaunting her contempt for the whole affair. Her shamelessness.

Stripped of all its regular ornaments for the pageant, the altar now held a wooden manger with a naked male doll hidden inside it underneath a dishtowel. Barrels of hay had been shipped in from the outskirts of the city and spread across the floor. Sister Aline was already miffed at the amount of work it would take to clean it up. She had allergies, she told us, but the pageant was an important event, and she'd simply have to suffer. She kept a handkerchief in her right hand and brought it out regularly, like a good luck charm, covering her nose to ward off the smell. Christmas lights were strung along the pews where the choir stood. When the night scenes were staged, all the church lights would be turned off and the tiny yellow bulbs would twinkle in the distance. The angels wore white dresses and cardboard wings attached to their shoulders by bent clothes hangers. Instead of real animals, we used a few sheep from the church Nativity set, plastic and easy to lift, and a couple of deer placed towards the back, painted brown to disguise their previous incarnation as Christmas lawn decorations. There was debate as to whether deer in Bethlehem would be historically accurate, but Mother Superior put her foot down, saying the audience would want other animals in the play besides sheep, and we would make do with what we had. Francine, who played Joseph, wore a shirt and pants cut out of a potato sack. She itched throughout the performance. When Mother Superior went backstage at the intermission, Francine was told to stop scratching or she'd be sent home early for the holidays. This comment put Francine practically in tears, which worked well with the play, a few parents commenting afterwards on the budding actress in the bunch; when Joseph returned to the stage for the manger scene, he seemed genuinely upset that he could do no better for the holy child.

The parents, teachers, and nuns sat in the pews as if we were performing in a theatre. Lights were kept on at the church entrances and on the stage only. Father McC. was our priest; he delivered Mass on Mondays when all the girls were in attendance, and also on Sundays for the Leftovers, and provided us with confessional services every two months, although we had no confessionals. He'd seat two chairs opposite each other, back to back, and we were supposed to pretend he didn't know who we were and we didn't know who he was. He enjoyed delivering his repentance instructions in Latin, then waiting for us to ask him for the translation, admonishing us to study languages other than English and French in order to be good Catholics. For the pageant he sat in the front pew with Mother Superior, both with their backs straight and staring ahead, without speaking to each other. Mother Superior took a Bible from the back of the pew in front of her and read. Father McC. counted something on his hands.

The collection plate would be passed three times: once at the beginning, again during intermission, and finally after the performance was over. Sister Aline told us this so we could warn our parents to bring more money or divide the money they planned to give. We would all remain onstage at the end of the pageant to sing a final hymn, the hymn of the school, "Our Eyes to Heaven," a translation of a Greek Orthodox hymn altered by one of the founding nuns to reflect the motto of the school. Sister Aline taught us the hymn with as much vigour as she taught the rest of the songs, but she hated it. In four-four time and with forced rhymes between words such as "school" and "adore," "heaven" and "stepping," the hymn, she believed, was not a sound translation. One day, in her disgust, Sister Aline muttered that she was sure it must have been a drinking song. As usual, however, she acquiesced under Mother Superior's authority and added it to our repertoire.

Before the performance, we were herded into the hallway behind the choir section, and before our group prayer, Sister Aline kept sneaking peeks through the doorway to judge how many people had arrived and found themselves seats. "Yvonne, your parents and your brother are here," she chimed. "Patricia, I think your grandmother made it." I wanted to ask if she spotted a woman in rose-coloured glasses holding onto a tall man's arm, but I didn't want to draw attention to myself. The odds were not in my favour that my parents would be attending. When I mentioned it to my father on the phone, he replied that a couple of hours would be an awful long time for my mother to sit on such uncomfortable seats. "Is it really important?" he asked. I said no, but hoped against hope that they might not have been able to keep themselves away, that they might not want to miss their oldest daughter perform in a pageant, that they might feel proud.

With only a few minutes left before curtain, Sister Aline, her handkerchief tucked into her fist, asked us to hold hands. She couldn't lose any opportunity to broaden our religious instruction. She'd told us once in class that when she was our age, the nuns didn't explain theology, and how you could love something you could not understand was beyond her. She wanted us to love our religion, not because we were born into it, but because we would choose it. Because of this decision she anticipated us all having to make, we did not sing a single song in the choir without listening to an exegesis of the lyrics in excruciating detail. She had such a gentle disposition, though, that we didn't resist her. We merely humoured her.

"Christmas is the day the prophecy begins to be fulfilled," she said, choking a bit on her words in her excitement or because of her stuffy nose and scratchy throat.

"You are made in God's image. And like God's image, there are complements in all things." She pointed to her own body to demonstrate. "We have two eyes, two hands, two legs. We are symmetrical. The same on both sides."

"Two breasts," added Francine under her breath, a row of girls in front of her, enough to ensure Sister Aline did not hear. I wondered if Francine had been privy to Rachel's bra showing as well and had made the joke for our benefit, but I kept quiet and concentrated on Sister Aline's sermon, hoping she might impart a few words to save me from disaster in front of the school. It was the birthing scene I was dreading, pretending to give birth to a child in front of all those people, regardless of whether the child represented the Son of God. A stupid plastic doll, without the features of a boy, but called a boy because it was bald and girl dolls were always sold with hair, reeked of mockery. I didn't want to hold that hollow boy child in my hands and rock it in my arms.

"This is why there are two parts in the Bible. The Old Testament and the New Testament. There are those who think you can disregard one or the other, but you can't. They lose their meaning. The Old Testament is the prophecy, and the New Testament is the prophecy fulfilled. The birth of Christ begins the miracle of Christ's fulfilment. Begins the process of complementing the past with the future. So remember when you are out there, you are making the prophecy come to life! God will be watching you."

I think she added the latter statement to comfort us, but it made me even more nervous to think of God sitting in one of the pews, like Caroline's mother or Rachel's father, assessing which of the children could sing best or deliver their lines most clearly and passionately, silently admonishing those who might fall short of their cues or forget their lines under the lights. If not God, we were acutely aware that Mother Superior was watching, and she was scarier than He was by a mile. Mother Superior would let you know if you'd failed her. She would call you into her office and then dismiss you from her presence. She would inform your parents.

When the lights were dimmed, Sister Aline escorted the choir onto the stage, and those of us in the play stepped out onto the church floor while the rest took their places in a row of pews to the left and waited their turn to join us in the final hymn. Father McC., though he was smiling up at us, was fidgety once the play began, shifting around in his pew, as if uncomfortable being seated with the rest of the crowd when he was accustomed to the lead role. He frowned. Mother Superior held the Bible against her chest.

When it came time for me to deliver baby Jesus, I did it exactly as I was instructed to: miraculously, without pain or discomfort. Hidden underneath the dishtowel in the manger, the baby rose fully formed into my hands; the shortest labour in the history of womanhood. Sister Aline had directed me for this climactic scene, and had insisted that Mary did not suffer from childbirth pain in the least, as she was free from sin. She said it was the simplest birth in the world. I doubted her, but at least I wasn't asked to scream or moan or hold onto the bundles of hay with my fists and yell at Joseph to fetch water, as we had seen in the movies. My labour was a fake. The pillow strapped to my stomach was removed by my own hands while the choir gathered in front of the altar in a straight line to shield me. As the force of the singing grew, Bella's voice leading the way, the singers parted and I was revealed, slim and smiling. The hell of being in front of everyone was nearly over.

The only thing left before the school hymn was Bella's rendition of "O Holy Night." Gabriel's costume, though also donated by the theatre group, was prettier than ours: a long white dress with ruffles along the hem, a set of wings made of silk. The crowd hushed. Bella's voice rose steadily, evoking both reverence and mourning. Her silk wings opened as she raised her arms, her voice transforming into triumph. The choir stood motionless behind her. We were instructed to freeze in our positions as she sang, but we didn't need to be told. The spotlight was hers.

Hear the Angels Sing.

O Night Divine, O Night that Christ was Born.

Illuminated, she was practically transcendent. Father McC. folded his hands in prayer. Sister Aline took out her tissue but delayed wiping her nose. Mother Superior stared fondly upon the school treasure. I was sure each parent in the audience wished Bella were their child. And then I was glad my parents hadn't come. I knew if they had shown up, they would have shared the same expression as the other parents in the crowd; they would have been stunned at the beauty of Bella's gift, they would have regarded her mother, who sat beaming though she didn't understand the English words, with envy. I was grateful to be spared.

I took the plastic baby from the manger and tried to cradle its stiff body lovingly in my arms as Bella hit her final note, which echoed under the wooden beams of the church. Every single person applauded. Some rose to their feet. When Bella took her humble

bow, they sighed with wonder. At the end of the performance,
I walked out with a trussed-up baby Jesus dangling by his feet from
my hands. Bella, distracted for a second from the glowing appraisals
of Sister Aline, stepped backwards in confusion. Take it, it's yours,
I said. And she did.

KIM WALKS WITH A black leather purse in her hand, a gift from Sister Josie, the string hanging down like a tail between her legs as she exits Mother Superior's office. I just happen to be near the office door on my way to get lunch. It is Thursday, and I like to have two large helpings at lunch and dinner because on Fridays I fast. I stop and wave to Kim, but she does not address me except to raise her purse slightly in the air. She turns quickly as if to enter the washroom to her right.

"Wait, Kim," I say.

She is not a difficult ward. She obeys her elders when she must and waits for me to catch up to her, fiddling with her purse string, weaving her fingers through it like a cat's cradle.

"It's good for you," I say. "The doctor will be able to tell you if you're well. Sister Ursula doesn't have all the equipment here."

Kim pouts. Her lips are puffy and wet from crying. Her pitiful expression makes her condition seem more hopeless. She had built up her energy to appear so healthy to Mother Superior, so well adjusted to her new surroundings, that she hoped a trip to an outside doctor would be deemed unnecessary. It doesn't surprise her that I am aware of what her meeting with Mother Superior was about; she already knows there are few secrets here.

"For the baby," she says. "Yeah, I know. Apparently I'm too skinny. All the weight's in one place and I'm going to bend out of shape."

Her knuckles are white, the purse string wrapped tightly around the skin. She does not wish to speak to me and scales the walls nervously with her eyes, as if she were being expelled from the convent, holding in her breath to keep from crying. It is worse than the day the policemen came.

"Mother Superior didn't say you had to leave, did she?"

"No," she replies, taking her free hand and wiping her forehead, rubbing it in frustration. "It's just that …"

She sucks in her lips and I lament how skinny she is, how much pain she might be in from her pregnancy. She has barely enough energy to lift herself out of a chair. The unborn child rides high and directly in front, and she is without any bulk on her obliques or lower back. And her pregnancy is barely half over. A healthy girl might not even look pregnant, just a little bloated, but Kim looks like she's strapped a ball underneath her shirt. Mother Superior is right to worry, I think. The baby needs more room to grow. Kim needs to build up her muscles or else the child might topple her.

"Are you afraid?"

"Yes."

I try to put my arm around her but she backs out of my embrace. She must be sick of being touched by us women, continually fussing over her body and trying to coddle her. She pats my elbow to assure me she isn't angry, she just doesn't want the comfort

I offer. Sister Bernadette strolls by and smiles at us, beaming brightly, one of her many manila folders under her arm, a skip in her step. Kim stares at her backside grudgingly.

"Is she always so happy?" Kim asks, imitating Sister Bernadette's stride by moving her arms into a march, an exaggerated smile pinched across her face.

"Hard to believe, isn't it?" I reply with a smirk. "She's a real happy nun."

This at least elicits a laugh.

"She's got a lot of faith, I guess," Kim says, dropping both her arms and her smile.

I point to the end of the hallway, the cafeteria entrance, to indicate she should join me for lunch. We walk together, our steps in unison. "Oh, I don't know about that. Faith doesn't mean much if you've never had doubts. She's just sheltered," I say without thinking who I'm talking to and inwardly scold myself. I do not know Kim well enough to be able to judge whether or not she will repeat this to one of the Sisters. And they think I act strangely enough; being critical of others won't boost me in their esteem. Putting me at ease, Kim nods and seems to accept my answer. She's probably seen enough already at her age to be able to understand a bit of these things. She relaxes a little, stops strangling the tips of her fingers with the purse string. The doors are open.

"I don't like clinics," she tells me as we stand in line with the Sisters for our meal. I take two servings of milk from the counter and place one on her tray and one on mine, without checking if she wants one.

"I don't think anybody does," I say, scanning an array of sandwiches wrapped in plastic. "Which one do you want?"

"Ugh, none thanks. I'm sick in the mornings."

"Oh, of course." I begin to suspect my initial reaction to her lack of appetite might have been wrong. She may care little about her own health, and she still does not voice concern over her baby's health, but in all the fuss to get her to eat, none of us had bothered to ask if she was throwing it all back up. Has it really been so long since we knew such things? Since we witnessed what women actually suffer through in their pregnancies? Standing side by side, Kim and I are both women, but our bodies are as foreign to each other as opposite sexes. Her body growing, transforming, and connecting with another life. Mine backing up, pulling away, in the beginning stages of menopause. The Change of Life, Sister Ursula calls it. A little early, but nonetheless. For us, it isn't a change really. Ought to be called The Pull Away from Life. Kim vomits in the mornings because her body is fighting an intruder, while mine is fighting the lack of one.

"What about some soup, then. Tomato? I'm sure we have it."

"Okay," Kim says, and ventures off to one of the tables. She selects two places for us among the many empty seats. There is no need for a convent of our size to have such a large dining area, so many of us try to spread ourselves out to make the room appear more lived in.

I choose two tuna sandwiches for myself and a cup of tea.

"Have you managed to find out who the father is?"

It's Sister Gwen. I can recognize the sound of her shoes anywhere.

At least I used to think it was her shoes, but it's just the way she walks, clamping down on her heel while sliding her toe to the side with every step. She also has a distinct smell, like pine, and Sister Sarah told me it is because she uses men's deodorant. Her sweat glands are overactive.

"Does it matter?" I say, staring her down.

"Suppose it wouldn't to the man," she replies, ignoring my disapproval, extracting herself a napkin from the dispenser and pushing ahead of me as Sister Gloria retrieves my soup order, setting the hot bowl on a plate with some unsalted crackers. "Good for her stomach," she adds.

I am a bit annoyed by their air of familiarity in regards to Kim, although I have no reason to make claims on the girl and her baby either. Many Sisters have been doing their part, spending time with her. She's like a communal project, the same as our regular church activities: a duty and a mission. Perhaps we hope to see how well we've affected her, and think that if she proves to be a good person and the baby a healthy child, it will be due to our intervention. But it's Kim who's intervened. Changed our routine, inserted herself. Now more than ever, I too need to know my time has purpose here, that I can help Kim even if I am unable to help myself. I hastily move past the line to sit with her and bump against the table as I do so. I snort and massage my hurt knee.

"You all right?" asks Kim, reaching for her soup, her black purse perched on the table beside her. I think about suggesting she take it off the table and place it on the bench, but change my mind and ignore her lack of table manners. She slurps, and I notice a space between her front teeth that causes her to whistle when she sips.

"Yeah. It's just Sister Gwen. She wanted to know who the father of your baby is."

Kim clangs her spoon against the ceramic bowl, spurting soup across the top of her dress, one I kept aside for her that is warm, with a turtleneck collar. She grabs a napkin to wipe at the spillage before it becomes a stain.

"The baby has no father," she replies sternly without looking up from her cleaning.

"Oh, is it a virgin birth then?"

She refuses to meet my eyes. Returning to her soup, she runs her spoon across the top of it without bringing any to her mouth.

"If you don't want to say who the father is, that's fine," I tell her. "Just don't lie to me and say that there isn't one. You didn't get that bulge across your waist from sitting on a dirty park bench."

I continue to eat my sandwich. It's got a good texture and must have been made today. Sister Katherine sits down beside us and eats with her arm across her plate as if guarding her food. She chews quickly, dabbing the corners of her mouth between every few mouthfuls. I am weakened by sleeplessness and am not any further along on the issue of who has sent me the candle holder. Four more envelopes have been returned, but to no avail. I've stored the cheques in my socks, and I'm not sure what I'm going to do. They are made out to the convent and so I cannot refuse them, but I need to wait until I can concoct a credible story for Mother Superior and Father B. They don't usually care where church money comes from as long as the cheques don't bounce, yet it is still a tricky business to lie about why I've been secretive collecting it. Maybe I would be better off if I went over the wall. Leave the nunnery for good and start a new life somewhere else, under a different name, become a florist or a secretary or a hostess in a restaurant. At least I'd be free of this. Free of my knowledge, instead of suffocating inside of it. Whoever is tormenting me might merely be waiting for me to do the right thing and end this life of hypocrisy. Belief in God isn't enough to be a nun. The word Believer originally came from the word meaning Approve. Sister Aline taught me that. One must approve of God and I'm not sure I do. God isn't a belief anyway. He's more like a rumour. Especially at this time, so close to Christmas, it is the possibility of His presence that makes us prepare the church for festivity. Hope for mercy. I've worked hard here in my repentance. Why am I being disturbed now? Who wants me to pay at a higher rate than I've already been paying?

I look at Sister Katherine suspiciously for a moment, wondering if we might have met at some earlier time. The probability is minimal, practically non-existent. There is no reason to suspect any of the Sisters here. Sister Katherine lifts her face up from her dish and I pretend I am staring past her to the window and the orchard outside. Not Sister Katherine, but perhaps one of the Sisters from St. X. School for Girls might have sent the silver candle holder. Sister Marguerite or Sister Aline or Mother Superior. I encounter Sister Aline once a year; she lives in another convent only twenty miles away, but she has never given me any indication that she knows what happened in Rachel's room all those years ago.

Sister Aline is fragile in her constitution; I imagine she would have broken her silence before now if she had any privileged knowledge. She was particularly distressed at the time, expressed a desire to investigate the circumstances but found very little. In fact, when we do meet at certain church events, she is content to reminisce about the old school, with only a tinge of regret that it is no longer running. Sister Aline adored teaching and the choir. She loved the girls, and her belief in our eternal innocence was unshakeable. I would bet it is not her. Mother Superior would be old if she were alive, but she isn't; she died of a heart attack eight years ago. Our Mother Superior received a letter and a photocopy of her obituary in *The Catholic Monitor*. But Sister Marguerite might still be alive. Maybe I can write to her convent and find out. I could pretend to be researching the history of how St. X. School for Girls came to be sold to the separate school system, to hire both male and female teachers and become co-ed. Sister Marguerite was particularly sad when the school shut down, I remember. She had been wary of the tide of feminism carrying off younger women and feared that Sisters were dwindling in numbers. Didn't I prove her wrong. Maybe she hid the candle holder in hopes of keeping the scandal hidden and only now, in her later years, felt the need to be free of it. Send it back to one of its sinful owners. Maybe she blames us for the loss of the school. That, at least, wasn't our fault. That ending was out of our control.

Kim picks up her bowl and drinks the last of the soup. She is about to leave the table and makes a show of it, standing up and whipping her tray off in a dramatic gesture. Suddenly I'm a bit afraid of her, of her power to hurt me. I need her and her baby here.

She keeps me focussed. At least I'm sure she knows nothing about me or my past. As I know little about hers. She won't even reveal to me who the father is. But that doesn't matter. Right now the child needs only its mother to survive. God could have sent His one and only Son down to earth in any form; He chose Mary for a reason. Even God knows that every child needs a mother.

"Wait, Kim," I say, rising with her to stack our trays and dispose of our napkins in the trash bin. "I'll go to the clinic with you if you like."

Her eyes widen in gratitude. She is more fragile than I give her credit for, I realize. I must be kinder to her. There is no need for me to keep forcing her to pay for her pregnancy. She'll have enough reminders and hard times ahead without any of us making her feel worse. I smile, gesture to her to sit at the table nearest the exit. She obeys.

"Drink your milk," I tell her, noticing she hasn't opened her carton. She drinks, and a white moustache forms across her upper lip. If it wasn't impossible, I could almost believe she was going to have a virgin birth. I wonder if such things might actually be possible. Could we ever be given gifts instead of burdens? Did Mary herself know which she had been offered the day the angel Gabriel came into her life? The trash beside us needs to be emptied. Crunched up paper napkins stick out the top, and wrappers and food scraps fill the bin. I am reminded of how much we waste. Even us.

At the clinic, after Kim is examined, the female doctor, hectic and overworked I can tell from her bloodshot eyes and her lab coat buttoned unevenly, comes out of the examination room to inform me Kim is in trouble. Although the existing weight is hard on Kim's slight frame, she also hasn't gained enough weight to ensure a healthy pregnancy.

"By six-and-a-half months she should be at least ten to fifteen pounds heavier," she says, demonstrating with a picture on a pamphlet, a row of cartoon women at different stages of pregnancy, their hands around their hips, holding up their progressively larger bellies.

"But she's only four-and-a-half months," I reply.

"No, no. She's six-and-a-half months along. Maybe closer to seven, but I'm trying to be conservative. Get her to eat." The doctor's tone is curt. She signals a nurse, who inserts a couple of files between her hands as if they were a mail slot.

"But she has morning sickness," I tell her.

"No. That's only in the first trimester. Get the nurse at the admitting desk to give you some information booklets. If she's throwing up now, then there's something else wrong with her. But I don't think so. I didn't find anything else out of the ordinary when I examined her. She's young. They're all worried about their weight these days. She's probably trying not to put much on in fear she'll never take it off. It's getting harder to get women to put on the weight they need when they need it. And then harder to get them to take it off when they gain too much."

"I didn't know," I stammer, a bit put off by the amount of noise in the clinic corridor. People pass by in such a hurry, boots stomping on the floors, while the nurses call out names, deliver instructions. There's the banter of those waiting on chairs, a child in a stroller crying while a tired mother shakes a rattle.

"That's all right. I'm sure you didn't know this surprise was coming months ago. Tell her mother to get her to eat."

She returns a folder to the reception area. Her short hair has split ends at the base of her neck, and her nylons have a small run up her calf from behind. A pregnant woman in her thirties and a man who must be the child's father follow her out. They look equally exhausted but relieved to see the doctor.

"She doesn't have a mother," I say to no one in particular as Kim emerges from the examination room, zipping up her jacket, head down, shuffling her feet across the floor and holding her belly protectively with her hands. She looks so downtrodden; I'm startled by an urge to slap her. I don't know what she told the doctor about the length of her pregnancy, but I'm sure she knows I won't be happy. She's lied to me once already today. She walks bravely over to me in a straight line, anticipating the anger in my face.

I take her hand harshly, squeezing her slim fingers, and press the elevator button.

"I'm ... I'm sorry," she stutters, and I shoot her an outraged glance to silence her. My entire body is tense. I can feel my back stiffening. The side of my cheek twitches.

Kim whimpers and I press the button again, although the light is flashing to tell me the elevator will arrive when available. I'm glad I decided to wear plain clothes instead of my habit. The effect is liberating. I can argue with Kim, express my dissatisfaction and scold her without being worried about how my behaviour as a nun might reflect on the Church.

"That hurts."

"Shut up." I stamp one boot on the floor, turn to face her. She's flushed. My grip loosens on her fingers.

"After I agreed to come with you … you lied to me. To all of us!" My voice is loud, and a few patients waiting in the reception chairs glance up momentarily from their magazines. The rattle keeps shaking.

"I'm sorry," Kim says quietly, squeezing the end of my jacket sleeve. "I didn't mean to. I didn't know."

"You must have known it was longer than four-and-a-half months! You must have known you couldn't hide it forever!"

I hiss the words at her and she averts her gaze, admitting guilt. I surmise from her erratic breathing that she is trying not to cry. A small group of people encircles us, all eyes on the flashing floor numbers overhead, indicating how long before it will be our turn. I feel swarmed, claustrophobic, and pull Kim closer to my side. The doors open.

"There are things we need to plan," I say to her. "It's so soon. There are so many things we need to get for you. To prepare. You haven't given us any time to prepare."

With the doors about to shut with the ring of the elevator bell, we rush inside, Kim's body and mine close together, her chin at my chest. She angles her neck to huddle against me and I tense up but comply. I lift my hand and stroke her hair, slightly damp at the forehead with sweat, and am aware I have taken on her and her baby whether I want to or not. I laugh inwardly at the thought that I too am now a mother, a victim of immaculate conception. *What will happen to you?* I think, and hold Kim even closer, potential life stirring within her. She slides her arms around my waist as the floor gives way underneath us. *We will not fall,* I say to myself like a prayer.

WHEN MY FATHER CAME to pick me up for Christmas holidays, discussing something intently with Mother Superior as I waited impatiently to get going, I noticed his body had grown tighter and thinner since I'd last seen him, the muscles on his face and arms shrunken, yet hard to the touch. The red and green sweater I remembered him wearing snugly the year before hung below his waistline, and the hair at his temples was practically white. He had grown a beard, a reddish-brown mix with a patch of black-brown at the chin, which contrasted starkly with the greying hair on his scalp.

"Why the beard, Daddy?" I asked as he drove a car I'd never seen before, on loan from a neighbour. I hadn't seen him since arriving at St. X. School for Girls on the bus. I wanted him to feel guilty for leaving me alone all this time, but I was giddy at our reunion, regardless of the friends I'd made. I didn't want to upset my mother by causing any trouble. She was probably too weak to deal with my problems. I couldn't let my anger out.

"Oh, this thing," he chuckled, stroking the bulk at his chin comically with his free hand. "I figured I might as well let it grow.

I've been so busy. Barely enough time to shave. Your mother tells me they're in style again?"

"Sure, Dad," I replied, though the pictures we cut out of magazines were of much younger men, with thin arms and legs, and they never had beards, their faces as smooth as satin. In my room, underneath the mattress of my bed, I kept a picture of an eighteen-year-old model from a magazine, his shirt sliding off his shoulders like a blouse. His cheeks, which I kissed with red lipstick Rachel lent me, were round, and his chin was free of hair, as if he'd never shaved in his life. As we watched boys walking by, I liked the ones whose skin appeared almost transparent. The one I particularly liked, Nathaniel, or Nattie, as I heard his friends call him, barely had eye-brows. He would stop by with other boys at the convenience store across the street from our school and we'd run over at lunch to meet them sometimes. Nathaniel knew Patrick but wasn't friends with him, so I don't know if he heard about Rachel or our club. He told me he played hockey and was going to be in the NHL someday. I thought he looked too skinny for that. He was shorter than most of the other boys; shorter than Caroline and me. But I liked the way he pulled licorice whips out of the jar and shared them with me and how his hair was blond and fine like Rachel's. I was sure it felt like silk, not scratchy like my father's new beard when he kissed my fore-head to greet me.

"Your mother is doing so well, Angela. She's like a whole new woman!" He was tapping the dashboard with his fingers, listening to jazz on the radio, humming contentedly, though it was clear he didn't know any of the words to the songs.

I hugged my small duffel bag with pleasure, a few clothes and a couple of pictures we had drawn in art class to give to my mother. I worked on a bowl of fruit for hours, contouring shades on grapes and apples. I was less successful than many in the class, but I knew that my mother would want to see something I'd done, and she'd praise me anyway.

"Does that mean I'm coming home soon?"

The thought made me anxious and relieved at the same time. I missed my mother, and I hated the nightmares I had in my room. Always filled with young children tending the wounds of women; my mother's face streaked with dirt and blood, her glasses smashed on the floor. The children had white hair and were horribly thin; they ripped paper off the walls with their fingernails as they cried. With small needles, they pricked my mother's flesh, draining her. I feared many times the ghosts of the past were seeping in through the walls, through the floors, as was rumoured. Yet I also knew that if I was allowed to return home, it would mean a new school and new friends, and I wouldn't be able to do the things I did with Rachel, Caroline, and Francine. I liked being part of The Sisterhood. The girls had accepted me. They made the isolation endurable. I didn't want to start all over.

"She's home," he hummed, bopping his head to the rhythm.

"Yes, I know Mom's home. She's home all the time," I answered. "What about me? Or Christine?"

"You're home for Christmas," he said and squeezed my arm beside him, then ruffled my hair.

"Am I going to be there all year?"

He stopped tapping the dashboard and checked the side and rear-view mirrors. "Did I miss the street? I think I missed the street, Angela," he said, squinting to make out the signs covered with snow as we drove past a park on a sloped road. "There should be a house here with a yellow veranda. I think I missed it. What was I thinking?"

He turned the car around.

The snow had fallen gently and steadily for a week. It lined roofs and trees, piled up on driveways and road signs, and made the city's breath exhale the fantasy of new beginnings. The festivity was getting to me, after the pageant and the treats at St. X. School for Girls and The Sisterhood's trek to the boutiques lining the Market streets, where we peered in the windows, ran our hands over expensive dresses, and spent our change on maple candy. Rachel bought me a gold-painted ring with a fake purple stone. It wasn't worth more than a dollar, but I adored it and slid it on my finger right away. It didn't matter if the stone didn't sparkle, I felt incredibly proud. "Sisters," she said as I opened the white box. We had our gift exchange right on the city street, not waiting to wrap the presents. I bought Rachel a bottle of perfume from the Hudson's Bay Company cosmetics counter. The clerk claimed many women who wore the scent attracted their future husbands. Rachel broke the seal and sprayed herself four times. Men and women carried boxes and bags, tissue paper and bows. On the frozen canal, couples and families skated in snowsuits and scarves, gliding across the ice, their faces flushed. The Christmas cheer was infectious.

Coloured lights in green, red, and yellow, strung around maple trees in front yards and evergreen bushes lining the streets, were plugged in and sparkling despite the afternoon whiteness, the sun directly overhead. Father said the city Christmas lights were overwhelming, nothing like what we were used to in the country. Every house was draped in light and sported a wreath on the front door or ornaments and tinsel on the windows and the lawns. Even our neighbourhood appeared lived in.

"Look at it all," he said as we drove. "I'm going to take your mother out to see the trees along the canal tomorrow."

I was about to tell my father I'd already been but decided against it. I hadn't heard of my mother leaving the house for anything except doctors' appointments. He might be hurt I hadn't invited them, or he might ask too many questions about Mr. M. I'm sure he wouldn't have thought it odd one of the girls' parents had taken us on an outing, but I wanted to keep Mr. M. to myself. My cheeks went red in the car, my heartbeat quickened. I could not mention Mr. M. in my father's presence. He might guess I had a secret. Instead, I agreed my mother would love to see the lights and decorations around the neighbourhood and downtown, and Christine and I could be taken later on in the holiday. I insisted they should have a nice day alone. My father was pleased.

As we drove he continued to be amazed by the decorations. Even though it was daytime, the lights made the snow glitter in the sun.

"Sister Aline told us the Christmas lights show God how much we thank Him for His son."

"I suppose she'd say so," replied my father gravely.

"I think they're to make sure He can see us."

He tapped the dashboard with his gloved hands. "And what did Sister Aline say?"

"She said He's watching us all the time. But I don't see how He can. There'd be so much He probably wouldn't want to see. Brushing our teeth, sleeping, taking notes in class. Why does He want to see all that?"

I was playing a bit, tired of pondering God and His ways, happy to be away from the presence of the nuns, their dark habits and conservative natures, their continual reminder of things beyond our control and their strange answers to our questions. *He works in mysterious ways* was what they said if they couldn't explain a passage in the Bible or answer a question about a recent event or hypothetical dilemma. It was what Mother Superior finally said when we asked why there were so many religions in the world and only one true God. It was what she said when we asked why children were orphaned and abandoned and left hungry if they were innocent. I was perplexed the nuns seemed to know so little about Him, their only knowledge obtained through the teachings of others, through confessionals and gospels. Sister Marguerite told us not to worry, others had searched before us and found the truth and we were lucky to follow. Sister Aline tried not to circumvent our questions, but her answers were equally incomprehensible to us most of the time. Ultimately, she said, God is a healer, and we are all his patients. The word Patient means Long-Sufferer and the purpose of God is to alleviate our suffering. Mostly she made little sense to us; we believed we had no experiences comparable to those in the Bible.

"I don't think He does," my father said, smiling in my direction as we approached the empty driveway.

When we entered the bungalow on Ashbrook Crescent, my mother was wearing her rose-coloured glasses and lying on the couch in the living room, Christine playing cards by herself on the floor. My mother's flesh was shockingly white, and the skin on her elbows and knees was pinched around bone. The lines on her face were deeper, even her chest was smaller and caved in. I couldn't believe my eyes. She had deteriorated so drastically in the last two-and-a-half months she reminded me of a plant at the end of its season, the way I knew our Christmas tree would feel to the touch in a few weeks: brittle, unable to drink water, the roots cut. She was a new woman, as my father said, but not the one I had been expecting. Had he grown blind? Was he trying to make me aware of the parts of her growing healthily, her teeth and her fingernails, perhaps? Had he stopped noticing any more? Or was it me? Had I not perceived how badly off she was when I left? She did smile more often, though, so it might have been that change in her he was speaking of so optimistically. I noticed over the next couple of days that she had new mysterious pills in a plastic container divided into sections, and more of them.

As I put down my luggage and wiped my wet boots on the welcome mat, Father ran over and placed a kiss on her lips. A pink streak spread across her cheeks.

"Look, Daddy!" Christine said. "Mommy missed you as much as I did!"

My father scooped Christine off the floor, her gangly legs dangling over his arms, accidentally kicking the cards astray, whirling her around.

"Oh, Joe. Watch out," my mother warned half-heartedly. "You'll make the girl all dizzy."

"Dizzy, dizzy. I want to be dizzy!" Christine squealed as I walked over and hugged my mother; her neck smelled of cream. Strangely, she had more hair than when I had left, darker and thicker. I ran my fingers over the top of it and found it rough, hard to separate. She gently pushed my hands away, taking them into her own and squeezing.

"Your hair?" I asked. "What—"

"It's a wig, Angela."

"A wig?"

Christine was simultaneously laughing and coughing, her long hair fanning out as Father spun, her heels kicking, his arms straining with the weight of her. "Yeah, Mom got a wig!" Christine cried. "It's pretty, don't you think?"

Father was running out of breath.

"You're getting too big for this," he said, lowering her to the floor.

"Yes, it's pretty," I said. "But—"

"My hair's almost gone."

My hand instantly reached out to touch her again. The wig went down to her shoulders, curled at the ends in an attractive bob. Each strand was thick and strong as I tugged. Until then I thought only movie stars wore wigs.

"Not too hard. It can come off," she said, readjusting the net to her forehead. "I can brush it, comb it, and cut it," she added. "I can put it up or down. And my head, it's as smooth as a baby's. Like yours was."

"Can I see it?" I asked.

"Later, Angela," she replied, a little sadly, pulling the blanket on the couch up to her chest. "You just got here."

"I like the wig," Christine offered. "You look glamorous."

Christine had also changed in the past couple of months. She was wearing rose nail polish on her fingers, and her bangs were held back with a stylish matching barrette. She had gained none of the visible signs of womanhood—the budding breasts or shifting bone structure—as I had in the last year, but she appeared less childish to me in some way. Maybe being on her own she had gained confidence, giving her strength I almost admired. She didn't seem distressed by Mother's appearance, nudging her calves playfully, then taking her tired toes into her hands and rubbing them. *She'll be a good mother*, I remember thinking.

The house was spotless, smelling of cleaners and disinfectants, the floors freshly mopped, their tiles slippery, the windows washed and the mantels scrubbed. There were only a few decorations: a pinecone wreath on the inside of the door with a bright red velvet bow, a plastic vine resembling fresh holly outlining the edge of the hallway, a few hanging cinnamon sticks that gave the room's air a spicy taste, and our simple red stockings hanging over the fireplace. Yet the entire house was transformed by their presence, bespeaking comfort. A green mat with "Merry Christmas" stitched on it lay in the corner by the window. A place to the left of the fireplace was reserved for the tree.

My father went into the kitchen to make sandwiches, and my mother asked me to bring her knitting bag out of her bedroom. In it were balls of yarn and an assortment of smooth brown sticks. She laid out the yarns on the couch according to their colour.

"We're going to make some Christmas presents with these," she proclaimed. "Look at the great colours you can get nowadays." She had balls in yellow, green, blue, red, and white. "There's more in the bag. Purple and pink, multicoloured yarn. Fantastic."

Her rose-coloured glasses, together with her wide smile, gave her a clownish appearance. The rather stark features of her face—the high cheekbones and long thin nose, her triangular chin—added to the effect. However, she had rarely seemed so light to me, so beautiful. Her hands moved as if skimming through water, effortlessly pulling out the strings. She held up a finished example of what we would be making: a star woven around the wooden sticks, crossed in the middle, the tightly wound yarn fanning out to the four points, front and back identical.

"Did you make that, Mom?" I asked, impressed by its exotic flair. We had made ornaments for the Christmas tree at the school—pieces of cloth pinned in sections to Styrofoam balls and clay cutouts of angels and trumpets—but this was a shape I'd never seen before.

"Yes, I did. They're quite easy, really. You'll see," she said in excitement, her words rushing out of her. "At first I didn't believe the nurse—I mean the neighbour, that I could do it. My hands were very sore the day she taught me. But once I got going, it was simple."

Christine was already rummaging through the knitting bag to find the purple yarn, and Mother passed me a large ball of yellow.

"Wool is a little more elegant, but it's more expensive," she added. "There's only two rolls in there. You can have one each if you like."

"Wool makes me itch anyway," I replied.

"That's right," she said, patting my head as she did when I was small. "I'd forgotten that. Well, the yarn's easier to work with too. Wool doesn't like to be separated."

Father came in with the sandwiches and some eggnog and sat in the recliner beside the fireplace, his eyes fixed on my mother as she demonstrated how to tie the first knot to keep the sticks in place and the way to wind the yarn in order to keep the pattern consistent. She had given up sewing and crocheting, and it was the only time in the last year I'd seen her use her hands with such concentration besides saying her rosary. In fact, the rosary was curiously out of sight for once, and its absence gladdened me as I thought that even my mother was capable of forgetting about Him once in a while and thinking of herself first. But the illusion soon vanished when she told us the name of the objects we were crafting.

"They're called God's Eyes," she said. "Those are the empty spaces." She held up her original piece and poked the air with her slender fingers. "His eyes."

Father got up from his chair to put some Christmas carols on the record player. "I think the name's strange," he said with a mischievous glance in my mother's direction. "Making God's Eyes. How about God's Legs or God's Hair or God's Lungs or God's Toes ..."

Christine and I started giggling. I thought of what God's legs might look like. I tried to imagine them with hair like my father's, dense as mesh.

"You're not making the empty spaces," he continued.

"Joe, you're so silly. Don't encourage him, girls," said my mother, and she tilted her head back to chastise him. "We are making the empty spaces. That's what the threads are for. You can't create the space without the yarn. But the yarn's not the creation. The creation is something unseen. God's Eyes. It's a perfect name." Her explanation was so sincere in her belief that she reminded me of Sister Aline.

"How come I've never heard of them before?" asked Christine, who had inherited Mother and Father's love of working with their hands. She was almost finished her first piece, albeit a bit clumsily, while I was still trying to get the rhythm of the turning.

"They're Mexican, I think the neighbour told me. They just hadn't been imported here yet." She said the last part with authority, directing a smirk at my father, who shrugged his shoulders and poured her a glass of eggnog from the jug.

The word "imported," brought from another land to ours, made me remember how Sister Aline had told us the Apostles travelled from land to land bringing their new customs with them, converting people to their beliefs. I envisioned thousands upon thousands of Mexicans in the heat on the equator, which Sister Marguerite had pointed to on her map in Geography class, running in the sands on the beach collecting branches and twigs in little baskets, picking up their sewing thread, and weaving their way into heaven. Conversion, Sister Aline had taught us, came when one spoke the Word of God. Becoming a witness, as in court. You had to speak for it to count, in front of everyone. The way we needed to speak at Confession or Confirmation to the priest. Yet performing an act of conversion instead of speaking thrilled me. Speaking with one's hands, as these faraway Mexicans might be doing, was better than studying catechism and reciting prayers, memorizing the words and writing them out ten or twenty times in lined notebooks, the nuns upset with any error. Conversion was a word I could use to make sense of what I had seen between Mr. M. and Esperanza in her room beside the furnace. Conversion by speaking through one's hands. But then, as my mother held up Christine's newly finished God's Eye, the empty spaces filled me with dread. Why were God's Eyes empty? Why did we need to frame them in order to see their emptiness? Earlier I had worried God was watching us twenty-four hours a day, but now I thought it must be the other way around. We were looking for Him. And He, instead of clearly showing us the way to follow Him, was showing us holes.

My mother continued to curl the yarn around the wood, sliding her glasses down her nose and then back up again to shield her eyes from the harsh sunlight, her motions monotonous. Christine was well equipped to follow suit. Being with my mother was what I'd wanted, and I didn't care for God or anyone else to share in what we as a family were enjoying together. My mother hummed, and I was determined to believe her song was for me and for me alone. She had lost her hair; she took pills and wore her glasses as she was told; she did everything as she was told, and she wasn't getting any better. At least she was spared the pain in her hands that day, weaving with serenity. I was slower with my craft, and I aimed to fill in the entire surface of my cross with the thread. Determined not to leave a single hair's breadth space open for anyone to see through.

THE MEMORIES OF THAT Christmas you would think should comfort me. My mother in such high spirits, my father's extreme tenderness towards her and her every need, his own laughter back and double in force. The whole family under the same roof during the holidays, making crafts and singing carols, eating and drinking seasonal treats, playing in the snow, staying up late, and the lights, the decorations, the smells designed intentionally to enchant the senses—pine, cinnamon, peppermint, chocolate, nutmeg. We played games and went sliding down the hill in the park in our snowsuits, pushing our bodies into the coldness. Throwing up the snow or packing it into our palms. Waving our arms and legs, making snow angels. Snow Angelas, my mother said when we returned, and I laughed at the thought of my own imprint in the snow, a snow fossil of me.

As one who believes in ghosts, it isn't surprising that I also believe in magic. Yet whose magic transformed those few weeks for us into normalcy and comfort, I do not know. Maybe my father did, with his wishes and his dreams, his love for my mother and for us. He bathed the house in light and warmth, keeping the fireplace burning day and night, the flames like pillars. He kept us busy making cookies, getting our hands sticky and sweet in the dough and chocolate chips, icing and sprinkles; or going outside to throw snowballs, stroll up and down the street peeking in at the holiday decorations in other people's homes, or walk down to the mini-mall to buy little gifts for each other. Maybe it was my mother or us kids, unwilling to give up on the holidays, bent on creating a foundation of happiness stronger than the frame of the weather-beaten bungalow on Ashbrook Crescent. My mother capable of moving from one room to the other with little fuss, up in the mornings bright and early, her wig washed and brushed, her clothes ironed. She may have watched television when she got tired, or asked us to read the newspaper to her when her eyes were sore, but she was with us, alive and full of conversation, her world re-energized. Maybe it was simply an act of faith, unnerving, unspectacular, but miraculous all the same. It almost had a sound to it—the sound of a quiet, humble joy. Not the noisy joy from Christmas trumpets or carollers, but the sound of paper crackling in a hearth or a child sleeping in a manger of hay.

Still, for those of us who love magic, but lack the skill to perform it, underneath all such joy lingers frustration. Magic comes in small doses. Someone else holds on to its secret, so you can never force it to materialize at will. And Christ was the master magician of them all. Coming back in the flesh. Not in a memory, or in a vision, but in the flesh. Come to earth, where his adopted family lived. He was not content with His spirit alone. He wanted a body. As I desperately wanted my mother to have another body, to be rewarded for her belief in God by Him transforming the sickness inside her into health. I knew the day I left, back on the bus to St. X. School for Girls downtown, that my mother's body was very weak. She could barely put her arms around me to hug me goodbye for another term. She removed her glasses. Her eyes were unable to focus. She said she hadn't slept the night before, because she wanted to remember this holiday forever. There was some part of her that was already floating away. But I loved her then more than I believe I've ever loved her. For a moment, I even loved her God for making her so beautiful, while I also cursed Him for making her so sick. I held her tightly. I caressed her fake hair and kissed her cheeks, and I was full of hope for the possibility of a cure, for a new life she could almost make me believe existed. "I'll see you soon, Angela," she promised. "And when I see you again, I will be better. I don't think I'll be allowed to suffer much longer. Have faith." Regardless of the evidence before me, telling me it wouldn't be, I did have faith in her words, until I reached the iron gates of St. X. School for Girls and realized my mother could no longer do anything for me. But for a single moment, daughter in her mother's arms, I knew faith. And I tell you, I can barely contain the memory of the happiness I felt on that Christmas as I have contained the guilt of my youth, hoarding it for all this time from others. The happiness is harder to forgive myself. Without her, the happiness has lost its meaning. Suffering ends; Christ on the cross rises again. But tell me, how do we forgive ourselves, O Lord, for the times we've been happy?

~ WINTER ~

white birds are rare, except for doves
and those who have lived out the winter
hanging against the sky like crosses

—PAUL-MARIE LAPOINTE, "Poem for Winter"

WHEN THE GIRLS RETURNED for the winter term at St. X. School for Girls, the festivity continued. Mr. M. organized an elaborate party for Rachel's fifteenth birthday. The party was held on her actual birthday, a school day, so every girl in the school could attend. The nuns were more than happy to oblige, and all the girls in the school, whether friendly with Rachel or not, were excited and made a point of mentioning the party to her, asking numerous questions about what activities were planned and what they were going to eat. The younger girls were particularly thrilled to be invited to a party with the older girls. "I asked for an ice cream cake," was all Rachel could say. "The rest is supposed to be a surprise."

Classes ended early so we would still keep curfew and have lights out at a decent hour. Mr. M. managed to enlist the cafeteria staff and Esperanza to help out with decorations. When we entered the cafeteria, it was as if we had been transported to another world. Blue and green streamers hung from the ceiling the entire length of the hall, twisted into spirals and merged at the centre of the room, where yellow, green, pink, and purple balloons formed a cluster like enormous multicoloured grapes. Yellow bristol board cutouts of stars were attached to the walls, high and low, in no apparent pattern, creating the picture of a night sky. The lights were dimmed. An area to the left of the cafeteria was cleared of tables and chairs to provide a space for games. There were presents with shiny wrapping and bows on the table beside it, which weren't for Rachel as we first supposed, but were for the winners of each of the games.

Mr. M. stood at the door, waving and calling to the girls as they approached the cafeteria. He was boisterous and energetic in his delight, laughing and teasing the girls as they arrived with presents for Rachel in their arms. He wore a three-piece blue suit, but tonight the formal dress didn't belong to the same world as his banking. Here in the makeshift party of our dreams, he was like the ringmaster of a circus, elegant and in control. The smell of his familiar musk cologne permeated the air around him.

Even the nuns were impressed. I noticed Sister Aline staring at the stars in the dimmed light with a reverence generally reserved for Bella. Sister Marguerite was gathering the girls together into groups, handing out the name tags Mr. M. said his wife had made for the party. He had requested a list of all the girls in the school, and the tags were cut out of yellow cardboard into stars to match the decorations, the names printed in blue ink. Safety pins were used to pin them on our chests. Mother Superior, walking around the perimeter and between the tables, inspected the table settings: the paper plates and napkins with "Happy Birthday" on them and a smiley-faced clown, the matching paper cups, the party favours—little whistles and horns, long paper tongues that rolled out and made bleating noises—and the pretty pink and yellow carnations that were centre-pieces on each table. Every detail was ordered, perfected. Between Mr. M.'s vision and the nuns' work, what I would have believed impossible had been accomplished. An aura of joy and wonder sur-rounded us.

"You're going to spoil them, Mr. M.," Mother Superior remarked after taking it all in. "I'm not sure we should have agreed to all this."

"Oh, Reverend Mother, it's only once in a girl's life she turns fifteen." Mr. M. could have mentioned he'd paid for the party, but he didn't. "You all did a wonderful job here," he said instead.

"I suppose," she replied distantly, as if remembering some-thing, maybe making concessions for the fact she had been fifteen once with dreams of her own. The deep furrow across her brow relaxed, and she picked up one of the decorative cups, admiring it. "It is amazing all the things you can buy nowadays, isn't it?"

She then turned her attentions to the staff, who were working on our dinner: fried chicken legs and potato salad with vegetables, and white bread rolls with butter. Plastic cutlery was being laid out on the tables as we waited for everyone. The aroma of chicken wafted around me, seeping down through the vents circulating air from the kitchen in the back, the fans chortling.

Rachel wore a bright orange dress of tightly knit wool and black shoes with a slight heel. She showed off to Caroline and me how well she could walk in them, although she teetered every five steps or so. Her father even allowed her to wear a light-orange lipstick, but not so much as to offend the tastes of the nuns. A thin leather belt encircled her waist, and the cuffs of her sleeves were a darker brownish-orange. Her hair was in a ponytail held up with a black barrette. Two blonde curls wove around her ears. On Francine, the orange would have made her freckles all the more visible and startling, but on Rachel, the dress brought out the sunny shade of her hair, the wildness of her green eyes, and the whiteness of her skin. Caroline and I could only admit that she was as beautiful as the decorations.

"You look like a movie star," Caroline teased.

"The good girl or the bad girl?" Rachel inquired.

"I guess we'll find out soon enough. Did you invite any of your boyfriends here tonight?"

Boys, of course, were not invited and Caroline knew this. Other girls were crowding around us now, fawning over Rachel's dress and shoes, giddy with excitement. We all began to talk quickly about how much we liked the decorations and how wonderful the food smelled. Most of the girls, like me, wore dresses to the party, but a few day girls did not have clothes at school besides their uniforms and wore them in default. Their outfits hampered the fantasy of being away from the school, but didn't destroy it. Francine, in a pastel pink dress, was the last of The Sisterhood to arrive. Her mother had sent some homemade chocolate chip cookies, which Francine had kept hidden in her room. She held the tray out in front of her like a badge of honour as we walked over to greet her. Rachel was thrilled.

"Let the games begin!" announced Mr. M. to the hall. A couple of the nuns turned, unaccustomed to hearing a strong male voice that wasn't a priest's. He instructed all the girls to group together according to their grades. Those not involved in a game could sit and chat, snack on cookies, or help themselves to some orange punch from a large bowl on a table at the entrance of the cafeteria, slices of fresh lemon and orange peels floating on the orange-red water.

We played pin-the-tail-on-the-donkey and plastic horseshoes, and the top three winners of each game were presented with clip-on earrings or a fake moonstone or a bag of jellybeans and lollipops.

"It's absurd!" Rachel said to me as we drank punch, waiting our turn to play. "You'd think I was turning five, not fifteen!" But the truth of the matter was we loved it. Rachel loved it too. There was a glorious freedom in playing the games of childhood we knew we'd probably never play again. And Mr. M. supplied us with the pleasures of both worlds. The presents weren't toys or plastic bubble pipes, but things young women did enjoy. Rachel spun around with the blindfold on her head and laughed so hard she could barely stand, her father trying to steady her in the direction of the donkey. We ate cookies and stuffed our faces with candy. Caroline showed us her bright blue tongue after winning a bunch of blue jellybeans in a guess-the-number-in-the-jar game. I won a pink bracelet bobbing for apples, the wet hair on my forehead plastered to my skin from dunking. Mother Superior and Sister Marguerite joined us in a boiled-egg-on-a-spoon race, and when they finished last, unable to manoeuvre properly in their constrictive habits, Mr. M. rallied us to cheer their valiant effort. The few girls who hadn't been wearing the paper hats handed to them at the door, upset at the possibility of messing their hair, were found sporting them before dinner was served. Our bellies ached, our jaws hurt, and we couldn't wait to eat more.

The kitchen staff and the nuns presented the trays of food. Instead of waiting in line, on this night we were being served. We asked the staff to pile the potato salad as high as they could. I ate four drumsticks. Caroline beat us all by eating six. Gluttony had no power to shame us that day. We licked the grease and crumbs off our fingers and asked for more. Francine's fork didn't touch the table until she'd finished eating everything on her plate. Caroline talked with her mouth full, and Rachel disgusted us by pouring punch over her potatoes and eating them. The nuns and Mr. M. ate at a separate table. He told them knock-knock jokes and complimented them on how well they'd done raising all these young ladies of tomorrow. Although by dinner some of the streamers were falling and a couple of the balloons had burst, the darling illusion remained intact.

When the ice cream cake Rachel had requested, three layers high and the length of a small window, was brought out with all of its candles alight, a darker underbelly was revealed.

"Make a wish, Rachel," Mr. M. said.

Rachel closed her eyes and concentrated for what seemed like an unduly long time, then puckered her lips to meet the candles. She left two burning, which Mr. M. and I blew out, already clapping along with the others. Some girls crowded around the table to watch and were slicing the air with their hands to indicate the size of the piece they wanted. The icing was pink and blue, spelling out "Rachel" across the top of the cake. While Mr. M. clapped furiously, Mother Superior approached from behind, tapping him on the shoulder, an apologetic and confused expression on her face.

"Mr. M.," she stated as confidentially as she could amidst all the people. "Your wife has arrived."

"My wife?"

Rachel looked up from her cake, knife in hand, about to take the first cut. Her father had his brand-new camera poised to capture the event. He handed the camera to Sister Aline, who had no idea how to use it and so asked Esperanza to take the picture. She managed to press the button as Rachel's eyes shut. The flash lit up the table while Esperanza glanced over in Mr. M.'s direction. She appeared uncomfortable, unsure of where she now belonged in the party. And Mr. M. didn't offer any indication of how he was going to handle the situation. Esperanza kept taking pictures, Rachel holding up her knife in a mock gesture of action. Mr M. adjusted the knot of his red-and-white striped tie, a gesture he performed while in thought or when taken off guard. He smoothed his other hand over his hair and began to follow Mother Superior. For once, she was leading him.

"I just don't have enough money for her cab," Mother Superior apologized. "As you know, we do our banking on Mondays."

"That's fine. Fine," Mr. M. replied, although his voice betrayed a touch of anger, directed towards the stairs he was about to climb to reach the entrance lobby of the school, the cafeteria being on the ground floor.

Esperanza took another couple of pictures as Rachel cut the cake and handed slices to Sister Aline, who accepted them on paper plates. Rachel seemed grateful the party wasn't halted and she directed Esperanza on how to adjust the focus for a broader picture of the room. I, however, felt anxious. I wanted Mr. M. to be the leader of the party at all times. And only the girls ought to have been there. Not Esperanza. I hoped that once Mr. M. returned, Sister Aline would ask her to leave. Notwithstanding, I helped Esperanza by distributing the plates, starting at the back of the cafeteria, then making my way to the front. Francine also helped, her body shaking from sugar intake.

"I didn't know Mrs. M. was going to be here," she said. "I haven't seen her in two years." Her words came faster than usual, her tongue sliding in and out of her mouth, trying to catch a smear of purple sugar on her lower lip.

"No?" I placed a few slices of cake on the table for the youngest girls in the school, who instantly started to devour the ice cream before it melted. Allowed to serve the food, like a waitress in a dessert shop, I suddenly felt a smug equality with Esperanza. If she could take the pictures, then I could pass out cake; Mr. M. would be pleased with both of us. Maybe I could even impress Mrs. M. by how well I performed on her daughter's behalf. I was sure Mrs. M. had never met Esperanza, and might dismiss her once she discovered she was hired help and not one of her daughter's friends.

"Well, we don't live on the same street any more."

"I've never met her," I said. Francine knew this, of course, but I felt I should say it anyway. I didn't know what else to say.

"Rachel won't like this," Francine added, turning with me to go back to the head table to retrieve more cake from Sister Aline. The nun was at ease in her motherly role, gasping merrily at the size of the slices, gazing at the top of Rachel's blonde head with pride, while the cafeteria staff stood back politely waiting for instructions. They made an effort to speak mostly in English, in short and blunt phrases they had memorized, but periodically slipped into Chinese when the new words escaped them. The two women behind me were repeating "ice cream cake" to commit the item to memory. Another one was shrugging. "Mrs. M.?" she asked, scanning the room as if the woman would materialize out of thin air.

Mr. M. returned fifteen minutes later with his wife. Most of the girls took little notice, content with their feasting, wearing party hats and blowing occasionally on a whistle or party favour, then bursting into laughter, cake dripping from their mouths. Several of the nuns rose from their table to welcome Mrs. M., who held onto the crook of Mother Superior's arm, not her husband's. Mrs. M. wore a white blouse with a ruffled collar and a tartan skirt of green, blue, and yellow down to her ankles. She shuffled, her left foot dragging behind her, and her free arm moved jaggedly, up and down. Her mouth was crunched into a bow, and a pink lipstick puffed out her lips, a slightly darker pencil stencilled around them. She was not a large woman, but held herself as if she were, dragging her body over to a seat near Rachel. Her big eyes were framed with blue eye shadow and her skin, although sagging around her neck, was tight on her cheeks and around her eyelids. Her hair was brown, which suggested to me for the first time that with age Rachel might lose the stunning blonde curls of her youth. It also struck me that Mrs. M. was holding in her breath, her posture rehearsed, as if it took all her concentration to walk.

Rachel did no more to acknowledge her mother than hand her a piece of cake, which was refused, Mrs. M.'s hand held against her mouth to indicate she did not want any, a girlish smile breaking through underneath. She marvelled at the balloons and streamers as Sister Marguerite brought her a cup of coffee with milk. She pointed to the colours surrounding her with glee.

When Mrs. M. finally spoke, she slurred. "My daughter's having quite the day," she said to no one in particular. The nuns agreed, told her a bit about the games that had been played and the girls who had won the prizes. I presented my pink bracelet to Mrs. M., waving my arm like an exotic fan. Mrs. M. smiled admiringly at the token and proceeded to list off the names of the girls, pronouncing each slowly as her eyes flashed around the room.

"Drink your coffee, Louise," Mr. M. told his wife flatly from where he stood behind her.

Caroline and I were excited to sit with the adults, eating our cake and trying to please Mrs. M. for the simple reason that she was Rachel's mother and we had never met her before. Francine, now also at the table, took a certain pride in the fact that she had. Mrs. M. looked like she had two different hairstyles, one on top brushed flat and another frizzy underneath. I wondered if she was wearing a wig, like my mother did. She appeared ill by the way her face was drawn, the manner in which she walked and spoke, and it occurred to me then that Rachel's mother might be suffering like mine. Tenderness welled up in me for her, and I wanted to share it with Rachel to show her I understood. But Rachel kept her elbows around her plate, her back arched in the opposite direction of her mother. She sucked in the sides of her cheeks each time her mother spoke.

"What did you get?" Mrs. M. asked her, holding her plastic cup to her lips. "Ouch!" she exclaimed, glaring at her husband.

"The coffee's lukewarm, Louise," he said loudly when one of the Chinese women heard and ran quickly over to check if she had hurt herself. Mr. M. waved her off, asking her to make more tea for the table. "Don't you dare ruin this for your daughter," he said quietly but not out of my earshot as he bent down and placed his palms squarely on his wife's shoulders.

"I haven't opened anything yet," Rachel said, indicating the table piled with gift boxes and bags. "Can't you see?"

Mrs. M. clapped her hands. "Gordon," she roared. "The girl hasn't opened any presents yet? It's her birthday!"

"It's a party," he replied. "We open the gifts after everyone has finished the cake." He pointed to my dessert, which I had barely touched. I smiled sheepishly and scooped another spoonful into my mouth. I too wanted to see Rachel open her presents. But Mrs. M. didn't seem to care about my unfinished cake.

"Says who?" Mrs. M. retorted, attempting to brush her hand across Rachel's hair, who in turn offered her a repellent curl of her lip.

"I say so, Mother," Rachel replied. "This is the way we do things here."

Mother Superior raised her finger. This gesture generally meant a warning of some sort. If a girl had overstepped her place, the risen finger would indicate it was time to retreat before she caused any real damage requiring punishment. Rachel wiped her mouth with a napkin and rose abruptly from the table.

"Where are you going, dear? I just got here," Mrs. M. pleaded, straightening the rose pin on her collar and flattening out her skirt with jittery hands.

"The washroom. And I don't need you to come with me."

Rachel left, and Caroline followed, bowing down politely in front of Mrs. M. before excusing herself. "It's nice to meet you," she said.

"Likewise," returned Mrs. M., apparently pleased with Caroline's manners. She tried to swivel out of Mr. M.'s grip. "See how kind the girls are to me," she said to him. "You see, they like me."

"Oh yes," he agreed, still holding her shoulders and rubbing them absently. "They are good girls." He winked at me as he said this and I returned his gesture with a smile, happy he had singled me out. I also realized Esperanza had disappeared, and I was glad.

Meeting Mrs. M. was like meeting a rumour. Rachel did not speak of her often, but when she did, she did not speak kindly. She ridiculed her for never leaving the house and for the number of useless afghans she crocheted. "Your wife could open her own store," Mother Superior said once when Mr. M. brought in an armful, a white one selected for my room. "Then I'd have two jobs, Mother," Mr. M. replied. On one occasion, Rachel went so far as to claim she had no mother; she never got to see her and she didn't speak to her, so how could Mrs. M. possibly be a mother? "She's just a ghost," she joked, "crocheting afghans in a rocking chair." She made a good

point. There were times when I felt it would be easier to say I had
no mother instead of explaining she was ill with a disease the
doctors hadn't yet been able to identify. I often feared people
thought my mother might simply have abandoned me. It wasn't an
outrageous leap; I had begun to wonder myself whether Mrs. M.
actually lived with Mr. M. And unlike Mrs. M., my mother had not
revealed herself in the flesh at St. X. School for Girls to put speculation to rest.

Although I was finished my cake and my belly ached from the
amount of food I had already eaten, out of politeness I did not wish
to leave my place at the table to walk off some of the discomfort and
use the washroom. I crossed my legs and waited anxiously to learn
more about Mrs. M. The nuns watched her with anticipation too,
as they might watch a pot heating to boil. She was offered a plate of
chicken and potato salad and nibbled at it, laying down her fork
each time she took a bite in order to sip her coffee.

"More, please," she asked Sister Aline, holding up her plate
with only half the potato salad gone and none of the chicken, the
skin stripped and shoved to the side. Had one of the girls asked for
a second helping before finishing what they had already taken, this
request would certainly have been refused. However, Sister Aline
walked into the kitchen where the leftovers were being wrapped and
piled up Mrs. M.'s plate accordingly.

The girls were getting restless now that the dinner portion of
the evening was over. They wanted Rachel to open her presents.
Many of the girls were hanging around the designated table, picking up boxes and shaking them, weighing them in their hands,

pointing out the presents they had brought, whispering the contents into each other's ears. A girl in one of the younger grades who I'd once seen counting out pennies to get a bag of chips from a vending machine hadn't brought a present, and rushed upstairs to her room to find something of her own to give. She came back with a book wrapped in newspaper.

Mr. M. removed the knot from his tie and was about to sit back down when Rachel and Caroline returned. Caroline stood behind Rachel while Rachel whispered something to her father.

"I'll do my best," was Mr. M.'s response, but he didn't exude confidence in his general way. He looked exhausted. He rolled up his tie into a ball and placed it in his suit jacket pocket.

"Are you feeling better?" he asked his wife, looking at his watch before placing his hands on her shoulders again. She turned and gazed up at her husband's face with bewilderment.

"Of course I'm fine. What are you implying?"

He removed his hands from her shoulders as Rachel joined the girls at the presents table. She practically ran, while Mrs. M.'s attention remained on her husband and the group at our table, including me and Francine, Sister Aline and Mother Superior. Mrs. M. wiped her nose with a handkerchief she pulled from the pocket of her purse. Caroline and I exchanged glances, unsure of whether we should stay until Mrs. M. finished eating or whether we should join Rachel, who hadn't waited for her mother. In fact, her mother hadn't touched any of the food Sister Aline had brought back from the kitchen, and I was beginning to suspect she really was ill and couldn't keep the food down.

"Do you think I don't know what's going on? What's been going on?" Mrs. M. said.

She was beginning to raise her voice now, and though I desired to leave the table because my bladder was almost bursting, I did not. Francine's kneecaps bumped nervously against the table underneath, creating a steady rhythm. She stared straight ahead, ignoring what was going on around her.

"Calm down, Louise. Don't ruin this for your daughter," Mr. M. told his wife, wagging his finger accusingly, then resuming his stance, smiling broadly but with difficulty. "She'll be fine," he told Mother Superior, who didn't budge.

"Do you think I can't hear you? That I don't know?"

Mrs. M. tried to rise, but Mr. M.'s hands bore down upon her shoulders, pushing her back into her seat. I did not know if she was alluding to what had gone on with Mr. M. and Esperanza, but I was relieved that at least Esperanza wasn't present. I tried not to look at Mr. M.'s rugged face, or his hair, or his hands now upon his wife, harsh and demanding in a way I'd never seen him touch a woman before. Not since being alone with him in my room, had I been afraid of him; I suspected he was in the wrong.

Mrs. M. hit her plate on the edge of the table with her arm and pieces of chicken and potato salad fell onto the floor. Bella walked by, on her way to get some punch, and with a swift gesture returned the plate to its position and bent down to pick up the food with a napkin.

Mrs. M. turned to touch Bella in thanks, but Mr. M. stood between them, creating a barrier with his broad-shouldered body. Bella stood demurely, the dirty napkin in her hands.

"Would you like me to get you anything?" Bella asked, acting as if she hadn't noticed the anger between them. And it worked. Mr. M. was caught off guard by her good-natured grace. He let Bella approach his wife.

"No ... no ... thank you. I'm fine," Mrs. M. replied.

Then Mr. M. laid his hand gently on Bella's back and told her it would be helpful if she went to join the other girls with the presents. Bella immediately obeyed and left the table. I was amazed by how Bella knew exactly the best way to behave, but it didn't surprise me. I inwardly chastised myself for being so slow and clumsy around the adults. I wished I could gain approval as easily as Bella could. "You too," Mr. M. added to Francine and me. We took a couple of seconds to gather our cups and plates for the garbage. We had barely straightened up from our chairs when Mrs. M. began pleading.

"Don't leave me!" she screeched, banging her hands in front of her, spilling her coffee on her tartan skirt.

Mrs. M. was crying, and the girls and the nuns alike could not help but stare. My mother cried often, but it was when the pills weren't strong enough and her skin burned. She cried in small doses, the tears weaving slowly down her face, and her moans were private. She did not cry in front of strangers if she could help it, although once at a doctor's office I did see her leave with a fistful of tissue. Mrs. M., however, was crying loudly and her tears gushed down her face, smearing her rouge and black mascara. Her face went red, and her chin, with a tiny extra layer of flesh underneath the cleft, pulsed with each sob. She clutched her handkerchief in her right hand, slamming her arms down into her lap, repeatedly stabbing at the coffee stain. Mr. M. said nothing, the way a parent might whose patience has been tried and who will simply wait for a tantrum to end. Mother Superior, her large frame now bent over Mrs. M. like an awning, tried to quiet her.

"Think of the children, Louise. Sister Marguerite will take you to lie down so you can collect your strength."

But Mrs. M. ignored Mother Superior and lashed out at the decorations on the table. She batted her hands at the stars on the walls as if they were determined to harm her.

Rachel pretended not to notice. She was the only one still interested in the presents, and she stroked a large red ribbon in her hands as if it were a cat, keeping her back to us, watching out the window as the sun set on a new blanket of snow outside. She produced the camera Esperanza had been using before and took a picture of the window, the flash reflecting off the glass back into the room.

It took three nuns and Mr. M. to drag Mrs. M. upstairs to the nurse's cot, where she would sleep for the next two hours. Although she did not strike out at any of the nuns, she tried to hold her ground, pleading with them to let her stay. She said she would be a good girl; they wouldn't need to worry about her at all. The smeared makeup on her face almost made it seem as if she had just been playing dress-up and had gone too far, that now she would keep quiet and wouldn't need to be punished. Mr. M. grabbed her by the waist and tried to direct her out with as much decorum as possible, but I could see his nails grinding into the flesh on her sides, his knuckles white with pressure.

"You see?" she screamed, turning her head violently in all directions to keep the attention that was hers. "You see? He's turned my own daughter against me."

"Please excuse my wife," Mr. M. said between kicking as discreetly as he could against the back of her shoes. "She isn't herself today." His smile was stretched so tightly across his face it might have had a wire in it.

"This isn't his party. It's my party!" she cried and stomped on his shoes. Mr. M. grunted and clamped his arm securely around her waist.

"Louise!"

"It's my father's money that pays for all these things. So it's my party! My balloons! My streamers! My cake! Mine!"

Mother Superior motioned to two of the nuns to come over. They looked like ravens picking up a piece of meat. They made a wall behind Mrs. M. as she tried to retrace the steps the nuns forced her to take, pushing her body weight against theirs. She nearly managed to overpower them.

"You should love *me!*" she howled, turning back towards the girls, poking her head out of the elbows and hands pushing her forward. "Me! Not him! Me!"

The last thing Mrs. M. did before leaving the cafeteria was to claim two party favours from the table closest to the door. "Mine!" she yelled again, the yellow tongues rolling out limp between her fingers. Another flash went off. Rachel's face was pressed up against the glass of the window. I thought I glimpsed Esperanza outside. I secretly hoped she was leaving the school for good.

Rachel finally opened her presents. A few minutes after Mr. M. and the nuns' return, the oppressive air lifted and the festivity resumed. Most of the girls forgot about Mrs. M. lying upstairs, forced out of the birthday party she had supplied. Attentions strayed back to bows and wrapping and the joy of opening presents: books and clothes, jewellery and paint sets, ornaments and treats. Rachel thanked each person, especially her father, who had bought her, through her mother's money, a new winter jacket and bright purple leather gloves, which she handed to me to caress. Besides Rachel's hair, they were the smoothest things I had ever felt on my hands. Rachel was like a princess holding court, her father, the king, presiding over all. The nuns, if they felt it at all extravagant, did not display their feelings. They watched over the proceedings with rare contentment. Sister Aline kept a list of each gift bearer, instructing Rachel to write thank-you notes to the girls and their parents. Mr. M. collected all the gifts in a large garbage bag to be taken upstairs to Rachel's room.

The outside courtyard lights now on, we ran back to our rooms to don our warmest jackets, wrap scarves around faces, and secure mittens on hands. We tumbled out the doors to enjoy the fresh snow of the new year. Girls in the grade just under ours built a lopsided fort in the corner of the lot, while Caroline and I rolled a snowball back and forth until we could no longer budge it, Francine and Rachel then joining our mission to make it as large as possible. Mr. M. made snow angels with the girls, a few of them dumping snow into his collar. He got up, laughing and brushing himself off, then caught them in his arms in the twilight. A couple of the nuns perched on the grey stone steps leading up to the school entrance, chatting and drinking coffee, the steam from their cups rising into the air and evaporating like our frosty breath.

Only when Mr. M. left us to give a taxi driver specific instructions and carry Mrs. M., groggy and disoriented, to the car, did I remember to remember her. Mrs. M.'s anger had calmed into a childlike uncertainty, and her flesh was limp in Mr. M.'s strong arms. She did look sick.

Bella had not joined us outside. "I've got studying to do. And I don't like getting wet anyway," she said to me when I asked her. But when the cab arrived, she ran out, her jacket unzipped. She held Mrs. M.'s handkerchief.

"You dropped this earlier," Bella said, and when Mrs. M.'s hand reached out the window to retrieve it, she held onto Bella's affectionately while we watched.

"Did you enjoy your party, dear?" Mrs. M. asked her, the blue-shadowed eyes foggy and dazed.

"Yes, I did. Thank you," replied Bella before retreating inside, not in the slightest embarrassed at being mistaken for Rachel by Rachel's own mother.

Rachel kept aloof in the background, patting dense snow between her new smooth purple gloves. She said she was aiming at the street light when she hit the side window of her mother's cab.

CHRISTINE IS COMING TO visit. "It's time I came and stayed with you," she said the day after Christmas over the phone. She knew I'd be busy making candles for Midnight Mass and then busy with my silent worship of the birth of Christ on the blessed day, so she had waited to call. My hands were still raw from moulding the wax and I wanted to get off the phone. I wasn't interested in hearing about the presents she and her husband had bought for their children or how tall their tree was this year. But she didn't mention it. She was the one who ended our conversation by announcing she'd like to come to Ottawa in a few weeks for a visit, but just for a night or two. My past is coming to get me, I thought with exasperation. She is my sister and I do love her, but I don't need more people around me. I'd even made a promise to myself about Kim: not to care too much for her, to concentrate solely on the health of her baby. As the Sisters made candles in the cafeteria space, converting the extra tables into workbenches and bubbling the wax in metal pots on the stove, then pouring it into moulds, I did my best to keep Kim at a distance, to instruct her in the craft and not engage in conversation outside of our duties.

"Is there something wrong?" she asked.

"I'm working," I told her. "We work here, just like any job."

She got the hint and offered to cut the wicks, sitting at the end of the table where the wax was brought out by Sister Katherine to be poured.

When Midnight Mass came and a hundred and fifty or so parishioners entered the church, the entrance was lit with white candles, imitating the night sky. I felt pride in our accomplishment and a sense of purpose in being so hard on Kim. It is essential for her to know we work here. Goods and services. I am employed in goods and services, like any retail industry. Kim was invited to sit at the front of the church with the Sisters but declined, seating herself in the back pew, out of sight. Father B. approved, said it was not right to make a spectacle of her baby on such a holy occasion. She went undetected, most of our parishioners excited by the prospect of gifts and food for the next day, the lonely ones comforted by the crowd. After the long service, I returned quickly to the solace of my room and have not been out much since. But today Christine arrives, and I am pleased to have Kim to present to her. To prove we contribute to the welfare of society.

I know how difficult it is for Christine to come visit me. She doesn't go to church, not on Christmas, nor at Easter. Her husband and his family are also Catholic, but she offers excuses about decorating and entertaining for the holidays, tells his side of the family she received Eucharist the night before. Her husband doesn't care whether or not she goes, and the children are enrolled in public school, attending church only when her in-laws are around. After I took my sacred vows she would only meet me at a restaurant or coffee house, or in a national park. "I don't dare go in there," she said about my convent. Sister or no sister. After a couple of years and many letters from me describing some of the Sisters and our activities in the community, she decided to give it a chance. Her old habits, however, persist. Although she visits at least once a year and converses with the Sisters, she moves through the convent's hallways as if it were a hospital and she feared contamination. She has outright refused to spend the night here before now, claiming the indulgence of hotel room service is too large a temptation to resist when she's away from home.

When she is due to arrive, I ask Kim to accompany me. I think she knows she is being used to some purpose, but cannot imagine what that purpose is. She is dressed up, having showered in the middle of the afternoon and asking Sister Josie to pull her bangs off her face. But she is still weak, barely supporting her skinny frame.

"You look nice," I tell her.

"You're wearing your habit?" she asks, a little taken aback to see me in it when we aren't supposed to be going anywhere outside of our gates. I told her that we'd have tea with Christine in the cafeteria but that I wanted them to meet beforehand.

"She likes to see me in costume," I reply, picking lint off my chest. "It makes her feel superior."

Kim stares at her shoes, shifting uncomfortably. She must suspect the reunion between sisters will not be an ordinary one.

I thought I was prepared, but even Christine has proven to be unpredictable this time. Her hair is dyed a strawberry blonde and pinned up in a twist, and even though she is covered up by a bulky coat, it is clear she has gained more weight since I last saw her in the summer. When she comes closer, I notice her eyes are heavily laden with mascara, which must be waterproof, because her lashes are impeccably defined, while her eyes themselves look bloodshot and irritated. She nearly trips over a piece of loose cement on the stairs, checking her sole to see if she's harmed the heel of her boot.

"God!" she exclaims and then waves her hand in front of her mouth in a sign of apology. "I'm just not used to you in that yet."

I am about to remind Christine that I've been a nun for twenty years, but decide against it. Kim just stands there with her hand extended, until Christine shakes it. She does not register Kim's pregnancy, her eyes stuck on me. She must assume Kim is a Sister she has simply never met.

"Well," Christine says as I take her bag from her and she circles her arm around the tops of my shoulders in an awkward embrace, "it's still good to see you."

Deep in my stomach, I feel a tightness. I sniff her freshly shampooed hair, so much like Kim's, and wrap my arms around her suddenly with the urge not to let go. She squeezes harder in return. I have the desire to run my fingers through her hair but refrain.

"This is Kim," I say finally. "She's going to have a baby soon. Maybe you could give her some advice."

Kim accepts her shame, closing her eyes intently and waiting for Christine to respond. She does not move away from the entrance or make an excuse to leave. She does not lower her face.

"First of all, don't have a baby on an empty stomach,"

Christine replies, patting Kim gently on the shoulder. "Let's get something to eat. Does that Sister Monica still make those wonderful shortbread cookies?"

"We ate them all over Christmas," Kim giggles, tucking her dark hair behind her ears, eager to press on to the cafeteria for the promised tea.

"Oh well," Christine says in my direction. "I'm sure Sister Angela has some hidden treats somewhere, don't you?"

I shift the weight of Christine's bag to my other shoulder and tell them to go on without me, that I'll catch up after storing Christine's luggage in my room. Several other Sisters are already waiting in the cafeteria to welcome her. They heard she's staying the night. Christine and Kim walk briskly away as if old acquaintances. I can even see Kim pointing to the various rooms on the way and telling her which Sister lives where. *Damn you, Christine,* I think, taking the stairs down one at a time.

Later in the evening, we retire to my room. Christine has been kind to Kim, has not made her feel the least uncomfortable for being in her condition. She treated her like any other Sister, and I could tell Kim enjoyed her jokes about the way we fought over toys when we were young, and her anecdotes about travelling overseas with her husband and children. "I didn't know you went to Russia," I interrupted. "I haven't sorted the pictures to send you yet," she replied.

She's sent me many over the years, tucked inside her letters. Aside from the wooden crucifix over my bed and the statue of Mary on the dresser, the only souvenirs I own are her photographs. In anticipation of her visit, I replaced them on my dresser, putting the candle holder away. One was taken on her wedding day. She married at City Hall and the reception was held on an upper floor of a fancy restaurant in downtown Toronto, where Christine and Father both live. In the picture we are facing each other, our eyes meeting and our hands touching, somewhat tentatively for sisters, but lovingly nonetheless. Christine is dressed in a long silk turquoise wrap, exotic against her white skin, and I have my hair curled and am wearing a white corsage on a plain grey dress. Although Christine's dark brown hair is tinted with blonde highlights and her eyebrows are dyed, it is apparent from our father's low cheekbones and our long thin noses that we are family. I placed the photograph prominently at the front of the dresser after deliberately smudging my fingerprints over it to prove I handled it often.

Another is of my parents on their wedding day, my mother with her white veil lifted, sitting prettily beside my father, who is dressed in a tweed suit with a lilac in his lapel; they are both smiling, a little nervousness betrayed by their stiff hand-holding. To the left of that is a photograph of our family before we moved to Ottawa, which Christine found and sent to me two years ago. Christine and I are standing beside our mother and father on our old property with the acres of land and miles of forest to the north. My father's nails, though he is trying to hide them in the photograph, are lined with dirt. My mother holds his hand tenderly and without shame. To the left of this I display a photograph of my father in the Caribbean with Christine and her children; my father has his arm around the oldest boy, proud and content, the blue ocean rushing in behind them.

Christine's boys, Peter and Leonardo, have only met me once, when I attended Leonardo's welcoming party after his birth. Christine asked me to refrain from calling myself Sister Angela in Peter's presence. She said it confused him. She told him I am his Aunt Angela, and when she tried to explain I am known by the name Sister Angela, he couldn't make sense of the relationships. Finally Christine told him people call me Sister Angela because I am her sister. I sometimes wonder if I would have made more of an effort with Christine over the last few years if she had given birth to girls instead of boys. Certainly, Christine and I would still have our problems, but I might have been more inclined to visit her in Toronto if I were going to visit nieces. A girl might have understood. And I might have needed her too. They are my nephews, but do not belong to me in any way. There is still a chance with these boys, I know, but the fact is I do not love them enough to make the effort. Without checking the photograph, I could not tell you the colour of their eyes.

Christine fingers the edge of our parents' wedding photo. It is strange to look at pictures after a person has died, I've always thought. Put a finger up to the photograph of our old property, for example, one single finger, let's say the thumb, and the forest is still as deep and dark and awesome, the trees producing leaves and growing taller, the wind still bending the treetops. But my mother is gone. She is no longer a part of that property. Unless you remove your finger, you could easily be convinced she'd never existed there at all.

"I know this is a hard time for you," Christine says, backing away from the dresser.

"I know you loved Mother," I reply, wondering when she'll leave to change into her nightgown so I can get into mine in private.

"Mother's been dead a long time, Angela. Someone like Kim needs your prayers more than she does." She unzips the top of her bag and I'm surprised to discover she's barely packed any clothes or toiletries. Her luggage is filled with food. She places a large bag of potato chips, two cans of pop, and a package of Swiss-chocolate rolls on the bed and then quickly closes the bag. But not before I notice a package of red licorice, assorted candy bars, and a box of Fig Newtons.

With her coat and blazer off, her body relaxed as she settles herself on the bed, the weight gain is even more noticeable now. Her legs have grown round and stubby, loose flesh hangs at her elbows, and her torso has two separate bulges, from her breasts down to her waist and from her hips to her thighs. I try not to stare but I've never witnessed such a drastic shift in her appearance. The striking new dye job must be intended to divert the eye as much as to cover up intruding grey. She must have put on fifty pounds since the birth of Leonardo. She should get her blood pressure checked. Maybe her family doctor has already mentioned something. I noticed she was out of breath after coming down the stairs.

She has a point about Kim, but I don't want to admit it. Kim is a welcome distraction, but she will be gone soon enough and will probably never think of me again. I figure the teenagers of today are like that, so what is the point of feeling something for her, something so close to love? The other Sisters might think I have regrets about my childlessness, that because I am heading into the barren territory of menopause, my unused eggs spent, I might be prone to delusions. They are already talking about my moodiness, my further withdrawal from them, my obvious anxiety. Christine's visit has enabled them to attribute my behaviour to the simple and common stress of family friction (which many of them also experience over their choice of vocation), but directing so much attention to Kim could be interpreted as excessive. The Sisters might jump to the wrong conclusions. Yet I do wish to be with her, this girl and her bastard child. They need protection. There is mercy for such children now, I know. Unwed mothers are everywhere, people live together outside of marriage, stepmothers and stepfathers abound, yet underneath there is still scorn for young teenage mothers. Girls who make grave mistakes.

"Don't you want to remember Mother?" I ask as Christine opens the bag of chips and flips the tabs off the cans of pop.

"What good does it do to remember? Why remember all the painful stuff? It's what I really can't stand about your religion, you know," she replies, shoving a few chips into her mouth.

"Please don't get crumbs in the bed," I say sheepishly, not wanting to acknowledge her insult, knowing how hard it is for her to sleep in the same room as me, let alone the same bed.

"OK, sure. I'll clean it, don't worry. Angela, I didn't come here to visit Mother, I came here to visit you. And I know it's a big anniversary coming up, but I don't want to be a part of it. And don't phone Dad to remind him either, OK? He's had it hard enough. Here," she says, handing over a cola, and I sip the sugary liquid, enjoying the fizz in my mouth despite myself. "Be bad for once."

I grab the package of Swiss-chocolate rolls, ripping open the plastic in a grand gesture. "Is that better, Christine? Is that what you want to see me do, be bad?" My voice begins to rise, and the little civility we have established in each other's presence vanishes. "You have no right to judge me and my decisions. You have no right to tell me what I can and cannot do."

She takes a bite out of a roll, and then another, devouring the dessert from end to end. The action is routine, although I do not recall her having a sweet tooth when we were younger. It was Mother and me who liked sweets; she and my father loved salt.

"I didn't come here to fight," Christine replies, shaking a few crumbs off her blouse. "I came here ... I came here because I needed to see you. There's a lot you don't know. There are still too many secrets between us."

"You have a secret?" I ask. "I thought you couldn't keep a secret if you tried."

"Is that what you think?" Christine eyes me offensively. Even when we are attempting to be lighthearted, none of our exchanges are very pleasant. She guzzles back some pop and makes a hiccup noise. "You don't trust anyone, do you? Except maybe your God!"

She knows where to hurt me. She thinks I throw Mother in her face, that I think I am as good as Mother because I've followed in the footsteps of the women who took care of her when she was orphaned. She thinks it's my trump card. Maybe it is sometimes, but not always. Tonight it's hers.

"How little you know about me," I counter sadly. "You're right. There are still too many secrets between us."

"Not just between us, Angela. Did you know Dad wasn't a Catholic before he met Mom?" Her eyes glower at me as I adjust the grey wool afghan on the bed, ironing out the creases with my hands.

My manner instantly betrays me. I shake my head in the negative and she fluffs the pillow and replaces it to the small of her back, leaning against the headboard. Then she shifts the waistband on her skirt, which has sagged beneath the bulge of her belly. Her clothes don't fit properly. She has red lines on her skin where the elastic had rested.

"Dad was an Anglican, and not a fervent one either. His family couldn't have cared less what religion Mom was, but Mom told him he would have to convert to Catholicism. He went to her parish and spoke to her priest. He did his catechism, was baptised, all before he even proposed. His parents never understood any of it. They basically concentrated on Aunt Heather after that, especially when Mom and Dad moved to Canada together."

I knew Father had recently retired from his construction work, work he wasn't suited to perform after designing tables and bed frames, chairs and chests in his tool shed, then doing the varnishing and finishing work, his tools carving the wood with a surgeon's precision. But after he moved to Toronto, he was forced into manual labour. He had no money and needed to live and bring up Christine and me. The last time I saw him was at the party for Leonardo. He shook my hand like a business associate, his attention on the baby dressed in a ridiculous sailor suit, a scarf with an anchor on it around his neck. He wasn't exactly cold; he thanked me kindly,

I recall, for bringing him a beer, but he kept his legs crossed in the other direction, uncomfortable whenever he dared look into my eyes. He didn't search me out to say good night when he left.

"He told me she was the most beautiful woman he had ever met. She was gentle and kind and had a way of making him believe in something beyond this world. He wanted to share in her God too."

"And—"

"And he came to hate Him, not her. Him." Christine fiddles with the discarded plastic of the dessert packaging, crunching it and letting it open back into its original shape in her hands. She hates Him too. She doesn't believe in anything except what is directly in front of her, proven by scientific principles. Graphs, statistics, polls. These things assure Christine there is a pattern to the universe.

I want to open up to her, tell her I hate Him too. That I don't understand His ways any more than the next person. That I am only trying to find the same peace Father found with Mother. I want to love Him like she did. But all the studying, the praying, the social work, the community of believers—none of it has revealed His face to me or made Him more human. He is a ghost, invisible; an infamous rumour. I want to tell her He frightens me, with His judgements and His evaluations, with His horrible voicelessness. That I haven't discovered Mother's kind and loving God, but am desperate to prove her right. I want to tell her about St. X. School for Girls, Mr. M., the candle holder, Rachel, all of it. How it is for me. How when I entered the convent at twenty years of age, Mother Superior took me aside, sensing something amiss. How she tried to make me confide in her. Questions about the men in my life.

Whether I had been hurt. Turned down. Jilted. The men in my life. Never the women. No one asked about the women. And then she asked the worst question of all: "Who has come for you?" We were in the orchard, the same orchard I now visit regularly to touch the autumn leaves in their seasonal bleeding and water the still-blooming flowers, trimming vines and stems, collecting the dead matter in my hands, worrying over the buried heads in the winter-time. I looked Mother Superior straight in the eye, without a quiver in my voice or a shake in my limbs, and said, "He has. Him." It was a bold-faced lie. I'd never heard Him speak or felt Him beside me. I didn't even love Him. It was Her, Her. She was the One I prayed for. She was the One I wanted to know. The only One who could bring me redemption. My mother, frozen in the snow.

"Why didn't he ever tell me?"

"Did you ever ask?"

Ask and ye shall receive.

My choices. I want to tell Christine, but I don't. It is too late. None of this can make a difference now. "They say God provides what we need, whether we know what that is or not." I take another sip of the pop.

Christine snorts, removes a Swiss roll from the cardboard tray. "They say a lot of things. Nothing gets done without other people, without money. Does God provide everything for you?"

"I don't know what I want," I reply, startled I would tell her the truth. But she doesn't take the statement seriously, treating it as part of our usual banter.

"I want my house paid for and my children to grow up bright

and protected, for Father to be happy, and never to die. Do you think I'll get it?"

There is no right answer when arguing with Christine. I am reminded of the re-enactment of Confession in catechism lessons. The priest would ask a string of questions for which we would be prepared to provide the answers. The right answers. "Do you love your God?" "Yes." "Do you love your mother and father?" "Yes." "Do you love your sister and brother?" "Yes." "Do you love those who do not deserve love?" "Yes." "Do you love yourself?" There is no right answer to that one. The question is a trick. If you said yes, you would be accused of pride. If you said no, of ingratitude.

"No," I say. "But who wants to live forever, Christine?"

"We all do," she replies, settling back onto the pillow propped against the headboard, putting distance between us, alarmed I should ask such a thing as she licks melted chocolate off her fingertips.

WITH THE NEW YEAR I still possessed a voice as unlike an angel's as before and was placed, once again, in the last row of the choir. I thought I would give it another try for the first few weeks back at school, but Sister Aline reiterated that God would appreciate my silent devotion as much as he would if I could express it. Francine was also stuck in the back row on the opposite side, whereas Rachel and Caroline were in the middle row. Bella returned to her solitary position in front of everyone, one step down, close to the altar. Her voice seemed to have grown even stronger over the break. Sister Aline's could no longer hold a candle to Bella's. "She must have been born singing," Sister Aline proclaimed to us, shaking her head in awe.

After Rachel's birthday party, we spoke more about Bella at Sisterhood meetings than we had the previous term. Instead of pretending she didn't exist, we mocked her—not for anything she did wrong, but simply because we could. We were tired of hearing the teachers praise her constantly. We were tired of comparing our voices to hers during choir. Caroline imitated Bella holding up her hand in class, echoing Sister with her answer to every question in class. Francine laughed at the way she ate her lunch, consuming each portion separately. I poked fun at her thick black eyebrows and predicted they would grow together into one when she got older and she'd have to shave the middle like a man. Rachel boldly claimed she'd be a virgin until her wedding day as the greatest insult. But our ridicule was nothing more than how we spoke of others in the school. It was a routine game. Bella was just added to our list.

The previous weekend, Bella had been a Leftover. Her mother and father were out of town and Bella stayed behind. Her parents wanted her to accompany them on the trip, but Bella insisted her schoolwork was more important. I couldn't believe she'd give up the opportunity for a brief vacation to stay at St. X. School for Girls, but she did. "What an angel!" Rachel cried in ridicule. "More angel than Angela!" It was the only time in Rachel's memory that Bella had stayed for a weekend in the three years Bella had been at the school. But it wasn't the same as for us. She was here out of choice, and for a single weekend. It wasn't enough to make us equals.

Mr. M. took us to a movie and invited Bella to come along. "I haven't been to a movie since summer," she said to the nuns, who had informed Mr. M. of her parents' trip. Mr. M. was happy to include Bella in his daughter's activities. "That's quite a girl. Her mother must be proud," he said to them.

Bella was shy with Caroline, Francine, Rachel, and me, staying close to Mr. M. He told her how much he enjoyed her performance in the pageant as we shuffled our boots across the slushy winter downtown streets to the theatre. "You've been given your gift for a reason," he said. "You don't want to waste it." She nodded with an adultlike understanding, though I wondered if she heard regret in his words, as I did. I had the urge to take Mr. M.'s hand, but he wasn't looking in my direction. He hadn't asked me how I was, or what I had accomplished in class this week, or any of the usual things we would talk about as a group on our way to the movies. His attention was on Bella. There was no physical reason to believe Bella was more womanly than the rest of us, but I sensed she was as she walked side by side with Mr. M. With a few more years added to her face, a passerby, noticing their comfortable gait and speed, their pleasant exchanges, might have thought they were lovers out on a stroll.

Waiting out in front of the theatre while Mr. M. bought our tickets, we shivered and jumped up and down in our coats and boots. Francine kept rubbing her nose in her mittens, and Rachel called her gross. Caroline pointed to a purple evening dress in the window of a store, her hands smudging the glass, while I noticed a woman pushing a metal shopping cart along the sidewalk, full of plastic bags in which there seemed to be clothes and blankets, her hair hidden by a knitted skullcap. We'd seen her before on our way to the theatre. Mr. M. had told us to ignore her. Once, Rachel had offered her some change, but she had refused it. "I do not take money from children. What have you ever done to me?" she'd said. It was difficult to watch her trudge along in the brutally cold winter, open sores on her lips, her few possessions grey with slush, and I turned my face to the window.

The movie was about to begin. Mr. M. and Bella emerged from the theatre with the tickets. They barely interrupted their own conversation to collect us. "You should spend more time with my daughter. You're such a good girl," Mr. M. said, his arm wrapped around Bella's shoulder.

It was unfair, I thought, for Mr. M. to make such a fuss over Bella when she would never need to go out with us again. He had yet to compliment Rachel, and she was wearing a necklace he had given her for her birthday, leaving it on her pillow as a surprise for when she returned from playing in the snow. Rachel tried to hide her frustration by covering up the necklace with her scarf, pretending he hadn't seen it when she put it on. But she had worn it especially for him. She had even asked him to help lift her hair. "Could you get it, Angel?" he had asked me. And so it was I who had lifted her soft blonde curls to reveal her neck, securing the clasp. How Rachel could be obscured by Bella when Bella wasn't singing astounded me. Besides, Bella didn't need Mr. M. Rachel needed him. I needed him. Maybe I could even understand that Esperanza needed him. But Bella certainly didn't need him. We were the ones who needed parents. We were the ones who were practically orphans.

"Let's invite the little bitch to a Sisterhood meeting," Rachel said, joyously swearing under her breath in the church as we took a break, sitting on the stairs, and Sister Aline approached Bella to praise her for her solo of "Lamb of God."

"Why?" I asked. "You don't even like her." Bella accepted her accolades humbly, then addressed a section on the music sheets that she wanted to clarify. Sister Aline spoke to her intimately, holding the crook of her arm and pencilling in a series of notes.

"We could trick her, have some fun," Rachel said flippantly. I don't think she had any idea what she wanted to do. And to be honest, I was intrigued by the idea of humiliating Bella, but I resisted.

"What's the point? She'd only tell on us," I countered.

"No, she wouldn't," Rachel replied. "She'd like to come. She'd just be too embarrassed to admit it."

"Are you sure? She wants to join our group? I mean, she seems happy being by herself." She did. The Sisters and teachers flocked around her like birds to a feeder. It was obvious Bella sought approval from the nuns and teachers more than she did from her peers. Bella had never shown the least interest in any of us unless there was group work to be done in class.

"Nobody likes being alone," Rachel said. "I'll ask Francine and Caroline about it, and we'll discuss it at the next meeting."

Sister Aline clapped her hands for our attention, and we all returned to our positions. I stood at the back, merging myself into the wall. It was stupid for me to be obligated to attend practice, I thought, if I wasn't allowed to sing, even if I was horrible. As I began to mouth the words of the Psalm, Bella's voice rose hauntingly into the air. She pleaded to the stained-glass windows of Mary and Jesus adorning the walls of the church for the mercy the Psalm claimed came with belief.

• • •

I WAKE WITH A pain in my side, forgetting for a moment I've shared my bed. Someone sleeping under the same blankets, a body beside me, the first time in twenty years. Christine's left hand, curled into a fist, pokes into my ribs. She makes mumbling noises as I sneak out of the covers to shower. By the time I return she is also awake, dressed in the same blazer, blouse, and skirt as the night before, spraying perfume in between her breasts and on her wrists.

"I'll shower later," she says, ignoring me as I adjust my wimple. I don't want to wear my habit again, but it would be inconsistent after wearing it the day before. I am now ashamed over how I acted in front of her and the position in which I put Kim.

"Did you sleep well?" I ask Christine.

"No. But it's not your fault."

In my single bed, Christine and I were practically on top of each other. I'd offered to get a cot, but she had refused. "Don't you think we should be forced to lie beside each other for once in our lives?" she asked. "I think you're right," I replied. And we both smiled, because for once we had agreed on something. But what a night beside each other was supposed to accomplish hasn't come to fruition for me. Christine is too large for the small bed, and we slept spooned, my body wrapped by hers, her back right up against the wall. At several points in the night, I almost fell off the side.

"It's cold in your room." I'm used to the cold; the tiles are freezing on bare feet, and the window lets in a draft. It snowed silently in the night, and the fresh white blanket glistens in the morning light, covering half the glass. Christine brushes dark-brown mascara onto her eyelashes over the layer from the day before.

"After tea this morning, I'll say my goodbyes and then let's go eat somewhere."

I know Christine said she'd stay here only for the night, but I thought she might stay at a hotel in the city for at least another day. She checks herself in a portable hand-held mirror she'd given me and which I had placed on the dresser before her arrival. She pinches her cheeks and plucks a few stray hairs from the ends of her eyebrows.

"So soon?"

"Yes. Anthony is working overtime on a case and I really should get back."

"But what about—" I pull the sleeves of my habit down over my wrists, irritated. I had decided to prove something to her this visit, and she's left me no chance. Kim had also begun to open up to her a little. I almost believed Christine might really offer her some advice on pregnancy that we childless women are not able to give. But she will leave Kim to us, just as her own parents have.

"I'm not going this year with you. I'm not going to visit Mother's grave. Anniversary or not." She finishes brushing her hair and twists it up, holding the sides flat with bobby pins. "I hope you understand."

"Yes. I understand." She has only visited the gravesite on a couple of occasions. It is near the hospital where Mother stayed. My father has not been since the funeral. But I go every year on the anniversary of her death. I go without flowers. I kneel beside her stone, brush the snow from the cold rock, and recite prayers I know she would have liked. *I will sing of the Mercies of the Lord forever: Thy*

Faithfulness to all Generations. I recited this one last year; it was on a banner in the church at St. X. School for Girls. Sister Aline would sing that line to us whenever we were lax in our attendance or dedication in choir. She believed we were offering the world mercy through the beauty of song. Music is a holy activity, she told us. Art is one of God's ways of bringing part of heaven down to earth. I know my mother would have agreed.

"OK, Christine. Where do you want to go?"

"Somewhere neither of us has been before."

"I'll have to think. I need to run some errands later."

"We can just wander."

I agree, although I'm not sure I can handle wandering without knowing where we are headed. I can't believe she is leaving so soon, when I haven't had the opportunity to share anything with her in the way she has with me. *Too many secrets between us,* she said. I know I must get rid of this heavy feeling in my side. I pack up the candle holder when Christine leaves to use the washroom.

WHEN KARL Z. THE THIRD asked me outside the gymnasium turned dance hall to show me his father's World War II medal that he kept in the pocket of his dress slacks, I went, not to impress him, but to impress Rachel. She was busy disco dancing with a senior and they were both acting ridiculous, pointing their fingers in the air and gyrating their hips to the music, the boy with a small white carnation in his lapel, she with her red scarf scooting down her neck at every turn. But she was dancing with a senior, and Caroline and Francine had only managed to dance with freshmen or sophomores. Earlier we girls had taken a break to trade notes and giggles about the various boys we had met: who had the best hair, who wore cologne, where hands had roamed, how they had managed to get away or what they had allowed them to do. Francine had let a boy touch the curve of her buttocks and Caroline had let one kiss the nape of her neck. We approached the discontented teacher at the drink stand and asked for sodas. Rachel had a small flask of gin in her purse. She'd taken it from her father's suit jacket. She told us the altar boys Father McC. brought with him for Mass stole the leftover wine from the chalice, so her theft couldn't possibly be as bad. We each had a single sip and forced the liquor down. I didn't feel much, but pretended to be slightly tipsy so I wouldn't have to drink any more. Rachel dumped the rest in the toilet. "I don't know how my mother can stand it," she said as she flushed.

When Karl Z. the Third asked me to dance, I was thrilled but afraid. Disco was too fast for my taste, and I couldn't imagine myself tempting him with my static moves. Caroline had tried to teach me before we headed out to the dance, saying her sister, Aimée, had taught her and it wasn't difficult once you found the rhythm. I told her I couldn't hold a tune. "You don't have to sing," she replied and I knew it was true, but I figured my deficiencies in one area would surely transfer to the next. Caroline plugged in her transistor radio, keeping it on low and adjusting the antenna when the signal faded. The four of us had spent Saturday afternoon in the washroom examining our hips and calves in the mirror, rotating our pelvises and swinging our arms, invisible hula hoops wiggling down our bodies. When a girl came in to use the toilet, Caroline would shut the radio off and we'd turn on the taps, pretending to wash our hands, though it was apparent we were up to something, our laughter giving us away.

"How do you know we'll be able to get in?" Francine asked.

"Aimée told me it's easy. She used to do it all the time," Caroline replied, demonstrating how to bend my knees a little when I swivelled my hips. The previous weekend, a boy in the Market had approached us while we were sitting near a flower stand. He said he recognized us from somewhere. We didn't know if he was lying or not. He said he went to J. High, which wasn't far from the Market, and they were having a dance next Saturday. We were immediately transfixed, imagining what it would be like to go. Caroline called her sister to find out if there was any way we could attend. "We'll just wait outside all together and some boys will ask us if we need tickets," she explained. "They want girls who don't go to their school there. They're bored with the ones they already know. And they'll pay for them too. The tickets, I mean."

"Foreigners," Rachel joked, pushing her developing breasts together in her hands, appreciating the effects of a forced cleavage. "We'll be foreigners for the night. Exotic belly dancers and snake charmers." She lifted her shirt, displaying her midriff, and tried to make her stomach undulate, grunting with frustration. "How do they get their skin so loose?" she said, letting her shirt fall back down.

"Ask Esperanza," I said.

"Do you think she can?" Caroline asked.

"She's Spanish, isn't she?" Francine replied.

"Oh, I don't know," said Rachel. "She was born here. I asked my mother once when she had an old Irish jig on the record player if she could still do any of the moves ..." She gave Francine a silencing look. "She can barely remember the name of her grandmother's village, let alone the dance lessons she took here when she was young."

"Takes practice," continued Caroline, each of us imitating the other in the mirror, bouncing and jumping up and down.

"They might play older music. I don't know. Isn't it supposed to be a semi-formal?" I asked.

"Yeah," said Caroline. "But it's different at mixed schools. They don't bother with all the old stuff—waltzes and foxtrots and boring junk like that. They've got better music, let the kids pick the music, you know. Same as the clubs." She hiked up her skirt so that a line of skin just beneath her buttocks was showing. "There's a whole other world outside of St. X. School for Girls. Here they treat us like nothing has changed at all. Sexual Re-vo-lu-tion never happened or anything."

We had read about it in one of the *Playboy* magazines Rachel had stolen off a stand. An article entitled "Why the Sexual Revolution Was Good for Men and Women," with photographs of women without bras, dancing in the open fields of California rock concerts, and muscular and tanned men running along the beach, playing volleyball. We practically peed our pants flipping through the pages of the magazine, hysterical with curiosity, never a picture without a woman in it, showing off a curve or staging a sexy pose. We imitated those poses for hours afterwards, asking each other "Do I look like her?" "Do I?" "Do I look like a tramp?"

"Did you grow up in a barn or something, Virgin?" Caroline jeered at my lack of knowledge about school dances.

"I guess so," I replied, sensing my face turning red. They all knew my family had moved to Ottawa from the country. My old school had fewer than fifty students in it. "I've never been to a dance before."

"Well, neither have I," admitted Caroline. "Aimée took me to a club once, but she made me stay quiet so no one would ask my age. And I wasn't allowed to dance. She told me I could just watch and tell Maman she had taken me to the movies." She wrapped her arms around my neck and moved close to me, her hips rubbing against my waist. "Aimée dances like this," she said. "She dances shameful, as Maman would call it. One of her boyfriends danced with me like this when she went to the store. He even kissed me, but I could hear Maman coming up the front stairs so I stepped hard on his foot."

Caroline was so close to me I could see a tiny brown mole between her nublike breasts. I was uncomfortable and pulled slowly away. She twirled around the floor, paying little attention to my withdrawal.

"Living in a barn," I told them confidently, "I've seen a few things."

"Oh, have you, Virgin?" taunted Rachel, tuning the radio to reduce the static.

"What did you see?" Francine asked warily.

"Well," I responded, turning Francine around so her back was facing me, feeling slightly dizzy at how I might shock them, "animals do it from behind," and I jerked against Francine's backside, tripping her as she moved forward to regain her balance.

"You're gross!" cried Caroline.

"Not as gross as kissing your sister's boyfriend!" I snapped at her, helping Francine up from the floor and patting her shoulder to show I hadn't meant any harm.

"That's grown-up," Caroline replied, her voice quivering. "He wanted me as much as he wanted Aimée. That's what I know."

"Forget about him," Rachel interrupted. "There are plenty of other guys out there for us to pick from. Five for each of us."

Caroline turned up the radio and we practised for a while longer, then went to pick out our clothes. Rachel lent me a plain yellow dress and a blue scarf with a bit of silver glitter on it. I thought I looked like a pencil crayon, curveless and ordinary. Francine, with her mousy hair, had much more cleavage. I had two nipples that stuck out like purple grapes. I was sure the boys at the dance would know I was younger than them, and not in high school at all. Rachel told me to stop worrying and just think older. I pouted as Rachel applied lipstick to me, aching to kiss another as Rachel and Caroline had. Francine hadn't either, but I didn't want to be the last one. So, in spite of my initial disgust at Caroline's admission, I told myself I was grown-up and had kissed my older sister's boyfriend when she went out shopping. Since the boys at the dance would practically be men, I conjured up the only two girls I'd seen talk to men in a comfortable manner: Esperanza and Bella. But when I imagined imitating Bella, I laughed. She would never go to a dance and let a boy touch her. She would never be a woman in the way Esperanza was a woman. I felt satisfaction at the thought.

"You've got nice hair," Rachel said, brushing it out as I brooded in the mirror. "And pretty eyes too. You'll be fine."

I'd already learned to feel pleased when I received a compliment from another girl. It could make me believe in my own beauty, as men's admiration, even Mr. M.'s comments, never seemed to. I was beginning to sense that a man will always want something from you, whereas when women compliment, it's because they mean it. As Rachel brushed my hair, my heart swelled with love.

My confidence buoyed by Rachel's words, when Karl Z. the Third approached me as I stood against the gymnasium wall, I ran my fingers through my hair, batting my eyelashes to show off the effect of my mascara, bought at Woolworth's, hoping my hazel eyes were framed as the girl who worked there had promised. He walked past me initially, and I was about to forget about him, figuring he was on his way to speak to an older, prettier girl, as a few boys had already done, when he turned on his heel dramatically and held out his hand for me to shake.

"Karl Z.," he said in a low gruff voice followed by a pause. "The Third."

I shook his outstretched hand, unsure of how else to respond. "The Third?" I asked, noticing a silver ring with a red stone on his index finger. He was dressed in black slacks and an aquamarine shirt, one button open at the collar, sleeves rolled up to his elbows. When he smiled, one corner of his lip lifted higher than the other and his opposite eyebrow rose. His blond hair, with streaks of darker brown on the top and sides, hung just past his ears, layered to a straight edge across his neck. In the sporadic lights of the gymnasium, his eyes appeared to switch colour depending on where he stood. They were either blue, or green, or grey; it was difficult to tell.

"The Third," he said again, dropping my hand and inserting

both of his into his pants pockets, his head angled downwards a few inches to my height. "My father and my grandfather were both named Karl. That's a nice dress you're wearing."

I felt an ache when he spoke, a desire to believe him. I had imagined Nathaniel, the white-haired boy at the convenience store, giving me a compliment, but it never happened, and then he'd lost interest. I wondered if it was because I hadn't let him do anything to me. I had never invited him to leave me notes in the school wall. I liked talking, just talking with him and hearing about his homework or the hockey team he played on.

I had no idea what to say to Karl Z. the Third, so I just stared, biting my lip, and tried to act nonchalant and grown-up, the way Rachel was. I could see her watching me with him. She waved, her jaw lowered in an exaggerated gawk for my benefit, urging me on. I told myself again that I had kissed a boy before. That I could be as special as anyone.

"Would you like to dance?"

"No," I said quickly, afraid I wouldn't dance as well as the other girls. Then I regretted saying no. His head turned to scan the dance floor and I thought that maybe he was going to approach someone else.

"It's just a bit hot in here," I said. "I'm taking a break. But I'd like to dance a little later." He had light-brown stubble on his chin, and his face was pleasantly oval, his cheeks pinched. I thought I could smell cologne when he bent down to speak with me, his voice raised over the music. I started to fiddle with the scarf around my neck, and I knew, as it moved across my chest, he was envisioning my body underneath the dress. He lingered. I breathed in deeply, punching out my chest.

"You're right," he said, shaking his shirt from the sweat, and I caught a peek of his white hairless chest, the bones of his rib cage visible. He was skinnier than I'd thought when he first approached me. He was almost all bone. The strands of hair falling behind his ears helped draw the eye away from the gauntness of his cheeks and chin. This observation made him a little less intimidating to me. "It is hot in here. Do you want to go outside? There's something I want to show you."

The music switched to a love song, and I kicked myself for refusing to dance. Slow dancing was far easier and more dangerous, as Caroline would say. But I agreed to go outside with him, after momentarily glancing longingly at the floor full of young men and women holding each other, resting their heads on shoulders, moving in rhythm.

"You never asked me my name," I said as we walked through the couples on the dance floor to get to the exit.

He stopped and offered his hand again for me to shake. I didn't take it this time, nervous about the female teacher roaming around, supervising the dance floor. He shrugged and put his hands back in their pockets. "So, what's your name?"

"Angela," I called into his ear. "Angela!"

"Ever meet a war hero, Angela?"

I was confused. He wasn't even old enough to enlist in the army. Karl Z. the Third strode along with confidence, inspecting the doorway for teachers before shuffling me quickly outside into the winter air.

Under the electric lights of the entranceway, the parking lot before us full of cars and vans and motorcycles, the skin on his face and hands glowed. I wondered if mine did too, hugging myself with my arms to keep the cold from my flesh.

"I should have brought my jacket," I said, annoyed at the weather. I imagined in the spring it might be more romantic to be outside with a boy.

"Nah," he replied. "Don't worry about it. It's just a little wind. It's not even snowing."

He wasn't cold at all, his shirt open and his stance relatively relaxed. He walked towards the snow-covered soccer field, the goal posts void of nets, and I followed, increasingly afraid of being alone with him and even more afraid of getting caught.

"I don't go to school here," I said as he kicked an imaginary soccer ball through the metal bars and raised his arms in success. "This looks like a big field. We just have a corner lot and—" I cut myself off. I might have been giving away that I went to St. X. School for Girls, a junior school.

"I know," he replied. "I mean, I would have noticed you if you did."

I wanted Rachel to come out and save me from what might happen. I wanted her to witness what might happen. I'm not sure what I wanted exactly, but I wanted Rachel to hear this boy who knew I didn't go to his high school because he would have noticed me.

I was getting cold and shivering, but wouldn't permit myself to show it; he wasn't wearing a jacket or blazer and might offer me his arms in default. Then he might feel me tremble and know I wasn't used to a boy's arms. We walked back to the parking lot, towards one of the concrete dividers. He patted the space beside him for me to sit. I did, gently pulling the skirt of my dress underneath me, my legs spread out straight in front, the same posture as he assumed. The concrete was cold but the hardness of the seat made it easier for me to curl my upper body and conserve some warmth.

"Are you the youngest in your family?" he asked.

"No." I said. "I have a sister. She's younger." I pulled up some frozen grass from the cracks in the concrete and started to sort it in my hands, letting the smaller strands fall through my fingers, keeping the longer ones, amazed that anything survived the winters here.

"I am," he said. "I'm the youngest by almost ten years. I wasn't supposed to live."

"Really?" I tried to appear fascinated, as the magazines said a woman should during conversation with a man.

"That's why I'm named Karl. My father says it's the name of a fighter." He curled his hands into fists and struck the air with a few short jabs. "My father was a fighter too. And my grandfather."

He squeezed himself closer to me, the tips of his fingers touching my tailbone. I breathed deeply, letting go of the grass, pulling out a new bunch, watching the entrance to see if a teacher was coming outside to check for students like us, far from supervision. A few boys stood in the doorway, smoking, the grey air rising towards the lights.

"The First and the Second," I replied. "Right?"

"Right," he said. "I wanted to show you this."

He put his hand into his front pocket and for a split second, my eyes wide with astonishment, I thought he was going to pull out his thing for me to look at, the way a boy did when we walked by a basketball court one evening on our way to the Market, safe behind the fence, taunting us with his strange bulge of flesh, his friends laughing. Instead, Karl pulled out a war medal, evidently preserved with polish and care. A purple ribbon was attached to the silver disc, but the night was too dark for me to be able to read the engraving upon it. He plopped the medal into my palm, on top of the grass.

"My dad helped save the Jews from Hitler," he said proudly. "He saved a lot of lives."

"Oh." I didn't know what to do with the medal except stare at it in uncomprehending awe. I recalled my mother mentioning Hitler, saying he appealed to the worst in people. An instrument of the Devil. I remembered those words clearly, for my mother wasn't the type to concentrate on the evils of the world. She preferred to recount the joys, the good works missionaries were performing all over the world, the miraculous displays of human endurance and faith of the saints. She preferred the New Testament over the Old.

"Did he save a lot of people?" I repeated back to him.

"Yeah, he killed a lot of Germans."

"Oh—" I didn't want to think about death or war, or what it must have been like to kill men in a foreign country. The conversation was getting away from me. I didn't want to sit in the night air discussing Hitler.

He started singing in an off-key bravado: "I got some medals from World War II. I wear 'em just like me granddad do."

I offered him back his medal as if holding a mouse by its tail.

"You had to kill the Germans to save the others," he said. "It's a trade-off, you see. Not really for the Jews, but for everybody. The Protestants too." He riddled the air with imaginary bullets.

"What about the Catholics?" I asked. I was getting colder and thought that as soon as he took a break from talking I would go inside. My legs felt numb and my teeth had begun to chatter, but if he noticed, he didn't mention it. He was beginning to frighten me a little, and I wanted to return to the gymnasium.

"Everybody," he said seriously, slipping the medal back into his pocket after holding it up to admire it a second longer. Then he shrugged, kicking up his legs to keep them from getting stiff. "So, what do you want to be?"

The question was beyond my reach to answer. I had no idea where I might end up, and the only work I'd had any real contact with was teaching. Before arriving at St. X. School for Girls, I had told my mother I wanted to be a nurse so I could save her. The only other person I'd shared my wish with was Rachel. I didn't want to explain myself to a boy I'd just met. Besides, I was no longer hopeful that if I did become a nurse my mother would recover. "Do you want to be a soldier?" I asked.

"No way. If the world goes to war again, it will be suicide. They can blow up the planet with the kinds of weapons they have now. I know a guy who went to Vietnam, and he paces up and down our street in his track pants and ripped T-shirt, winter or sum-

mer, and yells at people walking by that he has seen hell." He made
little exploding noises into the air and then laughed wildly until he
saw I wasn't joining in. "You got pretty eyes," he said, approaching
my face with his own.

He kissed me quickly on the lips. A small peck, just his lips
touching mine, fast, like my father did when he was very pleased
with me. A bit of salt was all, and a smell like that of Rachel's gin,
and it was over. I couldn't believe my first kiss could be so disap-
pointing. I wasn't prepared; I didn't pout my lips seductively like in
the movies or fling my hands around his waist in rapture. For all the
fuss of my adolescent dreaming, it could have been a mosquito taking a bit of blood from my skin. He slung his left arm over my
shoulder, and I wanted to go back inside and find the girls. I pulled
at my scarf, trying to cover up my arms, the fine hairs standing up,
my flesh irritated by the wind.

"You want to smoke," he said, his free hand pulling out a
hand-rolled cigarette. "It's good stuff. I had one earlier."

"No, thanks," I replied. "I should get back soon. My friends ..."

"Yeah, I guess they'll wonder where you are." He put the cigarette back in his pocket, wrapping it in a bit of tinfoil. "I probably
had enough of this earlier. The stars on your scarf seem brighter
than the ones in the sky." He chuckled to himself and let his palm
drop an inch to rub my left nipple, hard from the cold.

It pained a little, like a tickle. I held my breath. He rubbed
lightly, circularly, and I started to feel a pressure between my thighs.
I laid my head against his shoulder and moved my body towards
him to ease the throb. I thought of Esperanza and Mr. M., the way

they strove towards release and how badly I too needed salvation. How badly I wanted to find joy and feel such serenity. How badly I needed love. He kissed me again, this time parting his lips and licking my mouth with his tongue, forcing it upon my front teeth. I gasped. My hands roamed over his body, and he was bony, his fingers, his back, his arms. This boy who could speak of killing in one breath and then forget about it, kiss a girl he barely knew and rub her breast gently in the night air, was practically a skeleton.

A noise startled us out of our kiss. Or, more correctly, his kiss. I didn't kiss back, just moved my arms a lot the way I'd seen other people do, kept my mouth open but my tongue and lips still. He was wet and slightly slobbery. I couldn't believe I had anything of his in my mouth. I started to feel a bit shameful, giving in so quickly, without the façade of a fuss, and was glad for the noise. It was the fire alarm. A prank. The same boys who had been out smoking earlier were hiding behind a truck as the gymnasium cleared out. I rose from the concrete divider and straightened out my dress. He tucked in his shirt and wiped his lips with the back of his hand. I was about to leave him there.

"Hey," he said. "What do you want to do with your life?"

I said the only thing that came to mind, stealing Francine's mother's wish for her daughter. "I want to be a nun." My own mother would have been proud of my response. She believed nuns were chosen people.

Then I ran away from him to the entrance, where Caroline, Rachel, and Francine had found each other and were searching for me. It was getting near curfew and we needed to hurry back.

Caroline had told Sister Marguerite, who would be waiting for us in the dormitory, that her sister was taking us out and we were coming home in a cab. As we took a shortcut along a trail beside the soccer field that led to a road where we could catch a bus, Caroline spotted Karl Z. the Third smoking behind some bushes with one of his friends. They were howling with laughter, then stifling it under a few short coughs. The air was filled with a strong scent, sweet, like pine.

"You see that guy?" she said.

We all turned around. I recognized my first kiss instantly and was about to brag to the girls, sensing the right opportunity to divulge my secret, to have them include me in their praise.

"That guy," she said, pointing at Karl Z. the Third, "told me he wanted to show me something outside. I told him to get lost." She flipped her long hair over to one side and braided it as we walked.

"Good for you," said Rachel, slapping her back.

"I know a pervert when I see one," she replied, nodding for approval from the rest of us.

"Cute, though," said Francine.

"Yeah," Caroline added. "He's cute. But he probably thought I was easy or something. It's his school, you know. He'd know where to take you and you could end up chopped up in the back of the field somewhere. If it was at a place I knew, it might be different."

The fire alarm had stopped, although a single fire truck had been dispatched to the school, and we could hear its siren approaching, ringing loudly in our ears. "Where were you, Angela, when the alarm went off?" Rachel asked as she counted the number of boys she had met on her fingers.

"Me?" I was disgraced. I wouldn't be able to tell them now. "Oh, I was having a smoke with the guys out there, just underneath the lamp."

"You bad girl!" she teased. "Trying to keep them all to yourself?"

She grabbed my hand and squeezed it. I held onto Rachel's fingers tightly, afraid of letting go. I hadn't been chosen at all, only there and willing. The difference between Caroline and me was I had believed I was special. Karl Z. the Third's skeletal kiss dug a deep pit into my stomach the whole ride home.

AS CHRISTINE AND I walk to find a place to eat, three young boys all around the same age, retrieve plastic bags of stale bagels and doughnuts out of the cardboard trash boxes outside. They are obviously hungry, their bodies thin and their hair matted, legs shaking with the cold. They are wearing flimsy windbreakers and the baker is shooing them away, pointing to the alley beside the building. She continues to bellow as they run down the alley, pushing each other, the bags smacking against their sides. They laugh. Laugh amidst their hunger.

I am tired and do not wish to walk. I'm not fond of the bus service, but I have money in my pockets and Christine is struggling with her luggage. Under other circumstances, I would offer to carry it, but today I have a tote bag of my own. Christine says she wants to walk. She wants to see a bit more of the city before she leaves. The neon lights from the bars and restaurants, the lower-scale shops and dollar stores, and the churches with their sandwich boards and bells and stained glass, assault the eye. There are many races and religions competing to draw in crowds. All claiming to make something better out of what we've been given. Everyone is pulled by one thing or another in the city. By the lights or the advertisements, by the promise of food or the lure of music. We are in a poorer section of the city than I normally frequent. There are children here who should be in school.

A group of teenage boys and girls with a portable stereo between them smoke by the front entrance of an abandoned discount store, the debtor's notice taped inside the window, the rest of the glass plastered with newspapers and pieces of bristol board.

Christine suggests we turn at the corner. On the west side of the street is a sign announcing a buffet lunch under a green awning. There are petunias inside the window and a couple finishing up coffee. We can see no one else from outside the restaurant and decide to try it.

We enter and a middle-aged waitress, with deep wrinkles around her eyes, seats us near the back, beside a painting of an exotic landscape, the kind Christine likes to bring back from her trips. A tropical landscape with palm trees and large fruit hanging off the leaves, static and perfect, the colours bold and unblurred. A woman's sarong skirt is unravelling. She is walking towards the inviting blue ocean, caught by the painter in mid-step, her back tanned and contrasting with the bright blue of the waters. Her dark hair is swept around one shoulder, slightly damp. She is utterly perfect, I think, and look over at Christine, whose figure has turned frumpy.

The waitress serves two plates and directs us to a salad bar and a row of metal dishes not unlike those of the cafeteria back at the convent. I pile my plate with a Caesar salad, penne in tomato sauce, and a side of cooked broccoli and potato salad. Christine goes for the meat; she fills her plate with chicken in a white sauce, ham with bits of pineapple sliced onto it, a few shrimp in a fried batter, and a hot potato with sour cream and chives. She spoons a little coleslaw into a separate dish. We return to our table. We do not speak for quite some time. Christine chews quickly, barely waiting to swallow before grabbing for her glass of water to wash the food down. I enjoy the Caesar because the lettuce is fresh and the croutons have not yet grown soggy, but the penne is terribly dry and overcooked. I imagine Christine made the better selections.

"Looks like your food is good," I say to her.

"Not really," she replies, wiping the corners of her mouth with her napkin. "These buffets always look better than they taste. I guess that's what happens when you make things in bulk."

"Oh, I'm sorry," I say, forcing down the potato salad, which is too sour for my liking. However, having eaten all the pasta, I am full before my plate is clean. Christine leaves some sauce on the bottom of her plate and drags her last shrimp through it. She then gets up from the table while the waitress retrieves our plates.

"Can't go without dessert," Christine says, but I remain seated.

She returns with a slice of apple pie, a jello cup, and three chocolate chip cookies. I try not to gawk at her while she eats, but I do. Her hand hits her water glass, the ice cubes clinking. She drops her napkin, stops eating, but protects her plate from being removed from the table with her elbow. Cookie crumbs litter the front of her dress, and a smear of whipped cream is on her chin. I reach across with my own napkin to wipe it off.

"Don't mention it, Chris," I say, softly brushing her face, a little red lipstick smudging onto the napkin with the cream.

"Oh, God," she replies, her voice cracking, a tear falling from her left eye.

"It's only a little smudge," I tell her. "Nothing much, I swear."

"No ..." she replies. "No ... it's not that. I ... I'm a pig."

Her hands fall from her face and now she is fully crying, turning from me, reclaiming her napkin to wipe the mascara and tears underneath her eyes. She sniffles and struggles to keep her voice down. I do not know what to do. It has been decades since I've seen Christine cry.

"You're not a pig," I say, as her hands brace against her stomach. "You're just ... just hungry. You're tired from your trip."

She chuckles hopelessly and I feel sick. Her mouth is open and there is brown cookie on one of her bottom front teeth. She blows her nose, pressing the way one does with a nosebleed. She turns her chin up.

"Can I confess something to you?" she asks softly, her eyes upon the ceiling. "No more secrets."

"I'm not a priest," I reply.

"You're my sister," she says, leaning across the table, tugging on my sleeve the way she did when we were children. "I don't have any use for a priest."

At last we have found common ground. Neither do I. In all the years I've been holding my guilt like a huge crucifix across my back, I have never been able to tell a priest about it. I tried several times, going into churches where no one knows me, in regular clothes, and walking into the confessional, ready, determined to unburden myself, face God's penalty for what we did. Reveal it all as in a book. The words pressed into my heart like a prayer. Yet I was never able to. Instead, I would open my mouth and find myself confessing a relatively meaningless sin committed that week—coveting something or lying—express my dissatisfaction with myself and my failings, but never what happened that night in Room 313. I thought I was being a coward, and surely I was in some way, as if my guilt were my child and I was unable to let go of her. But I couldn't tell them, those men, what had happened. I know the priest would stress the fact we were girls, that we had committed a serious sin but judgement is in God's hands. I've never believed it. Not truly, not utterly, that it is in God's hands. In my nightmares it is never a man's hand seeking to touch me. It is a distinctly feminine hand, from its hairlessness, its fine knuckles. The smell of lilies. And here, after all these years, after all our fights, I only now realize that my sister can be wise. She is teaching me it doesn't matter what you confess, it matters only who you confess it to.

"I'm a horrible wife ... and mother." She speaks slowly, with difficulty, and I can sense her gathering her strength, her resolve to continue without giving in to tears or self-pity. She has dignity in her posture, her body gathered like tailored cloth. She wants to tell it straight. No dramatics. Facts are facts. But I dread her words.

"No, Christine, no—"

"I need to tell it my way! Don't interrupt me. Please ..."

"All right," I say, and the waitress returns with cups of coffee and a pitcher of milk. She ignores us and goes back to the kitchen.

"I cheated on Anthony," Christine whispers to me, then slices into her apple pie with her fork. She lifts the flaky crust to her mouth, biting hard. "I can't believe I'm still eating ... I'm going to be sick ... shit ... What the hell? I'm admitting I'm a pig, aren't I? I act like a pig."

I am shaking. I know in our litany of arguments there have been many times I wished Christine would just crack, unveil her immense weakness in front of me, let me in. She can dismiss me with a flick of her hand. A simple gesture to keep me out. And now what I've waited for is in front of me: Christine in all her distress. I am uncomfortable, despicable, wishing she would stop. I am the one collecting more shame.

"You don't—"

She slams her hand against the table. It makes a loud, hollow thud. Christine is not hysterical, only intent, and it's the intensity of her need that repels me. She can no longer keep it to herself. The weight gain, which I'd tried to avoid mentioning but wanted to acknowledge, is her weapon now.

"I'm going to tell you something. Haven't you said to me before I don't really say anything? Well, I want to say something. I want to say something, because I can't take it any more."

I keep my mouth shut, bite the inside of my cheek to remind myself not to interrupt her. I stir my coffee after filling it to the brim with milk.

"I'm cheating on Anthony ... with our neighbour." My eyes widen despite myself. "It's not him. I'm not in love with him or any-thing. He just talks to me, and at home I feel like I'm speaking to babies all the time. Peter's older, I know, but it's still not like a real conversation. And he asks me how I am and what I think, and sometimes I lie and sometimes I actually tell him something."

She pauses to take a bite out of her last cookie and I wait, in silence, for her to continue. I think of her lovely turn-of-the-century home, with backyard and terrace, sunflowers on the front lawn, a welcome mat and tea cozies, fireplace and polished wooden banisters. Everything in her life perfect. Like the painting behind her.

"I look at him. Anthony, I mean. Look at him at night, snoring beside me. He's an attractive man. Better looking than the neighbour. And I wonder why I'm not waking him up in the middle of the night to run his hands all over me, why I barely kiss him on the lips any more, or why I've started to think of our children as his children. It doesn't make any sense, I think, because I have this ache inside me," she says, pointing to her belly, "this ache that isn't being satisfied. Hunger pains."

She has stopped sniffling and crumples her used napkin in her hands, wipes her nose intermittently. I notice she has a scratch underneath her eye, the thinness of a paper cut.

"But it doesn't help. I thought it would. Because he is there, and I am hungry. I have needs. I know you might not know about that—"

I lower my gaze from hers, move a coaster across the table.

"No," I say. I do not lie. "But that doesn't mean I don't understand the feeling."

"True, true ..." she says, but I don't think she believes me. It isn't important anyway, the sex. Not to me and not to her. That's not what she is trying to tell me, I gather. She is talking about something that motivates the sex or cancels out the sex or redeems the sex, but I'm not entirely sure which. Unfaithful. Christine has lost faith in something. She needs to find out what it is.

"Anyway, I thought I could do something about it. But I can't. And now I eat. Constantly. I know you've noticed. How could you not? Anthony has too. Blames it on the children and the fact I don't get out much any more. Says it doesn't matter, that Italian men like a little meat on their women. Tries to make me laugh. But it's not that. It's that I'm just hungry all the time and there's nothing to stop me from eating. I'm guilty too, I guess. He doesn't deserve this from me. It's like I'm paying for something. Does that make sense? Do you understand?"

I do not lie. "Yes."

She is pleased with that at least. Takes a breath, finishes off her cookie in three short bites.

"That's the part that gets me. It's not so hard to be ... to feel ... so ..." She scrunches up her face. "What's the word?"

"Lost?" I ask.

"No, like dead. Inert. It's not hard to be inert and just going through the motions. Just hand to mouth. Hand to mouth. You don't even notice you're breathing any more. It's so much harder to feel alive!" And she leans over to put her face close to mine, as if to decipher a code I might have written on my skin. She is hungry; her eyes are hunger pains. I don't want to be here. For a slim moment of panic I think she is going to slap me, her forehead creased and the anger in her tense fingers threatening to lash out, but she merely rearranges the cutlery I haven't used into straight lines, taking the opportunity to speak near me.

"Nothing's enough."

I agree with her, nod my head and take her hand in mine, and she is like paper, crumpling in front of me, her tears falling again.

"I have to lose this," she says, patting her stomach. Her blood rushes to her face. She is red. She is stuffing herself. She might be dying. I am repulsed. I resent her for this. She has managed to hurt me in the worst way, has made me want to take her burden, she who I had assumed had no burden to take.

"And you, I always thought you were a cheater, you know. A cheat in life to go and lock yourself up in that place. To get away from life. But you're no worse. You're no worse than any of us."

"I'm no better, either," I say, giving in to tears of my own. The sickness in my gut churning round and round. The landscape in the painting taunting me with its blueness, its tranquility. The woman running towards the ocean, sure of comfort. The picture of relief. I want that. Hot sands on feet. Water. Coolness. Rest. I want to take the woman's place and let my skirt fall on the sand. Sure of my footing. My hair slightly damp.

"But you're no worse," blurts Christine. "I live like ... like ... like ... I'm a shell of a person. Something that was once a person!"

She pulls her back up straight. Looks in front of her, then at me, becoming aware once more of her surroundings. She wipes her forehead and collects herself. Her mascara has smeared around her eyes. Her hazel eyes, close to the colour of the tropical woman's back, are the only remnants of her previous self, her plain but sturdy beauty.

"A ghost," I whisper.

She does not hear me.

I am in need of the washroom, the push to go so strong I must get up. A pain stabs my abdomen.

"Angela," she says softly as I rise. "One more thing."

I don't know if I can stand any more. I need the closed door of the washroom, the water running into the sink and splashing over my hands, the seclusion of a stall.

"I don't want to see you for a while. It's just too hard on me. It doesn't seem to help us. Please, forgive me. I just don't want to see you again for a while. Until it feels like I'm coming because I want to, not because I have to."

I am stunned, but relieved at her words. Something is definitely happening that should be happening. There is a haze around us, propelling us forwards through a darkness and towards a light. This is what I think. Maybe I should have been more like Christine. Christine has always been practical. Yet I too know I have been practical in my own way. And I want to share with her how my world makes sense, if only she would take the time to understand. I want to tell her: *An Eye for an Eye.* The proverb has always haunted me, as do many of the Psalms I've sung or recited in class and in the convent. *Break my bones so that I may Rejoice.* That violence could be overcome with joy. *I will visit their Transgression with the rod.* The guilty would be punished and the just rewarded. *To the Righteous Good shall be repaid.* Life and death work on economy. The Divine

Economy of Salvation, as Sister Marguerite taught us. Christ paid for our sins with his blood. I could pay for my sins through work my mother would have been proud of. I could pay the debt. Spare the others. Balance the accounts.

"Forgive me!" I hear her say again.

But I am already thinking we are forgiven, that when I offer her the candle holder as I do now, the debt will be paid, the object redeemed by our forgiveness of each other.

"I have a gift for you," I say, unzipping my heavy tote bag, dragging it out from under the table.

"I can't accept a gift from you right now, Angela."

The silver candle holder is still wrapped in tissue, invisible to Christine, who has risen from the table and counted out money for our bill.

"I need to go now," she says, briefly touching my arm. "Thank you for the offer, but I can't bear the responsibility of a gift from you right now. It's not right."

It's not right. Is it right to remember and honour your mother's death or not? Is it right to eat yourself sick? Is it right to regret your past and want to save the world from a tragic fate? *There's never enough time to mourn,* I think. No matter how much time passes. There are new pains. New reasons to regret.

Forgive me. Forgive me for remembering you.

I rush to the washroom, unsure of whom I mean by you, who it is I need to forgive.

Returning to the table, I find all remnants of Christine's visit have been cleared away by the waitress. I button my jacket and pull the tote bag with the candle holder in it over my shoulder. The waitress walks over to me.

"Did we not leave enough for the bill?" I ask. I begin to dig in my pockets for more money.

"No," she says, handing me the receipt from lunch. "I thought you might need this is all." She hesitates a second more while I stand there, unable to exit the restaurant. "Are you all right?"

"I've just lost someone," I tell her and bow my head, folding the piece of paper.

"Your faith must be a great comfort to you," she replies, wrapping her fingers over my hand the way one grasps a door handle, her head shaking up and down insistently.

I tuck a stray hair back underneath my wimple. "Yes," I say, "it's an amazing crutch."

But she doesn't get the joke.

COMMON BELIEF WAS FRANCINE must have been the first to find Bella. She refused to come out of her room when the commotion began. Between the crying and the screams of the girls, and the whispering and crossing of the Sisters, their backs turned from us and their lips trained as the deaf are to communicating in silence, the hallways were overflowing. You could hear Francine moving inside if you stood by the door: erratic footsteps and the shuffling of objects, her heavy breathing. Many of the girls had already been asked to go back to their rooms or to gather in the cafeteria with Sister Aline, who would be holding prayer and serving hot apple cider and tea, and some of the more hysterical girls had been taken to the nurse, who distributed mild nerve pills. Throughout the panic, Francine never emerged from the retreat of her room. A few girls from our floor had tried to coax her out. I was not one of them. I stood as if caught in a trap between Francine's room and the stairs to go join those praying in the cafeteria. The nuns wanted to speak with her to determine if she had heard anything, whether Bella had confided in anyone about her situation. Everyone pleaded ignorance. That may have been untrue on The Sisterhood's part, but the fear was honest. We too were in shock.

Mother Superior, finally fed up with the knocking and pleading for Francine to come out, pushed herself against the door, her body the only one large enough to shift the oak dresser Francine had shoved in front of it. How Francine managed to move the dresser is beyond my knowledge. She must have been slowly working at it all night long, in small increments, leaning into the wood with determined will until the door was barred. When Mother Superior had successfully cleared the doorway, she stepped back. She had not closed the door, allowing Rachel, a girl named Philomena who had the room next to Francine's, and me a full view of Francine's quarters. We immediately understood Mother Superior's urge to retreat.

Francine was standing completely naked and staring out the open window, her back hunched over and the fingers of her hands curled around the ledge and an object I couldn't yet identify. I was struck by her nudity, her slightly stocky figure exposed, her buttocks sticking out in her bent posture. The floor was strewn with clothes: underwear, shirts, skirts, sweaters, and scarves. Her dresser drawers hung open and empty. When Francine turned to face Mother Superior, she revealed a face streaked in red scratches, her hair split and frizzy at the ends. In her hands was a hairbrush, gripped like a weapon. She had been brushing her hair ferociously, not stopping at the hairline, the wooden brush and its black needle-like bristles straightening the strands. Her pupils were twice their normal size, and she shook from the cold and an apparent lack of sleep.

"I have nothing to wear," she said to Mother Superior and turned back towards the window. She had a view of the north corner of our lot, the back of the building next to ours, a four-storey apartment building with a fire escape and a rusty trash bin. Snow fell, frost clinging to the windowpane, and the papers and books on her desk were rustling from the wind. Francine bumped her knees, shaking against the wall.

"Nothing is clean," she said, leaning her head out the window.

Mother Superior approached cautiously, her bulk shifting in slow steps towards her. She cornered her like a cat, holding out an open palm as if Francine were a wild thing. "Take one, Francine. It's Mother. Take one. Trust me, you'll feel better soon."

Francine took the tiny blue pill in her free hand and chewed it without emotion. I had never seen a girl of our age in such a hopeless state, her every muscle quivering.

Mother Superior stood behind her protectively until Francine slumped down underneath the window, the small flakes intruding, spilling their wetness on her forehead. Mother Superior joined her on the carpet, picking up the edges of her habit, tentlike, and she too was momentarily deflated, breathing coarsely in and out, waving at us to leave. Francine resembled Mrs. M. after the birthday party, when Mr. M. had lifted her into the cab. Did the nuns give her the same pills then? Mother Superior adjusted the silver cross around her neck to hang straight upon her bosom as I closed the door.

Rachel and I headed down to the cafeteria. Philomena went back to her room and slammed her door. Sister Marguerite, her entire body pointed like a stick, began knocking gently, calling her name. It was strange to see girls who were always plotting to leave their rooms suddenly determined to stay within their confines with desperate energy.

Francine slept in Mother Superior's arms. When her own mother came for her in the evening and carried her, straining underneath the weight, to her car parked outside the front entrance, we were told Francine had a bad stomach flu and would return in a week or so.

I never saw Francine again.

I AM BARELY BACK within the convent walls before Sister Bernadette rushes towards me. I cannot fathom what the problem is, but she seems distraught, taking long strides while her hair, in a twist at the nape of her neck, comes undone. My first impulse is that it must have something to do with Kim's baby. I find myself marching with undue haste, unable to contain my fear.

"Sister Angela! Sister Angela!" she says as we meet.

"What? What's happened? What is it?"

She has no need to catch her breath as I do mine. The short time with Christine has been like a dream. The fabric of my life has been torn, my own sister forsaking me. Refusing to accept the gift I had to give her, the only gift I have. My tote bag weighs on my shoulder like an enormous stone.

"A man called for you. Twice," Sister Bernadette says.

"A man?" I've never received a telephone call from a man here. Not once in the twelve years Christine has been married has her husband called, and it would pain my father too much to phone me. Even Father B. conducts his business here with Mother Superior alone and I generally receive messages from her regarding my various duties. No man has ever phoned the convent and asked for me directly.

"Yes. Mother Superior has his number, and she's being very secretive about it, so I thought I'd warn you."

Sister Bernadette immediately rises in my esteem. She does not pry for any more information and seems worried for me, as if I've broken a rule and will be reprimanded. My behaviour and moods being so erratic lately, the other Sisters might think I've done something stupid or reckless. She fumbles with my bag, taking it from me and slinging it over her shoulder, a courtesy I appreciate in my tiredness.

"What do you have in here?" she asks. "Did Christine forget something?"

"A gift."

"Oh, what is it?"

"You've seen it before. The silver candle holder."

I don't know why I tell her this, why I'm being honest. Sister Bernadette refuses to respond but appears to want to, clutching the bag a little more forcibly as if determining whether she ought to keep it herself.

"She didn't want it," I tell her. "You know Christine."

Sister Bernadette laughs. I am pleased she considers my flippancy appropriate. Lugging the giant weight for nothing. My throat is scratchy and I realize Christine has affected me more than I've wanted her too. I shrug and follow Sister Bernadette down the stairs to my room. We pass Sister Katherine and Sister Josie, whose conversation quickly halts.

"I know you've been going through a rough time," Sister Bernadette says as we reach my door. "I just didn't think you'd care to have any more surprises."

Sister Bernadette does not leave me. I open the door and she follows inside. She lowers the bag, resting it against the frame like a doorstop. I open it and remove the candle holder, placing it prominently on my dresser to address me once again. Proving it exists. There was a part of me over the course of the day that believed it would be gone, that by finally providing a gesture of good faith to my sister my debts would be paid and I'd be free. But nothing has changed. The air is stale, and I move towards the small window to open it. The little strength I have leaves me. I begin to cry.

Sister Bernadette bows her head to give me some privacy but stays planted in the room. I cover my face with my hands and sit on the edge of my bed, the familiar grey afghan offering little comfort. It is tucked in firmly and makes the room feel more like a prison than my home. Sister Bernadette probably assumes I'm thinking about the man who has called. I wonder if I can trust her.

Mr. M.'s round, bearded face intrudes into my thoughts, and the smell of his cologne assaults me. I'd never thought it might be a man who had found me out and sent the candle holder. But it makes sense. It's always a man intruding on the secret lives of women. If it's Mr. M., I think, I'll tell him everything. He had been there with us, taking care of the girls as if they were his own children. The afternoon I caught him in Esperanza's arms, I had judged him for his actions. I'd felt repulsed by his needs, the way he could let himself be led so easily towards a young woman who worked for us, doing our laundry and washing the walls. Yet I envied them all the same. We are not always capable of doing the right thing. Look at Kim. She is not to blame. But now, I suppose, is his time to judge. I'm no longer a child. Mr. M. probably assumes I can take it.

I regain a bit of control, enough to fumble through the outside pocket of my tote bag for a package of Kleenex. Sister Bernadette is at the dresser now, fingering the base of the candle holder, lingering over the foreign etchings. I cannot bear to tell her where it has been. She should clean her hands. Smell the blood on it and withdraw. I can't stand watching her. I get up off the bed, my tears not yet spent, and grab Sister Bernadette's wrist. I can feel her skin underneath her dress, pinched by my fingernails. I cannot let go.

"Please don't touch it," I say sharply. "It's not yours."

Sister Bernadette backs away from the dresser, trembling slightly. I've frightened her, so I've lost a possible ally. The messages waiting for me from some man will take on enormous significance. She will inform the other Sisters if they don't know already. She will tell them how my behaviour connects to the telephone calls. A story will surface.

She wants to escape me now but doesn't leave. Maybe she is here on behalf of the Sisters, to pry into what's going on.

"How's Kim?" I ask to divert her, releasing her wrist and

dabbing at my cheeks. She stands in her usual way, her sneakers rubbing to and fro against the floor. Sister Bernadette is incapable of
standing still. Her energy tires me. Her boundless hope.

"You should check on your messages, don't you think?"
she says.

I do think. "It can wait."

I know it can't. Rumours have a life of their own.

ESPERANZA WAS THE ONE to find Bella in the morning. Bella didn't show up for choir practice, and Sister Aline waited half an hour before starting our warm-up scales without her—a rarity, as she always insisted on punctuality. With Bella's impeccable attendance and her strong voice necessary for the solos, however, Sister Aline paced uncomfortably up and down the aisles of the church, her songbooks held tightly against her chest.

Rachel, Caroline, and I were in attendance, but Francine was not. We avoided each other's eyes, rereading the hymns we were to sing, sitting cross-legged on the red-carpeted stairs in front of the altar. Rachel and Caroline were distraught, messy, and short of breath, as if they had just come from calisthenics in the gymnasium. We were all exhausted and frightened, staying apart; not angry, but scared that if we put ourselves in each other's way we would unravel.

The three of us had helped Bella to the washroom. She was hurt but trusted us as we carried her, one arm slung over Rachel, one over me. Caroline kept watch of the hallway in front of us, drawing us to her every few feet with a forward movement of her hand, all of us trying to make as little noise as possible and hoping no one would be in the washroom when we got there.

"When does it stop?" Bella whimpered. Her entire body was in a cramp, her arms tightening against our shoulders, her knees buckling. "When does the pain stop?"

"Soon," Rachel kept saying, her small hands cupped around Bella's waist dabbed with blood. "Don't worry, Bella. Just wash up and it will end soon."

Her motherly stance surprised me. Rachel, the one so intent on hurting Bella, had instantly become her protector.

Water running in the bathroom was no cause for alarm. Many of the girls would leave their rooms in the night to get a glass of water or use the toilet. Caroline filled a jug of water kept beside the sink and handed Bella one of the white washcloths from the hamper. Bella entered the middle shower stall, her woollen skirt at her ankles, visible under the curtain. We could hear her wincing and scrubbing. Caroline prayed over the sink, *Hail Mary full of Grace, the Lord is with Thee,* her knuckles clenched to the porcelain. Rachel and I sat in front of the shower like uneasy guards.

"Is she ... is she going to be all right?" I asked Rachel, who had curled into a ball on the floor, her arms wrapped around her knees, rocking back and forth.

"I don't know," she admitted blankly, her eyes on her kneecaps, her lips close to the skin as she rocked.

"But you told her that she'd feel better—"

"How the hell should I know?" she spat back while keeping her voice down and continuing to rock. I didn't care whether she had the answers or not; I just wanted her to say she did. Whatever she said I would accept, so we could get to sleep without nightmares, so we could wash this night from our hands and forget. I wanted Bella to be all right. Her pain to end. Rachel was our leader. I didn't know who else to turn to.

Caroline recited the Hail Mary without pause, her head bent over the sink as if she were going to be sick. She was marking a bar of soap with her fingernails with each repetition, counting as one does beads on a rosary. Sister Marguerite made us say the rosary whenever we did badly on a test or disobeyed her instructions. We had to sit in the corner of the room and recite it softly to ourselves, then sign on a piece of paper when we had completed the assigned penance. It was worse than Confession. She always prescribed more punishment than Father McC. did. Caroline had switched to her native French after the first prayer, unmindful of the reprimands she usually received from Sister Marguerite when she did so. Matters between the English and the French had exploded into violence only a few years before. We had seen pictures and news reports regarding the kidnapping and murder of an English official. A bomb had gone off. Caroline's sister had warned her that even with time she should not be so forthcoming about her French background.

Rachel said little to Caroline, except to ask her for a glass of water. Caroline handed it to her, stopping her prayer in mid-line and then returning to it as if she hadn't been interrupted. I was afraid Caroline would leave us alone with Bella, as Francine had done, but Caroline stayed. I was tempted to join in her prayer, but I knew it wasn't going to be adequate punishment for what we had done.

After about fifteen minutes, Bella dropped the washcloth, its fresh whiteness turned a dark burgundy, the colour running down into the drain. *What else is down there?* I thought, horrified. *Under the ice of the canal?*

"I'm feeling better," Bella managed. "Just a little dizzy."

Caroline spat in the sink with a heave.

"It's OK. You can go now." Bella stayed behind the curtain. Rachel and I confronted each other with nervous smiles.

"Are you sure?" I asked.

"Yeah. I need to use the washroom first." Her voice was level, almost confident. She had stopped crying and I thought how odd it was that she was now embarrassed to show her naked body to us, after what we had seen.

Although we were filled with guilt over the bruises the candle holder might have caused, we believed her, eager to trust. We left Bella in the washroom sometime after nine o'clock. Caroline stopped praying. Rachel accompanied her down the hallway to their rooms and I left in the opposite direction to mine, noticing a light flickering on and off in Francine's like a signal.

My room was cold. I turned on my bedside lamp and curled under the covers, shivering, desperately hoping I could sleep soundly for once. Beside me on the dresser, the dried pink carnations I had kept from a centrepiece at Rachel's birthday party amazed me with their stubbornness. The original bright colour of the petals had faded, yet their skeletons were preserved, the stems upright in the vase. I brought them to my nose and breathed in their lingering perfume, trying to keep the night from my mind. The precious flowers in my hands, I said my nighttime prayers, careful not to crush them. But Bella, Bella would be dead by morning.

"Does anyone know where Bella is?" asked Sister Aline finally, approaching the stairs before the altar where the majority of the girls had congregated, seated on separate stairs, their knees kept together modestly, the hems of their skirts hanging to their ankles while Rachel and I sat on the top stair.

"I saw her last night," replied Yvonne. "I went to the washroom, and she wasn't feeling well."

Rachel concentrated on the red carpet in front of her. I stared at Yvonne, who didn't seem concerned, only relaying basic information with the same tone of voice she would use if you asked her directions to a classroom or what she ate for breakfast. Caroline got up and excused herself.

"Probably the flu," asserted Yvonne. "She said she didn't feel well in the stomach." She gestured to her midriff with her hands to indicate nausea and glanced around the room furtively, since girls frequently said they had the flu to disguise the fact they were having their periods. Some of the girls caught her euphemism and returned Yvonne's sympathetic glance.

"Maybe someone ought to check," mused Sister Aline absently.

"Francine's not here either," piped up Jessica, who was always meticulously on time for any class or event.

"Francine had to take a test she missed," Rachel muttered. "She told me so, yesterday."

"Well, all right then," Sister Aline replied, clapping her hands against her hymnal. "Angela, why don't you go check on Bella and we'll begin with the scales. Can't do much more without Bella. Just ask if she's in need of a nurse."

I rose, but it was difficult for me to do so. I moved slowly, the way a pregnant woman struggles to rise from a chair, my body weighing me down. I wasn't even sure whether I would actually go to Bella's room or just walk around the residence for a few minutes and return. I descended the stairs and crossed the threshold, shuffling my shoes, my cardigan tied around my waist. Rachel stared at me with dread. My black soles clicked against the wooden floor of the church as I departed, marking time.

I ran into Esperanza in the washroom collecting the laundry. The shower stalls were empty, their curtains pushed to the sides, and I lied, told her I was looking for a missing hair clip Mr. M. had bought me. At the mention of Mr. M's name, Esperanza immediately searched the drains in the showers and under the garbage can. She rifled through the laundry to see if it had slid to the bottom of her cart. The last time I'd spoken with Esperanza had been when she washed my nightgown.

"Did you find anything?"

"Not yet."

"Esperanza," I added, "I'm also supposed to check and see if Bella has the flu. She's not at choir practice."

"So, why don't you?" Esperanza retorted, hands against her hips.

"She's no friend of mine," I said and turned to sort through the garbage can, filled mostly with Kleenex.

Esperanza, accustomed to continual bending, prostrated herself on the cold floor, combing with her fingers under the sinks.

"So, what do you want me to do?" she said.

"Could you check on her for me?" I asked, my voice cool and controlled in a manner surprising even to me. "I don't want to have to take her to the nurse. I've got choir. You could get out of work for a while, couldn't you?" I knew from Rachel that Esperanza liked to deviate from her regular routine as much as possible, just for the sake of change.

"No. I'd still have to finish," she snorted, shrugging her shoulders in exasperation. "What does it look like?"

"What?"

"The hair clip. What does it look like?"

"Forget about it," I said, and I was on my way out to face my own punishment when Esperanza grabbed my arm, drawing me close.

"You trade me that bottle of perfume Rachel gave you last week and I'll go for you. I'll even sniff around the other rooms for your hair clip if you like. Maybe someone stole it."

It was then that I realized Esperanza rummaged through the

things in our rooms. I thought of a couple of missing magazines and tiny trinkets Rachel couldn't locate that I assumed she had been careless with, had left or lost outside the school. Rachel's father had bought her a bottle of perfume, a more expensive brand than the one I'd given her for Christmas, but she sneezed when she used it and passed it on to me. As far as I knew she hadn't shown it to Esperanza. I had been so pleased with the bottle itself, a blue-tinted glass in an oval shape, I hadn't worn the perfume yet. The only way Esperanza would have known about it was if she had pried into my top drawer, where it was hidden inside one of my socks. *She's taking things from me,* I thought angrily. *People are always taking things from me.*

Esperanza removed her cleaning gloves and draped them over the rim of her empty pail.

"Forget about it," she said, pushing her grey cart past me, bumping it against my side.

"I know about you!" I screamed.

Esperanza stopped her cart. She didn't turn around to face me, but gripped the handle tightly.

"I know about you and Rachel's father! I know!"

I attacked Esperanza from behind, smashing her up against her cart, then punching her in the stomach when she turned to defend herself. Esperanza, doubled over, rammed her head back into my ribs. Without a cart to steady my balance or catch my fall, I landed on my tailbone. A number of dimes I had in my blouse pocket, tokens from Mr. M. I hadn't yet spent, clattered to the floor. Esperanza raised her leg as if to kick me.

"You fucking bitch!" I screamed, raising my arms to shield myself. "Mr. M. is going to kill you when Rachel finds out! You hear me? Kill you!"

Esperanza lost her nerve and lowered her foot back to the floor. She smoothed out her apron. Then she dropped down to my level, taking my shaking fists into her own hands, dry and rough with callouses. Resistant at first, I soon accepted her grip like a child finishing a tantrum, aware I'd passed the point of tolerance. She then spooned herself behind me, her legs wrapped around mine, holding me as I cried openly, my anger dissipated into helplessness.

After I calmed down, red with tears and embarrassment, Esperanza loosened her grip and kissed my hair at the nape of my neck, the way my mother used to. I pressed her cheek to mine.

"I didn't mean it," said Esperanza. "I'll do whatever you want. Don't tell Rachel."

I shook uncontrollably, tried to collect the dimes off the floor as Esperanza got up. I barely noticed her leave for Bella's room.

KIM IS SHAKING ME, and I lift my hands against her in fear. Her hair appears white under the angle of the sun, but then my senses return to the waking world and I can see it is black and I am huddled in my winter coat on a bench in the snow-covered orchard of the convent, among the buried flower bulbs and stones. I try to speak, but all that comes out is a low moan.

"Are you all right? Do you need ... need a doctor or something? You fell asleep right in the middle of our conversation," she says.

"No. No. I'm fine, dear. Fine."

It is early afternoon and sunny, although the chill of winter is persistent. Ice along the maple tree branches sparkles. Kim has taken her gloved hands off my shoulders and now holds her belly like a package in front of her.

"You were screaming in your sleep," Kim says, her forehead scrunched up in confusion. "I thought maybe you were having a heart attack or something." She chuckles nervously, watching me carefully for a response, digging her boots into the hard ground underneath our iron bench.

"I'm sorry," I respond. "I didn't know I was ..."

"Well, I didn't really think you were. I thought you're too young to have a heart attack, right?"

"I hope so." I can't help but be a little amused and smile amidst my own embarrassment. The walkway is clear, not a Sister in sight, and the orchard is about thirty feet away from the road. Kim was no doubt torn about leaving me to get help. She has been so quiet in her stay here, she was probably afraid of a commotion. She is visible enough.

I let my back rest against the bench and pat the metal beside me. Kim sits down, her knees wide apart, more like a tomboy than a soon-to-be mother. She lifts her bangs by exhaling, her lower lip punched out. Her breath freezes in the air for a moment like fog.

"Oh, I suppose it's just stress," I tell her.

She looks at me quizzically. I am aware she too, no matter that she sought refuge with us, must think like other outsiders that a nun leads a very sheltered existence, that we are practically inhuman. It might even have been one of the reasons she wanted to live with us: to erase herself from the regular world. That we could be under stress or distress might be a revelation for her. I must admit, it was for me when I was her age. The nuns at our school existed in the hours we beheld them, that was all. Their private lives were of no interest. They seemed to merely do: schoolwork, chores, church activities, sleep. This was the extent of my imagination for them.

But I am stressed out. The phone call has unnerved me.

I couldn't sleep last night. When I went to return the messages Sister Bernadette warned me about, I used Mother Superior's office. Mother Superior paced outside the smoked-glass window the entire time. She couldn't view me entirely, but she could see my outline. And she might have heard me if I hadn't been careful about the tone and pitch of my voice. She must certainly have some legitimate suspicions now.

I put down the phone after giving my account and address information to the man. Mother Superior wanted her office back. She is possessive over the only computer in the convent, claiming it should only be used in emergencies and to keep the lines of communication open with other sects. But I think she was rushing me out in hopes I'd forget to cover my tracks. No one likes being lied to here, least of all our leader. It seems I'm becoming as mysterious in their eyes as Kim. Two girls on the run. I am relieved it is Kim who heard me scream.

The messages were from a lawyer: Mr. Y. He didn't wish to reveal the name of his client, but he called to ask me where I went to school and what my current occupation was. He said I could not be forced to answer his questions, but I would be of great help if I did. "How did you find me?" I asked. "Who is this for? What woman has hired you?" *Who has come for you?* But he refused to answer me. I was right from the beginning. Someone is toying with me. Would this lawyer find enough to have me arrested? "We'd like to pay you a sum for your time," he said when he finished taking notes. "I don't need money," I replied. "I'm a nun." "Oh, we are sure you'll think of something to spend it on. People always do," Mr. Y. said, although I suspect this will only put me further in debt. Yet when it comes to money, I suppose Mr. Y. is right.

"We have pasts too, you know," I say to Kim, staring at a solitary rock brushed free of snow, sitting at the edge of the orchard. There is a pull between us, the rock and me, and I rub my hands together as if feeling the coldness of it between my fingers.

Kim places her hands in front of her while I meditate. The sun is above us, not nurturing this humble spot, but killing it further, in conspiracy with the cycle of the seasons. Although winter offers some small consolations, I regret this time of year, with its gross injustice to plants and animal life: the way birds pack up and leave, how squirrels and raccoons must go into hiding after rummaging through garbage bags and hoarding nuts, huddled in holes in the ground or tight spots in attics. The trees have surrendered, let their lifeblood drip from them bit by bit through their weary limbs. It is these slow deaths that affect me most. The people too lose their colour with each new layer of clothing they don, space themselves farther and farther apart from each other, keep heads bent, hands in pockets, looking up only for landmarks along the way. The homeless of the city, who know deeply how blind the elements are to human suffering, come to church more frequently for a warm place and anonymity, carrying their regrets inside. Father B. offers them coffee sometimes, a bit of money out of the collection plate, asking them to vow not to spend it on drink, even though he knows they'll search for warmth in whatever form it takes. I overheard him once talking to a middle-aged woman with a Jamaican accent who walked to the front pew of the church and knelt down, leaving a shopping cart filled with her belongings by the holy water. When she finished, he put some change into her gloved hands and told her, "God loves you." "Of course He does," she replied loudly. "It is them." She pointed to the exit at the front. "It's them who don't, Father."

The wind helps, but I am still groggy, loath to go inside. There is tranquility out here, somewhat tainted by melancholy thoughts, but tranquility nonetheless. Kim is good company. She is a girl oddly detached from herself; she blends into her surroundings.

"You were calling someone's name, I think. I couldn't make it out," Kim says dreamily, as if the incident had occurred years and not minutes ago.

"Yes?"

"Uh-huh." Perhaps she thinks I've been praying.

"Oh."

The nights have been long, the candle holder on my dresser like a sentry. It is difficult to sleep in its presence, to relax. I nod off for only brief periods at a time and am aware it isn't enough. During the day my eyes are constantly closing. My legs and lungs tell me to stop moving, to take rest. But I continue on, not wanting to draw attention to myself. Yet no one has come. No one besides the lawyer, and he asked no questions beyond what I might have discovered about myself in the City Archives. He mentioned no other names to me. It's as if I've been followed by a ghost, by one of the children buried underneath the old St. X. School for Girls, and not a living person at all.

"Do you ever talk in your sleep?" I ask, thinking to indirectly change the subject.

Kim shrugs. "I think so." She pauses, hesitant whether or not to continue. "This guy once, he told me I did. But I don't know if I believe him. Probably just wanted to say I told him things I never did. He likes to think he knows everybody." She looks down at her belly again, and disgust spreads across her face as if she is just about to spit.

"Is he the one who—" I point stupidly to the evidence.

"No. I mean, I don't want to talk about it."

I shouldn't push her. I don't have the right. But I can't help myself, I want an answer.

"Have you decided what you're going to do yet?"

She is silent, flattens her hands against the metal beside her. It is clear she is about to get up and leave me.

"I suppose you don't want to talk about that either?" I say, raising my voice.

"No." A strand of her black hair blows into her mouth and she catches it between her lips, then brushes it away with her hand.

"Time isn't going to wait for you to decide, you know," I retort, clamping my hand on Kim's skinny thigh, twisting to face her.

"I know." She swings her legs, knocking the bench leg underneath. "Doesn't really matter though," she mutters.

"You should—"

"Look," she says swiftly, pushing my hand from her pants, a little large on her but donated by Sister Monica's sister. "I really appreciate everything you're doing, or trying to do for me. But ..."

Her hands shake as she does up the top button of her coat. Her face holds the despair of someone who would normally be in tears at this point but has already shed so many there are no more in reserve. She is practically blank, this girl. I am afraid her baby will be blank too.

"Well, Kim," I say, "if I'm not helping, then stop coming to me. I don't need to see you any more. I'm tired of your lies and your secrets."

I can tell I've shocked her. She studies me as if all of a sudden she doesn't recognize who I am.

"You're the one in trouble. Not me," Kim replies.

She leaves me in the orchard.

I STAYED ON THE FLOOR, my back against the washroom door, until I heard Esperanza scream. "My God! My God!" Esperanza cried down the hallway, her feet stumbling in her haste, her heavy ring of keys flung to the floor.

Esperanza ran down the dormitory stairs to get the nuns to phone for an ambulance. She had discovered Bella straddled across her bed, her white cotton sheets removed from the corners and bunched underneath her like a pile of dirty snow. Sheets stained reddish-brown with blood. Bella's head was bent into her chest, her black hair fanned in front of her. If she hadn't been bleeding, you might think she had merely fallen asleep in a sitting position. She had tried to stop the flow. She had tried to keep it from getting out, applying pressure on her wound as we had been taught to do in Health class. The clot must form in time.

As I heard Esperanza's footsteps race by, the clatter of the keys, and the echo of her screams in the hallway, I wept against the bathroom door, my body determined to keep it closed.

THE SNOWSTORM BEGAN EARLY in the day, a cold front sweeping through the province from the north-west, a wind blowing fiercely at ninety kilometres an hour. Streets inside the city were closed and the highways were difficult to reach, many of the ramps blocked by snowbanks the size of trucks. Citizens were advised to stay inside until the storm passed, the temperature reported at minus thirty degrees before the wind chill factor. The skin freezes in less than thirty seconds in such weather. Limbs go numb, the lungs rebel, and eyelids can be forced shut. Sections of hydro and telephone lines were down in various parts of the city, whipped off their poles or smashed down by the winds. The downtown core had generators as backup, but many of the houses and streets were cloaked in darkness, while outside, the world clothed itself in oppressing white.

My father was supposed to come downtown for Bella's funeral the next day, notwithstanding the snow and the difficulty to get there by car. All the parents were notified and advised to attend to help their children cope with the tragedy. He had agreed, but phoned Mother Superior back and told her my mother had made a doctor's appointment that couldn't be rescheduled, the waiting list was too long, and she might miss her opportunity to get better. At least that's what he told her to tell me. She may have believed him. Christine, too, would be absent. "She's too young to come," my father said. "Not to a funeral."

I had never attended a funeral either, and I hated him for abandoning me. A Leftover once again. Rachel's father would be coming. Caroline's mother, father, and sister were coming. Francine's mother was coming. But not Francine. She, apparently, still had the flu. Relatives of many of the nuns had begun to arrive as well. The school started to resemble a hotel. Each person who entered, dragging in the snow behind, was directed to one of the free rooms in the convent or school dormitory. Mother Superior stood like an idol in the entrance lobby, motioning to washrooms and the cafeteria, holding up in the face of all the questions. Meanwhile Esperanza toiled down in the basement collecting blankets and towels, extra cots from the boys' school down the street; her workload tripled. She was too distracted to speak with us any more, or was thankful to be busy. She didn't mention what had happened in the bathroom, and I gratefully ignored it too.

The nuns generally kept the church attached to our school locked after evening service. However Father McC. decided, due to the unexpected tragedy, that the church would stay open in the evenings and at night. Vandalism was a concern, but he opted to take the chance and leave it in God's hands to protect the place of His worship. "Keep the lights on. Maybe someone will be seeking guidance. We must provide," he said. Sister Aline informed us of the change so we would not be startled to see the lights on past their regular time or be alarmed by people entering the church at unexpected hours. The parking lot was filled with snow, despite the efforts of the staff and altar boys who had tried to clear paths for vehicles. Although most of the street's power was out, our school had its own generator. When I looked out my window, to the side of the large maple, the light from the church formed an arc around the entranceway. That light drew me from the staleness of my room, from the rattling of the shut window. As if those who entered the light would be protected. It spoke of possible warmth.

I was on my way down the stairwell to the church when I ran into Sister Marguerite, climbing up.

"Where are you going, Angela? It's way past bedtime," she said.

It was nearly midnight and the hallways were mainly silent, except for the water periodically running in the washroom, its sound reminding me of Bella's attempts to wash herself clean.

"I wanted to pray," I replied tentatively. "In the church."

Sister Marguerite regarded me suspiciously for a moment, and I was starting to panic from my guilt, rubbing my hands together to keep from sweating. I was alone here. I would have no father or mother or sister present at the funeral. No one to comfort me over what had happened. My last refuge seemed to be the church, the only place that would welcome me at this hour. I wanted to pray for Bella's soul, ask the Lord to take her up in His hands and reward her for the times she had sung for Him. Ask Him to overlook her small trespasses and the irrevocable act against the body He gave her that she had performed in a moment of weakness. She simply wanted to belong. Certainly He could understand.

I was disturbed that I hadn't yet shed tears over Bella's death. I wanted my mother, but knowing she couldn't be with me, I longed to fling myself into Sister Marguerite's arms, lay my head in her ample chest, whether she comforted me or not. She wasn't pretty, the left side of her face marked by a patch of yellowish discoloration, her manner withdrawn, but I wanted her to touch me then, on the shoulder or on my hair, to hold me against her. Sister Marguerite kept her lips pursed, her body straight and reserved. Her arms were occupied, holding a heavy cardboard box in front of her. Perhaps my clothes are inappropriate, I thought, looking down at the thick white cotton nightgown I hadn't bothered to cover up when I left my bedroom.

"I could change," I offered.

Sister Marguerite shook her head and relaxed her cheeks. "No. That's all right, Angela. You can go."

As I brushed past her, Sister Marguerite dropped her cardboard box, shocking us both with the thud against the concrete echoing in the hollow stairwell. She managed to save the box from tumbling down the stairs with her foot but some of its contents escaped. She let out a moan. We both bent down to pick up the mess, a pile of papers and notebooks we swept up with our hands. I recognized the diligent and letter-perfect handwriting, the name at the bottom corner of each of the papers. My hands removed themselves as if of their own will.

"I thought Bella's parents might like to have these," said Sister

Marguerite, her eyes blinking rapidly. "She was such a good student. Impeccable, really. It's unbelievable to think she ..."

Hurriedly she grabbed the rest of the papers and stuffed them into the box. Sheets protruded from its corners. She pressed them down, creasing the leaves.

The doctor was sympathetic. The medical report stated Bella died of internal hemorrhaging. Her parents were telephoned by Mother Superior, who assured them the nuns did not realize Bella had been feeling any pain, if indeed she had been before she died. Bella was never the type to complain, they explained. These things happen and answers are difficult to find. Accidents of nature. The body revolts against itself. In young girls in particular, there can be complications as the body grows into womanhood. She had not been to a doctor in over a year. The body can be like a bomb, ticking, ticking. Bella's parents were led to believe she was simply a tragic example of God's mysterious ways. An angel, Sister Aline said, her song so sweet God could not bear to be without her any longer. Bella's mother needed her husband to translate the English into Portuguese throughout the ordeal. Where Bella's father found the words, I couldn't tell you. "Bella is certainly at peace wherever she is," Sister Aline reassured them. "Have faith." Bella's mother cried out in Portuguese, wringing her hands and collapsing against her husband. No one translated what she said.

The girls were told the same story as Bella's parents: Bella died of internal hemorrhaging. She died in her sleep without pain. But the nuns suspected we knew how she was found. The nuns believed, as Esperanza did, that Bella had tried to perform an abortion on herself. The verdict was logical if scandalous. The wounds fit the description, if not her character. But facts were facts. Who could have guessed otherwise? There was no evidence to the contrary. The silver candle holder had disappeared.

On the day Bella was found, Rachel avoided me in the cafeteria. We sat at a table with a couple of other girls and drank the hot apple cider Sister Aline had asked the kitchen staff to brew for us. They were confused, pouring out the drinks into paper cups, unable to account for the crying and the stunned, shocked expressions and subdued movements of their normally boisterous consumers. They worked around us like nurses, scurrying from one to the next, asking us if we needed anything else, not waiting for an answer before they moved on to the next table.

Rachel, who took pride in being one of the oldest girls in the school, now appeared as helpless and childish as the rest as she sucked on her straw, drinking the warm cider into her belly. She sat next to Sister Marguerite like a good student awaiting instructions. Sister Aline put a protective hand on my shoulder, a little sorry perhaps that she had sent me to find Bella. I could not drink, but pretended to, blowing air into my straw when someone glanced over at me. The noise was unbearable. Sipping and crying and talking and shuffling. But the silence was equally unbearable when it came. Pauses of emptiness reminding us there was one less girl in the school now. I scanned the girls' faces, trying to determine who was crying because there'd been a death and who was crying because they'd been fond of Bella. I didn't know who Bella's friends were. We might have been her only ones.

The Chinese women in the kitchen had begun to boil hot water and stir soup, preparing for an early dinner. They chopped vegetables, cut up meat, and cleaned the free tables, never stopping to ask what had happened. I wondered, not for the first time, whether they cared about us or whether they regarded us as objects to manoeuvre around, the manner in which we usually treated them.

Even after Mother Superior came to take us to our common rooms and to speak with each of the grades separately, after the doctor had left and the official report had been recorded and Bella's parents had been notified, Rachel still did not speak with me. She slunk to her room and turned off her light as we were all told to do. She finally succumbed to the nuns' authority. I wanted to join her, crawl into her bed underneath whichever afghan was currently being used, but she did not want anyone with her. It was Caroline who stopped me and said, "I don't believe it. I've never known anyone who's died before, have you?"

I shook my head. Death was what happened in the newspapers and to relatives I'd never met. Death happened on paper, not in front of me. Death happened in the movies. Death happened overseas and in books. It happened in the Bible, but the good were resurrected or rewarded, and because we were told they went to Heaven, we didn't question their deaths. I couldn't imagine Death's face or Death's hands around Bella's body. What did He want with her?

"I'm scared," I said.

Caroline turned away from me to obey the nuns and retire to her room for the night, but I still caught what she said under her breath, possibly unaware she was speaking out loud. She said, *I don't want to die.* But that night, I wanted to. If I couldn't be beside Rachel, I wanted to go with Bella. Inexplicably, I felt closer to her than to anyone else.

As we collected the last of the papers off the grey concrete, I bumped my jaw against Sister Marguerite's cheek. Her yellow bruise was so close to my lips I could have kissed it. Some of the girls joked she had received it in a fist fight with Mother Superior one night, or she had painted it on her face on purpose to make us feel sorry for her and pay attention in class. The more plausible explanation was she had a disease, which allowed those of us who didn't like her to keep our distance from fear of contagion. My resolve to go pray was still firm, but I needed to know the truth about how she'd acquired the stain on her face. *The stains of sin,* I could hear her say, as she did about adulterous women in the Bible stories we read. I was fairly sure she was born with it and it must have been small when she was a newborn, gradually stretching out to cover her entire cheek, until it resembled in size and colour an autumn leaf.

"Sister, what happened?" I asked.

She had collected all the papers now, and she looked up, frazzled. "God only knows."

"I mean ... your cheek. The bruise," I said, pointing to my own face.

Perhaps the last couple of days had drained her of any protec-
tiveness. She barely hesitated to answer me, taking a short breath and
speaking with the same clipped precision as she did in class. "When
I was a small girl, I loved watching my father putting paper into the
fireplace. My father had these huge hands and he would chop the
wood outside, splitting it with his axe in short, blunt stokes. He kept
old newspapers in a pail by the fire, and he would use the poker to
place them in the spaces between the wood, close to the coals. They
would flare up and I thought they looked so beautiful. Like stars."

She was struggling now with her words, holding tightly onto
the sheets of paper Bella had written on. "You see, I had been warned
not to go near the fire, but I wanted to place the paper in myself.
I wanted to prove to him that I could. But I couldn't control it the
way my father could. The paper flew out and struck me in the face.
It burned off half my scalp when it landed on my hair." She touched
the left side of her head, the material of her wimple covering the area
the fire must have singed. "It was an accident, but I've been left with
this scar as a reminder of my carelessness. And my pride."

She straightened up abruptly then, tapping her toe, the
manner in which she ended all her classes. "You come let me know
you've returned," she said, waving her hand at me to get going. "It's
late, Angela. You need sleep." And I agreed, following the stairwell
down, the memory of her hair burning in my mind, praying pre-
maturely I'd be spared the scars of my youth.

I entered the church through the double oak doors adjacent to the
school. A stained-glass picture of Jesus on the cross, his perpetual

suffering on display, his brown crown of thorns the only opaque section of the figure, stared me in the face, and I turned immediately to cross myself with the holy water at the entrance. *The Father, The Son, and The Holy Spirit,* I whispered. *Forgive us our trespasses. As we Forgive those who trespass against us.* The emptiness of the church calmed me, its smell of pine cleaner and the thirty-foot-high ceiling with the triangular wooden arches. The felt banners we had made in Religion class, with cut-outs of white doves and small pillars of fire and letters spelling out words such as Peace and Glory, hung from the altar and from the pulpit. It was the lack of a voice I had been stalking, a silence, and it took a full minute for me to realize there was a steady metallic noise like the clinking of cutlery at the front of the church.

I tried to decipher the source of the sound. Some lights were left on, as Father McC. had promised, illuminating the altar with its white banner draped over the front, devoid of service ornaments. There were also lights at the entrances and exits, but it was difficult to see any image clearly more than a couple of feet away. An odd glow radiated at the left side of the church, near the front row of pews where the nuns usually sat at Mass with the elderly who found it difficult to stand in line for the Eucharist and were therefore first to receive Communion. Out of the glow emerged a figure with familiar blonde curls.

Rachel was in a nightgown too, of yellow cotton, and from her emanated a glow, a bright haze. She stood at one of the candle altars, and at her feet lay a green paper shopping bag, the kind we would buy for a dime at the department store in the Market when we went to browse for clothes and purchase candies and treats at the confection stands. One by one she lifted a coin with her right hand from the palm of her left, and slipped it in the locked copper deposit box. Clink. Clink. Clink. Each coin inserted through the small slot. Then she removed a long wooden stick from the jar to the left of the altar and lit a candle.

I watched her from the back of the church, kneeling in the last pew, my head peeking out from behind the backs of the benches for probably an hour. She moved in an orderly fashion and, as far as I could hear, she herself uttered no sound. Clink. Clink. Clink. Coins from the paper rolls in her hands into the deposit box. Then the wooden stick. The votive candle. She made her way, lighting the back row, wick by wick, then attacking the row in front of it, and so on until she conquered the entire altar. The section aglow, she would pick up her paper bag and shuffle down to the next stand, lay the bag at her feet, and begin again. As the box filled up, the sound of clinking was muffled. She had finished the altar on the far left side of the church pews before I entered. Her bag, however, was still full, her body revealing strain as she hoisted it.

She didn't pause between her movements, which was unusual. We were taught you paid to light a candle for someone and then stood still or kneeled to say a prayer in his or her favour. When my father remembered to send me money for the collection plate, I would keep a quarter aside and light one of the votive candles at the end of Sunday Mass for my mother. I generally said the Hail Mary after lighting it. But Rachel's lips were shut and she stared at the deposit box, not at the candles.

I could not bring myself to tell her I was there. I thought about the story Sister Marguerite had told us: Jesus in the temple denouncing the money lenders. Rachel's actions were not being obstructed. She was not hit with a thunderbolt or drowned in a flood. She was free to do as she pleased, alone by all appearances and her rolls of money plentiful. Her father's money, it seemed, was always welcome at the church. As she progressed, the church filling steadily with light, the stained-glass pictures glorious as the brightness grew, Rachel's actions were, against my will, pleasing me. The beauty of the serene church, a young woman in her nightgown, the dozens upon dozens of candles gave me a flicker of hope I hadn't felt since holding my mother at Christmas. The two-dimensional figures came alive in the light. Pictures of suffering and dying, yes, but the ecstasy of uplifted arms in Resurrection shone. The church breathed.

IT WAS UTTERLY STUPID of me. I can't believe it has come to this. I have completely lost even a tenuous control over myself. The convent walls, though made of stone, might as well be made of paper. I am exposing myself under the eyes of this place. The child I was is running around screaming murder. She is scared the walls and floors are going to crumble and bury her alive. In her nostrils is the stench of smoke. Her hands are stained with red. The women here can smell it, like strong perfume. There is nothing concrete separating my present from my past. My guilt spills over like water.

If I hadn't gone to see Father B. in the afternoon to discuss the accounts for the last quarter, it would have happened sooner or later. It was only a matter of time before I would be sent to Sister Ursula's office for a medical checkup, if not a strongly suggested psychological evaluation. It has happened to others. The confines of the convent can be suffocating for some. Sister Jessica, twelve years ago, was handed over to the Centre of Mental Illness near the same hospital where my mother was admitted when she was physically ill. Sister Jessica is still there. She believed she saw the Devil one day eating her dessert. She stopped eating. She withered away until there was nothing left. The gardener found her striking the heads off tulips with a kitchen knife, chanting *Thou be gone, Thou be gone!* But aside from her, no one has deteriorated that far since I've been here. Whenever someone starts to act strangely, one might hear the expression *We could have a Devil eating dessert on our hands.* It's a way to monitor, keep ourselves in check. They might already be saying such things about me. Father B. at least opted for the former, a medical checkup, after the incident with the wine. He chalks the entire episode up to nerves and the amount of time and energy I've spent helping Kim with her pregnancy. He should know about nerves, if not babies. Since the Bishop visited again, he's had his share of them. He's been unable to sit still or talk sensibly, paces around the church pews as if he will uncover a hidden stash of money or a great and revolutionary idea on how to sustain his traditional beliefs and still bring in more parishioners to the diminishing fold. I was intending to discuss possible changes to the rental of the church basement that might bring in extra revenue, although it still wouldn't add up to very much in the end. The accountant tells me it's not the make-it-or-break-it solution to our financial troubles. Neither are the cheques I've been stashing away until an appropriate moment to hand them over. Yet I felt the discussion might perk us both up, keep us focussed on the tasks at hand. A little more revenue is better than more debt, that's for sure. Father B. had been sneaking a drink of the said wine anyway, and probably felt a bit shamed about being caught in the act. Two guilty subjects we were, but I was the one who lost control.

I had also been planning to inform him about Kim's inability to decide on the future of her baby, to seek his opinion on what we should do about her, her delivery date being closer than we had at first expected. I didn't tell him about what happened at the hospital myself, but I'm sure Sister Ursula has informed him about Kim's lie. I figured the issue could be brought up at the end, after we'd made some progress, as a small aside. I don't trust talking to the Sisters about it; at least a man can keep a certain distance. The Sisters have plans for her I find ridiculous. Sister Humilita talks about sending her to live with her cousin, an eccentric woman who brings in broken toys at Christmas as charity gifts for poor children and bakes a single turkey at Easter, about five pounds, that she claims can feed the lot of us. She sits in the back at Mass, signing hymns with her eyes closed. Sister Bernadette has suggested that Kim might like to do tours of local schools speaking about planned parenthood. At least Sister Josie nipped that one in the bud, reminding Sister Bernadette of the humiliation Kim would feel. Besides, there has been no indication Kim can speak in public. She might find the thought of standing in a room of girls her own age, on display for her sin, abhorrent. Sister Maria says Kim should be on a strict regime of prayer, from morning until night, under her guidance. Father B. told her you couldn't force belief down the girl's throat. He says the same to the Bishop about the decline in conversions. Religion isn't about answers, he says, it's about helping people ask the right questions. But Father B. suspected all along Kim was lying about being a Catholic, a Christian even, and he let her stay with us regardless. It probably didn't surprise him to discover her pregnancy was further along than she led us to believe. He's probably known since before Christmas.

He has a good heart, cares about the child in the abstract if not in practice, still wishing she'd arrange her affairs with Mr. Q. so we don't have to take responsibility for her baby entirely upon ourselves. But I think it might be good for us, for me, to take responsibility for that baby. Kim's baby. She was brought to our home, after all.

Father B. was the one who spilled the wine. He had gone to get the mop and pail out of the janitorial closet. He couldn't have been away for more than a couple of minutes. The office door open, I knocked lightly beside the doorknob and walked in expecting to find him huddled in his chair, papers around him and staring listlessly. Instead, I found blood. Blood in the shapes of water flowers, wet and glistening across the floor towards the doorway. A trail of blood from the top of his pine desk, staining it, penetrating the wood, drops pattering onto the tiled floor, following the stream. Everywhere I looked, there was blood. On the crucifix above his window, the gold cross dripping with blood, Christ's head pricked with thorns, his side weeping its own blood. The missal pages steeped in blood. The plastic container of pens and pencils filled with blood. The smiling face in the picture frame, Father B.'s brother who lives by the shore in Nova Scotia, gums releasing blood.

As I fainted to the floor, Father B. returned just in time to save me from banging my head against the door frame. He caught me in the same arm that held the dirty mop. Its skeleton-like body sent me into further hysterics as I snapped back into consciousness. I wept with fear. I clutched onto Father B. as to a ladder. I told him, between tears, it was my fault.

"It is my fault," he said, holding me upright in his arms, trying to stop me from covering my eyes.

"No, no," I said, beating against his chest, trying to get him to unhand me so I could run out of the church and down the street, far away from this place that could read my heart like a book. Father B. held me, pinned, his arms wrapped around my shoulders like a straitjacket.

"No, it is. Sister Angela, I spilled the wine. That's why I went to fetch the mop." He was wearing his regular clothes, not his robes, at least. I could imagine he was a regular man and not the priest I had worked with and only exchanged a hug or a peck on the cheek with on holy occasions such as Christmas or Easter. His body was against mine and he was trying to calm me down. I fought him. I hit his cheek with my fist, nearly causing a black eye.

I don't remember much else. He had to wait for me to stop crying. I couldn't contain my fear, cringing each time I opened my eyes to see three decanters of wine toppled on the dresser. All I remember is his assurance that I hadn't done anything and he wasn't sure why I was so upset. He said I was stronger than he'd imagined, laughing self-consciously as he adjusted his white shirt and black pants after convincing me to sit still in his office chair. There was a stain on one sleeve. He wanted me to make an appointment to see Sister Ursula. He assured me the wine had not cost much, that it hadn't even been blessed yet.

Sister Ursula talks a great deal about the need for sleep. She is fifty, and her hair is white, though she dyes it a shade of ash blonde and forgets to have it touched up for six months at a time. The wrinkles around her eyes are veinlike and pronounced. Sometimes she has trouble with her knees, and you can see her wince when she kneels during Mass. Besides the yearly physical we are all required to take, I've come to her only sporadically over the years. She's examined us all. Besides looking after us, she relieves doctors at the medical clinic near the church three afternoons a week, more if any are on holidays. She says sleeplessness is one of the most serious problems of our age. People are so busy trying to accomplish the impossible, to juggle the various worlds they wish to exist in or are forced to exist in, that they don't take care of the most basic need of the human body: its need to sleep. Because they can keep their eyes open twenty-four hours a day, she explained once, people think they're fine and healthy. Maybe just a little tired, but nothing that can't be put off to a later date, because there are more pressing issues that need to be addressed: errands to run, money to make, kids to take care of, ways to get ahead of the competition at work. It's disgraceful, she reiterates. They don't see straight. The brain doesn't work the way it should. Everything in its proper place. The membranes become mutable. Facts are mixed up. Day is interpreted as night. You can see it in the body, she says. In brain waves. People are sleeping, dreaming, while they believe themselves to be awake.

I must try to sleep. This is her point. She does not push to know why I can't, but I offer her an explanation anyway, because I don't want her to listen to any of the rumours. I tell her it is because of the news. I can't tolerate reading another newspaper or watching another news report on television. The world is full of violence and disease and war and hypocrisy and hatred. I go on about the situation in Los Angeles between Hispanic and Black gangs, a news report by a doctor claiming sexually transmitted diseases are not only sexually transmitted any more and everyone is at risk for a massive infection from antibodies in the air, the investigation of a cover-up regarding a small town's water supply contaminated on purpose, the latest poll in the Living section stating that children of divorce are growing up angry and hostile. As I hear myself rant on in this manner, I wonder if I've gone too far. Maybe Sister Ursula suspects I've developed an unhealthy obsession or I can't distinguish between fact and speculation. She nods her head as she fills out a prescription for sleeping pills, assuring me they are very mild and many of the Sisters take them.

"Oh, yes," she says. "You'd be surprised. Often they complain of noises here. Do you hear noises?" She lifts her pen, poised to record my answer.

"I guess," I tell her uneasily. "My room's in the basement. I hear footsteps."

"But voices?"

"Not exactly," I say, a bit offended. "Not voices. I'm not crazy."

"I didn't say you were," she continues, checking my blood pressure and reflexes on the off chance my sleeplessness is an indication of a more serious medical condition. My knees and elbows react appropriately. My blood pressure is a tad high but within the normal range for my age. She cautions me to lay off the salt.

"Tell me more about what you hear," she says, after examining my ears and checking my throat, the wooden stick held uncomfortably against my tongue and then removed.

"Noise. Jumbled noise. Like my thoughts aren't letting me rest. I just can't seem to relax." I take a deep breath as she massages my breasts, my body spread out on the table. I know she is doing her job, but it feels strange to have anyone touch my body, which hasn't been touched in a non-medical way in over twenty years. I had one boyfriend before taking my vows. The Sisters in fact recommend it. They like the acolytes to have had relationships with men and sexual experience of some sort, so the choice to leave a life outside for one with God is not based on ignorance. We had talked of marriage and my father adored him because his family was tightly knit, had money, and was sending him to university to become an engineer. He ended up getting a scholarship too. He used to touch my breasts when we'd lie together on his bed. His fingers would linger over my nipples and circle them. And it felt warm and good. But there was something about his face that reminded me of my mother. His eyes squinted if the light was too bright in a room, and he couldn't handle any harsh noise, his fingers pressing against his eardrum to minimize his discomfort. The last time he spoke of marriage and of me taking classes if not a degree at a university, I told him it was over and I had decided to become a nun. It devastated him. My father refused to speak to me for months and thought I should see a doctor. My boyfriend thought I just had cold feet and waited a year before dating someone else. He was the last man to touch my body.

Sister Ursula finds no lumps in my breasts. I concentrate on my breathing and try to ignore her fingers on my flesh.

"Is there something in particular? I mean, in the news, that's getting you down? You talk about a lot of things, but is there a single one that's worse for you? That you think of right before bed, maybe?"

Sister Ursula is not my friend. She's too busy and I'm too quiet. But I've respected her the entire time I've lived here. She has performed good solid work for the last twenty years, having entered the convent only a few months before I did. The Sisters were ecstatic at the time, because interest in the holy life had already declined significantly from a stream of feminism unsympathetic to nunneries. Because we took our vows so close together in time, Sister Ursula and I were expected to become close friends. We didn't. She has her job and I have mine. She deals with people and I deal with things. But I feel her current inquiries are genuine and deserve a response. She works here. Mother Superior, who for years has suffered from rheumatoid arthritis, finds her only comfort in Sister Ursula's regular treatments. She calls her a lifesaver.

"I've been thinking about those high school kids in Colorado who killed their peers," I say, and find myself incredibly concerned about it once I bring it up. I thought I would use the news reports, always so horrible, filled with violence and amorality, to distract her from my own personal situation, but my stomach practically churns with nausea as I begin to speak about these children. Their faces on the news have haunted me, I now realize, as they surface in my mind. There is nothing in the set of their jaws or the glint of their eyes to foretell the future they would write. Although I do not mention it to Sister Ursula, in the year following my time at St. X.

School for Girls, there had been a similar incident. An eighteen-year-old boy at St. P. High School sprayed his senior class with shot-gun pellets, killing a classmate. Earlier he had raped and stabbed a woman, then set fire to his parents' home. The city of Ottawa grieved. The Catholic school was at a loss to explain the brutal violence.

"Yes," Sister Ursula says gravely. "That was particularly horrible." She brings the paper sheet I have been wearing over my half-naked body up to my chest to examine around my stomach. I imagine Kim must hate these kinds of examinations too. Although in her case the doctor is checking for life and how to help it grow, and in me for sickness and how to make it stop. Sister Ursula's hands press firmly on a spot that aches.

"Oh."

"Here?" She presses again, her hands spread against the skin, flattening my belly. "It hurts here?"

"Uh-huh." A spasm shudders through me. I grab my stomach and rub away the immediate pain. Sister Ursula prods a bit more before pulling the curtain for me to get dressed.

"I'm going to give you a prescription for some stomach medication too," she says. "Not sleeping can cause acid to accumulate in your stomach and a great deal of pain. If it doesn't work, come back to see me in a couple of days. OK?"

She doesn't manage her own pharmacy in the convent, so I will have to venture out to fill the prescription at the drugstore a few blocks away. Since it's open all night, I could wait it out until I really need the pills, but I'd cause far too much suspicion. Better to fill them as prescribed and not take them. I wonder what the side effects are. I am afraid the pills will give me more nightmares. I slide my habit back over my underwear and emerge from behind the curtain. Sister Ursula hands me the slip from her prescription pad with her coded writing on it.

"Do you think those kids were evil?" I ask her.

Sister Ursula places two fingers tentatively over her lips as if afraid of what she might say. She turns towards the window where frost has formed a pattern on the bottom of the glass. The winter light beaming in strikes her face and she squints. A butterfly is trapped between the glass and the screen. An orange monarch. I wonder if Sister Ursula has noticed. It must be dead.

"I don't know," she says hesitantly, cupping her hands together as if in prayer. Her blue eyes glaze over. "I think what they did was evil."

"But were they evil?" I am fully dressed now and relieved to be less vulnerable, to have my body to myself, but am not ready to leave Sister Ursula just yet. The thirst for a direct conversation overwhelms my desire to hide.

"They were children. I'm not sure they knew what they were doing." She places her stethoscope on her desk and picks up my chart, reading it over a final time before filing it inside a larger folder.

"They were teenagers. They kept a diary."

I can't believe I'm arguing with her over this. Especially when it's clear she isn't being evasive; she's unsure what to think about their souls. She doesn't want to damn them eternally, but she can't bear to suggest mercy either. I apologize. As Sister Ursula shuffles around searching for her appointment book, crossing off my name and taking a seat at her desk littered with stacks of papers, medical periodicals, latex gloves, and Kleenex, I lace up my shoes to get out of her way and thank her as I leave. Sister Humilita, who I hear is having problems with her bladder, is outside the door waiting her turn. I give over my place, take my prescription to be filled.

NO ONE EXPECTED HER to go through with it. You should understand that. No one expected her to comply. We thought she would cry and leave at the mention of the idea. We didn't expect it to grow the way it did, like weeds in a field, out of our hands and hungry.

Bella arrived on time. She had been told to be at Rachel's room by eight, after dinner, and Caroline, Francine, and I met a half-hour earlier. I was beginning to have doubts, and I could tell at least Francine did too. She sat on Rachel's bed, kicking her legs periodically, glancing at the clock. Caroline and Rachel spread out one of Rachel's mother's crocheted creations, a pale yellow afghan, on the floor, a makeshift mat for us all to sit on. They talked about Bella.

"Where should we seat her, in the middle? Or would that be too obvious?" Rachel asked.

"*Non,* seat her in the middle where we can all look at her from the corners. We can place the candle beside her." Caroline liked organizing; she enjoyed being next-in-command to Rachel in our ranks, sizing up the room as if it were a stage.

The candle holder was meant for ambience. It wasn't meant to be involved at all. But when Bella arrived, offering up tiny white chocolates as a gift, her hair tied up in a bun, her dark eyes expanding with curiosity, and her slim body taut as a string, Rachel was caught off guard.

The chocolate turned soft in my hands, and Francine stuffed three straight into her mouth so she wouldn't have to speak. I too didn't want to speak, hoping to leave everything up to Rachel and Caroline, but I wasn't that lucky.

"We decided we needed a singer in our group," Rachel began, motioning for Bella to sit and for Caroline to turn off the light.

The darkness was stifling for a moment, and I could have sworn there was pressure on my shoulder. *Who has come for you?* I heard, the way I heard things in dreams, unable to make out anything in front of me, or behind me, the formless ache of a body, taking up space, pushing me against walls and bedposts and trees. The same voice I heard as my mother was taken away from me in the dreams, unapologetic and cool. A male voice from the far reaches of the sky, taking away the people I loved. A match was lit, and Rachel's silver candle holder warmed the centre of the room, made our faces pale and hazy.

"I think I know what that one is," Bella said, pointing to an engraving, a circular drawing on the side of the candle holder closest to her, a curled creature. "It's called an ouroboros. It eats its own tail."

"That's gross," Caroline retorted, rolling her eyes in my direction. I bent my head to take a closer look, and the figure did look as if it were killing itself.

"Why does it do that?" I asked quietly.

"I don't know," Bella said, shrugging her shoulders. "My mother told me about it when we were reading a book on myths together. But the book didn't say why they do it."

"You mean you don't know everything?" Francine teased, her cheek still swollen with chocolate.

Bella's smile vanished while ours grew. Francine and Rachel were pleased Bella didn't know much about the etchings on the exotic candle holder. Her face was downcast, veiled by darkness as the light moved away from her, the wind from the open window changing the flame's direction.

Bella had made an effort to look nice. She wore a clear gloss on her lips and had carefully curled a few hairs outside her bun in the direction of her chin. A tiny blue beaded chain was woven around her neck. She had shown it to me earlier in the day, asking if I liked it. She wanted to wear it to the meeting. "I'm excited," she said, gently tucking the necklace into a velvet sachet. "It's my first time, you know."

I did know. Bella worked so hard on her studies that she rarely entered our adolescent world. You could catch her light on after hours, but not for the purposes of reading comic books or writing letters to put in the wall outside, but because she was practising her spelling or calculating math problems. She attended the school tea parties and birthday dinners, chatting and eating like the rest of us, but she didn't seem to know any of the girls. Outside her room, you could almost always hear her humming in anticipation of choir practice. I was starting to feel bad for what we were about to put her through, humiliation she didn't deserve; but another force held me back from warning her.

"We are The Sisterhood," Rachel began, her voice low in a mock-incantation. "We may be small, but we are a powerful group."

Francine laughed, her mouth now free of chocolates, her teeth glowing under the light. Caroline shushed her. Bella's lips began to tremble. She seemed caught between our legs on the blanket, as in a net.

"Would you like to join us?" Rachel continued.

"Yes," Bella responded after a pause. Her arm began to rise, as if she wanted to ask a question like she would in class, but quickly returned to massaging her knees.

"Well, before you join us, you must pass an initiation." Rachel stretched out the syllables in the word Initiation as if it might, like the engravings on the candle holder, intimate a secret power. Then she turned to me.

"Angela will tell you the rest."

I was taken aback. I had no idea it would be me who would be forced to ask the questions, give explanations, that I would be the one Bella would despise for tricking and scaring her. I started coughing, my hands waving in front of the candle, pretending the smoke was aggravating me, blinking my eyes. Bella stared at me intently, her lips parted. I couldn't leave or I was sure I would be teased, maybe kicked out of the group. I had agreed to the plan, after all. Did it matter who carried it out?

"Are you ..." I said after a few deep breaths, "are you a virgin?"

Bella made as if to answer, her face angled quizzically towards Rachel, her mouth open.

Francine, Caroline, and Rachel were biting their lips, stifling a few giggles. I couldn't speak and Bella wouldn't answer. Francine's blue eyes shone like wet stones in front of me, and I could hear Caroline swallowing the dryness in her mouth. The few pictures Rachel had taped to her walls, movie posters her father had given her, appeared living, part of our gathering. A young man in military uniform with a gun at his side, if stripped of his garb and manly occupation, could have passed for a girl, it occurred to me, his face curved and feminine, the delicate features incongruous with real warfare but exploited under the bright lights of the theatre.

Rachel might have tried to stop what was about to happen. I'm not sure. There was obvious dread in the room, and she began to rise, I remember, to snuff out the candle and perhaps pretend the whole thing was a jest, which it was. It was supposed to be. My left hand poking through a triangular hole in the afghan, I was reminded of Rachel's mother at her birthday party, incoherent and disorderly. And then my own mother, who slept in the dark with her hands across her burning eyes, a blanket up to her chin, her rosary curled like a cuff around her wrist. *Nothing was fair,* I decided. *Nothing about any of this was fair.*

"I said," I repeated strongly. "Are you still a virgin?"

Bella shifted uncomfortably, her left hand reaching up and fiddling with the tiny blue beads on her new necklace, sweat shining on her forehead over the flame.

"Yes," she said cautiously, her voice barely a whisper. "Aren't you?"

"No, none of us are virgins any more." I nodded to the three corners of the afghan for the other girls to return their assent. They did, like puppets, their movements exaggerated and quick. My voice took on a strength I'd never felt before, as if I were a teacher left in charge and demanding obedience to the rules.

"You can't join if you are one," I stated blankly, and Bella began rubbing her face the way an animal does when it's cleaning its fur. She wasn't even looking in my direction any more.

"But, I ... I don't want to yet. I don't understand," she mustered as she continued to rub her face and pull some dark strands of her hair in front of her eyes.

This was when Bella was supposed to make her exit, and we were to laugh. She'd be humiliated and we for once would triumph. Instead there was silence and Bella started to shake uncontrollably, her tongue edging in and out of her mouth as though parched. The silver candle holder wobbled as her leg shook against it, and she grabbed at it with her hand, close to the base, so the blanket wouldn't catch fire. A liquid stream of wax hit and solidified on the fabric. Bella's face turned red and the few tiny moles on her cheeks stood out markedly. My own heart was racing with a cultivated sense of fate.

Rachel was scratching the blanket, irritated the afghan wouldn't shed the wax, and Francine's hands groped across the carpet behind her, searching for stray chocolates. Francine's nervousness often resulted in her filling her mouth, whether with food or fingers or the ends of pencils. Soon she had a thick strand of her own red hair secured between her lips, and the soft noises of her sucking gave me a strange feeling of nostalgia to be Christine's age again. It was an odd sensation, that I was older than I was—older than these girls on the blanket. Maybe it was my fault I was left alone at St. X. School for Girls, I thought in that room. Maybe I was different, less deserving. Maybe I would be lost in the shuffle of Last Judgement, the way I always fell behind the rest of the girls when we walked through the city in a group. I had no voice. Would they abandon me too? Make me an eternal orphan? As I concentrated on the silver candle holder, the ouroboros closed its tired jaw.

"You don't have to do it with a boy. You just have to lose ... the ... skin. The skin that separates a woman from a girl." I spoke the last part hurriedly, unsure if it were true, only sure I wanted to appear knowledgeable about these things, to shock Bella.

I don't know why no one contradicted me. Rachel, Caroline, and Francine didn't budge. This wasn't part of the plan. I was supposed to tell Bella she'd have to lose her virginity to enter our club, knowing she wouldn't, and then we were to burst into laughter and she would know we had been kidding, that she hadn't been truly invited to join our club after all. I had no one else to blame now except myself. I don't know why I lied, but I set the shadows in motion.

Bella lifted her head. The skin on her cheeks and the tip of her nose was still red. Shocked yet unhurt, she was listening. Rachel was sitting on her hands, the tips purplish, and Caroline held one edge of the blanket in her fist, kneading it with her bony fingers. I gestured, unbelievingly, to the silver candle holder.

"You could use the candle holder. It's the right size, right Rachel?"

All heads turned to Rachel, who nodded assent, but I was sure, since she had been with Patrick, she would say the candle holder was probably much larger than a boy. Then we all eyed the object in question, judging its suitability for ourselves: the cold steel, the large base and small tip, the many carved ridges. I still expected Bella to leave. It was just a game. I was about to withdraw my comments, apologize for them in the morning, the candle holder sitting in judgement before me, the heat in the room claustrophobic, when Bella's voice, weaker than I'd ever heard it, said, "OK."

I was amazed and torn. I wanted to see what would happen to Bella but I didn't want to either. I had no idea whether it would work or not, or what it would mean to Bella to have her virginity snatched away from her. But curiosity won out over mercy. None of us realized Bella might be permanently harmed. Rachel took the candle, which had been burning in the shaft of the candle holder, and carried it to her dresser, where it momentarily illuminated her father's photograph. She turned the frame towards the wall, and lit a tea-candle instead. She didn't mind her father seeing her with Patrick, but not a girl by herself? I wondered. Perhaps she hadn't thought of him watching her from behind the glass until then. It was the only indication I ever had that Rachel might have been as afraid of ghosts as I was.

Caroline, Francine, and me, as I was now permitted to retreat into the shadows, sat on the bed, while Bella stood in the centre of the blanket. The yellow patch on the carpet resembled dead grass fried by a sweltering summer. Bella untucked her blouse, the white folds flattened against her skin with sweat. Her skirt remained around her waist though she hiked it up, extending her thighs to catch the material. She slipped off her underwear. They were pink,

I remember, pink like her fingertips, pink like the sugared candies shaped into hearts we bought for pennies at Woolworth's. She squatted and Rachel, once she had rubbed the wax off as much as she could, placed the candle holder on the floor between her legs and joined us on the bed. From our angle, it almost looked as if Bella were trying to find a position in which to urinate, her skirt in front of her, hiding in her modesty. Caroline sought my hand and I held on, pleading to myself over and over in my head: *Who has come for you? Who has come for you? Who has come for you?* I couldn't believe it was us.

She bore down upon it quickly. Bella moaned with pain, the suffering evident in her creased forehead alone enough to make me afraid for her. Her knees on the floor, her thighs closed around the base of the candle holder. Spots of red on yellow. Hands clenched against the bottom of her ribs, attempting to dislodge the foreign object. Her teeth clipping her bottom lip leaked a tiny trail of blood to her chin. She was still squatting, her face quivering as if in prayer towards the ceiling, wet clear snot cradled under her nose, in the space above her upper lip. She was still beautiful, if crumpled, her body slouched and surviving like a flower in a rainstorm. Black shadows from the candlelight moved over her like clouds, her face white as sheet lightning.

Rachel crouched before her. Bella fell against her and Rachel held her in her arms. The candle holder was still inside Bella, her body stuck to it, glistening with blood, red-black blood in patches over her legs. Finally, Rachel managed to balance Bella. She removed her hands from Bella's waist and grabbed the base of the protruding candle holder. I heard muffled noises from Caroline, who stuffed her face into Rachel's pillow, screaming into the feathers. Rachel cried out when she pulled, as if the object had been lodged inside her instead. They both fell against the floor. In the yellow haze, it was difficult to tell which girl was on top.

The candle holder lay discarded and stained beside them. Francine got up, her face pale, and stumbled out of the room, almost kicking Rachel and Bella on the way. Caroline was alone with her muffled screams; Rachel and Bella had become entwined like lovers. I was alone. There was no comfort for me.

When Rachel's face emerged out of Bella's embrace, it too had blood on it—an imprint on her forehead and on her blouse in the space between her breasts. Her cheeks looked chubby, bloated. Bella was curled in a ball on the floor, her hair falling out of the bobby pins, strands of black spilling from her bun, plastered to her face, her neck. Her hands pressed against her belly.

Rachel could barely speak. "Help me. God, help me," she begged through tears.

I knew we would see better if I turned on the light, but I didn't want to draw attention to Rachel's room. I didn't want to see Bella, not really see her, to be able to tell how bad it was. *God help us,* I echoed. It was the first time I'd uttered a sincere prayer within the walls of the school. Leaving Caroline on the bed, I slid to the floor and crawled over to Rachel, who was stroking Bella's hair reverently on her lap.

THERE ARE NO SUICIDES in a convent. Even now, when abortions are legal, handled by legitimate medical professionals, and where one can give power of attorney to family members to pull the plug on hospital machines, there is no such thing within our walls as a suicide. It is a sin, and the stains of sin, as Sister Marguerite would have called them, are not welcome here. The soul must be free of its own murder.

Sister Pina, five years ago, committed suicide—or euthanasia, depending what you call the deed done by a dying cancer patient. But in the convent, in the eyes of the church, she died of natural causes. She struggled, one of her breasts removed, her stomach and chest in great pain. Her skin had developed lesions, the sores shaped like hard pits of fruit along her arms. Throughout her chemotherapy, Sister Pina had trouble standing, could hardly keep solid food down, and her flesh had taken on a yellow hue not unlike jaundice. Mother Superior turned the other cheek when her nephew smuggled her tiny sealed baggies of hashish sent by crosstown courier; and most of us ignored the heavy smell clinging to her sheets and blankets, escaping underneath the crack of her door. Those who opposed were told to heed Sister Ursula, who, as a doctor, claimed no crime was being committed, only mercy. I remember sitting with Sister Pina one day, wheeling her outside to take in the spring air, admiring the red and white tulips planted throughout the rock garden in the orchard. Her hands gripped the arms of the wheelchair, steadying her as we went over the grass. She had refused the electric wheelchair Mr. Q. had obtained for her, saying it should be donated to a patient at the hospital or one who lived alone and didn't have all the Sisters she had to take care of her. She fell asleep in the sun that day, and I imagined her following the light shining down upon us: Pina rising from her chair ascending into the heavens. No wheelchairs or X-ray machines, no blood tests and cardiograms. The machines' broken screws and plates disintegrating with her bones. Imagined each pound she lost erasing a pound of memory. *What use is suffering?* I remember thinking. *What use is it if we can't leave ourselves behind?*

She took painkillers with her other medications, sometimes doubling the doses as she was told to do if she couldn't sleep. She hoarded her painkillers for five full days. The concentration of codeine in her system, we found out later, was enough to kill a horse. Sister Katherine found her in the morning. Her doctor was telephoned, an ambulance summoned. There was nothing we could do to bring her back. Her body was hard and cold as stiffened clay. The official report said Sister Pina died of cancer.

The depictions of martyrs have always seemed strange to me. The burning, the crosses. Rising fires, rising bodies. Christ, his feet nailed to the wood, his sides bleeding, crown of thorns. Joan of Arc, man's clothing over a woman's young body, draped by fire. Her heart, unburned in the ashes, sold as a relic, but the skin and bone destroyed. Saint Catherine martyred on a wheel of fire. A virgin sacrifice. Saint Christina who went further, the wheel of fire no match for her faith. She was rocked in an iron-hot cradle, sent into a burning furnace. Saint Ursula and her eleven thousand virgins slaughtered. Mutilated, tortured, piecemeal women. Saint Margaret. Saint Agatha. Saint Prisca. Saint Restituta. *Marry or burn,* St. Paul wrote. But we burn anyway. The symbols are wrong. On Ash Wednesday, the priest pronounces, *Remember, you are ashes and to ashes will return.* Ashes are the lot of us common sinners. Martyrs do not burn; they freeze.

I WASHED AND DRESSED in a black wool skirt and a black sweater that I had brought back with me at Christmastime, and I was combing through my wet hair when Sister Marguerite knocked on my door and entered the room. Mother Superior needed to speak with me immediately. Sister Marguerite looked concerned, her usually firm face softened. I held the brush in my hand, nearly paralyzed, and she opened my palm for me, releasing the brush from my grip.

"I'll go down with you," she said, placing it back on the dresser. "Take your coat. And take a book or something."

Rachel was in the hallway holding her father's hand, preparing to go down to the church for Bella's service. She too was wearing black, as was her father, whom I'd never seen in black. They were completely drained of colour. Rachel stared at me directly and I longed to run to her, beg her to take care of me, give her a sign we were all done for and Mother Superior knew everything. I was being summoned and would have to tell all, accept the shame and the punishment. The only time Rachel had spoken to me over the last three days had been to say that the silver candle holder was in the metal garbage bin outside. "We can forget about it," she had said. "I don't want it any more. My father won't notice."

I was hurried along by Sister Marguerite and began crying before we reached the stairwell, a textbook in my left hand. Finally I spilled tears over Bella's death, and this made me feel worse, knowing they had come only when I was threatened. The last glimpse I had of Rachel was her free hand, by her side, waving goodbye to me upside down.

Sister Marguerite ushered me into Mother Superior's office and left, and Mother Superior motioned to the chair on the opposite side of her tidy desk. It was free of papers, completely cleared of any books or items save a photograph of her family in a humble brown frame with a studio's blue background. In it the figures were poised on stools, with Mother Superior in her habit like a huge black-and-white banner behind them, no smile on her lips. The rest of the family seemed closer to one another. Their smiles, if not broad and beaming, implied comfort, their knees and arms naturally facing the other family members while their eyes looked towards the camera. The picture unnerved me. I had never thought of Mother Superior coming from anywhere or being a child of anyone. I rarely exchanged words with her, even in History class, and feared my face must have betrayed the guilt I was carrying. Heavy as lead, my legs numb and motionless in front of me, I wanted to sink into the floor. Mother Superior wore a silver cross that moved between her breasts as she breathed, and I couldn't take my eyes off it. I fixated on the silver like an oracle, hoping it would help me find the words to explain Bella's death.

"There is no easy way to begin," she said, pacing behind me then stopping and laying her hands firmly on my shoulders.

I jumped under her touch. Her strong and large hands were cold and intrusive. Was she going to strike me? Wait for my confession or send me to Father McC. crawling on my knees to beg for forgiveness? Would she call the police?

"Your mother died last night," she said authoritatively. "God has taken her to Him."

She continued to hold onto my shoulders as I tried to wriggle out of her grip and confront her. Had I heard right? Was Bella alive and my mother dead? Whose funeral was I dressed for? Why was her silver cross hanging so close to my cheek I could feel its coldness like bone?

She let go, put a glass of water in front of my face, and motioned for me to drink. She was a hundred years old to me, an endless survivor. Her eyes betrayed only a hint of concern, her face as stony and monumental as always, a bronze eagle. The water slid down my throat effortlessly, tastelessly. Death is a blessing in our faith. We were reminded of this daily. Sister Marguerite told us Death meant Peace. If one had cleared one's debts with a confessor, there was nothing to worry about.

"Sister Marguerite is going to drive you home immediately," Mother Superior continued, directing me towards the doorway. "It may take some time because of the storm, but you'll get there."

The door of Mother Superior's office ajar, I could see Sister Marguerite wearing her stylish green winter coat with the white faux-fur collar, a Christmas gift from a relative. My expression must have betrayed my bewilderment, for Mother Superior added, uncomfortably, "I'd take you myself, but I don't have a driver's licence." Wearily I stood, almost disappointed in this monolithic woman who could instill in me the fear of expulsion, but who was unable to take me to the trial, let alone carry out the sentence.

FATHER'S UNMARRIED SISTER, HEATHER, whom I had only heard of in passing since she lived in England, arrived by plane the day before and managed to make her way to our home by morning. During the past year, my father had told us that Aunt Heather would visit when it was more feasible. They had believed there would be plenty of time for us all to meet and to get to know each other before my mother's decline. Then my father warned Aunt Heather that Mother was very ill and asked her to come help him, since his own strength had been depleted over the months of caregiving. She had inherited the family home and a sum of money from their parents to live on and was between secretarial jobs at the time my father called. He sprang for the ticket. She had no idea when she finally arrived that the bride she had never met had already died.

She introduced herself when Sister Marguerite accompanied

me to the house on Ashbrook Crescent. Sister Marguerite had been silent for most of the trip, cautious with the car the convent communally owned and she rarely drove, doubly anxious due to the treacherous condition of the streets. I didn't know what to say to her, so I spent the time flipping mindlessly through a textbook filled with mathematical equations. We were learning algebra, how letters stand in for numbers; how to compute equations to identify the worth of a letter. It seemed too much like the Bible exegesis Sister Aline performed, the answers obvious only to those privy to the hidden meanings. Sister Marguerite regarded me distressingly at one point during the drive but said nothing. The three days had been hard on all of us. We'd all cope differently.

A woman stood directly on the threshold of our house, her auburn hair pinned on top of her head in a swirl, her makeup on thick, caking between the lines in her face. She wasn't unattractive, her eyes large and hazel, framed by black mascara and blue eye shadow, but her entire demeanour was one of exaggeration. Her face displayed an openness that startled me. She wore a purple dress with large sleeves and a black belt at the waist. Her skirt fanned out generously in front of her.

"Who are you?" I asked, suddenly fearful we had come to the wrong house or, because of my mother's death, the house had been sold overnight and these new people were using our things, sleeping in Mother's bed, and eating our food.

"I'm your Aunt Heather," she replied, taking Sister Marguerite's hand and then hugging her, burrowing her auburn hair into Sister Marguerite's shoulder. Sister Marguerite's stance held firm but she accepted the embrace. "Joseph's sister, from England."

Sister Marguerite turned to me as if for confirmation. I shrugged, dropping my book on the doorstep, irritated underneath my coat by the black wool skirt I was wearing, eager to find refuge from the cold, but unable to get past this woman who stood in my way. I didn't care who she was.

"You must be Angela," she said, cornering me next for a hug, but I pressed myself close to Sister Marguerite's side, distressed to touch a relative I'd barely heard of and had never met. She seemed hurt but smiled at Sister Marguerite apologetically, rubbing her elbows in the chill of the open door. Sister Marguerite pinched my arm and gave me a stern look of disapproval at my impoliteness. She was letting me go. I dropped my hand from her side to enter the house.

"Hello, Aunt Heather," I said. "My mother's dead."

AFTER MY APPOINTMENT WITH Sister Ursula, I run into Kim. She waits by my room, I gather, to reconcile after our exchange in the orchard. I've been avoiding her for a week, and though I don't mean to hold a grudge, I find that I do. When the Sisters meet at Mass or in the common room or the cafeteria, I make sure to lodge myself between them so Kim cannot sit with me. But I keep an eye on her. I want her to know she's hurt me and to judge whether she's hurting too.

Flustered, I am ashamed at my pettiness when I see Kim waiting there, her body slouched as she sits with her knees up against my door. Kim's presence here is ill-timed. I am reminded of my youth as if it were a flag waving over me. As Kim's young face looks up, I could be easily convinced I am standing in a hallway at St. X. School for Girls and she is quietly waiting for one of her young friends. With her hands against her cheeks, holding her chin up, she could be daydreaming about boys and dances, mentally calculating whether she has enough money to buy magazines in the Market. She's even wearing a blue cardigan, torn at the elbows, similar to the style we wore then as uniforms. One uniform for another. This is what I've accomplished.

I have just returned from Sister Irene's room. She was more lucid than normal and showed me she could hold the can containing her liquid meal by herself with her one good hand. She was straining, but she did keep the can up. Her fingers gripped the rim while the working side of her face spoke of victory. She even gave me a gift.

Sister Irene has come to the point where she is giving away her few possessions. If you walk by her room when the door is open, she'll scream as best as she is able with her partly numb mouth, then point at an object until you leave with it. When I went to see her this afternoon and read to her the Psalm *The Lord is my Shepherd; I shall not want,* she waved her middle finger jaggedly in the air. I didn't notice at first where she was pointing, because I was reading the lines she likes best as she attempted a smile, her head bent to her aching shoulder. *I will fear no evil, for Thou art with me.* Her skin has moved past its yellow hue to a dull brown. She is unable to wash her face without help, so I held a cool cloth to her forehead, wiped spittle from her chin, crumbled crackers into a bowl until they turned to dust. She likes to lick the salt.

She focussed on the typewriter, the same one I use when she needs to send letters. I suppose she thinks all her letters have been sent. It looks like an antique, although any typewriter must now be antique. But this one is made of metal, with the arms of each of the keys visible. I helped her after her initial stroke, when she wanted to inform her relatives and friends about her illness and ask them to come. The only one who heeded her plea was an aunt, so old and thin she could barely climb the two concrete stairs to the door of the convent. I felt little pity for Sister Irene at the time. She had been so critical of everyone, not just in words but in her actions, that I felt she didn't deserve to be remembered. But as I carry the typewriter back to my room, I think otherwise. She deserves to be remembered like anyone else.

And then there is the thing I can't shake from my mind. The keys on her typewriter. All are in working order except for the small *a*; the lower half of the letter does not complete the full loop back up to its curved spine. I typed the alphabet three times on a sheet of paper before leaving Sister Irene's room, demonstrating for her benefit how happy I was to receive this present from her. Each time the small *a* snagged. I hadn't noticed before. When I typed my form letter, I used only capital letters. I typed out my name. I pressed all the other keys. The ribbon is good, black, dark. A single key faulty. This same letter was faulty in my name on the package that brought the candle holder to me. *Who has come for you? How can it be one of us?*

Kim moves with the sound of my shoes on the tiled floor.

"I came to ... are you all right?" she says, using the wall to support her weight as she gets up. I do not offer her my hand to help, wanting to make it clear I am not pleased with her, but with the heavy typewriter in my hands, I also do not have a hand free.

My knees are sore. I need to sit, and I can't feign the motions of a casual conversation, so I just jut my chin to indicate she should move away from the door. She complies while I struggle with the door handle. I rush to the dresser, where I rest the typewriter. Kim tenderly inches her face in around the corner.

"Do you need anything? I can get it for you. Sister Ursula says I'm doing much better."

"I just need to catch my breath," I tell her and plop on my bed with a sigh.

"Oh."

She shuffles in, wearing one of the skirts with an elastic waistband that I salvaged from the rummage sale. It's a little large on her, like everything else, but she manages to keep it up by tucking her shirt into it. Her neck is slight, and the oversized clothes make her head appear larger than it is. A round face, like a doll's. The skirt should be hemmed and taken in. I'll direct her to Sister Humilita for the alterations, I think, before realizing she probably doesn't care about her appearance here in front of a bunch of celibate old women anyway. Let her fix it herself. Sister Humilita has enough to do. The old-fashioned wool habits have been replaced with cotton ones, which rip and fade more easily. Yet she makes do with them as long as possible, because it is a sin to waste anything.

"Are you just going to stand there staring at me?" I say, petulantly resentful. I'm worried about who she's been talking to, unwittingly perhaps exposing me to further scrutiny.

"I wanted to apologize," she says in a half-convinced voice as she shuts the door behind her and walks over to the bed. I don't move to make room for her to sit with me, although she could if she wanted to squeeze in close.

"Don't worry about it," I tell her. "I've long forgotten about it."

"Oh."

I've hurt her feelings now. Well, she hurt mine, I tell myself. Does she expect us all to spend twenty-four hours a day on her case? Does she think we have no one else to think about, no problems of our own? I'm exhausted by her ignorance. By her need for us to help her, save her. I want her to understand she is just one of many in this world whom we are meant to protect. She's nothing special. And if she doesn't appreciate us, we can find others who do.

"Look," I tell her, "I'm not feeling well. I need to rest."

Her hands are shaking. She has cupped them together in a handshake behind her back.

"Why don't you go see Sister Josie or Sister Sarah? Sister Bernadette? They're always willing to listen to a good story—aren't they?"

Kim doesn't respond to my comment, perhaps because there is no response. She hasn't had much experience conversing with adults, and she acts as if she hasn't heard me at all. She begins to admire the picture of Christine and me in the frame on my dresser. She ignores the candle holder and the typewriter. They don't seem to have any significance to her. In my mind, I tick off a point in her favour.

"You must miss your sister sometimes," she says, squinting for a closer view.

"I should."

Kim is in profile, but I can tell she's struggling to ask me something. Her mouth opens and closes and opens again. The tip of her tongue peeks out the side of her lips and retreats inside. Meanwhile,

I rub my forehead to fight off a headache I know will be full-blown by the end of the evening.

"I've been trying to figure out what I'm going to do … when I leave here." Her hand lingers on the oak wood of the dresser.

"That's good. It's about time you made plans."

She takes her scolding well, nodding submissively. "I just still can't decide anything. I don't know where I should go or if I should keep the baby. I don't want to be another mother on welfare who does nothing and is nobody."

"Don't you think that's going to depend on you?" I ask her. "I mean, that's why welfare's there—if you need it."

"But I don't want to take welfare," she says, covering her face with her hands and starting to sob. "I don't want to bring up a kid and just be poor. Just get by. I don't want to have to do it by myself."

Kim lifts her head and stares at the wall behind my dresser as if it were a mirror. She has begun to envision her future. It isn't a bright one, and I don't know if I should contradict her. She's fifteen, after all, and if she does keep her baby, what would she be able to offer him or her? The kind of life she doesn't want and it will resent, most probably. A life of counting pennies, of hardship, of hunger. Without an education, what would she be able to do? I cannot speak of these things with her, because suffering and poverty are accepted virtues within our walls. Yet, the only reason Mr. Q. hasn't forced her into school is because her parents don't want her back and Sister Ursula recommended she stay out until the end of her term. But what then? Certainly mothers have brought up children at sixteen before, but in today's age? Without a man? She's close enough to sixteen she won't be forced to give it away. She needs to decide.

"You could give it up," I say softly.

She shakes her head and turns around, meeting my eyes as I slide my hips to the end of the bed to give her room if she wants to sit. Her cheeks are wet, her olive face flushed pink. "I can't. I can't. I can't bring it into this world if I'm not going to take care of it. I can't."

"Then what, dear?"

She hoists her arms up over her head, her hands in two tight fists in a motion to bear down upon her belly. They fall like hammers. I let out a cry just as her fingers unravel before striking her own flesh.

She collapses on the bed and forces herself into my embrace. I hug her tightly, yet try not to apply too much pressure, not wishing to harm the baby, as I believed she wished to harm it. I know from my own teenage years that girls get ideas into their heads in such situations. Ride bicycles or use turkey basters, jump down flights of stairs or drink bottles of whisky. She's probably heard of other ways. She may be seven months pregnant and the clinics won't take her, but someone will. There's always someone willing to say they'll save you.

"Listen to me," I say, my voice cracking, unable to hold back the sorrow within me. "You can't do that. You can't think like that. You need to be brave."

I want to cup her jaw in my hands, force her to listen. She folds in my arms, the lingering smell of her morning shampoo in my face. I curl my hands around her until she decides to break free.

"I'm so sorry," she cries. "I'm so sorry. You're not feeling well and I shouldn't be here."

She's being sincere and I wonder how awful I must look to make her afraid for my health in her own distress. She must have heard about the wine from one of the Sisters. Maybe even Sister Ursula. I grip her wrists with my hands. They are delicate, like twigs. Her eyes, a muddy brown, are deeply set, the bottom rims edged with a row of tears.

"I hate my baby. I hate it. I wish it wasn't going to be born."

"Don't say that," I say strongly. "Don't you dare curse a life like that."

She tries to rise from the bed, but I hold her with the little strength I have left. My whole head is pounding and the room has turned into a cave, where we have little light and only each other.

"You see, Kim," I begin as she calms enough to listen to me and fumbles in her shirt pocket to produce a tissue. "I've been upset because of an anniversary. An anniversary of someone's death."

I cannot continue. The words stick like hair in a drain. Refuse to be extracted.

"Your mother?"

"My mother? No, not my mother. Not just my mother." But I'm surprised she knows. The Sisters have shared more with her than I imagined. I didn't even realize they knew the depth of that grief in me. I didn't know they thought it worthy of mention. For a few years after entering the convent, I could been seen crying on her birthday and on the anniversary of her death, but after that my grief was bound to this room, within these walls, where I believed no one could hear me. Has anyone been down here listening? Visiting my mother's grave once a year ought not to cause this kind of talk. But then there was Christine's visit, and they must know it will be the twenty-fifth anniversary of my mother's death soon. Our faith is big on anniversaries. Our faith is also big on suffering. And I know since I've spent nights with my ear pressed against the doors of other rooms, I shouldn't assume no one has listened at mine. Maybe Kim herself has. She doesn't make much noise when she walks and likes to go about in bare feet. Last week, when the air was warmer, I saw them outside my window. Square toes, blunt. The wet snow between them.

Kim is a sponge here, collecting information, but she can't know what fits where, how to put things into a pattern. No wonder she's confused. We pull at her in different directions, each trying to mould her into our own individual vision of the future. She can't make decisions and many don't want her to. If we all admitted it, that's what we'd find. No one truly wants her to help herself. We want to do the helping. It is the cornerstone of our profession. We need to be needed.

"No, a friend. A girl I knew when I was young. She was your age." I can't bear the holes in her cardigan. The girl is practically an orphan, I think. She's got nothing. She folds the tissue into square sections, keeping her face away from mine. I watch her movements from underneath a veil of approaching tears. The small orders of our lives.

It is my turn to collapse against her. And we cling to each other, her hands pulling on the material of my habit, me pushing against her neck with my shoulder blade. I can feel her whimpering breath and the skin of her cheek against my own. And it feels good to cry. I can vaguely make out the picture of Christine and me on her wedding day, the restaurant filled with clinking glasses, sisters sharing a moment together amidst the celebration. Two women who can rarely manage to spend an hour together without feeling miserable. The picture is where my eyes rest, regardless. Pulled to her. The candle holder momentarily out of sight. Christine's warm smile and turquoise wrap shine in my direction. I do miss her. I've missed her for years. Kim is young and scared. And though I've lived longer, I'm right here with her.

MY FATHER INTERROGATED THE nurses on night duty in my mother's wing, the doctor who had admitted her to the Children's Hospital, and the new specialist, a recently acclaimed ground-breaker in degenerative disorders. He generally worked only on children, but decided to take on my mother's case as it was so unique. The Children's Hospital, being brand new in Ottawa, was equipped with the latest technology, and my mother was given her own room in a research wing without many children. My father gathered up the facts of that night and held onto them with a confused but submissive complacency. The few facts were that she had previously been seen by the said specialist and complained of pain in her hands and trouble sleeping. This was in the afternoon, and later she was observed by an intern in the common room watching television. She asked a nurse to wheel her into her room, the wheelchair an apparatus provided for her over the last two weeks to help her manoeuvre around the hospital and for moral support, so she could attempt to make it to the washroom by herself instead of having to rely on the nurse or her bedpans. Her eyes were sore and she kept her rose-coloured glasses on, despite the doctor's optimistic prediction that she would soon be able to discard them and rely on specially prescribed bifocals. The operation had gone well, the healing around the lids improved by creams and drops over the last week, only her left eye covered with a bandage and patch to keep foreign matter from causing infection. Medical attention was now being concentrated on her dwindled muscles, her flesh grinding into bone at an astonishingly quick rate. After eating unsalted soup for dinner, she had been given her dose of night medication by the nurse on duty, one my father knew by first name and could recognize. The doctor had raised her sleeping pill dose by a slim margin to ensure she received the rest necessary to stabilize her condition. The two nurses on duty in her wing remembered nothing abnormal occurring, and they swore to their own alertness, corroborated by a few teenage patients who rang their buzzers in the night. When the morning nurse came by my mother's room early to take blood tests and dispose of urine bags, she found my mother's bed empty. The other nurses and the resident doctors on duty were immediately notified. They searched the wing first, the common room and the visiting lobby, the washrooms and the employee lunch room, expecting to find that she had fallen asleep after seeking out a snack or water. Then they searched the rest of the floor, the cafeteria, and the gift shop on the ground floor. They paged her over the PA system; they left messages with her doctors. Then they called the police. The hospital, my father was told, was officially shocked and bewildered and unable to uncover any concrete evidence of what had ensued on the night of the worst snowstorm of the season. It made no sense. How a woman drowsy and disoriented on painkillers and sleeping pills, who had just had an eye operation and had lost the workings of the lower half of her body, had passed completely undetected by staff or patients, and had walked through the snow more than five hundred feet in her hospital robe, was mind-boggling. If the event hadn't ended so tragically, her doctor said, they would have called it a miracle.

My mother was discovered beside the fountain. Not by the police or by hospital staff, but by a middle-aged man who had brought in his nephew with a case of seafood poisoning to Emergency. As he aided his nephew back to his car after the doctor confirmed he would be fine with some rest, the early light of dawn striking the new snow with blinding intensity, he thought he saw a half-buried article of clothing, a scarf, most likely lifted off its owner by the winds. He wasn't going to investigate further. The scarf was simply something he noticed out of the corner of his eye. The parking lot exit would have taken him in a curve in the direction from the fountain, towards a main access road to the highway. The oak trees lining the sides of the road would not have offered him a second view of the piece of clothing. The hospital had been sent a single snow removal truck for the night, to clear a route for ambulances. He had only to follow slowly behind the truck, concentrate on the signs, keep away from the snowbanks. He was cold and tired, and between the door of the hospital and the door of his car, his coffee, bought at the machine in the lobby, had chilled. But as he waited for his car to warm up, the pale-blue cloth waving in the wind like a flag nagged at him, the implication dawning that something must be weighing it down.

The fountain was built close to the Children's Hospital, near the separate lodging for parents whose children were being treated indefinitely. Drained of water in the winter, upon the first signs of spring the fountain would be running. Designed with a concrete base a foot and a half deep, it was painted a soft green and used as a wishing well by families and their children. Pennies, dimes, and quarters lay at the bottom, each thrown with the hope of getting well, of getting out of the hospital, of returning to warm beds and school recesses. The water flowed out from rubber tubes attached to the bottom of the statue erected in the middle of the wading pool: a blunt outline of a girl and a boy holding hands, without faces or eyes, two-dimensional as stick figures on paper, a triangular skirt and a curved head with the hint of curls at the shoulder to indicate a girl, and a round head with two rectangular legs to indicate the boy. The hands indistinct, melded together in the middle.

As the man drew closer, leaving his nephew to rest in the back seat, the notion grew that there might be a child caught in the snow by the fountain. He thought of the children in the hospital and how tempting the fresh snow must look to them, locked up inside. How many hours had it been? He panicked and started to run, his boots sinking into the two feet of snow, its icy crust breaking into clumps, spilling into his boots. It is difficult to run after a snowstorm when the winds are still strong. The air has weight and the coldness burns in the throat, practically bleeds through the lungs. The man was sweating profusely by the time he reached the pale-blue cloth furiously beaten by the wind.

There was definitely a form beneath the snow. He brushed off the top surface and began to dig at the surrounding ice. My mother was kneeling in the snow, prostrate, her fingertips closed together in a V around her face, thumbs frozen against her cheeks. He still believed it was a child he was collecting, her head freed of her wig, small tufts of brown hair around her ears and the back of her neck. The skin was laced a whitish-blue, similar to the hue of the cloth, which made him wipe his eyes, thinking his mind must be playing tricks on him. When he dug deeper and brushed away more snow, he saw the wrinkles on her hands, her face. What protruded was a larger form than he had supposed. Her breasts shrivelled into drained sacks, he did not know he had found a woman until he had fully dug a ring around her. The cloth was her hospital gown, which had risen in the night. She was bare and exposed, hairless between her thighs as well. He had no thoughts about how she had gotten there, only that he must get her out, digging and digging with his hands, alternately crying out and jumping, waving to attract the attention of anyone moving by in a car, the ambulance attendants by the entrance, or a patient gazing out the window.

He took off his coat and wrapped it around my mother, hanging the material off her shoulders as he did not wish to disturb her pose, afraid he might break one of her bones, his purpose to try and warm up her body. Poor man, poor Samaritan. Pulling her gently out of her white grave. He cradled her with his arms, lifted his eyes to heaven. When no one answered his shouts, he hoisted her up all along praying for her delivery. She was already dead. Her spirit had drifted in the night with the snow.

It is hard for me to envision him otherwise, the man who found my mother and attended her funeral, who finally managed to attract the attention of the ambulance driver and a doctor and two nurses who were working on that shift, who held my mother's back against his chest, her icy legs across his elbows, making the upper half of his body into a moving chair. A perfect stranger. The man who thought he was saving a child, but didn't turn away or feel less rage when he knew she was a woman. Knew deep in his heart she was already dead. There was nothing left to do except notify the family, if she had one. I imagine him perplexed by her pose, uprooted from the ground itself, her bones making a statue of her pain. Imagine the ground crying out as he set her free.

He came to the visitation with a bouquet of flowers, his wife waiting nervously in the background, uncomfortable in the presence of grieving strangers. But he had felt compelled to come, pay his respects and deliver a message. Like an angel, he came professing faith, said to my father as he shook his hands: "I came to tell you her face was serene. She did not look afraid. Not afraid at all." My father, holding onto his hands as if they were buoys in turbulent water, nodded in agreement. "She's made me think there is a place for us, after all this. There must be. She was praying. And she was not afraid." When he approached Christine and me on the cushioned bench between my father and Aunt Heather, he shook our timid hands as well, said he was sorry he hadn't been able to save her. Christine ran into his arms and hugged him, and his wife seemed flustered, coming up behind him and tugging on the back of his coat jacket. I joined him at the coffin when he knelt as a Catholic and crossed himself. They stayed for a quick coffee and left. He held my hand, that man, who from then on believed in a world beyond this one because he believed my mother had been praying peacefully when death arrived. He laid a bouquet of white roses down by the coffin's feet as one might at an icon.

My father, my sister, the doctors—all believe my mother died praying. But I know better. She prayed with her hands in her lap, with her rosary, not with them up at her face where her eyes burned. If she went to the fountain to pray, it wasn't for peace but for forgiveness. She had a way of knowing things, my mother. About her children. She could be found waiting upset by the door when one of us hadn't even been late coming in, sure that we had hurt ourselves playing, scratched a knee or bruised an ankle, and we had. I believe she knew what had happened to Bella. If she prayed, she prayed for the children. Children who were playing adults. Children who were going to be judged. I can hear her still, trapped in the walls of my convent room, whispering into my ears as I try to rest. *Angela, no, not you, you could not have done that to a child. A child. How could you be so blind?* Her hands were held up against her face, I know, because she was shielding her disbelieving eyes.

· · ·

THE SCENT OF LILIES followed our sleepwalking bodies, the sense of smell the only one that refused to be numbed. Lilies in decorative vases, in pots, in wreaths attached to the two ends of the coffin, on the pews of the church, in the entrance of our room at the funeral home, in Mother's black wig as she lay in her casket, preserved and alone. Mourners commented on the beauty of the arrangements and decorations, on the lovely scents. But we were cornered, molested by their pervading presence. The lilies bloomed, grew, filling up the air with her absence. Their long white faces, undisturbed, flouting us. Their petals smooth and silky. My mother's face powdered white and pink, her skin frozen in her slumber, a few lilies propped in her stony hands.

Here is Death, they said to me. *Pluck.*

KIM DOESN'T UNDERSTAND. She thinks that if you want to be a nun, the Church lets you be a nun. I'm light-headed, having spent Friday fasting and then taking a glass of wine after Mass. It is no longer required that we fast, but I like to do it every Friday. My body feels cleansed after the purging. Sometimes I sleep better. Having not had the courage to take the sleeping pills Sister Ursula prescribed and let my dreams, whatever they may be, take hold of me, wine is my last resort.

"It's a much more difficult process than that," I tell her.

She has come to Mass this evening with me and a few of the other Sisters, and has offered to keep me company while I go through this month's records for the rental of the basement. Besides the biannual rummage sale and the Lost and Found, this is my other responsibility. I am the person people call at the church office if they want to use the basement for events or meetings. My main client, of course, is Mr. Q. The government offers us a decent rate and is always on time with their payments. We hold addicts' meetings, mostly Alcoholics Anonymous, Alanon, and Narcotics Anonymous, but there is also an Overeaters Anonymous group that meets twice a month, plus workshops on finding work, producing résumés, on keeping a marriage healthy and functional, on stress management for the modern mother. At least four evenings a week the basement of the church is rented. Outside on the steps the clients wait and smoke cigarettes and drink coffee beforehand and during breaks. Sister Katherine once said to Father B. that if it weren't for the stained-glass windows and the heavy doors with a crucifix above the entranceway, a passerby could mistake our church for a rehabilitation centre. Father B. didn't mind. He laughed. "Isn't that what we are anyway? A rehabilitation centre for the soul?"

I think Kim is kidding, anyway. A pregnant fifteen-year-old girl who wants to become a nun is a bad joke along the lines of "A bishop, a rabbi, and an insurance agent walk into a bar"—the kind of jokes Christine loves to tell me over the phone. She thinks it proves she's accepted my lifestyle if she's able to laugh at it. Once she even sent me a cigarette lighter in the shape of a nun, the fire shooting out of her mouth. I threw the nun lighter in the garbage bin outside the first chance I got when no Sisters could see me.

"I realize that," Kim says. She points to a blank spot on my calendar for an upcoming Saturday night. "You'd think something would be happening here. They had a wedding every Saturday at my other church. Every single week. I loved watching them from my house, hearing the bells ring."

"That's the only time we ring the bell now, at weddings. We used to ring it for Mass, but the neighbours protested. Anyway, you can't foretell these things," I say. "People don't fall in love on our schedule."

I wonder if Kim wishes to be married. I can picture her in a white dress with a modest train, an empire waistline to push up her small breasts, and a white veil over her olive face. She'd be stunning, virginal with her petite stature, if she weren't pregnant. Yet I can still see her in my mind's eye, walking down the church aisle while the Sisters sit in their pews, while Sister Josie and Sister Sarah are forced through our connection with Kim to attend the same event and bring the same flowers, while Father B. prepares for the New Testament readings. But I cannot conjure up a man for Kim; Kim walks down the aisle by herself, her middle swollen to the point of bursting, two weeks overdue, as if the marriage being consecrated were not between husband and wife but between mother and child. The daydream thrills me.

Kim is in black today and could almost pass for one of us Sisters. She probably picked the black skirt and black sweater on purpose to blend in. She is still staring at the empty space on the calendar, circling it with her index finger.

"I think I'll phone back the gentleman who wants to give traditional Polish folk dancing lessons here. Maybe he'll start right away." He had spoken on the answering machine of the fact that dancing eases the soul. He also said he was willing to buy out someone else's time slot, because the girls who take lessons are generally from wealthier immigrant families who want their children to carry on traditions from back home.

"Do you have to fill them all?" Kim asks.

"No, but I need to try. The Bishop phoned again last week. Father B. is concerned about money. It will ease his burden if I can."

I am about to dial when Kim speaks again.

"Well, what do you need to do to become a nun?"

I put my pen down on the booking calendar. "Are you serious?"

"Why else would I ask?" says Kim, taking up the pen and biting the cap. "I mean … I'm just curious."

"Well, all right. First a prospective candidate for our convent, for example, needs to be recommended by a priest who's known her for at least two years and can attest to her character, her religious training, and to her honest desire to live a life in the service of God. Then she needs to have contact with the convent and the Sisters within for another two years after that. It's like an internship or residency, so she can decide if the life is really suited to her needs, or if she would like to try another convent. Then she is also required to go through a medical evaluation. She needs to be in good health. A psychological evaluation including a personality test is also mandatory."

"What? Why?" Kim glares with distaste while doodling on a piece of scrap paper.

"The life here is not for everyone. People think we live in silence and in solitude, but as you know we live with other people. More people than those on the outside do. We form an entire society, with rules and customs. A prospective candidate must be assessed as to whether she will be able to perform her duties, whether she will be an asset to the institution. Just like a job interview."

I am upsetting Kim. She doesn't want to hear about the

procedures. She wants to believe anyone can find refuge here if they so choose. She twists her lips and folds her arms in defiance of what I say to her. The cuffs of her sleeves extend past her arms, hiding her fingers. I wish we had a pamphlet on hand in the church to answer these questions, like those they have in the hospital for various medical conditions. Are you sleeping well? Have you gained weight? Ours could say: Have you heard voices? Do you think living with forty or fifty other women is your ideal vision of life? Kim doesn't want to be a nun. But she does want to live here, I gather. And she knows she can't stay. Her time is running out.

"Is it your soul you're worried about?"

She does not answer, regards my question as condescending. Or misunderstanding. I've never been good at assessing which when someone is silent.

"Are you worried about God?" I prod again. If Kim can barely talk about her child, who will become a reality in the next two months, I'm not sure why I think she'll be able to talk about God. But she tries.

"I want ... want ... I want ..."

I can relate. It is difficult to ask for what we want, especially when we cannot know if the request is acceptable or not.

"You want to be saved, maybe? From your life?"

Kim unfolds her arms, her thin ringless fingers peeking out from her sleeves. She makes a motion with her thumb as if trying to pinpoint her words before speaking them.

"I want comfort. I want to feel safe." Her eyes reveal an earnestness I've rarely encountered from her, or from anyone. She is stripped bare in front of me now. This must be how my mother looked when I listened through the walls and she asked father why she was being punished. Did she too want comfort and safety? I do not know how to answer Kim.

"Do you think that's what nuns have? Comfort and safety?"

"No. I guess not," she replies, unsatisfied, dropping the pen on the table and placing her hands flat out, squarely on her knees. "I know you live a hard life and all. But don't you feel good? Like you've been given something, I mean. That someone loves you? Maybe that you understand the mysteries of life?"

The Lord works in mysterious ways. Father B. lectured on it in Mass today. He would be pleased that one of his fold has been taking the time to meditate upon his teachings.

Oh, Kim, those things have never mattered much to me. I don't think the Lord works in mysterious ways. People live. People die. Some have babies, some do not. Some are poor, others are rich. Some get married, others stay single. A man gets hit by a car crossing the road to meet his lover. A child falls off a playground swing and wounds her knees. A bullet shatters glass. Body counts rise. People blow out candles on birthday cakes. We all return to dust and ashes. This seems fairly clear. Death, the equalizer of all life. His ways are not mysterious at all. In fact they are quite predictable.

But you, Kim? You are mysterious to me.

The mystery is why we carry on. Why any of us carry on. I glance at Kim's belly and think that it is mysterious. Not because it is life. But because it need not be.

"Comfort is for the dead," I say. "Death is backwards."

Kim laughs and I have no idea whether what I've said is funny or if she's laughing at me. Or maybe she's laughing at the idea she could have wanted to be a nun at all after living with the lot of us. Especially when she has to deal with our odd talk sometimes and our badgering and our harassing her to eat. She also knows that all of her motions and movements are recorded, noted, and discussed. That even we, who have come together under what would seem to be common beliefs, disagree with each other continually and have as much or as little in common with each other as strangers meeting at the coffee shop outside our church. Kim is more confused now than when she first entered this place. She is probably starting to learn that this is the real mystery of us all.

ON ASH WEDNESDAY, AFTER a solemn Mass in which our choir did not perform, but sat in the front pews on the left side of the church, Rachel and I went outside before afternoon classes.

Rachel had just checked the crack in the wall, under the brick at the corner, and was holding in her mittened hands a message from Patrick, rolled up, which she did not unravel. On her forehead was Father McC.'s thumbprint where he had blessed her with ash. We hadn't spoken in over a week, since I had been home for my mother's funeral. I had hoped my father would keep Christine and me longer, but he gave us up as soon as Aunt Heather was on her plane back to England. He shipped us off to get back to work, he said. But really he was paralyzed by my mother's death, wandering around the neighbourhood in his nightclothes, sitting up late by the fire watching the embers turn black. He had packed away none of her things, floating through the house like a ghost, haunting her, haunting the memory of where she had been. He mumbled few words to himself, but twice I caught him fingering her discarded rosary, saying, "There is no one to remind us any more."

Christine put up little fuss, which surprised me. She left with barely a sound, her school bag strap across her shoulder, a taxi waiting to take her back to her school, as a doctor had instructed my father that he shouldn't operate a vehicle under the medication he had been given to get through the week of visitations, the funeral, and the wake. It was I who had a tantrum.

"Please ... don't make me go back. Don't make me," I pleaded, catching up to him as he paced up and down the hallway, my arms tentacles trying to find the right place to latch on to.

He avoided me, shaking his head, pounding his hands against his sides. His breath smelled strong and sweet, and I knew he had been drinking after Aunt Heather departed. He had taken a bottle and a glass of ice and had closed the door of his bedroom. He hadn't showered or brushed his hair, which had an enormous cowlick—the kind Christine would get that Mother flattened out with water and a comb.

"Daddy, don't."

I didn't know how to explain that I couldn't go back to St. X. School for Girls knowing Bella was gone and my mother with her. My only consolation was that at least my mother had company. But it frightened me too. I imagined she had traded my love for Bella's. What haunted me most was that I was sure Bella deserved her love more than I did.

"But Daddy, I don't know how—"

My father locked himself in the washroom, pretending to take a shower. The water ran down uselessly, as I could see through the crack in the keyhole of the door that he was sitting on the toilet seat,

fully clothed, with his head in his hands. Not crying, but in a posture of prayer or sickness, an anger shaking his entire body like a
tremor. I knew the ground below him was frozen. Like the ground
my mother died in. My father had turned to ice.

"Does he want to see you again?" I asked Rachel, pointing to
her note.

"Who cares? He's not that great. I'm going to throw it out."
She didn't throw it out, though there was a trash can beside us, and
she refused to read it in front of me.

We sat on the remains of a snowman in our winter coats and
boots. The air was crisp and Rachel's hair flitted across her face.
My cheeks were cold, and I rubbed them with my mittens, blowing hot air onto my fingers to warm them up. Some of the other
girls were having a snowball fight, the white balls flying haphazardly through the winter day. Sister Beatriz, a nun whose primary
job was supervision, walked around the fence, supposedly the
chaperone of our lunch hour, ignoring them and their game. It was
my first day back and Rachel had not mentioned anything to me
about my mother's death, although the nuns had informed the
girls, and Father McC. had said the Ash Wednesday Mass in her
name. Her silence hurt me; I wanted Rachel to acknowledge what
I had been through. Since my father was unable to comfort me,
I ached for Rachel to.

"Esperanza is leaving," Rachel said finally, tucking her note
into her zippered pocket. "She told me so. At the end of term."

"We're all leaving at the end of term," I answered. St. X.
School for Girls was a junior school, and those of us in the upper

year would enter various high schools the following fall. We would need to start all over, at the bottom rung, making friends and finding our place in the new order.

"I know, but I kind of figured she'd always be here."

Rachel's green eyes glowed amidst the whiteness as she looked up and caught a snowflake on her chin.

"She's getting married," she said, getting up from our stump, brushing off her coat. "I didn't even know she had a boyfriend."

Neither did I. The night I caught Esperanza with Mr. M. came back to my mind. Certainly Mr. M. would find out she was getting married and leaving the school. But then again, as I had reminded Rachel, we all were, and Rachel being an only child, he would no longer have any reason to come back to St. X. School for Girls. It occurred to me then that he wasn't going to lose Esperanza, or Rachel, but all of us; his many daughters. He would be forced to stay at home with his wife, absent in mind if not in body. We were sentencing him to a life of loneliness.

I followed Rachel to the door, where I thought we would enter, but instead she sat down on the steps, muddy from the slush mixed with the dirt on the soles of boots coming in and out, the constant traffic.

"You know what they think about Bella, right?" Rachel asked, her left hand in her pocket, digging around, taking out a tissue to wipe her nose.

"Yeah."

It was Caroline who had told me how Bella was found. Not Rachel. Caroline, who had heard it from Esperanza, before

Esperanza was told by Mother Superior to keep her mouth shut. She would have told Rachel anyway at some point, but she told Caroline the day it happened, unable to contain herself. She told her because there was no one else to tell, having informed the nuns that they needed to call an ambulance. Caroline said Esperanza was crying; she kept crossing herself and saying that our school was a bad place. *Haunted*, Esperanza had said. *Haunted since before we came here. The dead here. The dead here stay. Haven't you heard them, crying in the night? Asking to be dug up. The children with their eyes covered died not knowing where they were.* "A bunch of nonsense," Caroline protested. "Just fooling with our heads because we call her Witch. She was just saying things because she'd found her and was scared." But we all knew the rumours, had played upon them in The Sisterhood meetings: the tales of the nurses who cared for the sick and laid them under the floors because there was no room to house them. The children without parents, without relatives, their arms broken, or lungs failing, their hair and teeth falling out, their skin filled with lesions. *The orphans.*

"Esperanza believes it," Rachel said, after noticing my distress, thinking it was because I thought we would get caught for what happened to Bella. But I wasn't afraid of that any more. The funeral was over and no one suspected us of anything. Rachel told me the silver candle holder was in the garbage. I wished it had been burned, but at least it had been delivered to the outskirts of the city, to a dump. The nuns only suspected Bella of a crime she never had the need to commit. "She believes Bella did it ... it, you know?"

I didn't want to imagine it. The nuns and the doctor could not figure out what object Bella had used to perform the abortion. There was nothing but blood and sheets around her. There was no likely object in her room nor in the washroom when they checked. Bella had washed away the blood in the shower stall, and she had taken her bloody washcloth with her, where it was found amongst the piled sheets. In the end they decided it wasn't necessary to know. Desperate girls used whatever was around—a coat hanger, knitting needles, eating utensils. They assumed Bella probably didn't know enough about such things, certainly not enough to know there were men and women in the downtown streets who would take your money and escort you to a place to have it destroyed; she was so scared that she obviously told no one about her plans. They didn't question her strange bruises and the object that might have caused them. She was dead; that was all they needed to know.

"Well, Esperanza said it's always the quiet ones you need to worry about, the ones you'd never think of doing anything. She knows about the stuff said about her ... and she said she's never been stupid."

The cars on the street drove by slowly, with their windshield wipers on, some brushed free of snow, others with up to half a foot on their roofs. Rachel watched them with an envious expression. She didn't want to be here any more than I did. We needed to get out, far from the place of Bella's death, far from our own guilt.

"Has she—"

Rachel shook her head. "No. Esperanza's never done it. She's a virgin. Told me herself. She said Bella was stupid to give in before getting married. That she'd never made that mistake. Called her a stupid slut. Not in a mean way, just mad. Stupid slut. She says she's only given in enough to get what she wants, but she's never sacrificed that. Your virginity's too sacred, she told me. Look where it gets you."

My heart was racing. We had judged Esperanza wrongly. Called her Witch and assumed she had delved into darker places than we had. Esperanza knew about men, not boys, and the difference was vast. Men could be bargained with. Boys took advantage because they didn't know any better. Esperanza knew about the places in the city that you could go to "fix" things, a "mistake," though Esperanza herself had never had the need. Esperanza would get married, be taken care of, might be able to stop working for good, though we had no idea who this man was and what he did for a living. Esperanza eluded us, was aware of all of our motions and actions but had never given a hint as to her own. I was the only one who knew about Mr. M. I was the only girl, I'm sure, whom she had kissed on the neck. I could hear her talking to Rachel, her mouth like a whip, scolding, the cleaning girl superior to those she cleaned for. The same mouth that kissed Mr. M. with a tenderness miles away from Rachel and Patrick's messy act.

"Do you believe her?"

"Yeah. Esperanza wouldn't lie about that. She doesn't have to."

The bell rang to signal the end of lunch hour. One of the girls in a younger grade pushed past us on the steps to enter the school. Some of the parents had kept their children at home since Bella's funeral, to help them get over their grief, so the school wasn't in full attendance and classes were sporadic. The snowball fight was winding down, a few girls giggling, shaking out their hair before coming in.

"I'm supposed to give you this," Rachel said, and at first I thought she was handing me Patrick's note, but she dug her hand into her pocket and produced a card in an envelope with my name on it. The handwriting wasn't Rachel's. There was a smudge on the side and the corner was creased from her coat.

"It's from my father," she said.

I opened the card. It had a butterfly on the cover, a yellow butterfly on top of a tulip, and if the block lettering hadn't announced In Sympathy, I might have found it pretty and taped it up in my room. On the inside was Mr. M.'s large scrawl of a signature and Rachel's name, also in Mr. M.'s handwriting. That Rachel hadn't signed the card herself upset me. I felt betrayed. Abandoned by both of them. A fifty-dollar bill was taped inside. It was the most money I had ever held, and I had no idea what I was going to do with it. The money didn't comfort me, but Mr. M., at least, had tried.

Rachel and I got up from the steps and followed the other girls up to our residence rooms to get our books for History class with Mother Superior. Rachel unzipped her jacket pocket, scrunched Patrick's note into a ball, and threw it in the snow. Our steps had grown sluggish. For once, we were in no hurry to get anywhere.

THE TWO CONVENTS of our order in Ottawa are having their annual lunch, a social gathering meant to keep us up-to-date on the activities of our parishes and our work in the community at large. We alternate the hosting duties; this year it is at the Convent of the Sisters of U. instead of at ours. Although the platters are sufficiently modest in their offerings, the number of them is slightly decadent. The dining hall buffet tables are covered with breads and fruits, plates of sandwiches and bowls of soup, and a long dessert table at the end with five varieties of tarts and cakes. It is a day I try not to think of waste.

Kim is our prize and she knows it. She hangs around the edges of the room like trimming, but the Sisters of the U. convent sniff her out at every turn. They are prodding her with questions, as my Sisters do, but to different purpose. They want to know if she's happy with us, who she is closest to, what she's managed to learn about our routines and activities. They are trying to get gossip, find out whether Kim's opinions and impressions coincide with theirs.

"Really," I hear one of their Sisters say. "Sister Maria barely speaks when she comes here. Are you sure we're talking about the same Sister?"

I dislike the day. It means I will have to have a conversation with Sister Aline, who insists on having her dessert with me every year. When they dine with us next year, I will be compelled to return the favour. Although I chose to serve in the same city as St. X. School for Girls, I did not choose the same convent that many of the nuns there did once the school was converted into a tuition-free separate school. Most of the nuns joined new convents, either closer to family ties that had strained over the years, or in townships and other cities where the nuns' teaching certificates were still valued. There were only two convents to choose from in Ottawa. I came to mine because I didn't want much contact with the nuns of the school. When the school closed, Sister Marguerite moved to Halifax and Mother Superior moved to Hamilton. Surely other nuns from St. X. School for Girls had transferred to the Ottawa convents available to house them when the school closed, but Sister Aline is the only one alive today whom I recognize from that time. Periodically at these dinners faces have triggered a vague recollection in my mind, but never concrete enough to put a name to a face. If anyone besides Sister Aline remembers me as a girl, they have thankfully kept it to themselves.

According to the usual routine, we get our soup and sandwiches, slices of melon or oranges, and pieces of leavened bread and sit in groups to discuss the various issues of the day. It is always the same. We begin optimistically, discussing the great advances we have made in our own convents and parishes, listing off the charitable functions and their successes to each other as if we were comparing grades in school. If that were the only story told, it would be one that included world peace and a glowing charity and economic boom for the poor of the city. It would tell the tale of a generation of men and women and children in healthy and happy homes, comforted by their faith and brought to God by Providence. The world would make perfect sense and everyone would live happily ever after.

Soon, however, the conversation drifts towards doubt and despair. Neither of our parishes has been able to sustain the support we once experienced. Many of the parishioners are not interested in prayer meetings or socials. We speak tragically about the high divorce rate, the gay rights movement, the decline of youth's respect for elders, of the fights in Eastern Europe and Africa over territory, of race wars and gang wars, of the decline in social services and education. We do not discuss the fact that many of us are here because we did not wish to be married or have families, because some of us are gay, or the fact that we know very little about life in Europe or Africa. Sister Maria told me that on her visit to the Sistine Chapel she learned that the votive candles were handled electronically now. You pay for your prayer and the candle only lights for a specified period of time before it is turned off. When I asked Christine, who had visited the Sistine Chapel herself on her honeymoon, about this, she said she had no interest in praying. She didn't go near the votive candles. She wanted to see the architecture. The mood, regardless of our full bellies and social decorum, flips from optimism to pessimism. It depresses me; not much of our work seems worthwhile.

Kim has chosen to sit with Sister Josie and Sister Sarah. I don't blame her. There is safety in numbers. Not in the masses of women collected here but in those who show genuine interest in each other, as Sister Josie and Sister Sarah do. The Sisters have clothed Kim in a long beige knitted dress that reaches to her ankles. It has a solid seam that runs directly under her small breasts, barely the size of a grown woman's let alone a pregnant one, accentuating the curve of her belly. Her burden is our badge, proof that we have been doing our duty for the unfortunate. A foreigner too, many like to think, although there is little to distinguish her as a foreigner except for her ancestral race. She was born here. She is Canadian. Sister Maria speaks worse English. Kim is more at home in this city than the rest of us. But here she is conspicuous and an exotic element, like the breadfruit on the dessert table that one of their Barbadian parishioners offered for our feast.

As I predicted, Sister Aline waves to me as we line up to select our desserts. She must be in her seventies now, but she has the fluid movements of a younger woman. Her smile is wide and her stride is confident, although she does ask for help carrying her tray back to my table. She will be singing later on, when we attend Mass. Her voice does not soar as it did when she was younger, it shakes at line ends like the tinkle of the bell the priest rings between prayers, but it moves me nonetheless. Perhaps because it is not perfect but almost so. There is a trace of the power she once held in each note, her eyes closed and her being unaware of those around her, the song taking precedence over the person.

"We meet again," she says, taking my arm affectionately as we move towards the table.

"As usual," I reply, placing our utensils out in front of us.

"We have much to talk about."

I drop her spoon on the floor, struck by her words, unable to bend to pick it up. The Sister beside us obliges and returns to her conversation. Sister Aline's eyes are upon me, seriously noting my composure. Her hand closes into a fist around her knife and she slices her piece in half. It occurs to me that I might have been wrong in thinking the candle holder has no connection to her. Sister Aline has been to our convent. She could easily have used Sister Irene's typewriter. I tried asking Sister Irene the names of anyone who had been in her room, but to no avail. She can't communicate. I feed her and read to her. She sleeps. She never taught at St. X. School for Girls. She can't remember my name most of the time.

"Sit, dear. Sit." Sister Aline taps her knife on the table as she speaks. Her power over me is obscured by my fear, but an internal nudge lowers my body to the attached bench of our table.

Sister Aline has a manner of eating that I've always found peculiar. Her face does not betray a single sign of chewing. The spoon or fork is brought to her mouth, her lips part, revealing tongue and teeth, the middle front two overlapped. The food is inserted and then it vanishes. The bottoms of her cheeks tremble, that is all. She must swallow her food whole, without tasting it.

"Is something wrong?"

I have not touched my plate. I must have been staring at her longer than I'd thought. The vanilla cake rests like a hat, intact and lordly. I decided against the breadfruit because I've always enjoyed the taste of icing. The more sugar the better. Sister Aline's plate has only a few blobs of icing left, crumbs around the edge.

"No. Not at all," I reply and take up my fork with a vengeance, shoving half the cake into my mouth and chewing thoroughly to avoid choking.

She wipes her lips with a paper napkin and then folds it in the middle of her plate. The sounds of chewing around me and in my own mouth make me aware of the activity surrounding us.

"We have an anniversary to celebrate, don't we?" Sister Aline says.

My jaw freezes and I start to cough, draw my own napkin to my lips. The moment has come. Twenty-five years has been enough time in limbo. How could Sister Aline forget Bella, her prized student, the tragic end of her life? How could anyone possibly believe the rumours surrounding her death? *I can't hide myself forever,* I think. *Like anything deep in the ground, I too can be dug up.*

And yet Sister Aline does not seem confrontational. She's concerned I may be choking and makes as if to rise. I wave my hand at her in a gesture indicating I will soon be fine, that I appear worse off than I actually am. My eyes are watering and my shoulders feel heavy. My body is trying to get out of here, break free from the past, from the person squirming inside of it.

"It occurred to me today that we've now known each other for twenty-five years. Do you think I'm right?"

Sister's Aline's tone is nostalgic, not alarmed. She regards me as an equal, someone who participated in a reality she too lived. The cake has finally turned to mush in my mouth, and I push it down my throat with my tongue.

"I know you are . . ." I do not know how to proceed delicately. Luckily, Sister Aline does not ask me to elaborate. She shifts a little in her seat, pulls up a sleeve.

"It's a blessing to be around people who know you. Who live the way we live, isn't it, Sister Angela?"

Sister Aline is being sincere, I realize. She has not come to talk of Bella to me. She does not know. She wants us to celebrate our mutual acknowledgement of each other every year. The quiver in her voice is tender.

"How have you been?" I finally reply.

"I'm well. Not as young as I used to be, but who would want to be young again? I've got more peace in my mind now than I ever did before. With each day I get closer to God in age, I suppose. He must be lonely with no one to understand what it's like to live and witness for centuries. But there's still more work I want to do. Mother Superior jokes we'll have plenty of time to rest when we're dead. I somehow doubt it. There are more children being born, more people to worry about. I think there'll always be more work to be done."

Sister Aline slaps the table with her hand, tilts her head backwards. Her smile is contagious. I find myself eating the rest of my cake as she describes the renovations in progress at their church: new windows in the rectory, revarnished pine pews, and a ceremonial vestment with gold trim for Father L. "A bit extravagant, I suppose," she says, shrugging her shoulders, dismissing her own criticism as soon as it is uttered. Sister Aline knows nothing about me and I know nothing about her. Our age difference saddens me, the lines around her eyes and on her forehead foretelling an eventual separation. Ours may be the longest and truest friendship I have ever sustained.

MR. M. TOOK RACHEL and me to buy graduation dresses. He said he had spoken to my father about it and that they'd worked out the details for the cost, but I knew he was lying. As far as I knew, he didn't even know my father's first name.

Rachel kept aloof for weeks, making excuses about upcoming tests and finishing assignments for class to get away from Caroline and me after dinner. She was not cold to us, simply curtailing, her eyes wandering over us vacantly. While she shut herself up in her room in the evenings, I sought any kind of distraction, latching onto Caroline, who also desired the company. Our twosome, however, felt incomplete. We were as if disabled, moving in stops and starts, fumbling in the most routine pursuits, the safest conversations. The ability to relax had left us. We might walk and speak and eat and play, but essentially we were sentenced, brought together out of necessity rather than choice. I missed Rachel's smile, her bold laughter, the way her curls bounced when she walked. I missed the colour of her eyes. I missed noticing the colour of her eyes.

Mr. M. directed us to the dresses on the ladies' rack at the entrance of the store. They had spaghetti straps and airy material, light to the touch. Attached were slips a shade darker than the dresses: a budgie yellow underneath a soft lemon, a burgundy under an apple red. The dresses had beads attached at the cuffs and on the hems, and I glanced at the price tags, which were considerable. I didn't want to owe Mr. M. any more than I already did and was uncomfortable as the saleswoman discussed the upcoming graduation with him, the two like conspirators as Rachel and I shuffled between racks, fiddling with the fabrics, ignoring each other with our eyes but stone sure of the other's presence on the opposite side. The store was one I knew my father couldn't afford. The saleswoman wore enormous gold rings with blue gems on the middle finger of each hand. She waved them around as if they were inconsequential. I was careful not to leave fingerprints or smudges on the cloth.

"Angel," Mr. M. called.

"Yes, sir."

"Sir, sir ... what's wrong with you girls today? Rachel, come over here. The lady wants to measure you. I'm sure you've grown at least an inch since the last time."

Rachel emerged from the back of the store where she had been picking out socks. She had collected three pairs in her hands, identically white.

"Put those down," Mr. M. said. "You can get socks any time."

"I'm the same height as I was last year. I've been the same height for two years now. I don't need to be measured."

Rachel stacked the socks on the counter beside the cash register so they wouldn't be left behind. The saleswoman smiled broadly as she bent over with her tape, a silver cap on one of her teeth.

"Yes, we'll get them. But the dresses, look at the dresses. Rachel, you might have grown in other places? Let the lady find out. Angela, what colour do you want to wear?"

Rachel glared, emanating hostility. I leaned against Mr. M. as if for protection and he absently patted my hair. I missed her so much I thought I was going to cry. Rachel broke away from the saleswoman, who hadn't finished measuring her bust, and grabbed the first dress in front of her, pulling the tape from under her armpits. The saleswoman sighed but tried to sustain a cheerful air, shrugging her shoulders casually for Mr. M.'s benefit.

"I'll take this one," Rachel said to the saleswoman. She held up a dusty-blue dress that hung down to her calves and was obviously too large for her.

"Rachel, that dress isn't half as pretty as some of the others here. Look." Mr. M. held up a purple satin dress with lace sleeves, a green flowered sash around the waist. "Now, this is a dress to dance in!"

"What would you know about that?" Rachel muttered. Mr. M. took the saleswoman aside and whispered to her. Her face took on a sympathetic softness, a poignantly exaggerated commiseration. "The girl has cramps," I heard him say.

"Angela," he called again. "Angel, I think you'd look best in red."

"Lift your arms," the saleswoman said, coming up behind me and measuring around my waist, neck, and chest. "I know just what to get you." She left immediately to rifle through a rack near the change rooms, twisting her neck around every few seconds to make sure we hadn't left.

Rachel was near. We had just been treated to a round of root beers before entering the store and I could feel her breath on my neck, sugary. "You don't have to get anything you don't want to," she said, smiling sheepishly.

I smiled back. She couldn't be mean to me the whole time we'd be out. She might even be apologizing, I thought. None of our moods could be predicted lately, changing faster than the weather. I accepted her efforts. "Do you like anything?"

"Sure, this one's nice," she replied, touching a peach-coloured dress with bows around the arms and three rows of ruffles along the skirt, meant to resemble that of a Southern belle. "Who cares, though? It's only going to be us and our parents. What does the stupid graduation matter for?"

The saleslady had lined up a number of dresses in bright colours—yellows, greens, and pinks—on an empty rack by the change room. "Come on, girls," she chimed, opening the wooden door. "It's rare I get to dress up such beautiful sisters as you two."

Rachel headed towards the change room, her head held high, kicking me in the heel as she passed. "She's not my sister. She's just an orphan we've taken on," she said to the saleswoman.

"Rachel!"

Mr. M. pulled his suit jacket closed in front of him, his fingers curling tightly around the material. He pretended to do up his buttons, his bearded face set in a frown. He did not scold Rachel any further, and the saleswoman fluttered around us, brushing our flesh lightly as she checked to make sure the dresses we tried were fitted to our bodies' shapes and not in need of tailoring. After twenty minutes Rachel had chosen an emerald-green chiffon dress with a heart-shaped collar and ruffles like sea waves along the hem. Mr. M. added socks, earrings, brooches, and two scarves to his bill, which also included my dress—red silk with a tight bodice, straight cut at the knees—and matching shoes with plastic bows on the back heels. I never got the chance to wear any of it.

THAT THURSDAY, SISTER MARGUERITE kept me after class. Easter was approaching, and I wasn't going to be a Leftover. My father was required to take me home for the holiday, the first holiday without my mother. He had telephoned, once, and in a hollow, distant voice said he was going to pick me up the following Thursday, after Mass. The coming Sunday would be Palm Sunday, my favourite church day besides Midnight Mass at Christmas, because we were usually given palm leaves to hold, to re-enact the procession. The leaves held a fascination for me with their weary strength, completely dried but difficult to tear. I would keep mine until it withered into nothing. Sister Aline had attempted to train Caroline for the solos in choir, but it hadn't worked. Caroline couldn't hold the long high notes in the style and manner of Bella. "From your diaphragm," Sister Aline instructed, sucking in her rib cage and exhaling her breath slowly, her arms rising with the expelled air. "You need to feel the air coming out of you. Control it." Caroline was a wreck. She studied the music sheets into the night, but her voice shook if anyone besides the rest of us girls and Sister Aline were in the church. Standing in front of people, performing, was not in her bones. In the end, Sister Aline needed three girls including Caroline to sing Bella's parts, each responsible for a single octave. And I grew suspicious whether Caroline was even trying. Caroline had sung better before Bella's death; maybe she could no longer bear to sing.

"That was a good report you gave," Sister Marguerite said, laying her hand on my shoulder briefly before turning her back to me to scrub the blackboard.

"Thank you." It was rare that I received praise, although I wasn't a bad student. I was merely average. My report had been on a passage from *The Book of Margery Kempe*, a medieval mystic who was convinced God spoke to her directly. She flew into wild convulsions and crying fits at the mere mention of Christ's Passion. She received letters from priests, bishops, and cardinals to tour around Europe; went on pilgrimages from church to church; and led a married life that was celibate and repentant. She wore hair shirts and flogged herself whenever she had impure thoughts. She asked one of her priests to write down all her visions, and she called herself by the name Creature. I had reported on repentance as an act of forgiveness from God.

"I bet she didn't want to sleep with her husband," Caroline whispered to me afterwards, alluding to Margery's demand that the priests allow her to travel alone and commit herself as a bride of God.

I didn't like her explanation. Saint Margery had affected me. Her endless stream of tears, her closeness to the thoughts of Jesus as she inscribed them. That her religious choice could be a practical matter to avoid the grossness or brutality or simple boredom of her married life took the mystery out of it for me. It didn't seem fair if she was faking her way into heaven.

With her back still to me, Sister Marguerite added, "Don't stop with your religious education. You're coming along nicely."

"Thank you," I repeated, about to leave for lunch, when Sister Marguerite let out a long breath with her last wipe of the blackboard and, collecting her papers, said, "I hope you will think of this place well."

Since our encounter in the stairwell, she had said nothing to me about the events of the last weeks. Then she had shared her story with me about how she had been scarred by fire as a child. I thought perhaps I was supposed to comfort her with assurances that I would not be scarred by my experiences here.

"Sure," I said as she inserted her papers into a folder and tucked them underneath her arm. I tried not to stare at the discolouration on her cheek, the reminder of her confession.

"It's a shame," she said seriously, shaking her head. "I want you to know I don't think it's right, what they're doing to you. It's not Christian."

I had no idea what she was talking about. Lately everyone seemed to be speaking in codes. Rachel, back in the dormitory the previous Saturday, with our dresses in paper bags and wrapped in scented tissue paper, had waited by her room and said, "It could be true, you know," before shutting her door, not asking me to come in, her father dropping us off at the entrance without staying for dinner. Mother Superior had told us in History that "Evil in the world is not the responsibility of God," after we had re-read a chapter on the Great War for the upcoming exam, the number of young men who had died in our city alone added in a footnote to our reader. No one spoke directly. Everything had to be interpreted.

The confusion I felt must have manifested itself in my demeanour. Sister Marguerite halted in her steps, then closed the classroom door, motioning to the nearest desk for me to sit down. She took the seat next to mine, and I almost chuckled at the sight she made lowering herself to my level, her dark habit's hem draping the floor, her body scrunched into the small desk.

"They haven't told you," she stated, angling her face towards the blackboard she had just scrubbed, lines of grey streaked across it in stripes, the crucifix above. "When were they planning on telling you?"

I remained silent. The chalk dust on her hands made her fingernails appear white. She looked as if she had been painting, chips of chalk on her habit and a smudge on her chin. I had the urge to wipe them off her, the way my mother used to whenever I was untidy. I wondered if Sister Marguerite had a mother, or only the direction of Mother Superior, who wasn't a real mother, just a mother in title. Maybe that's what made her feel responsible towards me. I had no mother. I had touched her cheek with my jaw. Maybe it was through touch that we connected ourselves to others. I certainly wouldn't have felt close to Sister Marguerite if she had turned away that night. I could still remember the scent of her hair, tucked in under her wimple, as she confessed the indiscretion that had stained her forever.

"Your father is coming to take you home."

"For Easter weekend," I offered. "He phoned." But why she needed to speak to me about it struck me as odd. Unless she was worried about how well he was coping with my mother's death.

"My dear Angela, I am not the person who should be telling you this," she said, interlocking her fingers, palms curved as in prayer, on the top of the desk, "but your father is not just taking you home for Easter. He's taking you home."

"What do you mean?" My father had made it quite clear he was sending me back to school against my will the week after the funerals. I couldn't imagine him changing his mind. My father did not relent after he made a firm decision. It was against his nature.

"Your father," she continued, "has not paid your tuition or room and board for this entire term. His cheques bounced at the bank. Mr. M. didn't want to tell us—it happened at his bank—but the teller, knowing his daughter is schooled here, brought the information to our attention. With your mother's funeral," she said quickly, the words spoken under her breath, "there is no hope of him being able to pay."

"I ... I ... don't understand."

"Your father is bankrupt," Sister Marguerite explained. "He doesn't have the money to pay for this school. It's not his fault. Remember God's commandment to honour thy father and thy mother. The school is in debt. Mother Superior feels she has no choice." I didn't understand whom she was asking me to forgive.

"Mr. M. gave me some money. He gave me fifty dollars," I told her.

"Keep it," she told me firmly. "It's not going to do you any good to give it to Mother Superior. You might need it."

There was no way we could repay the school. Sister Marguerite had made that clear to me. I was being sent away.

Caroline was probably right, I figured. Saint Margery was certainly a fake. Her God was far too easily understood by her. I emphatically left the book open in my room when my father came for me. For if I ever understood God, it was as a child understands a parent. To simply trust that all will work out. And this could be comforting, like my mother's arms when I was sick, her hands on my forehead, the gentle way she would lift a straw in a glass to my lips, read to me at my bedside. Or how it was in the end with her. Pouring her water and ensuring her rosary was wrapped twice around her dwindling wrists so it would not fall to the floor in the middle of the night. The dishing out of her pills and how she would make it a game, saying she must have been a good girl to get such a handful of treats. And I would pretend I wanted them too, tucking the blankets under her chin when she fell asleep. But He was different. He scolded and kept aloof. He said, *Don't touch anything. Don't speak unless spoken to. Follow my instructions to the letter.* And what happened if you didn't? What happened if you couldn't read the instructions, let alone interpret them properly? The answer was clearly punishment.

Sister Marguerite stood up, extracting her body from underneath the desk with a shove, straightening out her skirt, and settling the cross around her neck in the middle of her chest. Her face returned to the rigid expression it assumed in front of the class when she lectured. She wiped her hands quickly together, and I was a fleck of chalk upon her dress, discarded with a flick of her finger.

THE POWER IS OUT. Through my basement window there is no way of telling how much of the street has been affected by the storm. The winds howl and the space between the glass and the frame rattles repeatedly, causing me to shiver with each bump. More snow has fallen. The piles of snow, plowed earlier in the week into neat hills, will get even larger. Snowflakes lie prostrate against the glass.

Knock. Knock.

I mistake the noise for the window, for the storm, and wrap myself more snugly in my blanket, keeping my toes in, pinning down the cover. My hair is wet from an evening washing, and the draft in the room makes me tremble. When I place my hand against my stomach, I can feel latent warmth. I tried earlier to write Christine a letter and gave up. She has kept her word. She has not contacted me. I decide not to intrude on her wish to be forgotten.

Knock. Knock.

The weather haunts me. And now the noise. Insistent like a clock. Like the weather on the night my mother died. Our anniversary coming up. I cannot bear it any longer. I have taken the pills Sister Ursula prescribed for me. A double dose. My dream is for sleep, and it must be washing over me in waves. It is working. I have needed a good night's sleep for months. In my sleepy mind's eye I can see the orchard outside the convent and feel the wetness of the snow, the smoothness of the hidden rock in the garden against my hands. I am tearing into the ground, digging, bringing up something that was buried there by me long ago. It is long and heavy and I am alone in the night, after having snuck out with my nightdress on, the cloth barely obscuring my body. The candle holder. The silver candle holder is in my hands. Could it have been me? Could it have been me who kept it all this time buried in the garden, forgetting one day I'd need to face it? When Rachel told me where it was abandoned, did I retrieve it? I must have. It belonged to me in the end. The burden was mine to carry. Mine to rediscover. To package it up, here in the convent, deliver it back to myself.

Knock. Knock.

And this is how I imagined Death would come. The same as for my mother. The same horror awaiting me, although mine is deserved. Knocking at the door during a storm. I am nearly the same age as she was. I should not have the privilege of living as long. All the lights out and nothing to tell me where I actually am, except perhaps a smell that drifts away. Wrapped in my cocoon, this bed is the perfect grave. My hands dig deeper into the soil. I have the candle holder. But I am searching for something else. This isn't the only piece of evidence. What frightens me most is I do not answer the door. I do not try to hide. I do nothing.

The door opens.

"Angela."

A woman's voice. Faint but surely a woman's voice. I did not think Death would be a woman. But it makes sense to me as it occurs. Of course it's a woman. A woman knows about these things. Old age has not yet stung me, but many have died younger than I. Sister Ursula says it can happen when you lack sleep. Your heart can stop ticking.

"I am ready," I say, astounded by my confidence. "Come in. Speak."

Noise against the tiled floor. Shuffling. A hand scratching against the wall. Breathing. Breathing. Steps. Steps closer.

"Angela. My water broke."

I bolt upright in bed, brush a strand of hair out of my mouth. I cannot see the face in front of me, but I can feel it breathing a hot rush of air onto my face and lips. She must be right up against me. And then the weight on the mattress, pulling down. Two hands gripping the covers. The blackness a void.

"Who are you?"

"My water broke! It's all over the hallway! I don't know what to do!"

"I don't understand."

"It's Kim, Angela, Kim! I think the baby's coming. I felt pain and got scared. And then on the way down to see you ... on the way down ... my water broke. Oh, God, I'm wet. My thighs hurt. I can't see anything."

It is Kim. I had succumbed to the pills. Her voice sounded older. Much older than it does after I fumble around the room trying to figure out how to get her upstairs to Sister Ursula in the darkness of the power outage. And she used my first name, without my title. She used my first name like a friend.

I think I have a flashlight somewhere. When the fuse for the light in the basement toilet burned out last spring, I used the torch in emergencies in the middle of the night until the electrician could come by to fix it. Two weeks it had been, me creeping along the dark passageway with the faint light in my hands, creating shadows along the walls. Noticing the details I missed when the lights worked. The cobwebs in corners. The defects in the stones. The dirt in between tiles on the floor.

Crash. My lamp smashes as it hits the floor. I catch the shade in my left hand, then discard it as useless. Kim is leaning against the headboard of my bed, her hands clasped around her belly, moaning in pain. Her cries intensify by the minute.

"Hurry. Hurry. Please."

"Dammit," I curse openly. "Dammit!" Nothing is ever where you think it should be. The top dresser is empty. No flashlight. I can feel only papers, the typewriter, and the ceramic lamp I purchased at one of my own rummage sales that is now in pieces.

"Watch your feet, Kim. There's glass all over the floor."

I bump into the dresser. The angle of the wood hitting me against my chest, my left breast in pain. I try not to scream. I know it will only make Kim worse. In my sock drawer, I remember, are candles I've kept as souvenirs from various services: the Christmas and Lent candles we Sisters make ourselves. I seek out their bodies.

"I've got a candle, Kim. Hold on."

There is also a book of matches on the dresser, the pack I kept from the restaurant where Christine confessed to me. I had automatically dropped them into my totebag, not because I needed them but because I am used to hoarding what is free.

"Angela! I can't wait. I can't wait." Kim is stumbling around. I can hear her trying to get back to the door. My eyes are beginning to adjust to the darkness. Kim is no longer invisible, but a shadow whose movements I can follow.

"I've got it! I've got it!" I yell.

Inserting the candle into the silver candle holder, I wince, but take hold of it. Mine all along.

I strike a match. Kim holds onto the doorknob, her legs crossed as if she needs to use the washroom. I carry the silver candle holder against my sore chest, to keep the weight balanced so the candle, slightly thinner than the opening, won't fall forward and hit the floor, or fall backwards and burn my nightgown. I am awake. Determined. The fog of the pills lifts.

As I get closer to Kim, who is also in her nightgown, a long pale-blue cotton dress with small bows, the blood is apparent. Blood down from her thighs to her toes in thin streaks and patches. The candlelight makes it visible. Kim gazes at herself in horror and crumples the skirt of her nightgown to find out where the blood is coming from and how bad it might be. She holds in a cry. I take her arm and hook it into mine. She requires aid. I cradle the candle holder in the crook of my other arm. The weight, distributed in this manner, makes it easier to manoeuvre.

"Don't look at yourself," I tell her as I kick the door open with my heel. "Look ahead."

The place works. Upon reaching the first floor, I call out for help and Sisters come running in the dark, some with flashlights, some with candles, and some without any aid, using their voices against mine to feel out where we are. The Sisters are like trained police squads or firemen. All working in unison in a disaster, following the unwritten rules that they know to be the correct way of proceeding. Kim almost fell twice on our way up the stairs, and I want someone with a flashlight to take over for me. I am afraid I will burn her accidentally, trying to save her from falling. At the top of the stairs, the flame from the candle singed a strand of my hair. Kim coughed and plugged her nose momentarily before her labour pains started up again.

On the way to Sister Ursula's office, Sister Irene can be heard screaming.

"Baaahhh!" she roars. "Baaahhh!"

I am about to rush up and help her, but Sister Ursula stops me. By this time all the Sisters on the first floor are gathered around and, with little direction, divvy up the duties to be performed. Sister Rosalind goes to find Sister Bernadette, who has a cellphone, to call the hospital, our phone lines being affected by the storm. Sister Josie leaves to inform Father B. that the baby is coming, and Sister Frances runs up to the other floor to get any of the Sisters with medical training to help out. I think I shouldn't be here, even if Kim has asked for me, because I have no medical training, except for a St. John's Ambulance course that all the Sisters took together a couple of years ago. I breathed into a plastic doll. We did not learn how to deliver babies. So when I hear Sister Irene screaming, that is where I think I should be, assuming each Sister ought to use the tools they have to take care of each other. Sister Irene is my care. My presence might calm her down.

"Don't abandon the living for the dead," Sister Ursula says curtly. "Go to Sister Irene," she orders Sister Mary, another older Sister who spends most of her time in her room and handles the prayer meetings on Thursday nights with Father B. Sister Mary obeys.

Sister Ursula, with the help of Sister Katherine and Sister Sarah, manages to get Kim to her office and placed on the examining table. She keeps looking to make sure I am there. I tell Kim I will stay with her as long as she needs. I try to appear calm, but under the beams of light, everyone can see she is bleeding badly. Sister Ursula scrubs her hands and puts on plastic gloves. Sister Katherine gets some water and bandages and towels to place underneath Kim, while Sister Sarah wipes the sweat off her forehead and places a pillow underneath her neck. I place the candle holder outside the door like an offering.

"It hurts too much," Kim pleads. "Oh God. It hurts!"

It takes the three Sisters to convince her to open her legs.

• • •

Kim screams with all her strength, her lips contorted into a rectangular shape, all her teeth pushing the skin to the outermost edges. She grips the padded cushions of the table and the white paper rustles underneath her, her legs in the stirrups meant for internal exams.

"Try to push," counsels Sister Ursula, pulling her white lab coat over her pink pyjamas. "Now try to breathe evenly."

Four Sisters stand guard like bedposts, each holding a flashlight, and many other Sisters come and go from the room, snatching anything that can be used for light: candles, bedside lamps that work on batteries, key chains that glow, lighters. With the women around her, Kim's legs spread while Sister Ursula bends in between, the room resembles a vigil. The uttered phrases are low and precise, incantations.

Breathe.

Too much blood.

Contractions four minutes apart.

Ambulance on its way.

Too late.

"I don't want to die!" screams Kim, groping for my hand and then crushing it inside her own.

"You're not going to die," says Sister Ursula confidently. "You're having a baby. Now concentrate. Concentrate. Get me my forceps." The last command she directs to Sister Sarah, who searches for them on the shelves over Sister Ursula's desk. Two damp handprints are visible on the sides of her sweat suit. She was performing yoga exercises when the commotion started.

"I won't let you die," I tell Kim, who, with my words, squeezes my hand even harder. Her hair is drenched in sweat. Sister Katherine combs it off her face with her fingers, then tries to massage her temples. Kim convulses with pain. A faint trickle of blood runs down her lips. She bites the side of her mouth, following Sister Ursula's demands for concentrated effort.

"Push."

"Yes!"

"Push."

"Yes!"

Kim yells her words. Each *Yes* gaining in force, until she is on her own, pushing with all her might, throwing all her energy into the stirrups to set the baby free. The white paper beneath her is red from her waist down, the stain spreading. Sister Ursula attempts to hide it from her and mostly succeeds. Since I do not know anything about childbirth except from the few pamphlets I took home from the hospital the day Kim and I went for her checkup, I am unsure whether to panic. I was not present during Christine's sons' births, so I don't know how it was for her, whether the loss of blood is normal. However, Sister Sarah, returning with the forceps, who I know worked as a volunteer in a hospital when she was a teenager and helped deliver a couple of babies, gives me concern. She is calculating the loss of blood and spreading towels across and underneath Kim's legs. She is worried enough to leave the room twice to check on the ambulance.

Kim holds on. In the strange multicoloured glow of all the little lights, her face takes on a greenish-yellow hue. She is straining, bearing down upon her body, forcing it to comply. For the first time since she entered our doors, I can see the will to live written on her face, pulsing in every muscle of her body. She wants to live. She wants to push the baby out. And I am scared like I've never been scared before. I thought I'd become accustomed to fright, but this is different. This is not a known fear. This fear could end in many ways. If my hand weren't in hers, I'd be gripping my locket for strength. I'd be begging my mother to save us.

"Baaahhh!"

I turn my head rapidly, nearly yanking Kim with me, who holds onto me as if we were handcuffed. Sister Irene is nowhere in sight. The noise has come from Kim. Her face turns white and her neck goes limp. I begin to shake her.

"Sister Ursula! She's fainted."

"Get her a face cloth. And get me the liquid Demerol from the drug cabinet. And a syringe. Quickly." She says all this while between Kim's legs. Sister Frances hands me a face cloth, dousing it with cold water from the tap, a sympathetic nod exchanged between us. Sister Katherine produces the medication from the cabinet and hands it to Sister Sarah to load the syringe. Sister Ursula removes her green mask for a moment, standing upright.

"I'm going to have to extract the baby myself. The ambulance will be here to take them to hospital once this is over. She's going to have the baby here."

Although it is a tense situation, the announcement makes many of the Sisters waiting outside the door pleased. Several turn to each other silently and nod. Some hold hands outside the door. One or two actually go down on their knees and start to pray. Once immersed in a crisis, it is difficult to offer it up to anyone else's hands. The women here trust each other more than they trust people on the outside, regardless of the new technologies such people might bring to our aid. It is meant to happen here, this miracle or this tragedy. They will see it out.

The water seems to help. Although not fully conscious, Kim does regain her ability to hold her head erect. She glances around the room, stunned, her mouth open and droopy.

"I don't get it. I don't feel any more pain."

"That's good, Kim. Just push. Right?"

Sister Ursula nods, sinks back down to gauge the progress of the child and the damage to Kim.

"It's coming feet first," Sister Katherine whispers to me, shaking her head. "Not a single thing is going right."

I am about to ask her a question about this but she puts her finger to her lips, jutting her chin in the direction of Kim, who is staring up at me with such deep affection in her eyes that an outsider might think I am her mother.

"Am I dreaming?" Kim asks me, taking my hand and placing it on her cheek. "Am I giving birth?"

"Yes," I reply. "Yes, my dear, you are."

"Premature?"

Sister Ursula is the best doctor this convent has ever seen. That's what Mother Superior says, and many of the other Sisters are of like mind. I put my trust in her. Feet first or head first, this child is going to live. Both children are going to live, I correct myself. Both children are going to live. *Please.*

A couple of Sisters outside the door are humming. Or at least they seem to be humming, their voices melded together in unison, all intent on the same wish. I have the urge to pray as well, as I caress the hand in mine. Kim's eyes have grown heavy-lidded. She struggles to keep awake. Sister Ursula and Sister Josie hand each other instruments and talk in short, blunt phrases. Their voices drain away from the one inside my head.

A Psalm. A Psalm I sang at St. X. School for Girls, Bella in the front row, her voice echoing. The priest absent. Girls like me practising to please Sister Aline. Saying the words without knowledge of their meaning or impact. Saying them for the sake of saying. Girls wanting to hear their own voices rising into the air, the desire to create something beautiful, something holy.

The scalpel rising.

Kim falling asleep. A cut on her side, just under the rib cage. Sirens wailing. Sisters running back and forth, making room. A stretcher rolling. Sister Katherine telling them there is no time.

Remember not the Sins of my Youth, nor my Transgression:
According to Thy Mercy remember
Thou me for Thy Goodness' sake,
O Lord.

I remember the prayer and it is not to God that I recite it, but to the unborn child struggling to get out. It is from this child that I require remembrance and forgiveness. It is to this child I confess as if it were my own, as Sister Ursula draws it from the body, cutting out a space for it to emerge. Premature and small enough to hold in her two open palms. The blood of its life upon her hands, a tiny purple face. The sex hidden from my view.

Who has come for you? little one.

The men approach to secure Kim on the stretcher. Sister Bernadette has already gathered my jacket from my room. The power is still out, but the Sisters line the hallway with their candles and flashlights, illuminating the way for the men to follow, the cord cut and the baby wrapped in cloth in the back of the ambulance, hooked up to oxygen. The men have high-powered flashlights, but the women stand with their weaker ones, insistent on participating in the procession.

Death is backwards, Sister Irene. You were right. Death is backwards. Another ambulance is also here, come for the pale out-line of the woman I have just invoked. Her spirit lingering on. An intravenous tube tucked into the skin of her arm. The snow pound-ing down, dragging the boughs of trees to the harsh ground. The doors to her ambulance close as do ours. Goodbye, Sister Irene. Goodbye.

Sister Ursula removing her mask and hugging Sister Josie, waving at me still holding Kim's hand as we go. Two male para-medics bandaging Kim. The child breathing, artificially for now, but breathing. I have faith. I have hope.

The baby's purple chest rises. The closed eyes open for a moment, the white as pure as lilies.

Before you were born, you were already a rumour.

Speak.
Breathe.
Dear Child, *Tell me.*

The renovations have begun for the Day Care Centre. Kim cannot be convinced to return to school, but we try. When she comes to see us, that is. She visits less often as the many months wear by, reminds us how much work it is to care for a child on your own: the feedings, the diaper changes, the sicknesses, the constant supervision. She says that with the Day Care Centre in the basement of the church, she might be able to find full-time work. Yet she's elusive. I sense this is not entirely out of choice, but out of shame. She is thankful for what we've done for her, but now she desires her freedom. I can sympathize. And the child has grown well, despite the respiratory disease. Social Services makes sure the medicine is paid for. I figure in about a year or two, if Kim doesn't bring her child here for care, we will not see her again.

The Centre has solved my problem about what to do with the basement during the weekdays. We have arranged it so that there is a room for teaching with desks and a bulletin board, paint and pencils, and a blackboard. Glass walls divide the schoolroom, while the rest of the space is for playing. The toys, which have been donated by our parishioners as well as by a toy company Sister Bernadette has corre-

sponded with, can be brought in and out on carts and in bins, easy to clean and removable for wedding and wake receptions on the weekends. The addict meetings, workshops, and prayer groups are now held in the back offices of the church. Two partitions have been removed, and the rooms can hold up to thirty-five adult people, fifty children. I am pleased. The large donation from the employer of Mr. Y., the lawyer who had phoned the convent asking about me, provided the down payment on our loans. Although there was no return address or name listed on the enormous cheque itself, I know who it must be from. I sent a card to him. And I think I can still recognize the large sprawl as his signature. He must have simply wanted to make sure it was from me. I know he will keep my secret. I tell Father B. a little lie about it. I tell him this is what the cheque was specifically donated for: a daycare. What does it matter if it works in the end? Father B. had needed to do a bit of convincing to the Bishop, but the Bishop relented. It means the church can qualify now for various grants. The application forms are on Mother Superior's desk. Sister Bernadette is going to teach full-time there until word gets out and more children arrive and we need more Sisters to join in.

What I've discovered is not that I have been released from my burdens. Far from it. I've found more. But before, my burden was a hungry and scared child. I held on to it, gave it milk, watched it grow out of my arms, out of control, until it was far too dependent to make its way on its own. And as Sister Ursula told Kim about her weight, that she wasn't in danger because of the amount of weight she had gained, but the way it was being distributed, I've also found a better way to distribute my weight. Among my Sisters. I used to think that we were meant to walk in black because we were the mourners of the world. I had been assuming God was a man, a parent. He must be a child. And I shouldn't have been stuck on the present paying the debts of the past. I should have been asking whether the present can pay the debts of the future. It's a practical matter. There is no answer, only action. As for the transgressions of my youth, no one may have found me out yet. But like anything else, like a silver candle holder buried deep in the soil of a rock garden, I too can be dug up. I can be found. So can this. Forgiveness is not absolution as I'd once supposed. It's a carrying, owning one's sins. It will be found. It must be found. Then there will be confessions, and I will listen. You see, I live here. My name is Angela. You may remember me.

~ ACKNOWLEDGMENTS ~

For the U.S. publication of this book, I'd like to extend my sincere gratitude and thanks to Hilary McMahon of Westwood Creative Artists for her hard work and great enthusiasm and to Antonia Fusco at Algonquin Books of Chapel Hill for her empathetic reading of my nun and her keen eye.